Old Ghosts

Six Tales of Terror

By Joseph J. Christiano

Old Ghosts

By Joseph J. Christiano

Printed by

Tell-Tale Publishing Group, LLC
5174 Peri Street
Swartz Creek, MI 48473
www.tell-talepublishing.com

Nightshade Imprint

NIGHTSHADE

For my parents,

Joseph and Donna Christiano

emet

Wagner slid the MG 15 through the broken glass of the windshield. Schmidt stepped atop the rubble and caught the weapon as it slid down the nose of the aircraft. He stepped back and rejoined the others while Wagner climbed through the opening. He followed the MG 15's path down the nose and jumped the last meter to the ground. Dust and dirt plumed around his boots. He slid down the pile of rubble and nearly lost his balance. The snow was thick and deep but the plane's impact and slide had pushed most of it away from them. He pulled his coat tighter to his body. The December wind rippled his jacket and moved the dust around them. It whistled through the shells of the ruined buildings and sounded, to Wagner's ears, like the mournful cry of a banshee with bronchitis.

"Where did you find this?" Schmidt asked. He hefted the weapon, struggled a bit under its weight. He was smiling, probably satisfied with the weight and bulk of the thing. Perhaps it made him feel safer.

"It's my dorsal gun. It's the only one I could find that was still intact. Not much ammunition, though. I'd say it has maybe fifty, sixty rounds left."

"Did you find Von Valkenberg?" It was Mueller who asked. The pilot stood apart from his men. He had to have been as cold as the rest of them, but he showed no sign of discomfort. He stood with his arms folded across his chest and his perpetual scowl firmly in place.

Wagner nodded. "Some of him." He took a breath, and the tenseness in his shoulders revealed that even he felt the cold air invade his lungs. "He didn't make it."

"And the radio?" Mueller's voice held no hint of emotion. He may as well have asked about the weather.

"Destroyed." Wagner nodded at the gun in Schmidt's hands. "That's all I could salvage."

"Major, what are we going to do?" It was Neumann who asked. The short, stocky man with the long scar down the left side of his face shifted his feet and shivered. "We're miles from anywhere. We can't survive out here like this."

Mueller turned on him and his scowl deepened. Wagner had seen this expression from his commanding officer only once before. Six months earlier, when his bombardier missed the target by a few thousand feet, Mueller had exploded on the man. The rumor was Mueller himself executed the unfortunate officer upon their return to base, but it was only a rumor. He had walked around the rest of that day with the same scowl he turned on Neumann. "We are not miles from anywhere." His tone was still emotionless, but there was an edge to it that had not been present a moment before. "We are still in the Reich. Therefore, we are still inside friendly territory." He turned from Neumann and looked at the rest of his crew. "We will make our way west, toward the Fatherland, until we can link up with the *wehrmacht*."

"Major?" Wagner waited for Mueller to acknowledge him. He did so with an abbreviated nod. "Sir, I think perhaps we should wait for nightfall. I know this city is supposed to be cleared, but if there's anyone left, especially if they were part of the uprising, it won't be safe for us to travel during the day." He indicated the MG 15 with a nod. "Not with a single machine gun between us."

He waited for Mueller to turn that scowl his way. Instead, the Major glanced around the ruins of Warsaw. There was not a single undamaged building as far as the eye could see in any direction. Most had been reduced to shapeless piles of rubble and dust. Snow covered everything and yet the ruined city seemed more gray than white. Aside from the background groan of the wind, and the crackling of the dying fire which consumed the left engine of the Do 17, no sound reached their ears.

After a moment, Mueller turned to Wagner. The radioman may have imaged it, but he could swear he saw a sense of pride behind the Major's eyes. "Very well. We'll wait for nightfall, as the good sergeant has recommended. We can return to the inside of the plane. It will afford us some shelter from the elements of this goddamned Polish winter."

"There is no way I'm going back in there." It was Neumann who said it. He planted his feet in the snow and his hands on his hips. Considering who their commanding officer was it was close to an act of insubordination punishable by death. "That bastard might blow up on us."

Wagner cringed and waited for Mueller to draw his Luger. Again, the major surprised Wagner by not turning on the bombardier. His lips pulled back from his teeth in a bad imitation of a smile. "Very well. You can remain out here and stand guard. The crew and I will get some rest."

Neumann swallowed but said nothing. His silence was most likely all that saved him from a quick death.

Wagner silently thanked whichever deity kept Neumann from voicing a response. Mueller appeared calm, even friendly, but the truth of the man was quite the opposite. The major had not placed a hand on the Luger clipped to his belt but Wagner had no doubt the major would draw and fire the weapon if Neumann did anything other than remain silent.

"Everyone else, back in the plane."

Schmidt hefted the MG 15 and handed it to Neumann without a word. He clapped the short man on his shoulder as he walked past. He followed Mueller and Wagner inside the plane.

****

The sun had vanished behind the taller ruins of Warsaw and the three men inside the wrecked bomber were mostly asleep when the sound of the MG 15 cut through the silence of the city. Wagner leaped to his feet and smacked his head on the curvature of the bomber's fuselage. He winced but managed to hold in the epithets he wished to unleash. He ignored the pounding in his head and his hand went to the gun holstered at his hip. Mueller and Schmidt were likewise on their feet and the Major drew his Luger and moved rapidly toward the cockpit. Wagner and Schmidt fell into step behind him. When they reached the cockpit, they looked through the shattered windows around them.

Mueller took the center windows, eyes scanning the street and ruined buildings for any sign of movement. Schmidt was on the major's right side and did likewise. It was Wagner, looking out the left side of the cockpit, who saw Neumann. The bombardier was down on one knee, balancing the machine gun and aiming it down a side street.

"Neumann's on this side. He's got something."

Mueller muscled his way past Wagner and looked out the remains of the side window. He took one look at Neumann and climbed through the broken windshield. Wagner followed him out and ran in a crouched position over to the bombardier.

Smoke drifted lazily from the barrel of the MG 15, which Neumann pointed straight ahead of him. He looked scared. His eyes moved rapidly right and left. Mueller slowed his approach and Wagner guessed the major, too, recognized Neumann's emotional state. It would not do to run in behind him and be cut down by a burst from the machine gun. Mueller took a moment to look at the destroyed buildings that formed the alley down which Neumann aimed the MG 15. He had his gun in his right hand and looked for any sign of movement. With the meager remains of sunlight, and the gray monotone that was now Warsaw, he could see nothing.

"Report." It was Mueller, in full command mode.

"One man, running from the building on the right." Neumann breathed heavily, loudly. "I think I hit him."

"You think. Are you certain you saw someone?" Mueller could not or did not hide the doubt from his tone. He was obviously even less pleased with Neumann than he was before.

Neumann licked his lips. He did not look at Mueller as he said, "Positive, sir."

Mueller's eyes moved across the alley ahead of them. Wagner followed his gaze but saw nothing. "Let's assume Mr. Neumann is correct and we're not alone here. This is obviously a straggler, someone who through sheer luck managed to avoid the cleansing of the ghetto." He holstered his Luger. "Spread out. Let's find him."

The four men made their way cautiously down the alley. Their pace was slow; the alley was strewn with too much rubble and the snow was too high and thick for more than a light jog. Wagner was able to look through the destroyed second-story walls of the first building he passed. After a few moments Neumann held up one hand and brought them to a stop.

He eyed the building to his left nervously. Most of the outer wall facing the alley was gone but what remained of the interior was too dark for them to see in detail. Wagner kept his pistol aimed in the general direction of the building but he saw nothing. For all he knew there could be two dozen people inside readying an attack.

The same thought occurred to Mueller, apparently, because he turned to Neumann and said, "A single, short burst, Mr. Neumann."

Neumann nodded once and pressed the MG 15's trigger. The weapon's report was much louder than it should have been to Wagner's ears and it made his head throb all the more. He resisted the urge to block his ears and instead kept his eyes focused on the building. Neumann sent five or six rounds into the structure. Dirt, dust and snow kicked up.

The four men stood and watched and waited. Wagner heard what could have been a muted cry from within the structure. His eyes went to the spot. He tried to see through the darkness but it was absolute.

"There." Mueller pointed to the spot where Wagner heard the sound. "Another burst, Mr. Neumann."

Neumann did not bother with a nod this time. Evidently he heard the same thing as had Wagner and Mueller. He sent a dozen rounds into the darkness of the building.

Wagner winced at the pain in his head but he brought his pistol up and aimed it into the darkened ruins. More debris and snow jumped up when the high-caliber rounds tore through the darkness.

For a moment there was only silence. The wind picked up and moaned sorrowfully. It took Wagner a moment to realize it was not the wind at all. It sounded like an animal, wounded and dying.

"Christ, what the fuck is that?" Schmidt asked.

"Wagner, you and Schmidt investigate. We'll provide cover from here."

"Yes, sir," Wagner replied. He nodded to Schmidt, who looked reluctant and scared but managed to return the nod just the same.

A large pile of debris leaned against the building. Wagner dug in with his boots as much as he was able. He used it to scale the buried first floor of the structure. He needed to leap the last meter and just managed to get his hands on a section of the second story that jutted from the ruins. With a grunt he pulled himself onto the second floor.

The building had been residential, that much was obvious. He got the distinct impression he stood in what was once somebody's living room. There was no furniture but the bare walls were marred with dark patches where photographs and portraits might have hung. Partially collapsed walls and open doorways showed him a kitchen and the remains of a stairwell that spiraled its way through the center of the building. Nearly everything was covered with snow.

He heard a grunt from behind. He looked and saw Schmidt struggling to pull himself up and onto the second floor. Wagner reached down with one hand and helped the navigator. "Thanks," Schmidt said.

Wagner nodded wordlessly. The sky had grown darker and it was impossible to see into the building. Schmidt brought out his lighter and flicked it to life. He waved it slowly in front of them.

"Can't see a fucking thing," Schmidt complained.

"Quiet," Wagner said. "I thought I heard something."

Schmidt's eyes widened a bit. "Where?" He sounded nervous. He pulled his pistol and pointed it into the darkness.

"Ahead and to the right." Wagner used his own pistol to point Schmidt in the direction. He still saw nothing but shadows but he was convinced he heard something when Schmidt was complaining.

"What was it?"

"How do I know?" He swallowed. "Let's move."

Snow crunched beneath their boots. Wagner listened intently but he heard nothing but the sound of their footfalls and the wind. He reached a doorway, peered through it. It was most likely a dining room. The remains of a large light fixture hung from the ceiling in the center of the room. Wagner turned and took a single step from the room when he heard the sound repeated behind him. He stopped and spun.

The wind picked up momentarily and Wagner felt the temperature drop a few more degrees. He needed both hands to steady his pistol. The far corner of the dining room was complete darkness. He strained his eyes and ears but he came up empty. "Is someone there?" His voice startled him in its volume.

He heard Schmidt come running. He checked over his shoulder quickly to ensure it was, indeed, the navigator before he returned his attention to the dark corner. "Come out. I won't hurt you, I promise."

Schmidt joined him. He raised his weapon and pointed it inside the dining room. "Who's in there? Come on out right now." He sounded more than nervous, now; he sounded scared.

"Settle down," Wagner said. He nodded in the direction of the far corner. "Over there. I think there's someone in that corner."

Schmidt licked his lips and swallowed audibly. "Come out here," he said to the corner.

"I said settle down." Wagner held up both hands, palms out, and slowly holstered his weapon. "We're not going to hurt you." He tried to sound calm, and, compared to Schmidt, he did. He hoped it would be enough. "I promise. Just come out so we can see you."

"Fuck that,' Schmidt said. He aimed his weapon at the corner and pulled the trigger. Three rounds vanished into the darkness. One hit the wall; Wagner knew this because he heard the distinct sound of the bullet striking brick. The other two…

There was a grunt of pain. It was followed by a scream.

Wagner's hand returned to the butt of his gun. Before he could draw the weapon something large and fast erupted from the darkness. At first he thought it was a bear or perhaps a wild boar; it was big and covered with fur. At the last moment before the thing crashed into him he realized it was a man in some type of fur coat. The knowledge did him little good.

They went down in a heap. Wagner landed hard on the floor and the breath exploded from his lungs. He had the presence of mind to reach again for his pistol but he could not get a grip on it. The big man on top of him rolled onto his side and brought Wagner with him.

Wagner looked and realized the man used him as a shield against further gunfire from Schmidt. Wagner looked into Schmidt's eyes and wondered if the navigator might open fire anyway. He was clearly terrified. His weapon remained pointed at them.

The big man roared and sprang to his feet. Wagner felt himself lifted from the floor as if he weighed as much as a mannequin. The big man hurled him through the air directly at Schmidt. Wagner collided with him. Schmidt lost his balance. He backpedaled, arms pin-wheeling, until he reached the edge of the building's second story. With a yelp he disappeared over the side.

Wagner pushed himself onto his knees. He looked through the gathering darkness and saw the shape of the large man a few meters from him. In what was left of the daylight he realized the man was large but hardly muscular. The coat was all he wore from the waist up. Wagner could see the man's ribcage quite clearly. Blood flowed slowly from two bullet wounds on his chest. The tattered scraps of his pants revealed legs that did not appear thick enough to hold his weight. A third bullet wound bled quite profusely from his right thigh. Wagner was not a medic but it looked to him as if the man's femoral artery was severed. If that were the case he would likely be dead in moments.

The wounds did nothing to slow the man. He rushed Wagner and lifted him from the floor. Wagner caught sight of movement behind the man. A second shadow separated itself from the corner of the dining room. It was small, much smaller than the man holding Wagner a few centimeters from the floor. The child, no more than five or six years-old, crawled on his hands and knees and looked more frightened than anyone Wagner had ever seen. His eyes were large and wet.

Wagner returned his attention to the man. "Please," he said. "I won't hurt you. But you can't stay here. They know you're in here now. Please, go. Take your son and go."

The man spared a glance over his shoulder before he returned his eyes to Wagner. The child cried something but Wagner could not make it out. The man ran for the edge, Wagner still in his grasp and suspended above the floor.

With a roar like a bear the man hurled them off the building. Wagner tried to twist from the man's grasp but he lacked the strength to break free. They were in the air for only a moment although to Wagner it felt much longer. They landed hard on a pile of snow-covered rubble. Wagner felt two ribs crack even through the heavy insulation of his coat. They tumbled the rest of the way to the cold ground. The man released his grip on Wagner and they rolled away from each other.

Wagner spun off his wounded side and struggled to rise to his knees. A hand reached beneath his arm and helped him to his feet. He saw it was Schmidt; the navigator looked none the worse for wear.

Mueller and Neumann stood over the wounded man. In the dying light he looked much smaller than he had within the confines of the building. Tall, yes, well above two meters, but painfully thin. Neumann held the MG 15 inches from the man's head. Mueller held his Luger in his hand and his customary sneer on his lips.

Without comment Mueller put a single round into the man's abdomen. The sound of the gunshot was loud, and it echoed off the ruins of the city. The man groaned and doubled over into a fetal position. His blood stained the snow and, in contrast with the uniform gray/white of the ruined city, it appeared almost neon.

The echoes of the gunshot died, only to be replaced by a high-pitched scream. All eyes moved up to the second floor of the ruined structure. Mueller, Neumann and Schmidt raised their weapons. The small child Wagner had glimpsed in the shadows crouched near the edge and looked down at them. His eyes were wide, terrified. He looked at the man bleeding into the dust and snow. He screamed again and cried. Tears spilled down his cheeks; his entire body shook.

"Mr. Neumann, do you have any grenades?" It was Mueller who spoke.

"Just one, sir," Neumann said. His eyes darted between Mueller and the boy.

"Well, then?"

"What?" Wagner took a lurching step forward. He grunted at the pain in his side. "Sir, you can't. He's just a child, for Christ's sake."

Mueller turned his gaze on Wagner. His eyes were narrowed slits, his lips curled down so much his chin stuck out. Without taking his eyes from Wagner, he said, "Mr. Neumann, use your grenade."

"Yes, sir," Neumann said. He lowered the machine gun and pulled the single grenade from his belt.

"*No!*" Wagner broke from Schmidt's grip and sprinted at Neumann. Mueller spun and hammered his Luger into

Wagner's wounded side. His cracked ribs felt as if they exploded. Wagner gasped and went down in the snow.

At the same moment the big man shouted something to the child and reached a hand in his direction.

Neumann looked with naked surprise at Wagner. Their eyes locked. His arm remained cocked.

"Don't do it, Johann," Wagner gasped through clenched teeth. "He's just a boy."

Neumann's eyes went from Wagner to Mueller. Mueller said nothing. He lit a cigarette and glared at Neumann.

Neumann swallowed and pitched the grenade.

Wagner and the big man shouted at the same time. The child remained frozen on the edge of the ruined building's second floor.

The grenade tumbled through the air in an inelegant and too-accurate arc. It landed on the second floor a meter or two behind the child. A moment later it exploded.

The sound of the explosion was brief and immediately drowned out by a sound like rumbling thunder. Dust plumed from the side of the second floor and the child was lost from view. The interior wall that at one time separated the living room from the rest of the apartment bowed in and then collapsed. The thunder grew in volume as several more walls followed. More dust and debris was shaken loose from the structure. The third floor descended rapidly and pancaked onto the second. More dust and small bits of debris exploded from the building on all sides. Some of it pelted the crew of the Do-17 and the dying man lying in the dust and snow. The bottom-most floor, all but destroyed already, could not support the impact. Almost in slow motion, the building toppled. It fell to the south, away from the men in the street. The remains of the top two floors crashed into the building next to it. Bricks, glass, plaster and wood rained down on the deserted streets.

The sound was nearly deafening but Wagner managed to hear the cry (more of a wail) erupt from the wounded man. He crawled toward the collapsed building, one arm out-stretched for the boy now lost. He left a trail of neon crimson in his wake.

Mueller was the first to recover. He looked down at the pathetic man in the snow. He brought his Luger down hard. It connected solidly with the top of the man's skull. The man cried out. His head hit the ground and he lay still. His breathing was quick and shallow.

"For the love of God, why won't you die?" Mueller nearly did not get the question out before he laughed. He took one last drag on his cigarette and tossed the butt onto the man's back.

Wagner looked at the man and then at Mueller. But it was Neumann his eyes settled upon. The bombardier was covered with dust and he stared dumbly at the destroyed building. Wagner walked quickly to Neumann's side and slammed his fist into the man's jaw. Neumann squealed and dropped the machine gun. He staggered away from Wagner, tripped over some debris, and wound up flat on his back. He looked up at Wagner in total shock and rubbed his jaw.

"You fucking animal!" Wagner launched himself at Neumann. "He was just a child. You just murdered an innocent child." He grabbed Neumann by the collar of his coat.

A single gunshot broke the eerie silence of the city. Wagner and Neumann both turned in Mueller's direction. The major pointed the Luger at the sky but his eyes burned into Wagner.

"You forget yourself, Mr. Wagner." Icicles formed on Mueller's words. "That was not a child. That was a *Jew*. You would do well to remember that."

Wagner let go of Neumann and took an angry step toward Mueller. The Luger descended. Mueller aimed it directly at Wagner's chest. Wagner stopped in his tracks. His mouth worked but no sound escaped him.

"Nothing to say? Good." Mueller regarded Neumann and the bruise taking shape on his jaw. "On your feet, Mr. Neumann. Retrieve your weapon." He turned his attention to the man lying prone at his feet. The Luger swung away from Wagner and Mueller aimed it at the back of the man's head.

"Sir, don't." It was little more than a whisper but it was all Wagner could manage. His wounded ribs throbbed and shortened his breath.

Mueller turned his head slowly in Wagner's direction. The gun remained aimed at the man's head. "You object, Mr. Wagner? Perhaps you feel some love for this man. This worthless, *Jewish* man. Is that it?"

"Come on, Wagner, shut up." It was Schmidt who spoke.

"This man is a civilian, sir. We do not make war on civilians."

"We make war on all enemies of the Fatherland," Mueller replied.

"Damned right," Schmidt added.

Neumann mumbled his agreement as he massaged his jaw.

The man remained on the ground but he lifted his head and looked at the remains of the building. Tears spilled from his eyes and his body was wracked by sobs.

Mueller pulled the Luger's hammer back. He cast a sideways glance at Wagner and smiled. He remained in that position, unmoving, as if savoring what was to come. Then he released the hammer and slid the weapon back into its holster. He laughed, then, a throaty, unpleasant sound that filled the air around them. He regarded the dying man at his feet and spat upon his head. Slowly, the spittle trickled down the side of the man's cheek and mingled with his tears.

Schmidt laughed. He clapped Wagner on the back. "Looks like you got your wish, Wagner. Now this poor bastard gets to bleed to death slowly." He turned to Neumann. "That okay with you, Ernst?"

Neumann stopped rubbing his jaw long enough to favor them with a toothy grin. "Yeah, that's okay with me."

"I think it's dark enough now for us to move out," Mueller said. "Wagner, take point. Neumann, you follow him with the MG 15. Schmidt, you bring up the rear." He looked at each of his men, but his eyes lingered the longest on Wagner. "Move it."

Wagner remained in place a moment. His eyes moved from the dying man to the collapsed building and back again. Ultimately, Mueller was correct, insofar as the Reich was concerned. He had followed his orders and killed the enemy. That was the end of the matter.

He wanted to apologize to the dying man at his feet. Not that such a gesture would amount to anything. And he could not do so, anyway, without the others hearing him. What would Mueller's reaction be if one of his men attempted to comfort an enemy? Most likely he would shoot Wagner and leave him to bleed out next to his newfound friend.

He could shoot the doomed man, end his misery. But that would be an act of defiance and just as likely to elicit a lethal response from Mueller. Wagner wished the man to look up, to make eye contact, but it did not happen. The man continued to look at the collapsed building and sob.

Wagner swallowed the bile which threatened to erupt from his stomach and took point.

****

It was some time before Sobczynski was able to take his eyes from the collapsed building. He turned his head and saw the Germans were already three blocks from him. They moved slowly but only one, the man who threw the grenade that killed Poldek, held a weapon. It was only the white of the snow and the meager moonlight that allowed him to see the four dark shapes wend their way through the ghetto. The sky was not quite black yet but it would be before long.

He pulled himself along the ground until he reached the base of the pile of rubble that had until recently been their shelter. He placed one hand on the nearest mound of debris and wept. He did not know how long he remained there but the moon was high in the sky when at last he raised his head again. A wave of nausea washed over him and had he anything in his stomach he would have purged it. He waited for the world to stop spinning before he raised his head again.

There was another wave of nausea but he forced it down. He felt along his wounded leg. His pants were soaked with blood but the hemorrhaging had slowed considerably.

Either I'm running out of blood or the snow helped to slow it down. Probably both. It would make little difference. He would be dead soon and he knew it. But he had one last task to perform. He said a silent prayer God would allow him to live long enough to fulfill it.

He got one foot beneath him, then the other. He reached down and placed his hand on the rubble again and said good-bye to the boy he had found three years before wandering through the ruins. He had promised Poldek they would survive and since the German retreat from Warsaw and the Home Army's pursuit of them it seemed he would keep that promise. He should have known better than to make promises in wartime. Had he learned nothing from his experiences in the War to End All Wars?

He pulled his hand away from the debris and stood. His right leg threatened to buckle but he willed it to support him. He placed one hand over his abdomen and held it there. Fresh, hot blood seeped from the wound and trickled between his fingers.

He walked west, in the footsteps of the soldiers and toward the Vistula. He did not see the Germans again; they were much too far ahead of him for visual contact. That was okay. He followed their footprints in the dust and snow.

Hours later the sun made its first appearance of the day. It rose over the destroyed cityscape behind him as he reached the banks of the river. He did not pause and lurched the last few paces to the river's edge. His feet left deep footprints in the Vistula mud but somehow the mud did not try to ensnare him. He made it to the riverbank and dropped to his knees.

Without pause he shoved his hands into the freezing mud. He was aware of the cold seeping into his fingers but only on a subconscious level. He had no more than a few moments of life left to him and he needed the last of his physical and mental strength to perform one final task. He piled the mud in front of him and set about shaping it. He worked quickly, despair and anguish lending speed and strength to his failing muscles. "Helen," he whispered, "take care of Poldek until we can find his family. I'll be with you again in another moment."

His blood pattered onto the mud. He continued even after he could no longer feel his fingers or hands. The edges of his vision blurred and then turned black. He nearly lost consciousness. At the last moment he forced his eyes open and his frozen hands to move.

He seemed to be watching himself from a distance. That part of him, the part that watched, screamed for him to stop. *There has been enough bloodshed*, that part of him wailed. He ignored the cries. The freezing numbness worked its way up his forearms to his elbows. He paused only long enough to survey his work. He was nearly there. Just a few moments more…

He became aware he could no longer feel his legs. The pain in his right thigh and abdomen was gone completely. "Keep going," he whispered through clenched teeth.

He extended the legs another meter, created arms that were perhaps forty centimeters too long. The upper torso was barrel-shaped.

Sobczynski could not feel his arms at all and still he willed his hands to keep moving.

He formed the head a bit too small for the body but he was beyond caring. *You weren't created for an anatomy class, my friend*, he thought.

When the figure was complete Sobczynski looked it up and down a final time. He kissed his fingertips and applied them to the mud man's chest. Sobczynski's eyes closed for the final time. He lost what little balance he still possessed and toppled over. He lay in the mud next to the malformed figure. Slowly, his eyes still closed, Sobczynski reached out a numb and trembling hand and placed a single finger on the forehead of the mud man's body. His finger traced a single word across the forehead.

אמת.

Sobczynski dropped his arm and lay in the mud. He remained there until his body was discovered the following April.

****

Mueller looked at Neumann and suppressed the urge to shoot the man. He was clearly out of his element. His head whipped to either side so rapidly he might have been watching a tennis match. The devastation around them provided ample cover to any enemies that might have been in the area, but they had seen no one since the skinny man and the child. They had also failed to see any sign there was anyone still alive anywhere around them. Yet Neumann acted as if the Red Army was about to emerge from every destroyed building around them. Ridiculous.

"Why are you so scared, Neumann? Afraid the communists will get you?" He laughed, a short bark that startled Neumann and made him jump a little. *He's the last man who should be holding our only real weapon*, he thought.

"No sir, it's not that." Neumann's voice was steady but he was clearly exerting much willpower to make it so. "It's the Home Army. We don't know for certain they were all captured. There could be some elements of them still in the city."

"The Home Army." Schmidt snorted with just the correct amount of scorn. "Undisciplined pieces of shit. What did their fighting accomplish?" He spat on the ground. "Just another destroyed Jewish city, if you ask me."

"No one asked you," Wagner said from point. He did not turn as he said it.

"The Home Army was captured or killed to a man, Neumann. I don't think you have to worry about them." Mueller's voice was almost conversational. He purposely kept his disdain for Neumann out of his tone. He could always deal with the spineless son of a bitch when they rejoined the *wehrmacht*. For the present, he had to allow for the slight possibility there were remnants of the Home Army within the city limits. If that proved to be the case he would need every man he had. Even Neumann.

"Yeah," Schmidt piped in. "If you're going to worry about anything, worry about freezing to death." He laughed but fell silent and stopped dead in his tracks when Mueller turned on his heel and glared at him.

"Schmidt has a point, Major," Wagner said from the front. He stopped and turned. "We've been going all night. We need a break. And didn't we decide it was safer to move after dark?" He looked into the sky, where the sun continued its slow trek above the ruins of the city.

Mueller scowled. Neumann had turned and looked at him, just as Wagner did. He knew without looking Schmidt was also waiting for his decision. *Fucking Jew-loving piece of shit* was what his eyes said. But then he sighed his acknowledgement that they were right.

"Very well." He looked about. His gaze settled on what might have once been a church or synagogue but was now little more than a shattered shell. The building lacked a roof, and the north wall had collapsed completely. But the wind was coming from the south, so that would matter little. He pointed. "There. We'll rest there until dark. Neumann, give Schmidt the MG and help Wagner find some firewood."

"Yes, sir." Neumann held the machine gun out for Schmidt, who took it with much apparent glee. He followed Wagner toward the church.

An hour later Mueller polished off his ration and had to admit, if only to himself, he needed the fire as much as the rest of his men. He had thought winters in Berlin were bad; they did not hold a candle to this. The wind, while not oppressive, was constant and enough to cut through his clothing. His hands were nearly numb when Wagner and Neumann returned with the firewood.

They sat on the opposite side of the fire, warming their hands and smoking. They did not look at him or at each other. Their heads hung in a most dejected manner, and Mueller found himself more and more annoyed with them. Schmidt may have been a brainless kiss-ass but he believed in the infallibility of his superiors, including Mueller. He would prove useful if trouble arose. And there was always the possibility Neumann had been correct. If some remnant of the Home Army had escaped capture, they could well run into them. With but a single machine gun and two crewmen who were questionable at best, Mueller did not like their chances.

They would have to stick to the plan and continue their trek by moonlight.

Schmidt had eaten his ration as he stood next to a sizeable hole in the east wall. The MG 15 stood propped against the ancient brick next to him. He looked out on the shell of the city but thus far there had been no need of a lookout. There was no one out there, most likely no one within the city itself. The only sound which reached them came from the wind. It whistled through the remains of buildings and gave birth to dust devils in the streets.

"We'll sleep in shifts," Mueller said, breaking the silence and causing Neumann to jump, just a little. "Schmidt will take the first watch. Wagner, you relieve him in two hours, then Neumann, then me. Clear?"

The men nodded and said, "Yes, sir." Mueller leaned against the wall at his back and closed his eyes.

****

It was on Neumann's watch that the shit hit the fan. Wagner had succeeded in finally falling asleep when he heard the MG spit fire. He leaped up and moved as quickly as his wounded ribs would allow to the bombardier's side. Mueller and Schmidt were right behind him, pistols drawn. Neumann let loose another burst from the machine gun, and shouted something which could not be made out above the din.

Mueller grabbed Neumann's shoulder and pulled the man back from the wall. Neumann released his hold on the gun's trigger and had the presence of mind to point the muzzle at the floor. It was the only thing that saved him. The look in Mueller's eyes spoke murder, and the Luger in his right hand was aimed at Neumann's chest.

"What is it?" Mueller's tone was all business. He glanced through the hole in the wall, but saw no one on the street below.

Wagner and Schmidt continued to look in every direction. The street appeared deserted. What Wagner expected to see was a body, perhaps several, in the street next to the church. Neumann had to have opened up on someone. But there was no one there.

"I-I don't know," Neumann said, his words coming fast. "I never saw anything like it."

"What are you talking about, Lieutenant?" Mueller's voice was low, deadly. His eyes drilled into Neumann's .

"There's no one out there," Schmidt called back.

Mueller leaned into the man. "You better have one hell of a good reason for wasting ammunition."

"There was something there," Neumann said. He eyed the Luger, still pointed at his chest. "It was big, *very* big. It stood right out there and looked up at me. I swear, I've never seen anything like that in my life."

"What was it? Some kind of animal?" Wagner again scanned the street, and again came up empty.

"Must have been," Schmidt said. "Maybe a bear or something. Whatever it was, it looks like it took off. There's nothing out there now."

"You wasted all that ammunition on a bear?" Mueller did not await an answer. He tore the MG from Neumann's hands and tossed it to Schmidt.

"That was no bear," Neumann said.

"Sir, it couldn't have been a bear." Wagner stepped away from the wrecked wall and looked at the two officers. "Not this time of year."

"Thank you, Professor," Mueller said. He kept his eyes on Neumann. "Well? What was it?"

Neumann's eyes went from the Luger to the man holding it. He looked scared, but Wagner could not tell if he was frightened of whatever it was that had been outside, or by the man in front of him. Silently, Wagner encouraged Neumann to say the right thing. He did not like the look in Mueller's eyes. He did not like it at all.

Neumann took in a deep breath, his lips parted as if he were about to speak. Whatever he planned to say died in his throat. He caught sight of something moving from across the room, behind Mueller. His eyes went wide and the breath caught in his throat. He stammered and pointed. The other three men whirled in that direction.

At first glance, it did, indeed, resemble a bear. It was taller than a man, and wider. At first, Wagner thought it was dressed in dark brown (almost black) from head to toe, but that was incorrect. Upon closer inspection, he saw it wore no clothing at all. It appeared covered with mud. It possessed no neck and its too-small head sat atop shoulders that looked broad enough to support a halftrack. It stood in the doorway, between them and the stairs which led to street level and the outside. It said nothing, simply looked at them through the dark recesses which were its eyes.

"What the hell is that?" Schmidt sounded incredulous. Wagner thought the navigator would have rubbed his eyes had he not held the MG in his hands.

Mueller had forgotten all about Neumann. The Luger had dropped and was now pointed at the floor. The major turned and faced the thing in the doorway. Wagner could see the disbelief in his eyes. It lasted only a moment, however, before he raised the Luger and shouted, "Schmidt, fire your weapon!"

The thing took a step forward. Schmidt screamed something which could not be understood over the bark of the MG 15. He depressed the trigger and the first few rounds chewed up the wood floor in front of the thing. A moment later his aim improved dramatically. He thundered away with the MG, pumping 7.92 mm slugs into the thing.

It held its ground. It did not fall over, was not blown back by the impact of the rounds. It simply stood. Mueller yelled something and opened fire with his Luger. Neumann had drawn his pistol and was likewise emptying it into the mud man. Wagner had his own pistol in his hand, but it remained pointed at the floorboards. He stood and watched as the crew of the Do 17 dumped their ammunition and the object of their attention took every round.

"Cease fire, cease fire," he shouted, but he could scarcely hear his own voice above the barrage. There was simply no way anyone else could have heard him.

Mueller emptied the Luger and dropped the spent clip with practiced ease. He reached into his belt cartridge and pulled a fresh one. He slammed it home, moved the slide back, and resumed his assault. As Wagner watched, Neumann followed his commander's example and reloaded. Metal jackets rained down on the old and ruined floorboards, and still the thing stood, apparently oblivious to the attack.

Schmidt removed his finger from the trigger of the MG and looked at the thing in the doorway. His eyes bulged, his lips moved, but Wagner thought perhaps the navigator spoke only to himself.

"Cease fire, cease fire!" Wagner waved his arm in the air, and without the din of the machine gun, this time, the rest of the men heard him.

Mueller turned on him, his eyes swimming with rage. Clearly he was unhappy with a subordinate issuing orders. His eyes whipped from the mud man to the radioman. "Who do you think you are, *Sergeant*? You don't issue orders, *I* do!"

"Major, that thing is taking everything we throw at it. Or didn't you notice?"

Mueller took an angry step toward Wagner, but he was stopped in his tracks by a shout from Schmidt. "It's coming!"

Indeed it was. The mud man strode slowly across the floor. With each step, shells which had penetrated its body oozed from the mud and fell to the floor. Mueller turned to Schmidt. "He's wearing a flak jacket, nothing more. Schmidt, take him out. Point blank range."

Schmidt nodded, braced himself. The thing continued its slow advance. Mueller moved a bit to his right, and the thing seemed to single him out and it adjusted its course accordingly. Mueller's eyes went wide and he pointed at the thing. "Schmidt! Get him! *Now!*"

Schmidt swore under his breath and opened fire. More slugs tore into the thing's body, but it seemed not to notice. Schmidt stepped forward, finger still on the trigger. The thing ignored him. Schmidt ran the last few steps between him and the mud man, and jammed the MG's muzzle into the thing's belly. The gun penetrated perhaps four or five inches into the mud. It stopped and turned on Schmidt. For his last act on earth, Schmidt pulled the trigger.

An explosion of mud and gun metal pelted the bomber crew. Schmidt flew through the air and landed hard on the floor. Wagner dove for cover behind a small pile of debris. Mueller landed on top of him and Wagner felt his wounded ribs give way. Neumann screamed something and went down clutching his left leg.

When the mud stopped raining down on him, Wagner poked his head up and surveyed the room. Schmidt was down and was not moving. The MG lay perhaps five meters from him. The end of its barrel had opened like a budding flower. Smoke wafted from its shattered remains. Neumann was likewise down, but he was more than moving. He writhed on the floor, his gun a few meters away, forgotten. Blood saturated his left pant leg and he had wrapped both his hands around it. He screamed in agony.

The mud man stood in the same spot. Its midsection had opened up, and droplets of mud dripped from it and spattered on the floor. It seemed to show no discomfort from the blast. As Wagner watched, the mud began to reseal the hole in the mud man's middle. It flowed up from the floorboards and Wagner could actually see the thing add mass to its body.

Mueller rolled away and came up kneeling, Luger pointed at the mud man. His eyes went to Schmidt, who was clearly dead. Blood covered the navigator's face and chest. His eyes stared sightlessly at the afternoon sky above. No breath escaped him and frosted the air. Mueller's eyes settled on the ruined MG 15, and he swore. He eyed the mud man, who stood motionless in the center of the room.

Neumann remained on the floor. A pool of blood widened slowly around him. He screamed and whimpered and clutched his wounded leg with both hands, everything else apparently forgotten.

Mueller stood, then reached down and grabbed Wagner. He hauled the radioman to his feet. "We're leaving, Sergeant. Move, *now!*"

Wagner glanced at the mud man, who still had not moved. Mud continued to track its way across the floorboards from every direction and flow into the thing's body. Wagner looked at the wounded and screaming bombardier. "I'll grab Neumann."

"Forget him, he's gone." Mueller took a step toward the doorway and then seemed to change his mind. Instead, he strode past Neumann and approached the collapsed wall. "This way."

"Sir!" Wagner approached him, but stopped next to Neumann. "We can get him out of here right now." He protected his wounded side but tried to keep Mueller from seeing it.

Mueller pointed his gun out the wall and looked down. "We're going to have to jump. It's a good four meters. You think he can do that? Besides, the only thing that bleeds like that is the femoral artery." He regarded Neumann, coldly. "He's dead already."

"No," Neumann squeaked through gritted teeth. "I can make it."

"No, you can't." Mueller ran back to them, grabbed Wagner by his arm, and all but hurled him toward the collapsed wall. Wagner's feet skidded on the floorboards, and he nearly went down when he slipped in the pool of Neumann's blood. Mueller joined him at the wall. "He's dead. Maybe that thing will concentrate on him and give us time to put a little distance between us." He indicated the drop. "Get moving."

"Sir, we can't leave him here."

The mud man took its first steps since the MG exploded. Wagner could not tell if it targeted Neumann or Mueller, or even himself. Its steps were slow, deliberate, and straight. Mueller saw this and shoved Wagner through the opening. "Go!"

Wagner dropped like a rock. He landed on a pile of debris and rolled down to the street. Each impact on his right side sent lightning bolts of pain through his body. He yelped despite himself. Mueller followed him a moment later, and it was all the radioman could do to get out of his commander's way. Both men remained where they were for a moment, on their backs in the snow. Mueller was the first to regain his feet. He hooked an arm under Wagner and hauled him up. Wagner gasped with pain but managed to stifle a full-on scream. They looked at the collapsed wall a few meters above their heads.

Neumann had managed to crawl to the edge of the drop-off. His eyes were clenched almost shut and his knuckles were white. His lips had pulled back from his teeth with the effort. He screamed something incoherent. Wagner was certain it was a cry for help. He took a single step toward the church.

Neumann's expression changed in an instant. His eyes went wide and he struggled to hold on to the edge. Something jerked him back. Neumann's left hand lost its grip but he savagely held on with his right. "Help me, *please*! No, no, no, *no*!"

He grunted with the effort, his breath exploding from his lungs in a cloud of frost. His right hand maintained its grip on the edge of the second floor but it was clear he was losing the battle. All at once he let out a scream and vanished back inside the church. Several small objects pattered down the rubble and landed on the ground in front of Wagner and Mueller. The radioman gasped when he realized they were Neumann's fingers.

There was another scream from inside the church. It echoed off the walls of the destroyed buildings around them. Wagner turned his wide eyes from Neumann's severed fingers to where he had last seen the bombardier.

The mud man stood at the opening and looked down on them. In full sunlight, Wagner was afforded a better look at the thing. It had no eyes Wagner could see, although there were twin indents in the mud where the eyes should have been. It even had a crease which might have been a mouth. It did not appear to have fingers, but Wagner got the impression the thing was clenching and unclenching its fists.

"Move it." Mueller shoved him from behind.

Wagner stumbled on some pulverized concrete, but his feet started moving nonetheless. He cast several glances over his shoulder, expecting to see the thing chasing after them. It remained at the hole through which Neumann disappeared and stared after them. After covering several blocks, Wagner gave up and kept his eyes in front of him.

****

Mueller opened the door to the ruined hospital and looked inside. All manner of debris littered the corridor. There were several bodies on the tiled floor, all clearly dead. Each one lay in a long-dried pool of its own blood. Bullet holes marred the walls and floor around the corpses. Stretchers and other medical equipment were overturned and lay on the floor beside the people they were intended to save. The building seemed mostly intact from the outside, so he waved Wagner forward and entered.

The third room on the right turned out to have a few overturned beds. Mueller righted one and found it free of bloodstains and sat down. Wagner limped inside and looked at him from the doorway. Mueller could see the anger in his radioman's eyes. He ignored it. He swung his legs up onto the bed and lay back. He reached into a pocket and pulled out a crumpled pack of cigarettes. He shook one out, took a lighter from the same pocket, and lit up. He put one arm under his head and puffed on his cigarette.

"Are you going to stand there when there are beds? Get some rest. You're going to need it." He avoided looking at Wagner as he spoke. "Come nightfall, we're moving out again."

"You left him back there to die, sir." Wagner remained in the doorway. "I could have grabbed him and taken him with us."

Mueller sent a few smoke rings toward the ceiling. "To what end? He was already dead. He died the minute the shrapnel severed that artery. You know it, I know it. He would have slowed us down until he died." He puffed again. "You should be happy for him. He finally proved useful."

Wagner took a few angry steps into the room. "He was an officer. He was a member of your crew. And you just gave him up."

"Forget about him. That's an order." He lowered his voice for emphasis. "Now get some rest."

"I'm fine the way I am."

Mueller expected that. "Very well. Then make yourself useful and stand watch. Wake me when the sun goes down."

"If we make it out of here, I'm writing a report about this incident. *Sir*."

"And what are you going to tell them?" He puffed on his cigarette again and then butted it on the side of the bed. He propped himself up on one elbow and regarded Wagner. "We were attacked by a mud man? Is that it? They'll think you're insane. Or a liar. Neither of which holds much of a future in the Reich."

"I'm talking about you abandoning one of your own crew back there. He had a family, for Christ's sake."

"And you don't?" Mueller rolled onto his side and faced Wagner. "Aren't you always going on about Greta and how much you miss her? Oh yes, I hear everything my crew says. Greta and that little house in Brandenburg. And Helmut and Inge, of course. How old are they now? Do you want to see them again? Then maybe you should think about what you plan to say when we get back to Berlin."

He watched Wagner's eyes flash with anger. He had obviously hit a nerve bringing up the younger man's family. Mueller's hand drifted down toward the Luger just in case. He watched the sergeant bring his emotions under control slowly and with much effort. Mueller returned his hand to its former position nonchalantly. Wagner said nothing. He walked to one of the beds that had remained upright and sat down.

After a moment, he said, "And how will your report read, Major? What do you plan to say about what happened back there?"

Mueller was already on his back again. "Back there? Nothing. I'm thinking Neumann and Schmidt died in the crash along with Von Valkenberg."

"And what about liars not having a future in the Reich?"

Mueller smiled to himself. "It depends on the liar, and which lie is told." He coughed and cleared his throat. "That's much more believable than the truth, Wagner. Whom do you think they'll believe? Me or you?"

Wagner did not reply. He pulled his own pack of cigarettes from his jacket pocket. The pack was crushed and the few remaining cigarettes inside were pulverized. He crumpled the pack and tossed it away. "We should keep going."

"We're not going anywhere until we get some rest. And if you're thinking about deserting me…" This time he made no effort to hide his movement toward the Luger. He patted it with his hand.

"We're gonna die here, you know. If we don't freeze to death it'll be that creature back there. One way or the other, we're not getting out of here alive."

If he expected a response he was wasting his time. Mueller had already closed his eyes.

****

Wagner had a hell of a time trying to fall asleep. He walked the perimeter of the ward, checking outside the windows for any sign of their mysterious attacker and looking for any leftover food. He found neither and so he returned to the bed he claimed for himself.

The cold bit through his jacket and he pulled it a little tighter around his body. His ribs throbbed and any try at a deep breath drew severe pain. He lay in the filthy bed and thought about Greta and the kids. After twenty minutes of willing himself to fall asleep he rolled onto his left side and glanced at Mueller.

The major lay on his back. He had his lighter out and was holding the flame in front of a small photograph. Wagner squinted but he could not make out much detail. It appeared to be a family picture. He looked at Mueller and for a moment the cold-blooded son of a bitch who left Neumann to die was gone. He looked like nothing more than a tall, thin man who loved his family and missed them fiercely.

In the time he had spent as Mueller's radioman the major had never once spoken about anything other than the next mission and the glory of the Reich. That man was not present. For the briefest of moments Wagner caught a glimpse of the man Mueller had been before the war.

It lasted until Mueller glanced over at Wagner. The stern mask of a born disciplinarian dropped over his features like a portcullis blocking the entrance to a castle. He snapped his lighter shut and pocketed it and the photograph. "I told you to get some rest."

Wagner said nothing and closed his eyes again.

Much to his own surprise, he did succeed in nodding off. When he came to, bright moonlight was streaming through the windows on the far wall. He sat bolt-upright on the bed and swung his legs off. His ribs barked at him but not as much as they had before. He did not fool himself into thinking they were healing; the cold had simply numbed much of the pain. He glanced at Mueller, still asleep and snoring loudly. He lowered his head and ran a hand through his hair. In truth, he had needed the rest. He felt a little better than he had when they first entered the hospital. Still, he glanced at the rest of the overturned beds and could not help but think of the three men from his plane they had left behind.

He cleared his throat, and it sounded too loud in the quiet-as-a-tomb hospital. "Major, it's time to wake up."

Mueller did not wake, but he pulled his jacket tighter to his body and rolled onto his side. Wagner lifted himself from the bed and stretched his legs. His wounded ribs throbbed. He took a few steps toward Mueller when he noticed the shadow spread across the floor. He whirled.

The mud man stood in the doorway. It hesitated only a moment before it advanced into the room.

"Major!" Wagner yelled, and the panic in his voice penetrated the fog in Mueller's mind. The major snapped to in an instant and leaped from the bed. His hand went to the holster at his hip and he pulled the Luger. He pointed it in all directions until his half-awake mind focused on the thing in the room.

"What are you waiting for? Open fire!" Mueller depressed the trigger and the Luger barked. The first shot went wide but the next one hit the thing squarely in its chest. It did not slow its advance in the slightest. "Circle around behind it, Wagner. We'll catch it in a crossfire."

"It won't work," Wagner said. He had yet to draw his own pistol. He simply stood and watched the thing's relentless march. He had moved a few steps to the side, out of the thing's path, and he noticed now it ignored him. It seemed to home in on the major.

Mueller backed up as he continued to fire. The Luger went dry, and Mueller dropped the clip without thinking about it. He inserted a new one and continued to fire. The rounds clipped the thing's arms, its legs, and buried themselves in its body. Mud splattered with every impact but still it advanced.

It passed by Wagner no more than two meters away. Wagner stared at it, at where its eyes should have been. It walked into a beam of moonlight and Wagner saw the strange marking on its forehead. He leaned forward a bit for a better look, but it moved past him before he could begin to see it clearly.

It closed the distance to Mueller, who continued to shout and fire his weapon. He had backed up all the way to the wall now, between two large windows. He fired the Luger dry, and reloaded again as fast as he was able. He got the fresh clip loaded as the thing lifted its arms and reached for him.

Mueller screamed and swung his empty hand in a wide arc. It hit the side of the thing's head. Mud flew everywhere. Mueller tried to pull his arm back, but even from across the room, Wagner could see it was stuck inside the mud of the thing's head. It reached up and wrapped one of its hands around Mueller's right arm. It pulled the arm aside, and Mueller pulled the Luger's trigger and sent shots into the walls. Dust and pieces of plaster rained down on the floor. He screamed.

The mud man grasped Mueller's other arm, and yanked his hand out of its head. Mud dripped from the major's hand and wrist. His fingers seemed frozen in the clenched position. The thing held Mueller by his arms, and in moments, the Luger was once again empty.

Wagner took several steps forward, but stopped himself. Shooting the thing had no effect. His wounded ribs made the idea of physical combat laughable, and he had serious doubts a few punches and kicks would succeed where large caliber bullets failed. They were overmatched in every way.

Use the time to get out of here, his mind screamed at him. *You can get away while it's busy with Mueller.* But he could not. This thing had found them twice already. Wagner did not doubt it would find him again. All he would gain was time, a few hours at most. His ribs would not allow him to move quickly enough to keep ahead of the thing. Running was not an option.

And there was something else. He saw the terrified expression in Neumann's eyes as the thing grabbed hold of him and tore him away from the drop-off. He saw the old man sob at the results of the single grenade that destroyed his sanctuary and took the life of the young child. These images flashed across his mind's eye and he regarded Mueller again.

Although the major looked frightened he also appeared angry, even homicidal. There was no trace of the sad man who looked at the photograph and longed to be with his family. He had been replaced with a murderous monster.

The mud man lifted Mueller from the floor and then above its head. It released one of the major's arms and grasped his legs. Wagner knew what was coming. Mueller apparently did as well; he screamed impotently at the creature.

The mud man brought Mueller down fast at the same time it lifted one of its knees. Mueller smashed against it. His arms flailed at the air and his legs splayed at odd angles to his body. Wagner heard the sickening *crack* from across the room. He turned his eyes away from the gruesome tableau before him.

Mueller flopped onto the cold tiles and lay still.

After a moment Wagner looked up again. The mud man was moving in his direction. Wagner swallowed and steeled himself. "Get it over with," he whispered when the mud man stopped in front of him.

The creature did not move. It seemed to regard the radioman with its hollow mud eyes. At this distance Wagner could clearly see the strange marking on the creature's forehead. He stared at it for a moment and his mind filled with images of his childhood. He had not thought of Timothy Rabinowitz in years, so why was the memory of the little Jewish kid from the apartment upstairs now returning to him? If this was his life flashing before his eyes he would rather have seen Greta. Wagner returned his gaze to the creature's hollow eyes. It loomed above him but made no overtly hostile move. In fact it did not move at all.

Then Wagner whispered something before the thought even finished forming in his head. "I'm sorry." He swallowed and lowered his head. *Just make it quick,* he thought.

The mud man remained in front of him for another moment. Then it sidestepped Wagner and lumbered slowly toward the door. Wagner heard it move past him and he turned and watched it exit the room. He waited for it to return, convinced it was playing some type of cruel trick on him. After a moment he caught sight of movement outside the nearest window. He walked to it and looked out and saw the creature moving down the street, back the way they had come.

All at once the tension left him and he sagged nearly to his knees. He held onto the window frame to stop himself. He closed his eyes and forced himself to breathe normally. He remained that way for several moments.

"Sergeant, help me."

The voice was little more than a whisper and it belonged to Mueller.

Wagner opened his eyes and looked out the window again. The mud man was nowhere in evidence. Wagner turned his attention to the man lying on the floor five meters away.

Mueller lay on his back with his legs splayed at odd angles to his body. He was clearly broken but his eyes lost none of their customary forcefulness. "Wagner, you have to help me."

Wagner closed the distance to Mueller and looked down at him. He said nothing, simply stared at his former commander. After a moment, he turned away.

"Wagner, where are you going? Get back here and help me. That's an order, Sergeant."

Wagner made it a few steps before he stopped and turned and regarded Mueller again. He walked back slowly to his commanding officer.

Mueller's eyes lost some of their hard edge. "That's better. We have to get out of here. You'll have to carry me. We can use one of the mattresses as a stretcher until I can walk again."

Wagner continued to look down on him. "I think your walking days are over, sir."

Mueller's eyes hardened again. "Don't forget who you're talking to, Sergeant. I am your commanding officer and I have just given you a direct order. Get that mattress over here now!"

Wagner shook his head slowly. He watched Mueller attempt to move his arms, perhaps to grab Wagner and give him a shove. The limbs remained where they were on the cold tiles.

Wagner knelt beside Mueller and reached inside the man's shirt pocket. He removed the pack of cigarettes and shook one out for himself. He lit it and stuffed the pack into his own pocket. The smoke burned its way down his throat and filled his lungs and it felt wonderful. "Can't tell you how much I needed one of these, sir. And since it doesn't look like you'll have any use for them…" He took another big drag.

Mueller's lips pulled back from his teeth. "I'll have you shot for this, Wagner. So help me God, I'll have you shot!" His threat echoed off the walls and filled the ward. "Do you hear me, boy? Greta will be a widow and your children will grow up knowing their father was a traitor. Assuming they're allowed to grow up at all! Now help me!"

Wagner stood and smoked Mueller's cigarette and continued to look down at the man. When he was finished smoking he stamped out the cigarette and turned toward the door.

"Wagner! Goddamn you!"

Wagner made no reply and did not look back over his shoulder. He exited the hospital into the cold night air. Mueller's cries continued for some time, until Wagner had walked far enough away from the hospital so he no longer heard them.

He headed in the direction he hoped was west, toward Greta and Helmut and Inge. His thoughts were of them. He did not linger on the monster he left behind inside the ruined hospital.

But he was unlikely to ever forget the Golem.

It was in a book owned by Timothy Rabinowitz and inside was a crude illustration of a creature made by man. Wagner had asked the meaning of the Hebrew word scrawled into the man-shape's forehead. Timothy, a student of history and an avid reader of fantasy, was only too happy to tell him.

The symbol was *emet*, and it meant truth.

Somehow Wager doubted anyone would ever learn the truth of what really happened to the survivors of his crew's crash landing, but *he* knew. He knew the truth. That would have to be enough.

The Highwayman

Peña looked up in time to see the Muskrat place three large beer steins on the table. Peña placed his logbook to the side and took the stein closest to him. He held it up to Muskrat and Tombstone, the other man at the table, and took a long, slow pull. The golden liquid cascaded down his dry throat and it felt wonderful. He paused long enough to appreciate the sensation and then took another. The stein was nearly half-empty when he put it back on the table. He pulled his plate closer to him and dashed the steak and potatoes with salt. "That hit the fucking spot."

"It always does," Muskrat replied. Beer suds covered his mustache and dribbled onto his prodigious beard.

Muskrat was possibly the largest human being Peña had ever seen. It was not his height, although he had to be close to 6'7". It was not even his weight, although Peña suspected the man topped out somewhere in the neighborhood of 380 pounds. It was his girth and the tree trunks he called his arms; they looked large and powerful enough to crush a mountain gorilla. They were also covered with ink, which extended onto the big man's neck. Peña had never seen the rest of Muskrat (a fact for which he was grateful) but he got the impression there was not much skin left on the man's body that did not sport some manner of tattoo. In fact, Muskrat was probably what most people pictured when they thought of a trucker. In that respect he had chosen the right profession.

Peña's other tablemate nearly matched the 'rat in the category of badassery. He did not know much about Tombstone, other than he was originally from Arizona. He was not as tall as Muskrat but he carried himself as someone who could, and would, kick your ass at a moment's notice. He was bearded, as well, but his was scruffy and not the well-formed avalanche of hair that hung down from the 'rat's chin. He was tatted up, too, although not as much as Muskrat, or even Peña himself.

Peña put the first forkful of steak into his mouth and chewed. It was not particularly good but he was used to it and too hungry to go without. He chased the steak with the largest chunk of potato on his plate and then took another swig of his beer. He glanced out the window as he did.

The sky was gunmetal gray but the first evidence of black was starting to enter the picture. The big American flag next to the door flapped wildly in the wind. There was no snow, not yet, but it was on the way. He planned to be inside his sleeper before the first of the flakes made their way into Troy.

"Gonna blizzard on us like a motherfucker," Tombstone said around bites of his large pork chop sandwich. Barbeque sauce dripped from the sides and landed in small dollops on his black leather vest. "This is why I hate the Northeast this time of year."

"Fucking pussy," Muskrat mumbled and took another big gulp of beer. "Go back to the desert where you belong."

"Go fuck yourself," Tombstone replied.

Peña stifled a laugh with another mouthful of steak. They were quite profane with one another, his two tablemates; Peña suspected they took that kind of talk only from each other and a very select, and small, list of others. And no one outside the job, although he suspected Muskrat's wife most likely got away with it. He had never met the woman but the 'rat had showed him a photo once. She looked like the only woman on Earth who could handle the big man.

Peña drank more beer and emptied the stein just as Dia, the short waitress with the black hair, approached the table. She balanced three more large steins in her arms and placed one in front of each of the men. Peña looked at her questioningly.

"On the house, boys. Mike's new policy. Everyone gets a freebie at the start of the winter season. So enjoy." She smiled her pretty smile.

"Thanks, babe," Muskrat said. Tombstone nodded his thanks.

Peña raised the new stein to her. "Can you bring me a Coke, too?"

"Sure can." She took the empty from in front of him and made her way back to the counter.

Muskrat watched her go. "Sweet ass."

"Yeah, not bad for having punched out a bunch of kids," Tombstone added.

"How many she got?" Muskrat finished off his first beer and let loose a loud, long belch.

"Eleven or twelve, I think," Tombstone replied.

Muskrat nearly choked. *"What?"*

Tombstone broke into a belly laugh. "I'm kidding, I'm kidding. It's more like five or six. I'm serious this time."

'rat looked over his shoulder in the direction of the counter. "Hey mother, want another?" He was not stupid enough to say it with enough volume for Dia to hear him but it elicited guffaws from Tombstone.

Peña continued to work on his steak and the other men fell silent and ate and drank.

After a few conversation-free moments, Tombstone finally asked, "Whose turn is it this year? I never remember."

"Not ours," 'rat stated.

Peña raised his hand and frowned.

"Did your boss pick one yet?"

Peña nodded and swallowed the last of the potatoes. "Yeah. New guy. His first day is today, in fact. I saw him in dispatch when I was hooking up my load."

"Young guy?" Muskrat asked though a mouthful of fries.

Peña nodded again. "Young enough. Twenty-five, maybe twenty-six. I heard he got his class A just last month after he got home from Afghanistan."

Muskrat shook his head and Tombstone whistled through his teeth. "That's a lousy break. Guy went through shit over there and now he has to come home to this? That's kinda fucked up."

"There's no 'kinda' about it," Muskrat countered. He turned his attention to Peña. "Remind me never to work for your fucking company. To take a guy who just got back home after being in that shithole and give him this run…That's some cold-blooded shit."

"You want the job?"

"Fuck no."

"All right, then." Peña shrugged his shoulders. "I know it's a shitty thing to do, but it wasn't my call. Just be happy we've been doing this as long as we have and it's not us out there."

"Seniority has its privileges," Tombstone added.

The men fell silent and drank their free beers. Dia returned to the table with Peña's Coke and removed the empty plates. Peña ordered another round for his tablemates and chewed on a toothpick. Tombstone studied his logbook. Muskrat alternated his gaze from the weather outside to the cute waitress inside.

There was not much further conversation until the door opened and a blast of cold wind blew through the restaurant. Dozens of heads turned toward the door and men grumbled under their breath. The young man stepped across the threshold and closed the door against the wind. He stood there for a moment and ran a hand through his short, brown hair. A few random snowflakes fell and landed on his shoulders. Peña recognized him immediately and waved the kid over. The newcomer waved back and smiled and made his way to the table.

Peña slid his empty beer stein in front of Tombstone when the kid turned momentarily away and then pushed the empty chair with his foot. "Grab a seat," he said.

"Thanks." The young man sat and whipped off his jacket. "That was a nice ride to get here."

"Yeah, that part's a piece of cake. Muskrat, Tombstone, this is our new driver. Kid, meet two of the biggest assholes in the business."

The two burly men nodded at the newcomer.

"Hi. Rick Jordan, nice to meet you." He extended his hand across the table in Muskrat's direction.

'rat took the hand and shook it. "Muskrat."

"Tombstone," the other man said and shook Jordan's hand. "And don't believe anything this dickhead says. We're a couple of teddy bears, really."

"What's your name, kid?" Muskrat asked.

"Rick Jordan."

Muskrat shook his head. "No one around here's ever gonna call you that. What's your *real* name?"

Jordan nodded. "Sandman."

"That's better."

"You pick that because of your time in Afghanistan?" Peña asked.

Jordan shook his head. "No, but that did occur to me after I picked the name. It's a graphic novel series I read as a kid."

"Ah, okay." Peña glanced over his shoulder and, sure enough, Dia was approaching the table with another beer stein. Peña waved her off. It produced a confused look from the waitress but she obediently retreated the way she had come. "Well, welcome to the Northeast run, Sandman."

"Thanks." Jordan smiled and picked up a menu. "Anything good here?"

"Absolutely not," 'rat said. "What do you think this is, the Ritz Carlton? Nothing here is good. But it's edible, barely, and that's all that matters."

"The beer ain't so bad," Tombstone added.

"We can't drink tonight," Peña informed them. He looked gravely at Jordan. "Right?"

"Right," the kid confirmed. "First run. Hell, first day on the job. I'm not gonna blow that just to have a beer."

"Smart man," Peña said with a nod.

Jordan looked over the menu and Dia came over and took his order. She returned a moment later with a large glass of Coke for Sandman. The kid thanked her and downed half of it in one sip.

The conversation consisted mostly of the men asking questions about Afghanistan and what the kid did in the service. Jordan had been a corporal in the Army and served mostly as a gunner on helicopter missions. He saw plenty of action but he seemed reluctant to go into much detail. That convinced Peña the kid was not bullshitting them or playing up his role in the war. His grandfather had been the same way when the topic of Korea came up. Peña sighed to himself and wondered how Townshend's owner could have had the heart to pick this kid for this particular run.

Peña got the distinct impression both Muskrat and Tombstone felt the same way. Jordan was polite and seemed nice enough. Plus he had spent three years in the sand fighting assholes dead set on killing him. This was a lousy way to reward the kid for serving his country. But none of the men, Peña included, felt the least inclination to trade runs with him.

Tombstone was the first to call it a night. He said good-bye to Peña and Jordan, gave Muskrat a good-natured "Go fuck yourself" and headed out the door to his rig. The blast of cold wind that made it inside when Tombstone opened the door was enough to make Peña shiver. The wind was picking up something fierce and the snow had started. It was not a blizzard, not even close, but it was enough to make Peña not regret his decision to stay the night at the truck stop.

Muskrat followed his buddy out the door ten minutes later. He wished Jordan good luck and slapped Peña on the back. A second gust of icy wind accompanied 'rat's departure.

Peña ordered coffee for himself and his fellow Townshend driver. They drank the black liquid and talked about the run. Peña waited for a proper opening that would not feel forced when he brought up the subject of 228. The kid got close to giving him such an opening but he never quite got there. Peña wondered if he was being overly cautious; the kid trusted him, that much was clear. He doubted Jordan would even notice the abrupt change in conversation, but still he waited.

Another round of coffee and some cheese Danish later Peña was beginning to feel desperate. He glanced out the window into the yard. The number of rigs seemed the same, more or less. Most had their running lights on and diesel fumes spewed slowly from their chrome stacks. The wind whipped more snowflakes through the air; they played in the yard lights and around the yellow and red running lights of the big rigs. He imagined Muskrat and Tombstone snug in their respective sleepers, watching porn and stuffing their mouths with chips and salsa dip. He wanted to be in his own sleeper but first he had a job to do. He looked at Jordan again and caught the tail end of the kid's half of their conversation.

"…time-conscious are they?"

Peña tilted his head. "What?"

"I said, how time-conscious are they? At dispatch, I mean. I'm just asking because with the snow out there I might not be exactly on time to Lake Placid. How clear do they keep 87 North?"

And just like that Peña had his opening. He licked his lips and swallowed. "No one around here calls it 87 North.

Do that over the radio and everyone will know you're a rookie and they'll start breaking your balls. It's known as the Northway. Make sure you say that if you're going to say anything at all on the air. Cool?"

Jordan nodded. "Gotcha."

"There's a shortcut a little ways up the Northway. Look for the connector to Dixon's Pass. The official designation is Route 228. That'll take you to a much faster way through the Adirondacks and into Lake Placid with time to spare."

"Dixon's Pass."

Peña nodded. "Named after the first trucker to take the route. His handle was the Highwayman."

"So, is this guy a local celebrity or something? You have to do something right to have a road named after you."

"Or something wrong. He was hauling a load of plow blades to Ogdensburg. He didn't make it. There was a lot of snow on the road. He lost it going down a steep grade."

Jordan blinked at Peña. "And this is the way you want me to go? What am I, an asshole?"

Peña shrugged. "Kid, there isn't a road in America that hasn't taken the life of a trucker. I'm just trying to save you some time. The Highwayman bought it way back in '65. The route has been widened and maintained since then."

Jordan's eyes narrowed a bit. "What's it look like? Is it kept clear or am I gonna be fighting it all the way to the drop?"

Sharp kid. Knows all the right questions to ask. Just like the kid last year and the one before him. "It's clear enough. The fact is no matter which route you take you're gonna dealing with the snow. The roads are slick and there are some hills and downgrades you'll have to deal with. But it's a faster route to Lake Placid and that's what you need to think about."

Jordan nodded. "You've used it yourself."

"More times than I can count. It's safe enough as long as you don't drive like an idiot." That was when Peña put the icing on the cake. "And remember, I'll be with you. Lake Placid is kinda-sorta on the way to Malone so I can see you at least get to the town before I continue on north."

Jordan finished off his Danish and sat back in his chair. "You're babysitting me." He could not keep the disappointment out of his voice.

Peña shrugged. "You're a rookie. Tim and Sheila always assign someone to go with the rookies on their first haul so don't take it personally. And you're actually getting a break. I'm not gonna be in the cab with you watching your every move. So count your blessings."

Jordan held up his hands. "Sorry, I didn't mean to complain. It's just that after what I did in the war you'd think they'd trust me with this."

"They do. That's why you're riding alone. Got me?"

Jordan licked his lips and nodded. "Got you."

Peña stood up. "I gotta piss. I'll meet you outside. Where'd you park?"

Jordan glanced out the window. "Right next to you, actually. That's your rig with *Jala Peña* on the door, right?"

"Right." Peña took a rather large billfold from his front pocket, pulled a twenty and two fives from it and tossed them onto the table. "Since it's your first day on the job, dinner was on me. I'll be out there in a few."

"Okay. And thanks." Jordan slipped into his coat.

Peña walked into the men's room and closed the door. He voided his bladder and washed his hands. He caught sight of himself in the mirror and paused. Was he really going through with this? The kid was innocent. Sandman seemed decent enough, and he had served his country in time of war. 'rat and Tombstone were right. He did not deserve this.

"Bad luck," he whispered. The kid drew the short straw and it was as simple as that. He dried his hands and left the restroom.

The wind had subsided slightly although the snow had picked up. The cold hit him all at once but that was all right; his sleeper would be warm and so would the bottle of whiskey in the hidden compartment which no company owner or state trooper had ever found.

Peña made his way to his rig. Sure enough, Jordan had parked next to him. The kid was in his cab revving the engine and holding his hands in front of the heating vents. The rig he had been assigned was only a few months old and still looked new. Peña shook his head. *Bad enough what they're gonna do to him,* he thought of Townshend's owners. *They have to get an insurance payment out of it, too. Fucking pricks.* It was hardly a new idea. He remembered the kid from two or three years ago also driving a new rig. Tim and Sheila were hardly the only owners cashing in on what was a shitty necessity. *Probably gives them confidence to see the owners giving them a new rig. Poor bastards.*

Jordan rolled his window down. "Okay, how do you want to do this?"

Peña felt the heat from inside Jordan's cab and welcomed it. Not that it drove the cold from him, but he liked the idea of the kid at least being warm and comfortable. "I'm gonna follow you. I want to keep a few miles between us. It wouldn't do for me to come riding up your ass on a downgrade. So I'll give you fifteen minutes and then I'll follow. Once you get to 228 you'll probably have your hands full so don't get on the radio unless it's something serious."

Jordan nodded his agreement. "Okay. Anything else?"

"That's it," Peña said without hesitation.

"Okay, let's do this." It was probably something the kid had said any number of times during his service to his country.

Peña gave a curt nod and jumped off the running board. He climbed into his cab and watched the kid ease his big rig out of the parking spot. The truck moved slowly in the direction of the fuel pumps. Peña cranked up the heat in his cab and watched the pump attendants fill up the kid's rig. After a few moments Jordan pulled away from the pumps and headed for the exit. Peña watched him pull onto the main road and head for the Northway.

He made his way into his sleeper unit.

****

Sandman took the turn on the Northway and shifted up. The road was level and the snow accumulation was light and there was no sign of traffic in front of him. A mile up the road he saw another trucker coming from the opposite direction. He blew the air horn twice but the other driver did not respond. Sandman continued on.

He saw the first sign for the junction with 228 a few moments later. A mile farther and he came upon the turn. It clearly led into the mountains. He eyed the road and counted no fewer than three sharp turns within eyesight. He looked again at the expanse of the Northway in front of him. It was still level and free of cars and other trucks. Traffic lights flashed yellow at each intersection. The Sandman sat and thought.

It certainly looked like an easier path to stay on the Northway. He could call Jala Peña and tell him he was not taking 228. But the veteran driver had specified this route. If he stayed on the Northway it might make him look fearful to Townshend's owners and that he could not permit. The economy was in the shitter and he was fortunate to have landed this job; he could not take the chance of losing it or of inviting greater scrutiny from the bosses for a prolonged period of time. It was a fact drivers who needed a babysitter did not receive full pay for the haul. He needed the money and the benefits and so did Lori and the kids.

Sandman made the turn onto 228.

He negotiated all three of the turns he saw from the intersection with cautious ease. He downshifted one gear when he reached the first hill and crested it and got his first look at the enormity of Dixon's Pass. It snaked along the mountains, up and down steep hills. The road did not seem wide enough to accommodate two rigs at the same time and he wondered what would happen if he met someone coming the other way. A light dusting of snow covered everything. There was no evidence of other long haulers or pedestrian vehicles; the snow on the mountain road was undisturbed. It was not deep enough yet to warrant sending a plow to clear the way but Sandman did not doubt it would get there before long. Most likely before he was able to reach the end of 228 and the village of Lake Placid.

There was a decided lack of streetlights and guardrails for as far as he could see. The streetlights made sense; the road was not wide enough for a shoulder and there were far too many twists and turns for someone to string electrical cables. He paid it little mind once he noticed it; his truck's headlights and roof lights would be more than adequate.

The absence of guardrails concerned him a bit. He would not need them on the northbound trip but if he came back the same way he was less than enthusiastic about being that close to the edge with nothing between him and the Almighty but his driving skills. Perhaps he would come back via 87.

He sat back and his brow furrowed and he stroked his chin. From his vantage point he could still see much of the Northway. He glanced in that direction but Jala Peña had yet to catch up. Sandman debated waiting for his convoy partner/babysitter but he decided against it. He was not a child, and did not need someone to hold his hand. He needed his new bosses to know he could be counted upon to get the job done without someone looking over his shoulder. And if the man was experiencing engine trouble or something else that would delay him Sandman would have heard something on the radio. It remained silent except for some long haulers twenty or so miles south jabbering about the fucking Jets game from the day before.

He revved the diesel again and let out the clutch.

The snow crunched and compacted beneath his tires. The Peterbilt was heavier than the rigs with which he trained but not by a large degree. And the five tons of groceries bound for the supermarket in Lake Placid gave him some weight in the back to offset the sail that the trailer would become if a mountain gust broadsided him. Sandman felt good about this run.

He kept a steady speed on the first downgrade. He felt the tires slip a bit but he had no trouble keeping the new vehicle on the road. He upshifted before he reached the bottom so he would have enough momentum to climb the next hill. "Piece of cake," he said to himself.

He slowed and stopped when he saw the short, wooden cross on the side of the road. It was old and partially covered with snow. Sandman knew what it meant immediately. The name and date had been burned into the wood: E Karvellis 1972.

Sandman looked up the incline in front of him. "Must have lost traction going up. Shitty way to go." He nodded at the cross and started forward again.

He crested the hill and was rewarded with a straightaway for three more miles. He used the level road to pick up speed and make up time. When he moved beyond the range of the truckers to the south and their never-ending debate about the Jets he began to hum a tune to himself. The Peterbilt had a radio but he did not want to use it in case Jala Peña needed something.

It was pitch black outside the cab now and Sandman needed to concentrate. The snow was picking up; it shot through his field of vision in white streaks like the stars that zipped past the *Millennium Falcon* in hyperspace. The effect could be hypnotizing if he was not careful. He tightened his grip on the wheel and upshifted again.

The next upgrade was steep. Sandman came to a stop at its base. There were easily five, maybe six inches of snow on the road. He could probably make it but he was aware of what would happen if he lost traction on the way up; the consequences had been drilled into his head during training. He thought again about E Karvellis and the image of the man's memorial burned itself into his mind's eye.

He set the airbrakes and stepped from the cab. He could chain up in ten minutes, his average time at the training school. If necessary he would ride the chains all the way to Lake Placid. And judging by the rate of snowfall he might well have to do just that. When the deed was done he hopped back into the cab and reached for the microphone.

"Breaker, breaker for Jala Peña. You out there?" He waited for only a moment before the other driver's voice emerged from a burst of static.

"That you, Sandman?"

"10-4. Just a friendly FYI, I chained up. Snow's getting a little thick up here."

"Roger that. What's your 20?"

"No idea. I haven't seen a mile marker yet. I'm at the bottom of the first upgrade past the three-mile stretch of level blacktop, fifth upgrade overall."

There was a pause, then, "I know right where you are. I'm about three miles behind. You'd better get a move on."

Sandman frowned. *Just trying to give you a heads-up,* he thought but did not say. "10-4." He replaced the mic on its hook and put the rig in gear.

The upgrade was difficult to negotiate and the rig moved slowly. Sandman felt the wheels slip several times but he managed to keep his momentum and the truck eased forward. The snow whipped past his windshield and for the first time Sandman felt something other than excitement at his first run.

Even with the chains the road was becoming difficult to negotiate. He began to regret his decision to take this route. The Northway might have been more indirect but it was largely level and he would not have to deal with this nonsense. He glanced out the driver's window into the other lane. The road simply ended perhaps ten feet to his left. He could not see the drop-off, had no desire to see it, but he was willing to bet it was one hell of a sight. *Especially on the way down*, he thought. He was angry. Angry at Peña and Muskrat and Tombstone, but mostly he was angry with himself. He had allowed himself to be talked into this route and that pissed him off.

The Peterbilt finally crested the hill and Sandman looked through the windshield at the steep downgrade on the other side. The yellow sign to the right, abutting the mountain, read: 15% GRADE. It was the first evidence he had seen that human beings travelled this route since the old cross. Still, he swore. A fifteen-percent grade was not usually a problem but the snow made him hesitate.

"Oh, for Christ's sake, stop being a pussy."

He eased off the brake and the truck rolled forward.

He stayed in low gear, heard the snow crunch beneath the tires even over the wind and the sound of the cab's heater. He eyed the speedometer and nodded to himself. Sandman could not see the bottom of the hill yet and he wondered just how far down it went. He alternated between the regular brakes and the Jacobs and kept his speed below ten miles per hour. He suddenly understood why Peña had wanted a few miles between rigs. If one of them lost it on this hill…

Gravity clawed at the rig and seemed desperate to pull it along at a much faster rate of speed but Sandman maintained his slow pace. After a few moments his headlights showed him the bottom of the hill. He released a breath he did not realize he had been holding and released the brakes. The rig picked up some speed but it was manageable and he wanted to make up some time.

The road before him snaked around another outcropping of rock. Sandman began the turn—

"Jesus!"

A trailer sat at a dead stop directly in front of him. Instinctively he slammed on the brake pedal at the same moment his heart leaped into his throat. He had the presence of mind not to spin the wheel hard to the left; the drop-off was very close and a drastic course correction like that would send him over the edge. Instead he turned the wheel only slightly.

He felt the tires lock up and skid on the snow. The rig threatened to jackknife but somehow he maintained enough control to prevent that. The back of the stopped trailer loomed large in his windshield. He held himself as far from the wheel as possible and stood on the brake pedal.

The new Peterbilt responded to his actions. He watched the front of the cab swing wide of the trailer. If another truck picked that moment to come around the curve he was a dead man. Fortunately no other rig presented itself and Sandman avoided smashing into the newcomer. He fishtailed the trailer around the obstacle and jogged the wheel to the right. He was back in the right lane and in front of the stopped trailer. He came to a complete stop.

His breathing was fast, ragged. His hands and legs shook. He closed his eyes and took a few deep breaths. He could feel his heart crawl back down his throat and resume its customary place in his chest. After a few moments he opened his eyes. He glanced in the side view and saw the big rig sitting in its spot perhaps twenty feet behind. It was completely dark.

"Motherfucker." Sandman threw on his jacket and kicked open his door. Newbie or not this called for kicking somebody's ass.

The wind whipped at him and the snow stung the exposed skin on his hands and neck and face. He barely noticed. "Asshole!" He gesticulated at the dark cab. "You almost killed me, you piece of shit! Where are your fucking road flares?" He continued his brisk pace until he stood perhaps five feet in front of the cab.

The rig was old, the oldest he had seen on the road by far. It was not snub-nosed but compared to the newer rigs it may as well have been flat-faced. It was painted red but the color had faded to almost orange. Barely visible beneath the left headlight was the number 203. An old air horn sat on the roof above the driver's door. Above the flared front fender and written in faded chrome was the word, *Mack*. An equally faded piece of chrome in the shape of a bulldog stood at the ready to the right of the old nameplate.

It took Sandman only a moment to get over his surprise at the age of the truck. The anger returned and burned in his chest. He put one foot on the running board mounted above the fuel tank and grabbed onto the side view mirror bracket and hauled himself up. He looked into the cab.

It was dark but the lights on the back of his trailer showed him the cab was empty. There was nothing resembling a sleeper compartment and he concluded the rig had to be abandoned. He tried the door and found it locked. He held his face to the glass and looked inside.

The cab was wide but it lacked legroom. The seats were threadbare and he could see pieces of the cushion poking through the ancient leather. The wheel looked as old and weathered as the seats. Two gear shifts jutted up from the floor between the two seats. If the floor had been carpeted at one time there was no sign of it now; Sandman looked down on old and rusted steel and wondered who would drive this old piece of shit around, especially in this weather and on this route.

Then it hit him. He hopped off the fuel tank and walked around to the back of the trailer. It was much darker there than at the front but he could still see the lack of tire tracks leading up to the trailer. The snow was disturbed only by the tracks he had made in his desperate attempt to avoid the collision.

He looked up at the trailer. "Don't suppose you climbed inside to get out of the cold, did ya?" He reached for the handle before he remembered Peña would be coming down the hill very shortly. He sprinted back to his cab.

The change in temperature between the outside and the cab's interior was too much not too notice but Sandman ignored it. He grabbed his mic. "Breaker, breaker for Jala Peña. Copy."

He listened intently but heard nothing save static. He repeated the call and waited. Christ, if Peña was on his way down the hill…He glanced at his side view but he saw no sign of headlights coming up behind the dead Bulldog. He repeated the message again and waited.

After a few moments he heard, "Jala Peña, comeback."

"It's Sandman. There's an old rig stopped dead around a blind corner at the bottom of that hill. Keep your eyes open and your speed low. Copy?"

"Copy, Sandman. Thanks."

Sandman put the mic back and eyed the old rig in the side view. He contemplated going back to check the trailer but it occurred to him there was no point. It had been snowing lightly all day and had been coming down hard for the last two hours. The lack of tire tracks in the snow meant the thing had been sitting there for some time. Probably abandoned. He would report it once he cleared this goddamned mountain pass. He stayed long enough to drop a few flares behind the broken down rig and then he continued on his way

Dixon's Pass remained level but there were several sharp turns. Crags of rock jutted out above the blacktop in several areas and Sandman trusted they were high enough not to catch the top edge of his trailer. He reduced speed when he encountered them. He stole glances in his side view for Jala Peña's lights coming up behind him but he saw nothing but the snow swirling around in the big rig's wake.

"Probably taking extra care around that dead rig," he said to his cab. "Hell of a place to break down."

He kept his eyes peeled, too, for the driver of the old Mack. He doubted he would see him; Troy was much closer to where he broke down than anything else was. But he kept an eye out for the unfortunate hauler nonetheless. He saw no one.

He crested another upgrade. At the top he paused and looked out the side window. Two more wooden crosses stood near the drop-off. There was too much snow to read the names but he could make out one of the dates as 1985.

Beyond the crosses and on the other side of an ocean of darkness he could see the lights of Troy. They were microscopic pinpricks far below, as if the stars had descended from the sky he could no longer see through the driving snow. Sandman fancied he could see the truck stop but he was simply too far away and too high up to make out any detail.

He returned his attention to the road in front of him. The downgrade on the other side of the hill was not much compared to some of those he had seen already. He let go of the clutch and made his way down.

He was at the midpoint of the downgrade when he saw the lights in his side view. "He picks now to ride up my ass." Sandman shook his head and reached for the mic. "Jala Peña, this is Sandman. Got a downgrade here. You might wanna back off a bit." He replaced the mic and returned his hand to the gearshift. Despite Jala Peña's proximity Sandman was happy for the company. He had seen enough of Dixon's Pass and it would do him good to have another driver close by. If nothing else it would give him something to look at beside the endless mountain and the driving snow.

The lights of the truck grew brighter in Sandman's mirror. He spared a quick glance and shook his head. "What the fuck is he doing?" He could not see the other truck but it was close. He fancied he could hear the roar of its diesel even above the sound of his own engine. He reached for his mic again. His hand froze just short of his target.

The other truck popped into his side view. It was close, ridiculously close, dangerously close. Sandman's jaw dropped a few inches and he gaped at the image in his mirror. The lights were too low to the ground and too close together to be Jala Peña's rig. It looked, although Sandman did not know how, like the dead Bulldog he had seen at the bottom of the steep downgrade.

"Maybe he wasn't broken down at all." That still did not explain the driver's speed or his very close proximity to the back of Sandman's trailer.

Against his better judgment Sandman upshifted and picked up a bit of speed. His eyes darted between the windshield and the mirror. The truck behind him matched his increase in speed and remained seemingly mere feet behind his trailer. Sandman swore and applied more pressure to the gas pedal.

The other truck was close enough that he could keep its mirrored reflection in his peripheral vision and maintain his view of the road ahead. The bottom of the downgrade had to be close but he could not see it through the snow. He glanced at the speedometer and knew he was moving entirely too fast. "Crazy fucker, get off my ass," Sandman shouted. He wanted to reach for the mic but he needed both hands to keep the rig on the asphalt. His knuckles were white on the wheel; he felt his tires skid several times during the descent.

A signpost flashed by his window. Sandman was pretty sure it indicated the end of the downgrade. He wanted to slow and then stop at the bottom. This time he would pull the driver out of the cab and beat him while teaching him proper winter road etiquette.

The other truck bumped the back of Sandman's trailer.

His hands flew off the wheel and he was jostled in his seat. He gripped the wheel with both hands and resisted the urge to stand on the brake pedal; he had not yet reached bottom and doing so would very likely send him over the edge. Instead he turned the wheel to the right and tried to stay in his lane. His wide eyes looked in the mirror and he could no longer see the other truck; the back of Sandman's trailer glowed in its close headlights.

"Son of a bitch!"

The reasonable part of his mind, the part that tried to find a logical explanation for everything, offered a suggestion. Was it not possible the truck behind him had lost its brakes? The driver could not be intentionally trying to run him off the road. Sandman could simply be in the way of an out-of-control rig. It made sense.

Except that no trucker in his right mind would take this fucking route if his brakes, and the rest of his truck, weren't one-hundred-fucking-percent. That came from a different part of his mind, a more pragmatic part.

The Bulldog bumped him again.

He felt the trailer fishtail and he spun the wheel to the left and then jogged it to the right. The back wheels of the trailer came within inches of the drop-off but a fortuitous mound of snow prevented them from going over the edge. The trailer rebounded off the snow and Sandman spun the wheel again and regained some control.

The bottom of the hill was in sight. He gunned the engine and upshifted. The diesel roared and the clinking of the tire chains sped up. He caught sight of the left side of the rig behind him in his mirror. The sudden burst of speed had put a few feet of distance between them. Ignoring most of his training Sandman applied more pressure to the gas pedal and watched the bottom of the hill grow larger in his windshield.

He spared a quick glance in his side view and saw the old truck again close the distance between them. *So much for the no-brakes theory.* He floored the accelerator and reached the bottom. There was a straightaway for perhaps two hundred feet and then another curve to the right. He took the curve at fifty-eight miles per hour and amazed himself with his ability to keep the trailer from jackknifing. The rear of the trailer skidded on the slick surface but he recovered and upshifted again.

He looked in the side view again. The other truck was no longer behind him. "What…?" Its lights were nowhere in evidence; there was nothing but darkness behind the rig. Sandman eased off the gas pedal and downshifted. The rig slowed and then stopped. He set the brakes and stepped out into the snow.

He peered around the trailer and saw his mirror had not lied to him. The other truck was simply not there. He leaned against the open door to his cab and watched his breath frost the air. He was breathing heavily, something of which he had been unaware until that very moment. He remained that way for several more breaths before he walked slowly to the back of the trailer.

The bumper was caved in and the bottom of the trailer doors was smashed. The trailer's brake lights were gone. He looked back the way he had come, expecting to see the old rig roaring out of the darkness right at him. It did not present itself. There was nothing behind him except for empty road and rapidly-accumulating snow. Sandman checked the doors and found them secure. "Probably busted the lock, too." He inspected it and found it mangled. He kicked the remains of the bumper and shouted into the wind.

A moment later he was back in the cab. He grabbed the mic and said, "Jala Peña, copy." The radio was silent. He tried again, and a third time. He replaced the mic in its cradle when he realized he would receive no reply. "Fucking mountains."

Sandman sat back in his seat and rubbed his eyes. He let out a long, slow breath before buckling his seatbelt again. His wipers continued their pendulum swing in front of him and the snow continued to fall. He glanced at the clock on the dash and saw it was 3:38 in the AM. His GPS told him he was still 105 miles from Lake Placid. "No early arrival bonus for you," he said to the empty cab. "Not even a you-got-the-load-there-intact bonus." He watched the wipers continue their mindless trek back and forth across the windshield for another few moments.

He reached for the gearshift and almost released the clutch when he stopped himself. As much as he hated the idea of a babysitter Sandman knew he was better off waiting for Peña. Whether or not the driver of the old truck hit him intentionally it would not pay to simply continue on alone. If he encountered the old Mack again he would need Peña. Sandman took his hand off the gearshift and sat back in his seat and waited.

He nearly dozed off but he caught himself in time. The adrenaline from the close encounter had ebbed and he felt tired. This was nothing new; he had experienced this exact same feeling in Afghanistan. When the Black Hawk touched down after a mission he was always exhausted, even if said mission had not resulted in combat. The co-pilot, Lieutenant Webster, referred to this phenomenon as "Warrior's Remorse." Sandman was sure it had a technical name but he very much liked Webster's term. It was precisely what he felt now.

He glanced at the clock again. 4:17 AM. Where the hell was Peña?

His breath caught in his throat as it occurred to him his convoy partner had encountered the old rig and was even now wrecked on the road somewhere behind him. His first instinct was to turn around and go back for Peña. He glanced out the windshield and squashed that idea. The road was simply too narrow for any rig to navigate a 180-degree turn.

Sandman drummed his fingers on the steering wheel. He tried Peña on the radio again and received no reply. He tried a general message to any nearby trucker and still his radio remained silent. It was most likely the mountains and that was ultimately what made Sandman put the truck in gear and ease forward. He needed to get clear of the radio interference, if for no other reason than to get hold of Peña.

He picked up speed on the straightaways and down-shifted on the upgrades. This section of 228 was largely flat and he made up some time. He tried Peña every few miles but heard nothing back. He listened to the steady growling of the diesel and the sound of fresh snow being compacted beneath his tires. The clock read 5:09 AM when he saw the end of the mountain pass perhaps three miles in front of him and on the other side of a slight downgrade. At the same moment his radio returned to life. It hissed static but behind that were voices. He could not make out much of the conversation but he was okay with that. He seemed to have made it through the dead zone after all. He reached the bottom and made the hard right turn which would bring him to the last straightaway and get him out of the mountains.

The red Mack sat directly in front of him, its cab and trailer taking up the entire road.

"Fuck!" Sandman instinctively slammed on the brakes and cut the wheel to the left. The trailer's wheels locked up and skidded through the snow. The Peterbilt crashed into and through the Mack's trailer. The sound of the diesel was drowned out by the cacophony of tearing metal and breaking glass. Something large and heavy made it through Sandman's windshield and continued on through the passenger seat and the sleeper unit. It clipped his right arm on the way past and shattered his elbow.

Sandman strained to keep his good hand on the wheel and stood on the brake pedal. Icy wind and snow pelted him through the shattered remains of his windshield. He clenched his eyes shut and screamed.

The broken Peterbilt's momentum took it through the old trailer and out the other side. Sandman felt his own trailer's tires leave the ground and for a single moment the rig was suspended in midair. It landed with a jarring crash that broke both of Sandman's femurs. The trailer broke away from the Peterbilt. It crashed onto its side and skidded off the edge of the mountain.

Sandman was aware of none of this. He strained against the impact and it was everything he could do to stay conscious. After what felt like several hours the noise faded and the new rig came to a stop. It took Sandman several moments to realize he was no longer being thrown around the cab. Gingerly he opened one eye and then the other.

The rig's windshield was gone save for some broken, jagged safety glass jutting from the sides of the frame. The wind howled through the remains of the cab and snow had already accumulated on his arms and face. The front of the Peterbilt was smashed; steam escaped from the radiator like exhaust had once escaped from the stacks. His passenger seat was gone and there was a large hole behind it. He could see the remains of his sleeper unit; his small TV, his cupboards and bed were all gone. A few magazines flapped in the winter winds that tore through the opening. Something that might have been a plow blade had made it all the way through the sleeper and lay on the road behind the rig.

Dazed and not completely in control of his own actions Sandman watched himself open his door. He reached for his seatbelt and yelped. He was unaware of the state of his right arm until he moved it. The coat sleeve was gone and his forearm was covered with blood. He started to unlatch the seatbelt with his left hand when he chanced to look out the missing right side of his cab. He stopped dead.

The old Mack had survived the impact. Not only survived, it seemed its trailer was completely intact. There was no evidence that Sandman's rig had blown straight through it. The cab faced the open side of Sandman's rig. It did not move; its ancient diesel idled and a slow, steady stream of exhaust escaped from its single, short stack.

It took Sandman several moments to regain the ability to move. He pulled his eyes slowly from the idling rig and looked out his door. The Peterbilt had come to rest at the edge of the drop-off. Outside his door was nothing but empty air. He could not see whatever was below him; the darkness and driving snow obscured anything beyond a few feet.

He glanced into his side view but it was skewed from the impact and showed him nothing. He willed Peña to come around the corner just then but his convoy partner remained invisible. Sandman swallowed and turned his eyes back to the other rig.

The driver revved the engine and the old Mack started forward slowly.

Sandman took one last glance into the abyss outside the driver's door before he reached for the jagged edge that was once the right side of his cab. His right arm screamed at him but he ignored the pain. Something held him back and after a moment he remembered his seatbelt was still secured. He hastily unbuckled it with his left hand and reached again for the edge of his cab.

His legs joined the scream of protest from his right arm and that made him cry out. He did not waste time with a visual inspection of his legs; he clawed furiously for purchase on the torn metal on the other side of the cab.

The Mack jogged the wrecked Peterbilt only slightly when its bumper came to rest against it. Sandman mumbled, "No, no, no no," and continued to reach for freedom and safety. He looked up at the dark windshield that now loomed over him. He could see the silhouette of the driver. Sandman reached out to the man with his right hand. "Please, no."

The old rig began to move forward again. Sandman felt his cab moving sideways. It tilted wildly and he felt himself slipping off the seat. The microphone escaped its cradle and dangled in front of him. He ignored everything but the faded red truck just a few feet away.

The Mack's headlights reflected off the ruins of Sandman's rig and for a single moment he could see the other driver quite clearly. He was an older man whose plaid shirt seemed fifty years out of date. His salt-and-pepper hair was close-cropped and flat on top. His right sleeve was folded over the bulge on his arm that could only be a pack of smokes. He was grinning and Sandman thought he could see the blackened stumps of what at one time might have been teeth. The driver was smiling widely at him.

The ancient diesel roared a bit more loudly and moved forward with a burst of speed. It shoved the newer rig sideways. At the last moment before he and his rig went over the drop-off, Sandman thought he heard the other driver laughing.

****

Peña awoke to the sound of sirens. He rubbed his eyes and climbed from his sleeper to his front seat. He blinked at the brightness coming through his windshield. The snow was still coming down but the sky had brightened considerably and he thought he could see a patch of sunlight to the east.

He rubbed his shirtsleeve at the fog on his windshield and peered in the direction of Dixon's Pass. Several fire trucks were making their way toward the mountain. He scanned the parking area of the truck stop and saw several of his fellow drivers standing around and pointing in the general direction of 228. Peña's lips compressed into a thin, pink line.

He put on his coat and stepped out into the snow. The temperature had dropped since the night before. It was jarring after spending the night in his warm sleeper with his flannel sheets and thick blanket wrapped around him. He shivered and wondered if that had anything to do with the frigid air.

He spotted Muskrat and Tombstone standing near the 'rat's rig. He trudged through the snow and joined them in looking at the mountain.

"Morning, Jala," 'rat said without looking at him.

"Morning." Peña did not look at either man. Instead he gazed at the rising bulk of Dixon's Pass. The fire trucks were already out of visual range but he could still hear the faint scream of their sirens.

"Guess 228 is open now," 'rat said. He, too, did not look at the other men.

"Another sacrifice, another safe season through the Pass," Tombstone added.

Muskrat nodded. Peña stood still and simply looked at the mountain. "Think this shit will ever end?"

Tombstone harrumphed. "Doubt it. From what I've heard this has been going on every year since someone figured out what the fuck was happening there and came up with a way to beat it. How long has that been? Forty-something years, right?"

"Forty-nine," Peña said. "It's been forty-nine years."

"Forty-nine wrecks." Muskrat swallowed audibly.

"Fifty if you count the Highwayman himself," Tombstone countered.

"Thank you, Mr. Algebra," 'rat said with little humor.

The three men remained standing in the falling snow and looked at the mountain. The cloud cover was indeed loosening its hold on the sky. Several shafts of pale sunlight illuminated patches on the mountain.

Peña could not see the fire trucks wending their way through the curves and hills of 228, nor could he hear them any longer. But he knew where they were going and what they would find when they got there. He thought briefly of the young man who had been assigned the task of opening the mountain road for the rest of them. He smiled a sad smile and eventually managed to pull his eyes from Dixon's Pass.

"I'm gonna grab a bite before I head up there," Tombstone said. "It doesn't hurt to start the day off right. And spending some time looking at Dia is never a bad thing. It'll give the fire department time to clear the road, too."

"I'll join ya," 'rat said, his voice flat.

"Me, too." Peña started to follow his two friends toward the restaurant entrance. He stopped and turned and looked back toward the mountain. He lingered there for only a moment before he raced to catch up to his breakfast companions.

<u>Gamer's Glossary</u>

AFK—Away From Keyboard.

Aggro—The target of someone's hostility.

Buffs—Artificial and temporary augmentations to one's abilities.

Devs—Game developers.

Emote—Non-combat actions, such as dancing or waving.

GM—Game master. Can fix problems or dispense discipline.

IG—Ingame.

LFG—Looking for group.

Newb—A new player. Short for "newbie."

NPC—Non-player character. A game-generated character.

Rez—Resurrection.

Spatial—Speaking or acting in public for everyone to see.

God Mode

Jeremy Stewart felt the tension building in his shoulders and back. He realized he was leaning forward much closer to the monitor than usual. With conscious effort he leaned back in his chair and flexed his back muscles. The tension in his muscles eased somewhat but he remained anxious. He took his hand from the mouse long enough to take a long pull from his soda glass. He eyed the image on his monitor. Ceradus and Jazla were in the distance killing time by destroying the Death Dealers that surrounded the area around the tomb entrance. Trawolf knelt on the ground next to him and meditated. Windows had just loaded in next to Trawolf. That left three more on the way. Jeremy cursed silently and willed them to move faster.

It was an unwritten rule among the players that you did not enter the Vault of Shadows without a full group. It was Jeremy's first time and he was lucky enough just to be there. It would earn him no friends by jumping the gun and starting the heroic instance before everyone arrived. Least of all Ceradus, who had somehow talked the others into taking Jeremy along. It was probably the most frustrating aspect of playing Realm of Heroes. No group wanted to bring an inexperienced player into the Vault, which begged the question, how was one to gain experience? He had tried several times to join a group that planned to run the Vault of Shadows but he had been rebuffed (kindly in some cases, less so in others) each time. He had an easier time joining the groups that ran the lesser instances like Knoll Invasion and Queen of

Swords and he felt he was becoming quite good at both. But the groups had always balked at keeping him around for VoS.

Until today.

So entering the Vault before the whole group arrived was out of the question. He could join Ceradus and Jazla and kill some Death Dealers but he did not want to waste his potions and spells before the instance started. So he would stand next to Trawolf and Windows and wait.

He allowed himself a quick run to the bathroom to empty his bladder. He had been drinking glass after glass of soda since the group formed a few hours before. They had run through both KI and QoS as well as Haunted Slaveship (his second time) and Ravenwood Manor (also his second time). That added up to a lot of drinking and the last thing he wanted was to be AFK when the rest of the group finally arrived. When he returned to the computer he saw Attoseo and Shokata had arrived. The latter was running to join Ceradus and Jazla. That left Valen as the last one to arrive.

Jeremy swore to himself. He tapped his fingers on the computer desk. He paced back and forth in front of it. Each time he looked at the monitor he saw Valen was still absent. The group voice channel was mostly silent. He wanted to put his headset back on and suggest they go in anyway but that would have been foolish. He was the newb in the group and the others would either tell him to shut up or else demand Ceradus kick him out and get someone else to take his place. Wizards like Jeremy's character, Raak, were not difficult to come by; he could be replaced easily enough. So he paced and swore and waited for Valen to get his shit together.

After another few moments he heard Valen's voice in the group channel. "Okay, guys, sorry about that. Had to rebuff. I'm on my way now. Be there in a minute."

"Finally!" Jeremy exclaimed. He took his seat and put on his headset and waited. A moment or two later Valen finally loaded in next to him. Jeremy guided Raak to the Vault entrance. He reached it without incident, the Death Dealers having been killed by Ceradus and Jazla. He stood before the entrance and waited for everyone to join him.

Singly and in pairs the rest of the group made their way to the entrance. In his headset Jeremy heard Ceradus say in his British accent, "Okay, all in." Jeremy clicked on the glowing rune stone on the ground in front of the entrance. His monitor went black before it showed him a load-in screen he had never before seen. It showed a skeletal figure in a black robe casting a spell. Green energy crackled from its bony fingers. The text below the ominous figure read, *The Shadow Mage Rules the Vault of Shadows*. "Only until he meets me," Jeremy whispered softly enough that his mic did not pick it up.

The load-in screen was replaced by a large circular room. The stones that made up the floor and walls were nearly black. Veins of gold ran through the stones and formed eldritch symbols. Biers stood at intervals along the walls; green flames burned within them. Eight NPCs, Death Dealers who looked much meaner than their brethren outside, stood unmoving around the room's perimeter. On the far side of the room a woman in a black robe stood upon a dais. The name above her head was Shadow of Hate.

Jeremy gasped at the sheer coolness of the room. His heartbeat picked up the pace. His hands felt sweaty. He licked his lips until his smile broadened. He had waited a long time to see the inside of the Vault. The first room alone rewarded his patience. It was by far the coolest place he had seen yet in the game. He took a moment to savor his triumph. It occurred to him to take a screenshot and he did so. He might even use that as his desktop wallpaper.

"Okay, Raak, this is how it's gonna go down," Ceradus said in group voice. "Jaz is gonna tank Hate while the rest of us concentrate on the Death Dealers. Don't attack Hate at all until all the Death Dealers are dead. Cool?"

"Got it," Jeremy replied.

"And when we do go after Hate," Trawolf added, "don't use any spells above level 15 or she'll rebound them onto the whole group."

"Right," Valen added.

Shut the fuck up, Valen, Jeremy thought. *Like I need your slow ass telling me anything.* Aloud, he said only, "Understood."

He waited for the others to move. Trawolf and Shokata knelt next to each other and meditated. Valen and Windows took up residence in the center of the room. He guessed, correctly, as it turned out, their placement was so all group members would be within range of their healing spells. Jeremy had never seen an instance where two healers were required. He squirmed in his chair with excitement. This was going to be epic.

Trawolf and Shokata got to their feet at almost the same moment. Ceradus said, "When you're ready, Jaz."

"Okay," said only the second female voice Jeremy had heard in the game. "Going in now."

Jazla pulled off her hood and drew her staff. Jeremy saw her pointed ears and realized she was the first female elf monk he had seen in all his months of playing. She ran across the room, past the two healers in the middle and toward the dais. She struck the Shadow of Hate with her staff and commenced to run back and forth across the dais, the black-robed woman on her heels.

Two Death Dealers went live. Jeremy's screen lit up with color and his speakers both hissed and boomed at him. His health dipped but he was not concerned. He targeted the closest Death Dealer and unleashed his *firestorm* spell. Orange and yellow flames erupted from his wizard's staff and engulfed the hapless NPC. Jeremy watched its health drop like an anvil. A moment later the Death Dealer fell to the floor, lifeless. He turned his attention to the second. Others in the group had it well in hand; Jeremy did not get a shot at it before it, too, dropped.

Two more went live and ran at the group. Jeremy targeted the one nearest him and cast his *water whirlwind* spell. A tidal wave appeared and wrapped itself around the Death Dealer. The NPC spun in place. Shokata the shadow knight ran to it and began to attack it with his sword. Jeremy watched the Death Dealer's health plummet. "I don't need your help," he whispered, again conscious of his mic. The Death Dealer collapsed and the wall of water dissipated.

When its companion went down as well the next pair went live. Jeremy could not believe it but he was growing bored. These guys were simply not in his league and present-ed no challenge. He eyed the Shadow of Hate, still chasing Jazla back and forth across the dais. She would be a more worthy foe. He tried to target her but one of the Death Dealers ran between them. Jeremy released the NPC from his target lock and moved toward the center of the room.

The two healers stood their ground, taking turns glowing bright blue as they worked their healing spells on the group. Jeremy eyed his health bar and was not surprised to find himself at full health. Of course. Because these Death dealers were pussies. Why was everyone so cautious about this instance? Thus far he had seen nothing he would not be able to solo.

He placed his target cursor on the Shadow of Hate.

"Raak, what are you doing, mate?" Ceradus asked. "You have to come back here with us. If you're in the center you might draw aggro and the clerics could be attacked."

"Get back here, Raak," Trawolf growled. "You're gonna fuck this up."

Jeremy ignored them. They would not be so paranoid and scared once they saw what he could do. He doubted he would have any trouble finding a place in an instance group once word spread of how powerful he was. He smiled at the thought.

He returned his attention to the Shadow of Hate. He looked for a powerful spell on his toolbar and selected *raise dead*. Instantly the fallen Death Dealers stood as one. They ran in tandem for the Shadow of Hate. The NPC ceased her pursuit of Jazla and began to fight the resurrected Death Dealers.

"What the hell are you doing?" Jazla asked. She was either unable or unwilling to hide the surprise in her tone.

"Raak, cancel the spell," Shokata said.

"You're gonna get us all killed," Windows added.

Jeremy laughed. "Relax, guys, I got this."

The Shadow of Hate succeeded in killing one of the Death Dealers. The remaining three were joined by two more of their recently-deceased brethren.

"No, you don't got it," Trawolf shouted. "Cancel the spell you fucking newb!"

Jeremy frowned. He had been playing Realm of Heroes for nearly a year. When would he no longer be subjected to that goddamned derogatory term? He had been less than impressed by Trawolf thus far; now he began to loathe him. "I am not a *newb*," he said in as menacing a tone as he could muster. "Why don't you shut the fuck up, Trawolf?"

"Guys, hurry it up," Valen said. "Most of my heal spells are on cooldown."

"Mine, too," Attoseo added.

Jeremy glanced at his health bar. His brow furrowed. It hovered around fifty percent. "What the hell?" he asked no one. A quick glance to the left side of his monitor, which displayed the health status of everyone in the group, told him his companions were likewise losing health. He could understand their health being low; they were locked in combat with the last remaining Death Dealers. His own health, however, should have been at full. No one had laid a glove on him since the first Death Dealers went live. How was he losing health? His heart began to speed up when he saw the Shadow of Hate's health was nearly full.

"Raak, cancel the fucking spell," Trawolf shouted.

Another of the Death Dealers fell at the Shadow of Hate's feet. Jazla stood among them and hit the main NPC with her staff. "Guys, I can't get aggro back," she said. "She's concentrating on the Death Dealers."

"Ceradus," Shokata cut in, "kick him from the group before we all die."

Ceradus' reply was immediate, his voice, calm. "Raak, you have to drop the spell, mate. They're right, we're all gonna die."

Jeremy felt his heart racing in his chest. Could they seriously be considering kicking him from the group? Perhaps they were, but that was only because they had yet to see how truly powerful he was. He targeted the Shadow of Hate again. "Guys, calm down," he said. His voice was measured despite his rapid heartbeat and the hostility directed toward him. He selected his *magic overload* spell and hit the key.

Raak's most powerful spell enveloped the Shadow of Hate. Magical energy crackled and lanced through the hapless NPC like bolts of multi-colored lightning. His speakers crackled with the satisfying sound of an enemy being, not simply defeated, but annihilated. Jeremy allowed himself a smile.

Until Raak collapsed to the floor, dead.

Jeremy's smile vanished. He checked his health bar and saw it was empty. From his vantage point he could see Valen lying next to him. Jazla's corpse lay on the dais. He quickly checked the health status of the others in the group and found they, too, were dead. The resurrected Death Dealers were gone; the Shadow of Hate stood in her original place upon the dais, her health bar full. A text box appeared in the center of his screen. It read: *You have been slain. Where would you like to resurrect?* It listed the three closest healer huts and waited for him to indicate his choice.

"What...?"

"Fuck. Ing. Ass. Hole," Trawolf said. He enunciated each syllable as if he were attempting to speak in a foreign language.

"What the hell was that?" Attoseo asked.

"That was this piece of shit newb not listening to anybody and fucking the whole group," Windows added.

Jeremy continued to stare at Raak's corpse as if the simple act of doing so would reveal he had been mistaken and his wizard was, in fact, still alive. But, no. His corpse still lay on the cold, dark stone of the Vault of Shadows; his health bar was still empty. The Shadow of Hate remained in her original place upon the dais. And to add insult to injury the Death Dealers had respawned as well. They stood at their original positions around the room's perimeter.

"Ceradus, if you don't kick his idiot from the group I'm leaving," Attoseo proclaimed.

"Me, too," Shokata added.

Jeremy sat back. There was no way Ceradus would kick him. They got along pretty well, they had grouped before on some of the other instances. Ceradus knew he was a powerful and valuable wizard. Let these other whiny pussies leave. There was no way he would be kicked.

The status bars on the left side of his screen which indicated the health (or lack thereof) of the other group members vanished. His headset speakers went silent. He stared in utter amazement at the screen. He leaned forward again. "Guys?" He heard his own voice echo back to him. It was his only reply. "Ceradus? You there?"

The other members of the group began to vanish one at a time as they chose a healer hut. A moment later he was alone inside the Vault of Shadows. He stared at the screen for some moments. When he realized he had been kicked from the group, he typed, */tell Ceradus Hey, what happened?*

He swallowed and waited for a response. His chat window remained empty. He typed, */tell Ceradus you there?* Jeremy began to drum his fingers on the desk. He reached for his keyboard again when a single line of green type appeared in his chat window.

Ceradus tells you, sorry mate. youre not ready 4 vos yet. maybe next time.

/tell Ceradus did you really kick me? i thought we were friends. This was true. Jeremy had met quite a few people in Realm of Heroes but the only one with whom he felt even the slightest friendship was Ceradus. He was still trying to wrap his head around being kicked from the group.

Ceradus tells you, gotta go. ttyl.

Jeremy would have slammed his fist on the desk if the sound would not wake his mother in the next room. As it was he barely managed to restrain himself. He looked at the last message in his chat window. Perhaps Ceradus was calling it a night. Now that he thought about it Jeremy was certain it was the reason he had been kicked from the group. In fact he was probably not kicked at all. The group had simply been disbanded. Ceradus lived somewhere in England and he was five hours ahead of Jeremy. He glanced at the alarm clock on the nightstand next to his bed. 11:04 PM it read. He knew Ceradus was a hard core gamer but even he had to sleep sometime. He felt a little better when he concluded he had, in fact, not been kicked from the group at all.

His eyes moved from the chat window to the Shadow of Hate standing triumphantly and patiently upon her dais. The Death Dealers stood at attention around the room's perimeter. Jeremy stabbed the Shadow of Hate's image on the monitor. "Next time, bitch, you're all mine." He selected the closest healer hut and chose that as his destination. Raak's corpse vanished from the Vault of Shadows, leaving the Shadow of Hate to savor her victory. For the moment.

After the NPC cleric resurrected him Jeremy exited the healer hut. He took a final look around the area and saw no one. It was as good a place as any to logout. He exited the game. He turned off his computer and got ready for bed.

****

Jeremy logged in right after breakfast. He felt confidant about the coming day. He looked forward to his rematch with the Vault of Shadows and hoped it would not take too long to get a group going. He loaded in and found himself outside the healer hut. "Okay, let's see who's on."

He checked his friends list. The only name highlighted was Ceradus. He smiled and typed, */tell Ceradus wassup*. He waited for a reply. His chat box remained blank. Jeremy's brow furrowed. He retyped the greeting and waited. Ceradus did not reply. "He's busy," Jeremy said. "Okay, let's get some buffs." He needed to be ready when the group formed. It would not do to join the group and then be the lone holdout who was not buffed and ready. He summoned his mount (a giant spider he named "Fang") and made for the nearest tavern.

The place was rocking. Jeremy glanced at his alarm clock and saw it was 8:34 AM. "Not bad," he whispered. Several enchanters were present. They danced about the area and wove spells for the paying customers. Jeremy picked one named Allura and typed */watch Allura.* He had used her before and she was a decent enchantress, friendly and quick with the buffs. He kept an eye on his chat window and followed the various conversations going on amongst the players.

It appeared many were gearing up for PVP. Jeremy had never entered the PVP zone; he preferred battling NPCs to his fellow players. Not that he felt Raak was not up to the challenge. He felt he would do well if he chose to enter the blasted landscape of Highmoor and fight player versus player. In fact he was quite confidant he could mop the floor with almost anyone if they were foolish enough to attack him one on one. But he had bigger fish to fry this day. He looked forward to seeing the Vault of Shadows again.

When he had watched Allura long enough he sent her a message and asked for his buff. The buff window appeared and he watched with satisfaction as she increased his abilities. He accepted the buff and gave her a generous payment. She thanked him and he exited the tavern.

He typed, */tell ceradus you there?*

After a moment Ceradus replied. *Ceradus tells you, in highmoor mate. serious pvp goin on.*

He had been correct. Ceradus was too busy to reply to his earlier messages. Jeremy felt better immediately. He typed, */tell Ceradus brt.* Highmoor was on the other side of the Haunted Swamp. Jeremy rode Fang to the ferry and made the trip to Highmoor. He had seen the place once before when he was new to the game and wanted to explore the different realms. His level had been too low to enter the ruined city at the time. He was less than crazy about being there now but he could afford to wait a bit until Ceradus and the others were finished fighting other players. Then he could reenter the Vault of Shadows.

He disembarked from the ferry and stepped onto the staging area adjacent to the PVP zone. Numerous players stood at the edge of the zone, seemingly unwilling to cross the invisible line that would automatically shift them into PVP mode. On the other side of the line stood a small hill. Beyond that he could make out the shadowed ruins of the city of Highmoor in the distance.

The names of most of the players on his side of the line appeared in blue letters above their head. That meant they were opposite faction and would be enemies if he encountered them in the PVP zone. A few were in green which meant potential allies. Jeremy moved Raak closer to the line.

He looked over the assembled players but did not see Ceradus. "Must be in the city," he whispered. He found two familiar names in the crowd. Windows and Valen stood next to each other. He started to approach them when he noticed perhaps fifteen players crest the top of the small hill on the other side of the line. They were all green to him; his faction held the PVP zone. He scanned over them and found Ceradus. A few people away from him stood Trawolf.

/tell Ceradus hey im here.

In his chat window he saw, *Ceradus nods to you.*

He expected more but he reminded himself the enemy players were about to launch their attack. *Probably doesn't want to get caught typing a message when that comes,* Jeremy thought.

He took a quick headcount and realized the enemy players had a numerical advantage over those of his faction. It would be close but he thought his side would lose. "They need me," Jeremy said. He was uninterested in PVP but he thought it might gain him some friends among his allies and some much-deserved respect from his enemies. Jeremy's heart began to race. Was he really about to cross the PVP line? Before he could change his mind he moved Raak forward.

He ran up the hill and stood next to Ceradus. He typed */hi5 ceradus*. Raak performed the emote. When Ceradus made no move to acknowledge his presence Raak took a few steps back. When the enemy players crossed the line he did not want to be the first person they saw. His armor was not the greatest and his defensive spells were weak. Raak was all about offense. Best to stand back a ways and let the tanks absorb the initial attack.

A moment later the enemy players crossed the line. Instantly their names changed from blue to red. "This is it," Jeremy said. "Let's see how many I can get right off the bat." He placed his curser on the ground in the center of the enemy group and let loose his *firestorm* spell. The column of fire appeared among the enemy players. Some ran around it but most of them simply ran through it. None dropped. Jeremy's eyes narrowed.

The melee fighters among the enemy raced up the hill and began their attack with swords and maces and staves. His own melee fighters met them. Spellcasters on both sides unloaded with everything they had. The image on his screen lagged with the effort of trying to display the various graphics. His speakers crackled.

He moved his cursor across the field of red names and selected one at random. It turned out to be Valen. Jeremy smiled and thought of the night before. He unleashed *paralyze* and *energy drain* on top of each other. Valen stopped his advance and Jeremy watched his target's health drop rapidly.

He smiled. "That's what you get, asshole," he said. He paused a moment to savor the victory. He selected *blade fury* as his next spell. His finger hovered above the key. Valen's health suddenly shot up to full. Jeremy looked at it twice before he remembered the guy was a healer. "Stupid, stupid," he said. "Should have thought of that."

He hit him with *blade fury* anyway. The magical swords sprang into existence and hurled themselves at their target. Valen's health dropped again. Jeremy looked over his toolbar for the next spell. His eyes went momentarily to his own health bar and he froze. His health was at one-quarter and dropping. He looked frantically about.

Windows stood perhaps fifteen meters away. He unleashed spell after spell at him. "Fucking asshole," Jeremy said. He took his target cursor off Valen and placed it on Windows. Windows's health was close to full. "Let's see how you like magic overload." Jeremy hit the key at the same moment Raak fell to the ground. The spell remained uncast. The annoying text box sprang up with its equally annoying message, *You have been slain. Where would you like to resurrect?*

"Damnit!" Jeremy looked at the options and chose Highmoor. There was a healer's hut fifty meters behind the PVP line. He could resurrect and get right back in the battle. He loaded in to the tent, waited for the healer to pronounce him healthy and ran back outside.

The battle continued but there were fewer taking part. He saw a great many bodies on the ground. Two enemy players ahead of him crossed the line and rejoined the battle. Raak was right behind them.

He targeted one of them as he ran up the hill. It was a wizard. Jeremy hit him with *paralyze* and stopped him in his tracks. He then hit him with his *anti-magic bubble* to stop the wizard from casting anything for a full minute. Jeremy ran past the disabled wizard without a second look.

The battle had moved to the other side of the hill. Several allied players were in the distance running for the ruins of Highmoor. A few melee fighters remained near the hill but they were outnumbered and dropping fast. Jeremy drank his invisibility potion. He watched Raak become a vague outline on the screen. He swung wide of the battle and headed for Highmoor. He stopped once and looked back. He saw only enemy players left. One was a monk and another, a paladin. He counted two wizards and at least one cleric (Valen) with them. He had to get to Highmoor and warn whoever was left of the coming attack.

He saw the crumbled wall which marked the boundary of the city ahead of him. He passed through and got his first real look at Highmoor. It appeared much like any of the major cities in the game but the developers had taken the time to cast it in ruins. Scorch marks marred almost every building he saw. Many structures lacked a roof or one or more of its walls. He thought this very cool. He spared a moment to take another screenshot.

A small group of friendly players were clustered near the ruins of Highmoor's public marketplace. He set Raak on auto-run and typed into spatial, *They're coming in behind me. Lots of them.*

A cleric named Urchin had survived the initial battle and was busy casting healing and protection spells on the group. Raak stopped among them. Ceradus was there but

Jeremy did not know the others. He counted seven in all. They would be outnumbered at least two to one. He faced the direction where he expected the enemy players to enter the city. As he did he watched Urchin take up a position behind the rest of the group. Jeremy eyed his buff bar and realized he had received none of Urchin's protection spells. *I arrived too late is all*, he thought. "I can survive without them."

The players in the group talked among themselves. Jeremy kept track of the spatial conversation in his chat window. There seemed to be a strategy and every player had a job to do. Except no one had addressed him. What were they doing? He was easily the most powerful of those assembled. Perhaps they had such faith in him they felt he needed no specific assignment. He smiled. Their faith would be rewarded when they saw what he could do.

The enemy players poured through the collapsed sections of Highmoor's perimeter wall. There were more than Jeremy expected. Worse, they were spread out. His area-of-effect spells would not be as useful as he had hoped. He looked for Valen but did not see him. "Must be hiding in the back. Pussy." He aimed his *firestorm* in the center of the enemy's line and loosed it. Only two melee fighters were affected. Neither dropped. Jeremy saw the tell-tale blue glow from behind them and knew he had found Valen. He could not see the cleric through the ebbing flames of the *firestorm* but he knew he was there, healing the melee fighters. Jeremy grimaced.

He typed into spatial, *Incoming*. He saw no reply. *They're gearing up. Smart players.* He cast his *lightning bolt* into the group. Again he succeeded in killing no one; the blue glow from Valen's healing spells was beginning to annoy him.

He waited to see what the players at his back would do. The enemy moved in closer. The players on his side did nothing. Jeremy turned.

He stood alone near the marketplace. He looked wildly left and right. The group had retreated behind him. They ran for the remains of a two-story building in the distance. He was alone. He turned back to the onrushing enemy. No fewer than seven melee fighters ran at him. Jeremy looked quickly over his toolbar. *Water Whirlwind* was his only real option. He hit the key. Three of the seven melee fighters were enveloped within the spell; the rest managed to avoid it and charged him.

At the same moment the fighters attacked, Jeremy found himself surrounded by a purple glow. His health bar dropped by more than half instantly. "No, no, no," he shouted. Whatever spells were directed at him, coupled with the four fighters' attack, were too much for him to face alone. He started to run.

He made it perhaps five meters before Raak dropped to the ground. Windows and Valen approached him while the rest of the group ran past. In his chat window he saw, *Windows spits at you.* Beneath that he saw another message: *Valen laughs at you.*

Jeremy's cheeks turned red. His lips pulled back from his teeth. Raak was not dead, simply incapacitated. If these two assholes did not attack him while he was down and simply ran after their buddies he would recover. He could then attack them from behind and get a little revenge. He watched the incap clock tick down. With one second left he saw Windows swing his mace. The text box appeared on his screen. *You have been slain. Where would you like to resurrect?*

Jeremy slammed his fist onto his desk. "Motherfucker!" He was too angry to consider what his mother would say if she happened to be within earshot. But no, she was most likely still downstairs with the television on, enjoying her breakfast and perusing the coupon section of the newspaper.

He stared at the screen, at Raak's corpse. Valen and Windows had moved on. He was alone near Highmoor's blasted marketplace. Alone and dead because the asshats who were supposed to be on his side had abandoned him and left him to fight the entire enemy group by himself. Raak was powerful, there was no doubt, but that had been asking a bit much. "If not for your asshole cleric I coulda taken *all* of you."

He selected the healer hut outside the PVP area. After the healer pronounced him fit he exited the hut. He approached the PVP line but he did not cross it. Instead he typed, */tell Ceradus wtf happened to you?* He awaited a reply. It occurred to Jeremy someone must have alerted him to the group's retreat and he had simply missed it in the chat window. He scrolled up, past being spit on and laughed at, but found nothing. There had been no warning. They simply left him behind. He continued to wait for a reply until his mother called up to him to get ready to accompany her to the Potomac Mills Mall.

Jeremy stared at the chat window and willed Ceradus to reply. His chat window remained empty. He started to type another message when his mother shouted up to him to get moving. Jeremy said, "Okay, mom." His fingers hovered above the keyboard. He needed to know why the others had left him to die. There was no response from Ceradus.

Jeremy logged off and got dressed.

****

The mall was torture and he could not wait to get back home. He helped his mother bring in some shopping bags and then he bolted upstairs. He logged in to the game and found Raak where he left him.

There was a major PVP battle going on in front of him. Both factions fought for the hill just past the PVP line. The players were moving around too quickly for him to get an accurate count but he thought there had to be at least forty people in there slugging it out. He could not tell which side was winning or if one side outnumbered the other. It looked like mass chaos to Jeremy. He caught a glimpse of Shokata and Attoseo; they were running around like madmen. Valen was there, as well, staying well away from the action. He glowed blue or green as he healed the players on his side. "Fucking pussy," Jeremy whispered. The sight of the guy who killed him near the bazaar nearly made Jeremy cross the line, but he held back. There was too much going on and he could not keep track of the action.

He typed */tell Shokata hey sho. wanna run vos?*

He received no reply. It seemed Shokata was busy trying to keep himself alive. He tried the same message with Attoseo. He waited for a reply but received none. He pulled up his friends list. Two names were highlighted, Trawolf and Ceradus. He was a bit upset with Ceradus so he typed, */tell trawolf hey traw. wassup?*

Trawolf made no reply. Jeremy took a quick bathroom break and hurried back to the computer. He looked at his blank chat window. His message to Trawolf was the last item displayed. He typed, */tell trawolf wanna run vos again? im available.*

He drummed his fingers on the desk. Why was everyone ignoring him? He was about to retype the message when his chat window came to life. *Trawolf tells you, get lost newb. you suck.*

Jeremy gasped. He reread the message. His eyes narrowed with fury. He needed three attempts to type his message correctly. */tell trawolf fuck you fucking loser.*

The reply was immediate. *Trawolf tells you, rofl. get a clue fuckhead.*

Jeremy started to type a reply when a new message appeared in the chat window. *Trawolf ignores you.* Jeremy stopped typing. There was no point. Trawolf was apparently such a douchebag he had placed Jeremy on his ignore list. That meant he would not see any messages Jeremy sent. Jeremy rapped his knuckles on the desk. "Cocksucker."

He typed, */tell ceradus wasup?* He was mad at the guy but he also wanted to be in a group that was running instances. Even if they did not run Vault of Shadows again at least he could run the others. He waited for a response. What he saw was, *Ceradus ignores you.*

"What the fuck?" Jeremy said through gritted teeth. "What's his fucking problem?" He wished he could send another message but Ceradus would not see it. Even if they were standing next to each other he would see nothing from Jeremy. That was the whole point of the ignore option. But why would Ceradus do that? Trawolf he could understand because the guy was clearly an asshole. He had expected better from Ceradus.

"Fine." Jeremy found Valen still doing his best to stay out of the melee taking place on the hill. He placed his target cursor on the cleric. Before he could talk himself out of it

Jeremy guided Raak across the PVP line. Maybe he could not do anything about Ceradus and Trawolf but he could at least have a bit of revenge on Valen. And Windows if he had the balls to show himself.

He cast *blade fury* at Valen and watched with satisfaction as the cleric's health took a sudden dip. Valen ran back a few steps, clearly looking for his attacker. Jeremy closed the gap between them and cast his *paralyze* spell. Valen stopped moving. "Now you're dead, asshole."

Valen's health inched up toward full and he glowed blue. "No, you can't heal yourself fast enough. Not this time." He cast *ball of lightning* and watched the blue electrical energy envelop Valen. Jeremy's lips pulled back from his teeth. "How's it feel, dickhead?" Jeremy drew his dagger. It was not a particularly formidable weapon but it would make the kill up close and personal and that was precisely what he wanted. He approached Valen; the cleric continued to writhe helplessly within the ball of lightning.

Jeremy stabbed him once. Valen's health dipped but not by much. That was okay. Jeremy wanted to savor this one. He stabbed him again. The cleric's health was close to nothing. Jeremy paused long enough to smile. He said, "Now we're even."

Raak fell to the ground. Jeremy's jaw dropped. *You have been slain*, the game informed him. *Where would you like to resurrect?* "What the fuck just happened?" The ball of lightning dissipated with Raak's death. Valen glowed bright green and his health climbed to full. Shokata ran up beside him and Jeremy saw, *Shokata pats Valen on his head*, in his chat window. Immediately after that came the message, *Valen spits on corpse of Raak.*

Jeremy pounded both fists on his desk. He stood up rapidly and his chair fell over. He looked at the screen, at Raak's corpse and the last message in his chat window. Jeremy started to shout something, anything, but he was aware in the back of his mind his mother was home. If she heard him there was a good chance she would make him log off. He stifled his rage just enough to prevent himself from screaming. He punched his mattress with everything he had.

It took him several moments to calm himself enough to sit at the computer again. Raak still lay upon the ground. The sounds of combat continued but the battle had moved beyond the hill. Several players who had apparently been killed raced back across the PVP line. Jeremy had seen enough. He selected Valley of Power as his resurrection site. The hills of Highmoor vanished.

After the load-in screen he found himself in his home city. He checked with the healer and then left the hut.

He spent another hour hanging around the tavern in Misthaven, hoping to find a group that needed a wizard. Most of the messages he sent were ignored, a few were answered with a polite but firm *no, thanks*. Jeremy logged off.

****

After dinner that night he logged back in. He found the tavern was crowded. Enchanters were busy handing out buffs and the conversations in spatial moved so quickly he had a difficult time keeping up with them in his chat window. He checked his friends list and found no names highlighted. Ceradus had been removed from the list, presumably when the dickhead added Jeremy to his ignore list. "Fuck him," Jeremy said.

He tried again to join several groups. He finally got lucky and was invited into a group that planned to run all the instances except, naturally, Vault of Shadows. He added the group's leader, a ranger named Laybin, to his friends list after they completed the first instance, Knoll Invasion. They blasted through Queen of Swords and the Haunted Slaveship. He was killed once during Ravenwood Manor, mostly because the group's cleric, an incompetent newb named Snootz, did not know how to properly heal the group members. It was the only hiccup in an otherwise decent instance run.

He asked about doing Vault of Shadows but the group members began to leave. He typed, */tell laybin hey, good runnin with ya. if you need a wizard again look me up.*

A moment later the reply came, *Laybin tells you, thanx but prolly not. you were a little 2 wild in there. and windows is our usual wiz. but thanx again.*

Jeremy's heart sank. Windows again? And if they were friends then it would not be long before Windows told Laybin about him. Jeremy hung his head. *So much for that group.* He logged out but before he did he removed Laybin from his friends list.

****

Jeremy awoke the next morning and ate a quick breakfast. He went back upstairs to his room and turned on his desktop and logged into the Realm of Heroes forums. He had made a decent amount of money during the previous night's instance run (it was the single decent thing about the night before) and he was looking to spend.

He started to peruse the various wares being offered before he noticed he had a new private message. He clicked on it. It was from someone named Blacktooth Grin. "Never heard of him," Jeremy said. He nearly deleted the message without reading it; credit farmers were known to spam the forums from time to time. "Do you feel boring to farm credits?" was one of their poorly-translated messages. They always went on to proclaim the benefits of selling ingame credits, for real money, of course, and included an email address where you could sign up. Jeremy hated the credit farmers with a passion he usually reserved for bullies and jocks. His finger moved toward the delete key before he stopped himself.

"Greetings, Raak," Blacktooth's message began. "I am aware you've had some trouble recently in the game. I can help."

Jeremy looked at the timestamp on the message. 12:01 AM this morning. "This guy doesn't waste any time," Jeremy said. He checked to see who was online in the forums at the moment. He found Blacktooth's name right away. He clicked on the instant message button and typed: *How can you help?*

Jeremy sat back in the chair. The reply was immediate.

I have an item that I would be willing to give to you that will help your game play immensely. Interested?

"Yeah, right." He typed: *If this item is so uber why would you give it to me? And what is it?*

The reply came so fast Jeremy was certain Blacktooth had already typed the message and simply waited until Jeremy was finished. *It's called the Staff of Ultimate Darkness. It's yours if you want it. Just say the word and we'll meet up and I'll give it to you.*

The corners of Jeremy's mouth turned up in sarcasm. *Never heard of it. I'm not a newb, you know. Go sell that shit to someone else.*

He moved the mouse toward the End Chat button but Blacktooth's reply was too fast. *Of course you've never heard of it. It's something only the devs are supposed to have. I happen to have one. I'm sure you would find it extremely useful.*

"This asshole doesn't give up." Jeremy sighed and typed: *And what does it do, exactly?*

It allows you to play the game in god mode.

Jeremy paused. He looked at the words again. *God mode.* Every gamer knew about it. Most, Jeremy included, loved the idea of being invincible in the game. It was a login code that allowed the player, always a developer or at least a game manager, to do whatever they wanted to do. Jeremy had never heard of an ingame item that worked in god mode but he had to admit, if only to himself, he did not know all there was to know about Realm of Heroes. He stroked his chin.

Do I take your silence to mean you are interested?

Jeremy took a moment before he replied. *Are you a dev?*

No. Just someone who dislikes bullies. I know how they treated you and I want to do something to help. Do you want the Staff or not?

Jeremy swallowed. *You expect me to believe this? If it's so valuable why give it away?*

I already told you. If I'm wasting my time…

Okay, okay. Where do you want to meet? And when?

I'll be at the Dune Wastes at coordinates 813 111 in one hour. I'll see you there.

Jeremy's brow furrowed. He had been to the Dune Wastes only once before and he had not survived the experience. Sand dragons were all over the place and they were too tough for a single player to defeat. He was unsure if he could even reach the coordinates without being killed.

He was about to suggest an alternate meeting place when he noticed Blacktooth had left the conversation. He checked the list of all the players online in the forums and did not see his name. "Logged out pretty fast." Jeremy exited the forums.

He sat back in his chair and rubbed his eyes. "This is all bullshit," he said. Blacktooth was probably friends with those assholes Trawolf and Valen. It was certainly a setup. Make him waste his time going out to the middle of nowhere just so he could be killed by sand dragons. They would probably be close by, near enough to see it happen but far enough away not to draw any aggro onto themselves. He had no wish to entertain those idiots.

He took a quick shower and threw on a clean pair of jeans. He poured himself a soda, grabbed a bag of chips and returned to his room. He sat at his computer and logged into the game. He planned to see if there were any heroic groups forming that did not include any of the assholes from the previous two days. He felt he deserved another go at the Vault of Shadows. He would go through the other instances if necessary but only if it would get him into VoS.

The moment he logged in he received a message in his chat window. *Blacktooth tells you, come to the coordinates. im here right now. i have the staff.*

Jeremy looked about and saw numerous players going about their business. His chat window was alive with conversation. "Shouldn't have a problem finding a group today." He moved in the direction of the tavern. He kept an eye on his chat window for anyone looking for a wizard for a heroic run. He saw none by the time he entered the tavern. Several enchanters flitted about the stage area and a large crowd of players watched them. Jeremy picked one he did not know, an elf named Jaecee, and watched her.

Blacktooth tells you, you comin?

Jeremy ignored him. It took only a moment for the message to work its way up and off his chat window, pushed out by the conversations taking place in spatial. He watched Jaecee until he timed out. He requested his usual buff and she complied. He tipped her generously and found an empty corner of the tavern.

He sat at a table and watched the spatial conversations. Two separate groups were each looking for a cleric to join their instance run. Thus far no one had asked for a wizard. He sat and waited.

Blacktooth tells you, where you at? i cant wait all day.

Jeremy continued to keep track of the conversations in the tavern. He saw Laybin enter, get a buff from an enchanter, and leave. He nearly sent a message to him about starting a group. It would not matter; even if that dickhead was looking for a wizard he would not accept Raak. "I was too wild," Jeremy said sarcastically. "Fuck you, too." He alternated his gaze from the chat window to the door. Players continued to come and go. Some he recognized but most were strangers to him. He typed into spatial: *wiz LFG heroics. psm.* He did not need to add the "please send message" at the end but he did anyway. He watched his chat window and waited for someone to take him up on his offer.

Blacktooth tells you, last chance. im leavin in 2 mins if you don't reply.

"For fuck's sake," Jeremy said. He sat up and typed */reply go find some1 else 2 harass. im not a newb.*

Blacktooth replies to you, i see you need a demo. get rdy.

Jeremy laughed, a short bark that was louder than he expected. He reached for his keyboard, ready to blast the shithead with a scalding reply. He was able to type nothing. The tavern disappeared and he was staring at a load in screen. "What the fuck?" He hit the ESC key but the load in screen remained. He hit it several times. "What just happened? Am I locked up?"

The load in screen was replaced by a view of endless desert and sand dunes in every direction. Several large and aggressive-looking sand dragons moved slowly about the area. Jeremy panicked. He would be unable to defeat even one, let alone the seven or eight in his immediate area. He was about to die.

Blacktooth says, Greetings, Raak, appeared in his chat window.

Jeremy spun about and saw a black-robed wizard standing perhaps ten meters from him. He held a black staff in his hands. Some type of gem, a deeper void of color than the staff itself, rested at its top. Jeremy could not see the wizard's face, which was new to him. Unless the player or NPC wore a helmet their face was visible. He should have been able to see Blacktooth's face; that he could not made him uneasy for reasons he could not articulate.

"What…" Jeremy typed: *how did you do that?*

Blacktooth says, you needed a demo. i gave you 1. want the staff?

Jeremy's eyes narrowed. *how did you get me out here? even GMs cant do that.*

Blacktooth says, the staff lets me play in god mode. you 2. all you have 2 do is take it.

Raak says, why so charitable? why give this 2 me if its so powerful?

Blacktooth says, you need it more than i do. those peasants don't pick on me like they pick on you. and with this theyll nvr pick on you again. guaranteed.

Jeremy started to reply when the trade window opened on his screen. He watched the black staff appear on Blacktooth's side. On the bottom of the window he saw the message, *Blacktooth accepts trade*. Jeremy checked the box that indicated he accepted it as well. The trade window closed and in his chat window he saw the message, *Trade completed*.

Jeremy opened his inventory and the staff appeared at the bottom. He clicked on it to equip it. His old staff vanished from his hand and appeared in his inventory; a gray box surrounded the Staff of Ultimate Darkness, indicating it was now equipped. He closed his inventory and saw the black staff in Raak's hand.

Blacktooth says, try it on 1 of the dragons.

Jeremy turned Raak in the direction of the nearest dragon. He targeted the creature. The crosshairs that indicated a target lock were black instead of the customary red. He moved to click the mouse but his finger paused over the button. Instead he typed, *youre gonna get me killed.*

Blacktooth says, no im not. attack it.

Jeremy shook his head. In all the time he had played the game he had never attempted anything as foolish as attacking a sand dragon by himself. Not even when he was a newb. He took a deep breath and reestablished the target lock. The black crosshairs reappeared. Jeremy swallowed and unleashed the staff's power.

A beam of black light erupted from the staff. It streaked through the air and exploded against the dragon's brown scales. The creature toppled over and landed hard on its side. Smoke poured up from the carcass.

Jeremy blinked more than once to make certain he was not imagining the results. The sand dragon remained on its side, smoke continued to cloud the sky, and the creature remained dead. In his chat window he saw the message, *You have looted a crystal pearl from the corpse of a sand dragon.*

"Holy shit," he whispered.

Blacktooth tells you, have fun with it.

Jeremy typed as quickly as he was able: *i cant use this. if i get caught cheating it's a lifetime ban.*

Blacktooth tells you, you wont get caught. GMs will nvr know you have it. they cant see it. thats part of playing in god mode. good luck.

Jeremy typed: *take it back. ill get tossed off the game 4 good.*

But Blacktooth had vanished in the time it took Jeremy to type his message. He stood alone in the middle of the Dune Wastes. Several sand dragons continued to wander around him. He opened his inventory and selected the Staff of Ultimate Darkness. He double-clicked on it to uneqip the item. The staff remained in his hands; the gray box continued to surround the item in his inventory. He tried again and received the same result.

"Screw this." He typed, *Drop Staff of Darkness.* Nothing happened. "What the fuck."

He heard one of the sand dragons roar and he spun to face it. It was far off, seventy-five meters or more but it was charging toward him. How had he drawn aggro from so far away? He paused and watched it but there was little doubt the creature was coming after him. Jeremy targeted it and hit the attack button. Black energy surrounded the dragon and it dropped dead in the sand.

Three more of the beasts roared their disapproval and charged him. He targeted the area in front of them and used the staff. This time a zone of blackness sprung into being in front of the sand dragons. They charged blindly into it and died instantly.

Jeremy looked at the smoking carcasses. Had he really just killed three of them with one shot? He had. He checked his chat window and saw he had succeeded in looting another crystal pearl, a sword of destiny, an elixir of invulnerability and nearly six hundred-thousand gold pieces. In moments he had the greatest loot day he had ever experienced in Realm of Heroes.

Jeremy sat back and stroked his chin. He guided Raak toward another group of dragons. He targeted their area. The black crosshairs contrasted quite nicely with the brown-yellow of the sand. He hit the attack button and all five sand dragons dropped at the same moment.

Jeremy giggled. "This is fucking awesome," he said to his room. He looted more rare and valuable items, including a

Valdereen chestplate, a piece of the most expensive and sought-after armor in the game. He squealed his excitement.

He nearly summoned Fang but something made him hesitate. Instead he placed his cursor on the staff in his hand and examined it. A window opened on the screen and asked him for his destination. He selected Misthaven. The Dune Wastes vanished and the load in screen was up for only a moment before he found himself in the small town.

He checked the duration of his buffs and noticed there was a new icon there he had never before seen. It was black with an even blacker jewel in the middle. He placed his cursor on it and it was identified as *God Mode*.

He typed, */tell blacktooth this staff is awesome! thanx!*

The reply was immediate. *Blacktooth is not a valid player name.*

"Huh?" Jeremy checked the spelling for errors but found none. He retyped the message slowly and carefully and received the same reply. The only explanation was the player behind the character had deleted Blacktooth from the game. "Why would he do that?"

Jeremy continued to look at the message in the chat window until he saw one come up in spatial from someone named Chewhefner. Jeremy laughed at the name. "Good one." The message was, *need wiz 4 heroics run. ki-qos-hs-rm-vos. psm.*

Jeremy's heartbeat picked up. A group running through all of them, including Vault of Shadows. Jeremy quickly sent a message to Chewhefner and a moment later he received an invitation to join the group. He scanned through the names of the group members and sighed in relief when he saw none of the assholes from his previous groups were present. Knoll Invasion was first up. Boring as hell but it would give him an opportunity to get used to his new staff. He used the staff to teleport himself to the meeting place and he awaited the group's arrival.

****

Knoll Invasion bored him to tears. It was the easiest of the heroic instances even before he received the staff; with it, none of the invading knolls were even worthy of his attention. He blasted entire groups of the dog-men into nothingness with one click of his mouse. Since he spent most of the instance guarding the healers hut none of the others in the group witnessed how easily he dispatched the NPCs. In the grand finale of the instance when the knoll king arrived the others in his group were too busy attacking him and his bodyguards to notice Jeremy hanging back. He waited until the king was near half-health before he used the staff. It blasted the king and killed him instantly. Several members of the group were clearly aware something unusual had occurred but they had been too distracted by the combat to realize what had happened. They divided up the loot and moved on to Queen of Swords.

That bored him as well. As each of the Queen's henchmen went live Jeremy resisted the urge to simply destroy them instantly. He waited until they were already wounded before he put them down. When the Queen herself attacked, Jeremy allowed the fighters and monks to get some hits on her before he took care of business.

The Haunted Slaveship and even Ravenwood Manor came close to putting him to sleep. He assisted the others when he felt they would notice his inactivity but otherwise he allowed them to do most of the heavy lifting. He had wiped out six or seven sand dragons by himself; the NPCs in the heroics were suddenly small change to him. The biggest test of the staff was coming up. Jeremy wanted to be certain he was ready.

After Ravenwood Manor he loaded in to the area around the Vault of Shadows. He was the first to arrive and so spent some time wiping out the Death Dealers that surrounded the vault's entranceway. They were not particularly tough before; now he was able to destroy entire groups of them with one keystroke. They dropped items that might have excited him the day before; now all they did was clog up his inventory. He eased off a bit when the other members of the group began to load in. He waited impatiently for the stragglers to show up. When all eight of them were present he made his way to the entrance. He drummed his fingers on his desk and waited for them to enter the vault. He was the last to enter.

The Shadow of Hate stood in the center of the dais, the Death Dealers stood at their positions around the room's perimeter. Chewhefner ran through the rules while Jeremy stifled a yawn. "C'mon, already." He was anxious to start. There was a newb in the group, apparently, judging by Chewhefner's instructions to another wizard named Sufferance. Jeremy whispered, "Blah, blah, blah," softly enough for his headset mic not to pick it up. The two clerics, KJ and Ewoge, took their places in the center of the room. The monk was Skyreth and when Chewhefner was satisfied everyone knew what to do, he sent the monk to attack the Shadow of Hate.

Jeremy followed his usual routine. He remained on the sidelines until he thought his inactivity would be noticed. Then he nuked whichever Death Dealer happened to be live.

When the last one fell, Chewhefner informed Skyreth and the monk began to run around the room's perimeter. The Shadow of Hate ran after him.

For all the buildup it was actually quite boring. Jeremy guided Raak around the room along with the others in the group. He kept his target lock on the Shadow of Hate but resisted the urge to attack her. It was not long before KJ took notice. "Hey, Raak, you gonna get in on this?" he asked in group voice.

"Fine," Jeremy said. A beam of black shot out from the staff at the Shadow of Hate. The NPC dropped instantly. "There."

"What the fuck?" Ewoge asked.

"What was that?" Skyreth added.

"That, my friends, was me being badass." Jeremy sat back in his chair and folded his hands behind his head.

"What did you hit her with?" Chewhefner asked. "I've never seen that happen before."

"You've never had me in the group before," Jeremy replied.

"He's exploiting the game," KJ said. "That's a lifetime ban, idiot. Chew, you have to kick him. We might get nailed, too. I know a guy who got banned for a month because someone in his PVP group found an exploit. The devs consider that guilt by association."

"Hey, I'm not getting banned because some asshole found a way to cheat," Sufferance added.

Jeremy sat up in the chair. "Hey, I'm not exploiting anything. You'd better not kick me from the group. I'm far and away the most powerful one here. Without me you all go down in flames and you know it."

Two of them began to laugh at him. Jeremy's cheeks turned red.

"Sorry, kid," Chewhefner said, "but I don't play with hackers."

Jeremy started to protest. He stopped when he realized he had indeed been removed from the group. He sat bolt upright in his chair and slammed his fist onto his desk. "No, you fucking assholes!"

The rest of the group stood in the room for another moment before they made their way down the open passageway on the east wall. They were going to continue the instance without a full group and their only remaining wizard was a newb. Jeremy watched them leave. "I hope you all fucking die." He typed, /escape and left the Vault of Shadows.

He stood and paced around his room. This was twice he had entered the Vault and failed to go beyond the first room. He slammed his fist into his open palm repeatedly and swore just softly enough his mother would not hear him. After several moments he returned to his chair. He needed to vent some steam or he felt he would explode. He used the staff to teleport himself to Highmoor.

Several players of his own faction stood at the PVP line. Atop the hill stood numerous enemy players. Several conversations were going on in spatial chat. He ignored them and scanned the enemy ranks for familiar names. Immediately he saw Valen and Shokata. He looked over the rest but saw no one else he knew. They would have to do.

Raak stepped to the line. Valen saw him. In his chat window Jeremy saw, *Valen points at you and laughs.* The corner of Jeremy's mouth turned up.

Raak stepped over the line and stood his ground.

Instantly the enemy players unloaded on him. The fighters, Shokata among them, raced down the hill toward him. The wizards and clerics unleashed spells at him. Jeremy's monitor lit up with a graphics display so bright and multi-colored he squinted. Raak remained on his feet. Jeremy glanced at his health bar and saw it had not moved a centimeter. His grin became a smile.

The fighters, five in all, reached him. The swung their swords, staves and halberds at him. Raak simply stood among them.

Some of the players on his side saw an opportunity and crossed the line. Jeremy ignored them, too. He continued to stand his ground while the fighters tore into him and the wizards and clerics bombed him with spells. He should have been dead seven or eight times already yet his health bar remained full.

The attacks on him lessened somewhat as the enemy players suddenly had other targets to consider. The graphics display dimmed a bit and Jeremy could see clearly the action going on around him. Two of the allied players were already dead. He counted no casualties among the enemy. That was about to change.

He targeted Shokata and unleashed the staff. The fighter fell dead instantly. He selected another, a monk named Voorhees, and killed him, as well. The other melee combatants had moved on to other targets. Raak stood alone at the line.

Jeremy looked at the top of the hill. He did not see Valen but he knew he was there. The pussy had probably retreated a bit away from the combat so he could safely heal those in his group. Raak charged up the hill.

Jeremy smiled when he was proved correct. Valen stood at the base of the hill casting healing spells. Raak walked slowly and casually down the hill. He could have simply killed the cleric from long range but he wanted this to be up close and personal. He wanted to watch Valen die.

The cleric turned in his direction. A moment later a shimmering, translucent wall sprang into existence between them. Jeremy laughed and walked up to it. Valen appeared as a heat mirage on the other side of the wall. He ignored Raak and continued to heal the people in his group.

Jeremy typed, *hows it hangin valen?*

The cleric ignored him; keeping the members of his group alive was clearly taking most of his concentration. It did not matter. Raak stepped through the translucent wall and stood directly in front of Valen.

It took the cleric a moment to realize something had gone wrong. When it dawned on him Raak had somehow gotten through his shield he quickly backed up.

Raak swung the staff like a sword and smashed the side of Valen's head. The cleric fell dead. Jeremy nearly leaped from his chair. He threw up his arms and pumped his fists. "Yes, that's what you get, cocksucker. Fuck with me again and I won't be so nice." He looked at Valen's corpse upon the ground. He sat down again and typed a command. In his chat window it read, *You spit at corpse of Valen.*

Jeremy clapped his hands together. Three kills in less than as many minutes. He looked about for more targets.

****

The following day he was forced to accompany his mother to visit his grandmother in Towson. He faked his attention to her pleasantries and endured her endless questions about his return to school in September ("A sophomore already? I can't believe it. You got so big so fast, Jerrybear."). What he wanted more than anything was to be back home in his room watching Raak lay waste to the NPCs who inhabited the Vault of Shadows. And, he had to admit, anyone stupid enough to come at him in Highmoor. He was willing to bet Valen would leave him alone from now on. Shokata, as well, if he had a brain in his head.

He choked down his grandmother's chocolate cake and tried to occupy himself with the Marlins/Nationals game on TV. It was a close game and Strasburg was pitching his ass off but Jeremy found he could not get excited about it. Not when there were NPCs and enemy assholes awaiting his return to Realm of Heroes. His eyes went from the television to the clock on the wall and back again several times.

When his mother at last finished off her latest cup of coffee and began to help his grandmother with the dishes Jeremy started to calculate his arrival time back home. By the time they actually left her house he knew it would be too late to log into the game.

They arrived back home at 10:37 PM. His mother, in fact, made it a point to tell him to get ready for bed. He stared longingly at his dark monitor and wished he could spend some time in the world it contained. He knew his mother would never allow it. He decided to let her have this one. It's not like the game was going anywhere. It would still be there tomorrow and so would the Vault of Shadows.

****

The following day he logged in and saw the email icon flash at the top of his screen. He clicked on it and saw it was from someone named Glickspar—Developer. Jeremy's brow furrowed and he clicked on the email. It read:

You have been reported to the development team for possible

exploitative activities. When we conclude our investigation you

will be informed of our findings.

Jeremy gritted his teeth. Someone ratted him out. It was either Valen or Shokata, although he could not rule out the possibility it could have been Chewhefner. He suspected Valen, if only because the guy was obviously an asshole dweeb who could not stand having his ass handed to him in Highmoor the other day. So be it. He would take Raak to Highmoor and if Valen was stupid enough to be there, he would deal with him again.

Valen was not in Highmoor. In fact he saw only three players inside the PVP zone, all allies. There were no enemy players in sight. He walked up to the line and stopped. He saw two of the allies right away. Ceradus and Trawolf stood to the left of the hill and toyed with some low level NPCs that inhabited the PVP area. The third was someone named Jinzza, whom he did not know, although she appeared to be another cleric.

Raak waved to Ceradus before Jeremy remembered the dickhead had placed him on his ignore list. Ceradus would not see the gesture. He wished there was a way for allied players to battle one another in PVP but the devs had never allowed it. Too bad. He would have liked to teach Ceradus the same lesson he had taught Valen two days before.

He crossed the line and took up a spot atop the hill. Jeremy sat back and waited for the enemy to start showing up.

It took some time during which Jeremy nearly fell asleep. He waited atop the hill for more than an hour before enough of an enemy force congregated on the safe side of the PVP line. Several allied players had also showed and felt secure enough to cross the line first. They took up various positions and awaited the enemy players.

Jeremy saw Snootz, Windows and Laybin among them. Good. He had no problem showing them the error of their ways in kicking him from the group before they had even run VoS. He paid attention to spatial chat, mostly out of boredom. Until they crossed the PVP line he could not touch them. The conversation going on among the enemy players was banal to say the least. They seemed to talk about every-thing but the game. They also seemed in no rush to start the battle, which caused Jeremy to squirm in his seat. He wanted nothing more than for them to cross the line.

He licked his lips when the idea occurred to him. He typed, *hey windows wheres your boy valen? i humiliated his ass the other day. wanna try your luck?* On the heels of that he typed, */laugh at Windows.*

In spatial he saw, *Windows says, haven't seen him ig in a couple days. must be sick or somethin.*

Jeremy shook his head. "Like hell." He typed, *nah, hes just mad cuz i embarrassed him here.* Then he typed, */dance.* Raak began to dance about the hilltop.

He kept an eye on the enemy players. He thought they now outnumbered those on Raak's side. Not that it would matter beyond prompting them to begin the assault. Jeremy drummed his fingers on the desk and waited for them to grow enough balls to cross the line.

He looked to his right and was surprised to see Ceradus was near him. So were Jinzza and Trawolf. Whatever. He did not need them. He did not need anyone.

The enemy players finally crossed the line and his monitor lit up with pyrotechnic displays of magical power. Jeremy sat back and allowed both sides to do some damage to each other. A few long range attacks found Raak but his health did not waver. Jeremy crossed his arms and put his feet up on the desk.

The battle raged around him. A single enemy monk ran to him and began hitting Raak with his staff. Raak regarded him for only a moment. He had a difficult time targeting any of the enemy players he knew. There were simply too many people running about for Jeremy to target a specific person.

He placed his target cursor on the ground. It would be much less personal this way, but he wanted to get some killing done and the last thing he wanted was for the enemy players like Laybin and Windows to be killed by someone else and decide now was not the time for PVP. Perhaps they would start another group to run VoS. He did not like that.

He placed his cursor among the largest group of combatants and loosed his staff. A cone of black sprang into existence and engulfed the majority of the PVPers. The roar of the spell filled his speakers. When the cone dissipated Raak saw nothing but bodies on the ground.

He tilted his head and leaned in closer to the monitor. Among the dead were several allies, including Ceradus and Jinzza. "How'd that happen?"

He was not alone in his surprise. All combat had ceased in the PVP zone. Allies and enemies stood still and looked about. The chat window came to life.

WTF?

What just happened?

Is the game bugged?

Who did that?

Did anyone see how that happened?

Raak stood off to the side. He surveyed the field of corpses. Slowly his lips pulled back from his teeth and he smiled. He picked off the enemy players one at a time. When he was finished with them he targeted his allies. A few moments after his initial attack he had Highmoor to himself.

He surveyed the area. There were more than two dozen corpses around him. He sat back and waited for them to start vanishing as their players chose their healing hut. None did. The corpses lay where they fell. "Get up, get up," he said. "Killing you once isn't good enough. Resurrect and get back in here." The corpses remained. Were the players too frightened to rez and return? He thought perhaps they were. "Buncha fucking pansies." Raak walked toward the PVP line. "Fine, fine. I'll go. You guys can have Highmoor for now."

He crossed the line and teleported himself to Misthaven.

****

Jeremy logged in the next morning. He checked his friends list and was not surprised to find it empty. He was right outside the tavern in Misthaven where he had logged out the day before. After he laid waste to the PVP zone he had tried to find another group. No one replied to his messages so he logged out. He was hoping to get a good instance run going today. He sent out a few messages in spatial chat but received no takers. There were not many players inside the tavern, anyway, and only one enchanter. He did not wait for buffs; it would be too long before the enchanter got to him and besides, he did not need any buffs. He exited the tavern.

He teleported to Highmoor. There were three players present, all allies. They stood at the line but were not PVP active. He walked to the line and stood beside them. He typed, *any pvp goin on?*

One of them, a ranger named Ynot, replied, *no. been like this since last nite. no1 around*

"Damn," Jeremy whispered.

He left Highmoor and went to the Vault of Shadows. He did not bother with the Death Dealers outside; they attacked him on sight but they were utterly unable to cause him any damage. Jeremy entered the Vault. He was not at all certain the game would allow him entry because he was not part of a group but he loaded in without a problem. The Shadow of Hate stood upon the dais and her minions took up their customary places around the room. "Let's see what happens."

He dropped the Shadow of Hate and all the Death Dealers within the room with one use of his staff. His grin became a smile and he clapped his hands together. "Yes!" He looted the corpses (nothing particularly valuable turned up) and went on to the second room.

The Shadow of Fear was the main NPC in the second room. She stood in the center, arms at her side. The walls here showed the signs of ancient battle. The mystical runes which decorated them were broken in places by scorch marks. Even the stones which made up the ceiling were blackened. He had to admit, the room looked cool. He took another screenshot.

Three cloaked figures that resembled Death Dealers ran from the shadows and attacked Raak all at once. He removed the target lock from the Shadow of Fear and placed it on the three cloaked attackers. They went down with one shot. He retargeted the Shadow of Fear and dropped him. He looted the corpses and found a chainmail breastplate. The second-most valuable suit of armor in the game and something most fighters and knights coveted. He placed it in his inventory. If nothing else he could show it to some of the jerks who talked shit to him and wave it in their faces.

The third room's boss was the Shadow of Power. When Raak crossed the threshold this boss set the room on fire. The flames did nothing to Raak; a quick check of his health bar showed he had taken no damage. His smile widened even further. He stood untouched among the flames and imagined a group of players fighting the Shadow of Power and the rapid, panicked conversations going on in group voice as they tried, rather pathetically, to defeat her. He killed the Shadow of Power and looted her corpse. She gave him nothing but gold pieces but that was okay with him. He had little use for any of the loot items, anyway. He made his way toward the final room in the Vault.

The Shadow Mage stood upon a raised dais much larger and more ornate than the one in the first room. He stood in front of a large, black altar. Jeremy's heartbeat picked up. He had never before seen the Shadow Mage except in some screenshots placed online by other players. It was said he was the single toughest NPC in the game. He had wiped out entire groups with ease. Jeremy smiled.

He ran up the dais and stood before the Shadow Mage. The black-robed figure stood still for a moment before the air around him crackled with purple electricity. He unleashed a spell that should have killed Raak instantly. The wizard took it with no loss to his health.

Jeremy sat back and allowed the Shadow Mage to hit him with spell after spell. He glanced at his health from time to time but he need not have worried; Rakk, it seemed, was impervious to harm. After a few moments he targeted the Shadow Mage. He used the staff and the Shadow mage fell dead upon the dais.

Jeremy clapped his hands. "Yes!" He took a quick screenshot of the corpse so he could post it in the forums. He doubted he would have any trouble finding a place in an instance group after that image made the rounds. He looted the corpse. The Shadow Mage gave up a fresco depicting himself fighting a group of adventurers. The second item was a Ring of Invincibility. It was a powerful magic item but one for which Jeremy had no need. He placed it in his inventory.

He looked about the room. The devs had gone out of their way to make the last room in the Vault as creepy as possible. Giant spider webs covered most of the ceiling, iron braziers stood in each corner and purple flames sputtered within them. Runes which glowed green and purple decorated the walls. It was a very cool effect. Jeremy nodded his appreciation to the people who put the room together. It was a shame they could not have come up with a more powerful guardian to protect it.

He left the Vault and returned to Highmoor. A few more people had showed up but it was still nowhere near the size of the crowds he had come to expect in the PVP zone. He recognized none of the players so he teleported himself back to Misthaven.

The tavern was slightly more populated than it had been earlier. There were three enchanters present and they went about their business. Some of the patrons watched them but several others stood to the side and chatted in spatial. Jeremy glanced at his chat window.

Ewoge said, *cant believe it. 2 in 1 day. wtf happened?*

Sufferance said, *don't know 4 sure. if they found ceradus like they found snootz then it had 2 be coordinated. idk.*

Worthington added, *did they live close 2 each other?*

Sufferance replied, *no. ceradus lived in england i think and snootz is down here in tx with me. pretty fucked up tho.*

Raak moved closer to the crowd. He typed, *what happened?*

Ewoge said, *2 of our friends died yesterday.*

Raak raised an eyebrow. *really?*

Sufferance said, *really. sux. they were good guys.*

No they weren't, Raak thought. *They were pieces of shit. I'm just pissed I won't get to kill them ingame again.* He typed, *does any1 know how it happened?*

There was a pause before Sufferance answered, *don't know about ceradus but snootz was found by his wife. he was at the computer slumped over the desk. mighta been a heart attack. he was only 36 tho. kinda young 4 that.*

Raak typed, *that's 2 bad. wassup now? any1 wanna pvp?*

At first no one relied. Then Sufferance said *not in the mood.*

Ewoge added, *yeah not playin today. gonna logout in a few.*

Raak swallowed and drummed his fingers on the desk. "Assholes," he whispered. For the hell of it he targeted Ewoge. He would be unable to kill him outside the PVP zone but it would make him smile a bit thinking about it. He hit the key which activated the staff.

A lance of black energy shot from the staff and enveloped Ewoge. He fell to the floor dead.

Raak looked with disbelief at the screen. "Holy shit."

Sufferance said, *WTF!*

Worthington said, *howd you do that???*

"I don't know," Raak said aloud. He moved the target cursor to Sufferance and waited for the color of his name to change from blue to red. It did not. He activated his staff, anyway. The same black energy which felled Ewoge wrapped itself around Sufferance. When it dissipated Sufferance lay next to Ewoge.

"Oh, this is so cool," Raak said. He smiled broadly. He placed his target cursor on Worthington but paused. He became aware of many eyes turned his way. He looked at the enchanters and their customers. All activity in the tavern had ceased. The players looked at him and at the two bodies on the floor. "What are you looking at?" He removed the target from Worthington and placed it on the floor amidst the other players. "Ba-boom!" Raak shouted.

His view of the room was obscured by blackness. He sat and waited impatiently for it to clear. When it did he looked upon nearly a dozen bodies on the floor. None moved. He was the only non-corpse within the tavern. Or was he? He caught movement from the corner of his eye. Worthington, it seemed, had been outside the area of effect. He disappeared out the tavern's backdoor.

Raak considered chasing him down but he decided against it. He could clearly kill Worthington (and anyone else, it seemed) at will. There was no need to chase after him. All would eventually fall to Raak.

He turned back to the corpses in the room. His smile widened. He had another hour or so before his mother would be home and an hour after that before she got on him about not mowing the lawn. He had time.

He left the tavern and looked for more players.

****

The pickings had been light after the tavern in Misthaven. He decided to surprise his mother and have the lawn mown by the time she got home. After dinner he was eager to get back in the game but his mother informed him they were going shopping for school clothes. It was not his favorite activity before he found the joys of being the biggest badass wizard in the game; now it was torture. By the time they returned from the mall it was late and he was tired. He went to bed and slept soundly.

When he logged in the following morning he received a message. It read:

Your account has been deactivated and you
are hereby banned from Realm of Heroes for
exploiting the game and your fellow players.
If you have any questions or you would like to
challenge this ban you may contact the development
team. Sincerely, Glickspar—Developer

Jeremy stared at the message for some time. He did not know when his hands had curled into fists but he had squeezed hard enough to leave crescent moon-shaped slits of blood in his palms. "You can't do this," he whispered. "You have no right!"

He continued with the login. There was no chance the game would allow him in and he knew it. "Fucking Glickspar," he growled. He wished the Staff of Ultimate Darkness was a real-world item. He would not think twice about using it on the self-important dickhead who had the balls to banish him. But it was not and he would be unable to exact any kind of revenge on Glickspar at all. The fucker would get away scot free with banning Raak from the game.

The image on his monitor flickered and then went dark. "No, no, no," Jeremy said. He smacked the side of the monitor. "Don't do this to me." The monitor flashed back to life and flickered some more. It filled with snow and his speakers crackled static. The blackness returned and it was broken suddenly by lines of code. They scrolled up the screen much too quickly for Jeremy to even begin to read them. After a few moments the code vanished. The login screen reappeared.

Jeremy nearly smashed his fist into the monitor. He regained control of himself and worked to steady his breathing and heart rate. He inputted his user name and password for what would most likely be the last time. When Glickspar's message greeted him again he would sign off and never see Raak again.

The developer's message did not reappear. Instead what he saw was the character selection screen. Jeremy's jaw dropped. Was it that easy? Perhaps the developers had forgotten to remove his account login information. It was possible he could still play, at least until they discovered their error. Jeremy selected Raak and the character selection screen changed to a load in screen. Jeremy sat back and held his breath.

Raak appeared standing in the middle of the street in Misthaven. He clapped his hands together and pulled his chair closer to the monitor. "Yes!" The devs had fucked up and he was still able to play the game. He licked his lips and headed for the tavern.

There was one enchanter present and three other players. He did not know the three fighters but the enchanter had buffed him a time or two before. That was hardly going to stop him. He placed his target cursor on the enchanter, an elven woman named Allura. He struck her down and watched with amusement as the other players turned and looked at him. "That's right, bitches, I'm back." He targeted Weki, the nearest fighter. "Hiya, Weki," he said. He hit the key and the character went down in a cloud of blackness. "Bye-bye, Weki." He turned to the remaining two characters.

After they were dead, he left the tavern. The streets of Misthaven were deserted. "Where the fuck is everyone?" He teleported to Highmoor. There were a few enemy players present. They stood at the top of the hill. He saw no allies in the area. "Just four of you?" Raak snorted his derision. *Barely worth my time*, he thought, until he noticed Skyreth and Trawolf were among them. Raak's eyes narrowed and he smiled.

He approached the PVP line but stopped when his chat window filled with a message in red type. Red always meant a message from the developers and it was always sent with the highest importance. He read it.

Attention all players: There is a problem with RoH and the servers needs to be shut down for emergency mainte-nance. Please logout within the next 60 seconds. Thank you. The Development Team.

"Oh, no you don't," Raak said. He crossed the line. Above one of the players the letters LD appeared. That one had logged out. Skyreth and Trawolf were undoubtedly in the process of following him. Raak could not allow that to happen. He placed his target cursor on the ground amidst the three remaining enemies and let loose with the staff. All three players died instantly. Raak crested the hill and stood among the bodies. The fourth player had (escaped) despawned but Raak was not worried. He would deal with the coward later.

He stood among the corpses and waited for the game to shut down. He continued to wait even as he continued to stand among the dead. Nothing happened. Raak watched the clock on the bottom right of his screen continue to tick away. It was well past the 60 seconds the devs had given for safe logout yet he remained in Highmoor. "What the hell is this?"

He saw two players load in to Highmoor. He stood his ground on the hill and waited for them to approach the PVP line. Their names were in purple. Raak had never seen that color font in the game before. He paused until they came close enough for him to read their names. One was Inehao—Developer. The second made Raak smile. His name was Glickspar—Developer.

In his chat window Raak saw, *Glickspar says, wtf are you doin here? you were banned.*

Beneath that, *Inehao says, whatever you did 2 the game plz stop. youre overwriting the code. youll damage the whole game.*

Raak's smile widened. "Will I, now?" He typed, *make me stop. beat me and ill leave and nvr come back.*

The two devs stood in silence for a few moments. Raak knew they were talking among themselves. They were probably in an office somewhere in California trying to decide how to handle him. Let them talk. Whatever they planned to do would fail. He was unbeatable and all present knew it. He was just like—

The devs play in god mode, too, he thought. "Uh oh." Two against one and they were, in theory, his equals. "This could be bad." Raak sat up straight in his chair and gave the devs his full attention. He had already forgotten about the three corpses at his feet.

After a few moments Inehao and Glickspar stepped away from each other and advanced slowly to the PVP line. They were far enough apart that Raak's target cursor could not highlight both of them. He chose Glickspar. If they were to beat him at least he would have the pleasure of killing that haughty piece of shit before he went down.

They stood at the line and seemed to be gathering up their nerve. It did not occur to him until the other devs loaded in that they were waiting for reinforcements. Three more devs appeared and approached the line. Raak did not even bother with their names. It would not matter. Five against one were not good odds when the enemy had the same abilities he himself possessed. Raak swallowed and thought about what he would do without Realm of Heroes in his life.

The five developers crossed the line at the same time. He kept his target on Glickspar and used the staff. The developer was wreathed in black energy before he dropped. Raak blinked. "I just killed a dev!" he squealed. "Gotta be the first time that's ever happened!" And even though he was a moment or two away from being killed himself, he could at least take with him the knowledge he had carried out his revenge on Glickspar.

The remaining devs stopped in their tracks. Raak paused long enough to wonder what they were up to before he targeted and killed the second developer. The last three enemies continued to stand in place. They made no attacks against him, no moves of any kind. "What are you waiting for?"

He killed another dev. He waited for Inehao and his buddy to nuke Raak right out of the game but they continued to stand still. "What are you doing?" He selected the last of the new arrivals and killed him. Only Inehao remained. Raak moved his target cursor onto the developer.

In his chat window he saw a message in purple. *PLEASE STOP! YOU'RE KILLING US FOR REAL!"-- Inehao, Developer.*

"Yeah, right." Raak used the staff again. Inehao dropped.

Raak waited for the devs to resurrect at the healers hut and come back. There was no way they could allow him to do that and keep his character or account. There was no doubt anymore that he would be banned for life. If so, it had been one hell of a last day ingame. He only wished he could continue to play, if for no other reason than to brag to every-one how he had taken five devs at once without them getting off a shot. No one would believe him but that was okay. He knew the truth.

The bodies remained where they fell. Raak scratched his chin. "What's the holdup?" He continued to stand among the corpses and he waited for them to start despawning. He waited some more. The devs and the enemy players he killed continued to lie among the short grasses on the hill.

He waited a few more moments before he grew bored. He crossed the line again and teleported to Misthaven.

The place was a ghost town. He saw no one in the streets. The tavern held only the bodies of those he had killed. Somewhere in a dim corner of his mind he was troubled by the players' inactivity. They had all had plenty of time to resurrect at the healers hut. So why had they not done so?

"The server message," he said to the empty tavern. Of course. Everyone had logged out when they got the message from the devs. But the game had not been taken offline. Therefore it was only a matter of time before players started to log back in. Raak took a seat at one of the tables and waited for the players to come back.

****

He awoke with a start. He realized he had somehow fallen asleep at the computer. He shook his head to clear the cobwebs and rubbed his eyes. His legs were still asleep and he flexed them and rubbed them and waited for the pins-and-needles sensation to fade. After a few moments he was able to focus. He looked at his monitor and saw his screensaver. He shook the mouse and saw that Raak remained seated in the Misthaven tavern.

He had the room to himself save for the corpses of his earlier targets. He shook his head again and squeezed his eyes shut. He remained that way for several more moments, mostly to convince himself he was not dreaming. Why was the server still active and why had these fools not gone to the healers hut? He shook his head again.

He became aware of voices downstairs. He recognized his mother's right away. She was engaged in conversation with a man and a woman who did not sound familiar in the least. He got up and walked to his bedroom door. He put his ear against it but the voices remained muted. His mother sounded agitated but he could make out nothing of the conversation. He opened his door a crack and peeked out.

It was nearly a straight shot from his bedroom door to the front door with only the hallway and short staircase between them. His mother stood inside the foyer and she spoke animatedly with two people he could just barely glimpse. The woman wore what he came to think of as a business power suit; knee-length skirt and pressed jacket. The man was dressed in a three-piece that looked more expensive than most of the furniture in the house. He caught sight of the wallet and badge in the man's hand.

"We're not here to harm your son, Mrs. Stewart," the man said. "We only want to ask him some questions. Please."

"We have a warrant, ma'am," the woman added. "We don't need your permission. This conversation is a courtesy. We need to speak with Jeremy. It is imperative we do so at once."

His mother protested. The woman placed her hands on his mother's arms and tried to lead her into the living room. The man glanced up the stairs and spotted him. "Jeremy?" He began to ascend to the second floor.

Raak shut the door and fumbled with the lock. From the other side he heard the man say, "Jeremy. Son, you're not in trouble but we need to speak. Open your door, please."

Raak stood with his back to the door. His breathing and his heartbeat had picked up the tempo and sweat sprung up on his forehead. They weren't local cops, he was certain, not dressed as they were. That meant only one thing. What could they want with him? He glanced at his computer. Raak stood among the dead in the Misthaven tavern.

(PLEASE STOP!)

Would the feds actually investigate someone exploiting an online video game? He doubted it but why else would they be here?

(YOU'RE KILLING US FOR REAL!)

Raak's eyes grew large and the breath caught in his throat. "No way."

The doorknob twisted and it snapped Raak out of his shock. He gripped it with both hands. The man on the other side knocked quite loudly. "Jeremy, open up. We're with the FBI and we need to ask you a few questions." The pounding continued. "Open the door, son."

Raak eyed his window. He was certain he could reach it before the fed could get the door open. But then what? His bedroom was on the second floor of the family's split-level. It was a good twenty feet or better to the ground. Could he make the jump? Maybe. Probably. Would it matter? His eyes returned to the computer monitor. Raak stood impassively in the center of the tavern. The Staff of Ultimate Darkness remained gripped in his right hand. "That's what I need," Raak mumbled.

The door jumped a bit and threw Raak a few feet away. The boy leaned against it and absorbed the next blow from the other side. He looked at the lock and saw the door frame had splintered a bit.

"Jeremy, you have to open this door," the man said. "By refusing to do so you are interfering with a Federal warrant."

"Jeremy, honey, just open the door," his mother cried. Judging by her voice she was at the bottom of the stairs. "It's okay, nothing bad is going to happen." Her voice quavered. She was clearly very nervous, perhaps even scared.

"Jeremy, I'm going to ask you to step away from the door, son. I don't want you to get hurt when it opens. Do it now, please."

Raak's eyes were wild. He looked at the window again but it was no longer an option. The man would be through the door any second. He was out of options. He stepped away from the door.

It was blind luck he spotted the staff when he did. It stood propped in the corner of his room where he usually threw his dirty clothes. His eyes bugged. His mouth opened but no sound came out. He knew without knowing how just what the staff was. He recognized it as his only chance. He raced across the room and grabbed it.

The black crystal at the top of the staff seemed to pulse when he held it in front of his eyes. He looked more closely at the crystal. Although the hand that grasped the Staff belonged to Jeremy, the reflection in the compound features of the gem belonged to Raak the black elf. One hand went to the black crystal and felt along its facets. It was cold and he thought he saw something even darker flit about within. His other hand caressed the polished black wood of the staff itself. A single tear spilled from his right eye. It was even more beautiful in person than it was in the game.

His bedroom door flew open. The man stepped in. Behind him the woman in the power suit stepped into the doorway. The man held his hands up. When he spoke his voice was calm, authoritative. "We're gonna need you to come with us, Jeremy. We have some questions for you about that game you play. Realm of Heroes, right?"

Raak said nothing. He stood in the corner of his room and held onto the staff.

"It's very important that you come with us now, son."

"You're not in trouble, Jeremy," the woman said from the doorway. "We just want to talk, okay?"

The man held out his hand.

Raak smiled at him and activated the staff.

****

It was two days, forty-six miles and twenty-seven innocent lives later before a National Guard sharpshooter got lucky.

****

Tony Santiago had had one hell of a day. The never-ending stream of customers had been bad enough. When the computer system went down and took the cash registers with it his shift became a nightmare. For nearly ninety minutes he had been made to stand at his register and listen to customers blast him and his store, as if badmouthing his employer meant anything to him. He watched with quiet satisfaction as many of those in the store grumbled and swore and left. When the computer system finally came back online there was almost nobody left in the store. That was fine with him.

He was so frustrated by the whole ordeal that he had actually agreed to sit in Maria's car and smoke a joint with her after closing. He did not like the girl one bit; she was a scumbag and she looked like one. But she always had some killer weed and it was just what he needed after all the character assassination he had endured. When he was good and stoned he got out of Maria's car and into his own.

The drive home was uneventful and relaxing. His mother had left dinner and a note explaining that she was out for a few hours with the woman next door. That was fine with Tony, too. He did not think his mother would know he was high but it did not serve to take chances. He wolfed down dinner (chicken patties and mashed potatoes) and chased it with some root beer. Since no one was home he went out back after dinner and smoked a fatty from his own supply. Not as good as the shit he smoked with Maria, but it was good enough.

He went downstairs to his room and turned on his desktop. Usually after a shitty day at work he would login to StarForce 3000 and take out his frustrations on alien NPCs and enemy players in the PVP zone. Lately, however, he had had difficulty finding groups who would allow him to join. The uptight assholes who populated the game simply had no time for his intense brand of play. He contemplated letting his subscription expire, but he had to date resisted the urge. It was still a good game, still fun, even if most of the other players were jerks.

He sat down at the computer and logged into the game. He selected his favorite character, Ca'dik the pirate, and loaded in on the planet Neferus. He checked his friends list and found it empty. Naturally. The few people in the game he actually liked were never on this late. He saw the email icon flashing at him. He clicked on it.

It was from someone Tony did not know, someone named Blacktooth Grin. The message began: "Greetings, Ca'dik. I am aware you've had some trouble recently in the game. I can help."

Tony nearly deleted the message but something stopped him. He decided to give it a read, if only to amuse himself. When he finished the message he began to type his reply with much excitement.

Phantom Pain

Cynthia wept in the dark. The tears came freely, as they so often did these days. She was aware of the cold wind entering through the open window at her back, but only in the same subconscious manner in which she was aware of her breath frosting the air. It was noted in a dim corner of her mind, the same dim corner wherein she spent most of her time since the accident. She had been running mostly on autopilot the past three weeks, trusting to instinct to keep her fed and bathed. In truth, she could not remember a single meal or shower since her days of being a mother and a wife. She was neither, now, and it was this thought that occupied most of her cognitive process.

She recognized the cold steel of the .22 caliber in her left hand, was aware of its weight, but that, too, was only a subconscious glimmer. Her mind spent the vast majority of its time focused on Megan and Tom, as it did so now. Behind the many images of her late daughter and husband was a voice that belonged to neither yet sounded familiar to her nonetheless. It was soft at first, so soft she could not make out what it said when she awoke in the hospital minus her family and most of her right arm. The voice had been increasing in volume every day since and she could understand it quite clearly now.

Just put it in your mouth and pull the trigger, it soothed. *The pain will vanish and you'll be with them again. That's what you want. That's what* they *want. One quick and painless instant and you'll all be together again.*

If Cynthia believed in the afterlife she would have taken the advice already. She would have done it the moment she came home from the hospital, not even waited for her sister to leave. But she did not believe in the afterlife, or God, or much of anything else.

Oh, she used to. She was raised Catholic, went to Catholic schools and attended church on a semi-regular basis. But that had been another life, another person. That Cynthia Daniels was a married woman with a young daughter, a good career and a good life. That Cynthia Daniels had her shit together. The Cynthia Daniels sitting on her bed with the window open behind her at 3 AM on a mid-January night in New Jersey was not her. Not anymore.

"Shut the fuck up," she whispered to the voice. It was the first time she had spoken to it, indeed, the first words she had spoken in a week. Her voice sounded strange to her, a startling and unexpected presence in the dark.

She rubbed her forehead with the back of her hand. She removed her finger from the trigger as she did so. It was a subconscious move, something her husband had ingrained into her head when he trained her in the .22's use. Had the move registered with her she would have laughed.

Instead she dropped the gun onto the bed. She tried to grasp her head with both hands before she remembered she was one shy. She looked at the bandaged stump of her right arm as if seeing it for the first time. In the darkness of the bedroom she could just make out its silhouette.

Then she did laugh. It was a short, garbled bark that sounded as ugly as it did loud in the blackness around her. She tried to stop herself but the laughter continued unabated. That dim part of her mind informed her she would have sounded insane to anyone who heard her laughter. She tried to reply but she was unable to get a word out.

The laughter might have lasted as long as twenty minutes. When Cynthia regained control she watched herself stand up and walk into the bedroom suite's bathroom. She turned on the tap and held her mouth to it and drank quickly and deeply. The water felt almost warm in the freezing air around her. She drank until she felt she would burst and then she returned to the bed.

The moon came out of hiding in the cloudy sky and cast her bedroom in a ghostly light. Her eyes fell on the framed photo on her nightstand. The happy little girl that smiled back at her had no idea, no fucking idea, what lay ahead of her. The sun was shining on her, the trees behind her were green and full of life. She was dressed in her favorite outfit, the pink tee shirt with the rose stitched off-center to the left and her denim shorts.

Cynthia realized she could not remember when the picture was taken. Megan looked to be about five-years-old so that would make the photo…she did not know. Fresh tears spilled from her eyes and the photo became a blurred mess. She reached for it and then stopped herself. Her eyes went to the .22 but only for a moment. She returned her gaze to the photo and she blinked back the tears and tried to see it clearly.

She was so focused on the photo, she did not realize it when she passed out.

****

"Jesus H. Christ, Cindy, it's fucking freezing in here."

Her sister's voice cut through the fog. Cynthia's eyes fluttered open. She closed them just as quickly when the harsh daylight streaming through her window assaulted her. She groaned and rolled onto her side and pulled the covers over her head.

She heard Karen close the window with enough force to rattle it in its frame. "Did you have the window open all night? You did, didn't you? What is wrong with you, Cynthia Rose?"

Karen was the only one who called her that. It had been a favorite of their mother's whenever she did something wrong. At some point after the old woman died Karen had taken it upon herself to act as mother/guardian/all-around boss. Cynthia had to admit her sister had gotten the inflection down pat. She even sounded like their mother.

"You're gonna die of pneumonia at this rate. Get up and get dressed and I'll have some coffee ready for you downstairs." Karen's footfalls thudded across the hardwood and then she was in the hallway and headed toward the stairs. "And you might want to wrap yourself in that comforter before you come down," she called over her shoulder. "The whole fucking house is ice cold."

Cynthia remained under the covers for several more moments. When she finally pushed the comforter down the bed she saw the gun. Her eyes moved instantly to the door, but her sister was busy downstairs. Karen had not seen it. Cynthia scooped it up and placed it in the nightstand drawer.

Her eyes fell on the photo of Megan and she paused. *Pick up the gun again,* the voice said upon its return. *Pick it up and take care of business. You'll even have the added bonus of doing it with your sister here. That'll add to the table conversation at the next holiday dinner.*

"That *would* be a bonus," she croaked into the empty bedroom. Her voice was rough, sounding nothing like her.

"But not this minute." Cynthia closed the drawer and freed herself from the blankets.

Karen was right, the house was frigid. She heard the heat kick in as she made her way to the bathroom. After she relieved herself she grabbed a sweatshirt she did not remember discarding on the floor and put it on. Cynthia scooped up the comforter and wrapped it about herself and made her way down to the kitchen.

Karen was at the counter preparing two cups of instant. Cynthia sat at the table wordlessly and pushed a small pile of mail away from her. She plopped the existing half of her right arm down and looked at the limp, empty part of the sleeve. It flattened itself on the tabletop and looked like a dead snake. She tucked it back inside the comforter.

Karen droned on about the foolishness of leaving a window open all night while she worked on the coffee. "It's January and this isn't Hawaii," was the only thing Cynthia heard. She tuned out the rest. Her sister's voice became a mindless, endless droning in her ears. After a few more moments Karen placed a steaming cup in front of her and took a seat at the table.

Cynthia remained silent. She stared into the dark liquid still swirling about in the cup. Her eyes moved to the graphic on the cup itself: WORLD'S BEST MOM, it proclaimed. Cynthia nearly burst into tears. She would have had she been alone. Then again, if she had the house to herself she would not be in the kitchen drinking coffee, let alone out of this particular cup.

"I'm here for you, Cindy," Karen said. Her voice was warm, or at least the closest to warm Karen could get. She patted Cynthia's arm. "You know that. Bill and I are willing to do anything to help you through this. I know it's been tough."

Cynthia came close to laughing. She got it under control but could not prevent herself from smiling.

"You can't keep going like this, honey," Karen continued. "What happened was a shitty deal but it happened and we have to deal with it."

"'Deal with it,'" Cindy echoed quietly.

"Yes, deal with it." Karen took a sip of her coffee. "You can't go on like this. This—" she indicated the kitchen, "—is fucked up. It's eight degrees out there at most and you're sleeping with the window open. People die that way."

Cynthia nodded. "People die in all sorts of ways."

Karen opened her mouth to say something before she apparently thought better of it. She sat in silence and drank her coffee and perused the accumulated mail on the table. She picked up the new issue of *Today's Woman* and held it up, cover facing her sister. "You have another byline, Cindy. That's good news. They're using your name on the cover more and more these days."

Cynthia glanced at the magazine and looked away.

"Have you done any writing lately?"

"Sure, sis, every day. That's exactly what the grief counselor suggested. She said it's the perfect way to forget my family."

Karen's lips turned down and she returned the magazine to its former spot on the table. "That's not how I meant it."

"I have to get out of here, Karen." Cynthia spoke before she knew it. Both the spontaneity and the truth of her statement startled her. She looked at her sister with something akin to shock.

Karen paused in mid-sip. "What are you talking about? Go where?"

"Away from here." Now she seemed unable to stop herself. She swept her eyes across the kitchen. "This house. This town. These." She reached for the pile of unopened mail with her right hand. She stopped herself when she realized she no longer possessed a right hand. Her arm hung frozen in midair. The empty part of the sleeve dangled a few inches above the tabletop. She looked at her sister and they locked eyes. Karen eventually looked away.

"I can't be here, in this house. It's driving me insane. I have to get away before something bad happens." She cringed at the last part of her plea. Had she really just said that?

Karen looked at her with wide eyes. "What are you saying?" She reached across the table and placed a hand on Cynthia's right arm. "Honey, you're not thinking about…"

Cynthia looked away. She took the coffee cup and downed most of its contents in one gulp. The hot liquid filled her and for the first time in twenty-four hours she felt warm.

"Oh, Cindy, honey, no, you can't." She pulled her chair closer to the table and reaffirmed her grip on Cynthia's arm. "You have so much to live for. What do you think Bill and the kids will say if you go and do something stupid? It'll crush the girls. You know how much they love their Auntie Cindy. Please, just think about what you're saying."

Cynthia had to admit her sister sounded sincere. Perhaps she even was. She sipped the rest of her coffee slowly.

"Baby, just think about what you're doing," Karen said. "You're talking about a permanent solution to a temporary problem."

"My daughter is dead, Karen." Cynthia was surprised by the tone of her voice. She sounded lifeless. "My husband is dead. That's not temporary. That's as permanent as permanent gets."

Karen removed her hand from Cynthia's arm. "That's not what I meant. And you'll see them again someday. But that day is a long ways off. You have to believe that."

"Don't give me that God shit, okay?" Her voice no longer sounded lifeless; it sounded angry, forceful. "If He's so fucking great how could He do that?"

"He's—"

"He's an asshole!" Cynthia slammed her fist onto the tabletop. Her coffee cup danced a few inches away from her. "You don't understand, Karen. Your kids are fine. Your husband is fine. Mine aren't. They're dead and that's it. I'll never see them again. So keep that God bullshit to yourself. Understand me?"

Karen opened her mouth to speak, closed it.

"I'm going to the Cape for a little while. While I'm there I may or may not decide to eat a bullet. But that's *my* business, not yours. Got me?"

Karen remained silent. She stared at her sister with undisguised shock.

Cynthia finished her coffee and pushed the cup away. "Thanks for the coffee. I'll clean up later. You can let yourself out." She pushed her chair from the table and pulled the comforter closer to her body.

She made it two steps toward the stairs when Karen asked, "Want me to adjust your bandages before I go?"

Cynthia stopped. She did not want to admit it but it was about time for an adjustment. Her doctor told her it would need to be adjusted several times per day to maintain compression and keep a blood clot from forming. Wordlessly she pulled her half-arm from the sleeve and held it out to her side. It took Karen only a moment to tighten the bandage.

Cynthia left the kitchen.

****

She watched from her bedroom window as Karen backed her car out of the driveway. When the silver Volvo was gone Cynthia sagged against the wall before collapsing onto the bed. In moments she was sobbing uncontrollably. Her body convulsed as the anguish poured from her. By the time she got herself under control the sky outside her window was transitioning from blue to purple. She got her arm under her and rose to her knees.

She had not expected Karen's visit to go down the way it did. She had not anticipated the anger on her part. It had been so long since she felt anything that at first she was unaware of the anger at all. When it rose to the surface she found herself utterly unable to control it. That her sister was asking for it was undeniable but she still felt a little guilty. She would call her tomorrow.

She also had no idea as to the origin of her comment about going to the Cape. She meant Cape Cod, of that much she was certain. She and Tom had been there twice before they were married and once with Megan when she was six-teen-months-old. But that had been it. It was not a tradition in their family, and it held no special place in her memories that was not shared by their trips to Newport, Rhode Island or Martha's Vineyard. So why the Cape?

It'll be deserted this time of year, the voice said. *You can do it with no one around and they won't find your body until long after the fact. It's as good a place as any.*

And that was true. Cynthia was not certain if she intended to put the gun in her mouth, but if she decided to go that route at least she could do it alone and not have to worry about Karen or someone else walking in at the wrong moment. So the Cape it would be.

She went online and looked for a very specific house for rent in Dennisport. It was an old Victorian that she and Tom had tried to rent a few times. It was always already booked or closed for maintenance. She saw it on the list with the word AVAILABLE beneath the photo.

"Finally! Right, Tom?" The price was lower than she expected, most likely owing to this being the off-season. She booked the house for five days and paid with her Visa.

She nodded off a few moments later. It was the first night since the accident that she slept soundly.

****

Cynthia awoke the following morning and glanced at the alarm clock on Tom's nightstand. 8:09 it informed her. She got up and began the morning routine she had last performed the day of the accident. She showered (taking care to keep the bandage dry) and got dressed and made the bed. At the sight of Megan's photo, she sat on the bed and held it to her chest. The tears threatened to return but she was successful in keeping them down. There was no reason to cry; chances were good her pain would be over shortly.

She adjusted her bandage by herself and it took several attempts before she got it right. Then she went down to the kitchen and started the coffee.

The pile of bills was in the center of the table, neatly stacked. The new *Today's Woman* sat next to it, liberated from the pile. The coffee cups from the day before were rinsed and sitting in the sink. "She's nothing if not organized," Cynthia said to the empty kitchen. She made her coffee and sipped it and strolled leisurely into the living room.

Numerous sympathy cards sat on the coffee table. Cynthia did not remember placing them there and was certain she had not. Her sister, again. It was an obvious attempt by Karen to force Cynthia to see that people cared. Cynthia knew as much without the cards. She and Tom had good friends and family. The cards had come in the mail a dozen at a time for a week or two after the accident. She had opened the first few but soon stopped herself and never went back to them.

She sat on the sofa and put her coffee cup down and picked up a few of the cards. She made it through four of them before the tears came back. She threw the cards on the table and lay down on the sofa until she was cried out. Then she got up and returned to her bedroom and began packing a bag for the Cape.

It took surprisingly little time to pack. She figured she would be there no more than three or four days before she made her decision. One way or another she would need only a few days' worth of clothes. She was zipping up the bag when she stopped and got the .22 out of her nightstand. She sat on the bed and turned it over in her hand. It was small and cold and perfect. She buried it in the middle of her suitcase. Her permit had expired a few months before the accident and she had not gotten around to renewing it. She would simply have to avoid being pulled over between Rahway and Dennisport.

She scooped up the framed photo of Megan and placed it gingerly into the suitcase. She kissed her fingertips and brushed them against the glass covering the child's smiling face. Then she zipped up the suitcase and lugged it down the stairs.

She took the photo of her and Tom at their wedding. They held hands and beamed smiles at the camera. Her hair was blonde and she remembered dying it from its customary light brown that very morning. His hair was short but thick and jet-black. She had forgotten how much hair he had back then. Christ, when was the last time she had looked at this photo?

She was young, twenty-three. He was a year older and only two removed from the police academy. She remembered, for the first time in years, how disappointed Karen had been at not being her maid of honor. That job went to Chrissy Allen, Cynthia's best friend since third grade. Chrissy, whom she had not spoken to in six years, at least. "If I make it back, I'll call you."

The photo went into the suitcase next to Megan's.

She paused in the kitchen and looked at the pile of bills. Then she made her way into the garage.

Her side was empty and would be forever. Her minivan was likely still at Johnson's Auto Salvage, awaiting some insurance adjuster to proclaim it totaled. *That's a no-brainer. Fucking thing's the very definition of totaled.* That left Tom's Camaro. She was at once thankful that he had elected to get the automatic transmission; it would have been impossible for her to drive a stick. It was a small block V8 and would guzzle gas but she had no option. She tossed her suitcase into the backseat and got in on the driver's side.

Moments later she was pulling out of the driveway. She did not watch her house recede in the rearview.

****

She gassed up a mile from her house and guided the Camaro onto the Jersey Turnpike. Her GPS informed her it was just over 270 miles to her destination. Traffic was heavier than she expected but she scarcely noticed. She thought of the photos in her suitcase and what lay concealed a sweatshirt or two away. She started to reach back to touch the suitcase before she reminded herself she had no right hand. She kept her eyes on the road.

Cynthia took I95 along the Connecticut coast. It was a boring ride but there were plenty of rest stops and she made use of most of them. She saw the exit for Foxwoods and remembered going there once with Tom before they were married. She added it to the list of places she never wanted to see again.

She arrived in Dennisport nearly six hours after she pulled out of her driveway. Tom's GPS unit guided her flawlessly to the old Victorian. It was enormous but it seemed well-maintained from the outside. A recent snowstorm had dumped eight or nine inches of the white stuff on Dennisport. The Victorian's driveway and walk were cleared of all snow. Cynthia spotted shoeprints in the snow snaking their way around the side of the house. She pulled into the driveway and waited for Mr. Douglas to show up with the keys.

Ten minutes later she caught movement out of the corner of her eye. She turned in the direction and saw someone disappear around the side of the house, where the footprints in the snow had led. She opened the Camaro's door and the blast of cold air hit her like a punch. It took only a moment for her stump to start throbbing. Cynthia winced and stepped out of the car. She zipped up her coat, put her hand in her pocket and trudged through the snow.

She reached the side of the house and peeked around the corner. Whomever it was ducked behind the back of the house. Cynthia followed the footprints in the snow. She peeked into the Victorian's backyard and saw two kids in their mid-teens huddled together. When they saw her one of them quickly put his hand behind his back.

"What are you doing here?"

"Nothin'," said the taller of the two.

"Really." Cynthia stepped into the backyard and stopped when she was perhaps ten feet from the boys. "What's that behind your back? And what do I smell?"

"Nothin'," they said in unison.

They looked nervous, as nervous as Cynthia would have been had she ever been caught like this back in the day. She held out her gloved left hand. "Hand it over."

The taller kid, the one not hiding the illegal smoke behind his back, looked dejected. He nodded to his accomplice and said, with resignation in his voice, "Give it to her."

The smaller kid looked both reluctant and very, very worried. He hesitated, looked to the taller kid for confirmation, and took a few steps in Cynthia's direction. He pulled his hand out from behind his back and showed her the still-smoldering joint.

Cynthia waved him forward and held out her hand. The kid placed it into her palm and backed away quickly, as if afraid she would bite him. Cynthia looked at the joint and then at the two boys.

"You know this is illegal, right? And that my husband is a cop?"

The color drained from the boys' faces.

"If I see you doing this shit again I'm gonna have him arrest you. Understand me?"

They nodded with their heads down. Both had planted their hands in their pockets.

Cynthia inclined her head in the direction of the street. "Go home."

They shuffled their feet through the snow slowly until they passed her. Then they ran for all they were worth. The taller one quickly pulled ahead of his companion and the other boy had to strain to keep up. Cynthia watched them go. When they were out of sight she allowed herself a faint smile.

She looked at the joint in her hand and placed it into her pocket.

When she walked back to the front of the house she spotted a Ford Expedition pulling into the driveway. The monstrous SUV stopped a few feet from the Camaro's rear bumper. The driver killed the engine and stepped out.

Mr. Douglas was impossibly fat. The thick coat he wore could have fit Cynthia's entire family within its folds, back when she had a family. The simple act of extricating his bulk from the driver's seat caused his forehead to break out in sweat. He looked at her from beneath the brim of his Red Sox cap and waved. "Mrs. Daniels?"

Cynthia nodded and completed her return trip to the driveway. "Mr. Douglas."

Douglas smiled and held out his hand. He pulled it back quickly when he saw her empty coat sleeve. His face turned red and Cynthia let him off the hook by offering him her left hand.

"Nice to meet you."

"Nice to meet you, too," Douglas replied and took the offered hand. "Sorry about that."

"It's okay, really."

The fat man reached back inside the SUV and pulled out a thin briefcase. "I have the rental agreement right here. Shall we go inside?"

"By all means." Cynthia stepped aside so the large man could get past her.

"Do you have any luggage? I'll bring it in for you. No reason for you to go through all that."

Cynthia shook her head. "Thanks for the offer, but I can manage."

"You're sure?"

"Positive."

"Okay, then." Douglas led the way up the walk and opened the front door with an ancient brass key. He crossed the threshold and waited for Cynthia to step through. He hurriedly closed the door behind her. "Christ on a crutch, it's cold out there. Pardon my French."

Cynthia looked about the foyer. It was large and covered with what she was willing to bet was the original hardwood. A large grandfather clock ticked away to the left of the door. On the opposite wall stood a coatrack and a chest-of-drawers with a large mirror attached.

"This way, Mrs. Daniels."

Douglas led her into the living room. One wall was dominated by a large fireplace. He pointed to it. "There's wood under a tarpaulin out back. I can bring some in for you and start a fire if you'd like. Take some of the chill out of your bones."

The living room was enormous. Three full-sized sofas and twice as many end tables were positioned around the room. An equally-large coffee table stood sentinel in front of one of the couches. A giant flat screen sat in an entertainment center to the left of the fireplace. A cut-crystal chandelier hung from the ceiling in the center of the room.

"Mrs. Daniels?"

Cynthia pulled her eyes away from the living room and regarded her host. "Yes?"

"The fireplace. Would you like me to get it started for you?"

Cynthia nodded absently. "That would be nice, thank you."

They walked into the kitchen. A breakfast nook took up one corner of the room. The appliances appeared newish and clashed with the rest of the décor. Small teacups hung from hooks above the center island.

Douglas indicated the breakfast nook. "Please, have a seat."

They sat and he produced the rental agreement from his briefcase. He went over the details and when she was satisfied she signed her name. When the paperwork was taken care of she returned to the Camaro and retrieved her lone suitcase. It was dark by then but the snow on the ground made it easy enough for her to see the slick spots on the walkway. She reentered the house to find Douglas kneeling before the fireplace and coaxing a small flame to life. She took her bag upstairs to the master bedroom, a cavern of a room with a king-sized bed against the wall and three full-size dressers. She returned to the living room to find the fire burning bright and warm.

Douglas handed her the keys. "If you need anything, anything at all, don't hesitate to call me. My number's the fourth on speed dial, after police, fire and ambulance. Can't be too careful these days."

Cynthia nodded absently. "Will do."

He started to extend his right hand before he caught himself and switched to his left. Cynthia shook it absentmindedly.

"Enjoy your stay, Mrs. Daniels."

"Thanks."

He let himself out.

Cynthia walked to one of the windows facing the driveway and watched the giant SUV back out of the driveway.

****

She readjusted her bandage again while she waited for the coffee. She took the warm cup into the living room and sat on one of the sofas and turned on the television. She cycled through a few channels before she came across Nickelodeon and *SpongeBob SquarePants*. It was Megan's favorite show. Cynthia watched it and sipped her coffee and cried.

She added a log to the fire around 9 PM and watched the sparks shoot up the chimney. *SpongeBob* had given way to a show Cynthia had never heard of so she channel surfed until she came across a local news station.

She watched the news without actually watching it. The talking heads droned on and on and she caught not a word of it. Nor could she see the screen clearly through her tears. They were showing a child's photo, a young girl who might be the same age as Megan. It made the tears spill from her eyes quickly enough to form miniature rivers flowing down her cheeks.

When the tears eventually stopped she got up and went to her coat on the rack by the front door. She fished around in the pocket until she found what she was looking for. She looked at the joint with no expression.

It's been a long time. The voice spoke to her for the first time since that morning. Cynthia was amazed to realize she had forgotten all about it.

"You're right about that."

The last time she smoked had been the night before Tom entered the academy. It would not do to have a cop's girlfriend smoking weed so he had asked her to quit and she had done so. Had that really been twelve years ago?

Go ahead. It'll be just like old times.

"For once we're in agreement."

She grabbed the grill-starter Douglas had used to start the fire and lit up. She coughed on the first hit and the second. She remembered well enough what she was like when she smoked too much so she saved the rest for later.

Two hours later the fire was nearly out. Cynthia turned off the television and went upstairs to the master bedroom. She rifled through her suitcase until she came upon the framed photos. She placed them next to each other on the nightstand. She sat on the bed and looked at the happy people behind the glass. The tears made it as far as her eyes but she blinked them back.

"I'm so sorry, baby." Her voice sounded strange and unwelcome in the silent house. She pulled the .22 out of the suitcase and placed it next to the photos. Then she turned off the lamp and lay down. She was asleep ten seconds later.

****

In the dream Megan was alive and happy. That Cynthia knew it was a dream was irrelevant; she was with Megan and that was all that mattered. The little girl ran across the backyard of their home with Cynthia in tow and trying to keep up with her. It was not easy, running half-hunched over so the little girl could hold her hand. She was getting short of breath but she did not care. Any chance to spend more time with her daughter, even imaginary time, was okay with her. And there was the added bonus of having both her arms again. She appreciated that, too. Cynthia was never one to overlook the little things.

Megan continued around the side of the house and Cynthia suddenly stopped short. The little girl jerked back with a, "Hey! Mommy!"

They no longer stood in their backyard. This looked like the backyard of the Victorian sans snow. Cynthia could even identify the spot where she had confronted the two boys. How had they gotten here? Cynthia willed the Victorian's grounds to vanish and the dream to return them to their house. She and Megan remained in the backyard in Dennisport.

"Mommy, what's the matter?" the little girl asked. "Why aren't you playing with me anymore?"

"Something's not right, baby," Cynthia replied. "We're not supposed to be here."

"It's okay, Mommy. I like it here. Josh and Susan and Nicole are fun to play with. I wish we could stay here forever!"

Cynthia knelt down in front of Megan. "Who are they, baby? Are they your friends?" There might have been a boy named Josh in Megan's class but she could not remember. The other names did not sound familiar. Cynthia was certain Megan had never made mention of either of them.

"They're my best friends!" Megan shouted happily. She tugged on Cynthia's arm. "C'mon, Mommy, let's play!"

Cynthia did not want to play. She wanted to get back in the car with Megan and get the hell out of Dennisport. *Would the car even be here? It's just a dream, after all.* That was true. Perhaps they would not need a car. Cynthia closed her eyes and tried again to bring them home. The sounds and smells of Dennisport continued unabated.

"Why isn't this working?"

Cynthia realized she no longer held Megan's hand. Her eyes popped open and she saw her daughter running deeper into the backyard. The tree line was perhaps twenty feet away. Cynthia knew she would be unable to intercept Megan before she got there. "Megan, wait!" Cynthia got to her feet and chased after the little girl.

She could hear her daughter's laughter up until the moment she vanished into the trees.

Cynthia reached the tree line and peered into the woods. There was too much shadow, too many trees, and she could not see Megan. She called to her. The little girl's laughter echoed back to her but Cynthia could not pinpoint her location. She called to her again.

Megan's laughter was replaced with a scream.

Cynthia crashed headlong into the woods. Thin branches poked and tore at her clothes and skin. She gasped and stopped in her tracks when her right hand caught something hard and sharp on the bark of a tree. She looked at her hand. Blood flowed freely from the gash on her right palm. She looked at the tree next to her. A nail protruded from an ancient piece of wood nearly embedded within the bark. The piece of wood was small, about the size someone would use for a ladder rung that led to a tree house. Cynthia looked up and saw the weather-beaten remains of just such a structure about fifteen feet above her head. It was old and rotted and she could see the sky through the rotted holes in the floor and walls.

Megan screamed again. It was somewhere ahead of her and to the left. Cynthia took a single step in that direction…

And awoke in the bed.

She sat bolt-upright and screamed her daughter's name. Her voice bounced off the old walls and echoed back to her. The sound was much too loud in the silent house. Cynthia's heart raced and she was bathed in sweat.

Her right hand hurt like crazy and she moved to massage it with her left. Her hand grasped empty air and it took her a moment to remember its twin was gone. She reached across her body and turned on the lamp and looked at the stump of her right arm. Roughly fourteen inches from where her arm ended was the source of the pain.

Her mind snapped back to the hospital on the day of her release. The doctor had told her something then, something she had barely heard. She searched through the memory and cursed herself for not paying attention. He had said something like this could happen. It was even common among amputees. That was the word he used: *Amputees.* And that's what she was now, right? Most certainly. But what was it he said?

After a moment it came to her. *Phantom pain.* That's what he had called it. He warned her she might experience an itch or some other sensation coming from her missing limb. It had not happened to her before now.

It was quite unsettling, so unsettling, in fact, that she momentarily forgot about the dream. She would have sworn her right hand was injured and bleeding. The pain was real and all the more maddening because she could do nothing to stop it. "Because there's nothing there."

She pawed again at the missing hand, but the pain persisted. She even looked at the sheets to see if she had bled on them. The sheets were pristine except for the dark spots where her sweat had stained them.

Cynthia lay back down and stared at the ceiling. Her right hand throbbed and she eventually closed her eyes and told herself it could not possibly hurt. *It's probably been incinerated by now,* she thought. *It's not even ashes anymore. It's nothing. So stop with the pain already.*

She managed to fall asleep again nearly an hour later. This time she did not dream.

****

The pain in her missing hand was still there when she awoke, but it had receded into more of a dull throb. She could live with that. The dream as gone, or most of it was, anyway. She remembered being in the woods and cutting her hand on something, but the rest of it was lost. She felt she could live with that.

After using the bathroom, she went down to the kitchen. She made herself a pot of coffee and sat down to watch the morning news. The half-smoked joint sat in a saucer on the end table along with the grill starter. It went well with her coffee. By the time she started her second cup Cynthia had the munchies in a big way. She had completely forgotten how hungry she got when she was high. The cupboards were empty save for a container of sugar and the salt and pepper shakers. The fridge revealed a bottle of congealed ketchup and a pitcher of water.

Cynthia went upstairs and showered. Once she was dressed and her bandage snug she hopped in the Camaro and went looking for a grocery store.

Apparently the Stop and Shop would have to do. In the bread aisle she spotted one of the boys she caught in the yard the day before. She scowled at him just enough to let him know she remembered him. The boy stuck close to his mother and generally avoided Cynthia's gaze. He was obviously hoping she would not come over and tell his mother what she had witnessed. Cynthia smirked.

She continued her shopping, picking lightly from the shelves. *No need to go all-out*, said the voice. *You'll probably be dead in a day or two. Just get a few things. Why waste the money?*

Cynthia agreed. Her cart was perhaps a quarter full when she headed for the cashier.

There was not much of a line but she got behind an old woman who slowly navigated her way through her coupons. The cashier, a young girl with brown hair and braces, shot Cynthia a sympathetic smile.

Cynthia perused the tabloids next to the register. She found the latest issue of *Today's Woman*. Against her will, her eyes went to the bottom right corner and her byline. *Juggling the Big 3: Wife, Mother and Career Woman by Cynthia Douglas*, it proclaimed.

Cynthia stared at the byline. She had written that particular article a lifetime ago, when she had a husband, a daughter and a right arm. Christ, had it really been only three months ago?

I have a new article you can write, the voice said helpfully. *It's called,* Losing Your Family and Your Mind In One Easy Step, by Cynthia Douglas. *How does that grab ya?*

"Fuck off," Cynthia whispered.

Later she would be grateful the old woman was too focused on her coupons to have heard. The young cashier, on the other hand, heard her loud and clear. She stifled a laugh.

In the slot next to *Today's Woman* was the local newspaper, *The Dennisport Beacon*. Taking up most of the front page was the same photo Cynthia saw on TV the night before. The little girl looked to be about seven-years-old. She was blonde and smiling and dressed as if for a school photo. The headline read: *4th Child Feared Missing*.

Cynthia turned away from the headline before her tears could make another appearance. She could not bring herself to think of another mother losing her daughter. She avoided looking anywhere but at the cashier until she was able to leave the store.

****

When the groceries were put away Cynthia made herself a bowl of soup. She took it into the living room and sat on the sofa and turned on the television. She ate her soup

163

and watched an old HBO documentary on the Red Sox/Yankees rivalry. She was not much of a baseball fan herself, but Tom liked to brag that he bled Yankees blue. When the soup was gone she got one last hit out of the joint and then she went upstairs.

She readjusted her bandage (she was becoming quite good at it) and lay down on the bed and looked at the two photos she brought with her from home. The tears came unexpectedly and after a few moments she was bawling. She picked up the photo of Megan and looked at it through her tears. Her right hand started to throb. She wiped it on the sheets, but the pain persisted.

Instinct moved her to put down the photo and look to see what was wrong with her hand. Of course, nothing was wrong with it. It simply was not there.

Cynthia struggled into a sitting position and sniffled. She glanced down and caught sight of a dark stain on the sheets. She wiped the tears from her eyes with her hand and focused on the dark spot.

There was not much blood, only a small, thin streak dotted with a few random droplets. Her hand immediately went to her side, but it came away dry. She sprung off the bed and regarded the bloodstain. She felt along her right side but there was no wound anywhere.

Her brow furrowed. "What is this?" Her voice was small, barely a whisper. She reached for the stain, but stopped herself a few inches shy of her target. "This isn't real. This isn't real." She closed her eyes tightly and counted to ten and opened them again. The bloodstain remained. It glistened in the failing light coming from outside the window.

She held up the stump of her right arm to the light and examined it closely. What remained of the limb was dry and clean, as was its bandage. A foot or so from where her arm ended her hand throbbed a steady and painful beat.

Cynthia hurried from the bedroom and made for the bathroom. Its window looked out on the backyard. She glanced at the tree line, perhaps 100 feet from the back of the house. The property line was pretty well delineated; the trees began and went back as far as she could see. They were thick and Cynthia imagined they looked quite lovely in the summer. Now they looked like an army of skeletons preparing to march on Dennisport.

"The nail," she whispered. She still could not remember much of the dream, but she remembered the nail sticking out from the board on the tree and the remains of the tree house above.

She ran down the stairs and grabbed her coat off the coatrack. "This is nuts," she said to herself as she squirmed her way into the heavy coat. "And you're a nut for actually going out there to look."

She was in the kitchen headed for the back door when her cell phone rang. She looked back to the living room, where it sat on the end table. She paused, mere feet from the back door. She could see the tree line through the window from where she stood. Her right hand had made the transition from throbbing to a moderate ache. Her left hand rubbed empty air.

Her cell rang again. "Damnit."

She marched into the living room and picked it up. The screen displayed a picture of Karen with her number at the top. Cynthia sighed and answered it. "Hello?"

"Cindy, it's me," said the somewhat cheerful voice at the other end. "How are you feeling? Did you go to the Cape?"

Cynthia shook her injured hand. "Yeah, I'm here."

"Is everything okay, honey?"

Cynthia blew air through her pursed lips. "Everything's just ducky."

There was a pause and Cynthia could see her sister pacing around her kitchen while her children played in the living room. "You don't sound ducky."

Cynthia's patience was already wearing thin. "What do you want, Karen?"

"I just wanted to see if you're okay." She managed to sound both hurt and indignant at the same time.

Cynthia sighed and, before she knew what she was doing, she plopped down onto the sofa. She let loose a long, slow breath. "I'm sorry, sis. You know this hasn't been easy on me. I'm sorry I keep taking it out on you."

"Don't apologize," Karen replied. "Please, don't. God knows if I went through what you're going through I'd have lost my mind already. You're a lot stronger than I am, Cindy. I mean that. Now why don't you come home? The girls are asking about you and we'd like to have you over."

A ghost of a smile played across Cynthia's lips. "I rented the house for a week. I'll be back on Friday. Maybe we'll get together that weekend."

"Okay, if that's how you want it." Karen seemed incapable of keeping the disappointment from her tone. After a moment's pause, she asked, "You're not thinking about doing anything stupid, are you? You know what I mean."

"Not at all," Cynthia lied. "I'm just trying to get my head together. Okay?"

"Okay," Karen confirmed. "Call me tomorrow, just let me know you're all right."

She should have known Karen would hear the lie in her voice. "Yes, mom. Talk to you later, okay?"

"Talk to you later," Karen repeated.

Cynthia hung up before her sister could say anything else.

She put the phone down long enough to rub her eyes. Then she picked it up and turned it off. She got up and walked back into the kitchen and looked out the back door.

The sky was dark purple. The snow on the ground made for some light, but not enough in her opinion. There was no way she was going out there now. Her excursion into the woods would have to wait until tomorrow. She walked back to the foyer and slipped out of her coat and hung it on the rack.

She did not notice the absence of the phantom pain in her right hand.

****

This time the dream started with her already crossing the boundary of her rented backyard and entering the woods. Megan held her hand and led the way. Cynthia's bare feet penetrated deeply into the snow. Her balance was off and she needed her free hand to steady herself on the trees around her. Megan seemed to have no such trouble negotiating the terrain. They found the derelict tree house and stopped and Cynthia looked up at it.

"Check it out, Mommy." Megan's invitation was simple, matter-of-fact.

Cynthia saw most of the rungs were missing from the tree but she felt enough remained to allow her to climb safely. She started her ascent.

A large square was missing from the floor and she poked her head through the opening. Most of the interior was covered with a thin blanket of snow. Cynthia saw a bench on every wall; three of them were rotted and had already collapsed. The fourth would soon join its brethren but it held stubbornly in place for now.

Faded pictures cut from magazines and newspapers were tacked to the walls. Most were weather-beaten and faded beyond legibility. A few were intact enough that Cynthia could see they were of hot cars and hotter models. Poking up from the snow was a pile of magazines. She brushed the snow away and saw they were comic-books. The Amazing Spider-Man, the Incredible Hulk and the Justice League of America all stood guard within the remains of the tree house. Cynthia started to pull herself up.

"Mommy!"

The scream came from somewhere nearby in the woods. Cynthia dropped down a rung and saw her daughter was not where she left her. She peered into the woods. "Megan?" The girl's cry still echoed about the skeletal trees. "Megan, honey, where are you?"

Megan did not cry out again, but Cynthia could hear the child whimpering from somewhere to her right. She descended the decrepit rungs and landed in the snow up to her shins. Her head whipped about. "Megan? Where are you, baby? Mommy's here."

Cynthia caught sight of movement almost directly in front of her line of sight, perhaps forty or fifty feet away.

"Megan?" She started off in that direction. The snow grew deeper the farther she moved from the Victorian's backyard and it slowed her progress. Moments after leaving the tree house behind she was up to her knees in the white stuff. She sloughed forward as quickly as she was able.

She stopped for a moment to get her bearings and listen. She heard nothing; the woods were silent. Her breath blossomed in front of her like a cloud and remained in place. Cynthia waved a hand to clear the air in front of her.

She heard a child's cry from somewhere ahead. She started in that direction, but slowly, the snow making fast movement impossible. She spied a small, dark form kneeling in the snow perhaps twenty feet away. The child's breath frosted the air and its shoulders quaked. Cynthia could hear soft sobs escaping from small lips.

"Megan!"

Cynthia took off as quickly as she was able. Five feet from the child she felt something buried in the snow catch her foot and she went down hard. She coughed snow out of her mouth and rubbed it from her eyes. The child remained kneeling in front of her. Cynthia reached out with her right hand for the child's shoulder.

A large and powerful hand descended from behind her and landed on her shoulder with so much force Cynthia cried out in pain. She spun and beheld a large, unkempt man looming above her. His ugly face was twisted with rage. "She's *mine*, bitch!" the man roared. He hauled Cynthia out of the snow with one hand and held her suspended a few feet above the ground.

Cynthia gasped and struggled to free herself from the man's iron grip. Her feet scissored empty air. It was becoming difficult to breathe.

He pulled her closer until they were almost nose-to-nose. "They're *all* mine. Best you leave it be."

He released his grip on her and Cynthia plummeted to the ground.

She screamed into the dark, empty bedroom. Her breathing was fast, her heart felt like it would burst through her ribcage and land on the other side of the room. Cynthia closed her eyes and massaged her chest with her left hand. Tears spilled from her eyes, and she muttered, "Jesus H. Christ.

****

Moments later the details of the dream were fading fast. Cynthia remembered the tree house and the child kneeling in the snow and the large, ugly man grabbing her, but little else. She stumbled to the bathroom and drank directly from the tap. Then she knelt by the toilet and vomited it all back up. When her stomach was empty she came to a sitting position on the cold tile and leaned back against the vanity. She sat and cried until the sky outside her window began to brighten.

She went back to the bedroom, tossed on her robe and went downstairs. She made a pot of coffee and sat at the breakfast nook and tried to ignore the pain coming from her right hand. Cynthia sipped her coffee and looked outside, at the tree line on the far side of the yard.

There was no doubt in her mind the tree house was real. It sat in the tree no more than a couple hundred feet from where she drank her coffee. It was old and falling apart and there were rotting wood benches and comic-books within. After her coffee she would shower and go to see the tree house for herself. She did not know why she felt the need to see it, only that she must.

Thirty minutes later she came back downstairs and put on her coat. Ten minutes after that she was deep inside the woods and looking up at the tree house. It appeared precisely as it had in her dream. She reached out with her hand and touched the board with the nail sticking from it. Her fingers caressed the nail and the board to which it was attached. Her right hand started to throb.

Cynthia grabbed at the next rung and steadied herself. She was confident the ancient rungs would support her weight, just as she was certain she could make the climb with only one hand. She ascended the ladder.

The hole in the floor through which she had entered the tree house in her dream was the access hatch, now long gone. She hoisted herself up until her upper body was inside. She looked about. It appeared no different than it had the night before. The slightly raised pile of snow on the floor turned out to be the comic-books she had spied in her dream.

She picked up the copy of *Amazing Spider-Man*. On the cover he battled a portly bald man in an expensive suit while people fled the scene in terror. "Could have used you a few weeks ago, hero. Where were you then?"

Spidey was too preoccupied with the fat man to answer her question. Cynthia tossed the book aside and looked about some more.

The tree house was unremarkable in every way. Cynthia guessed it was just as unremarkable when it was first built. So why was she out here? "Just to see it for myself," she said aloud. And now she had. It was time to get back inside.

She climbed down carefully. Her right foot slipped on one of the rungs. Instinctively she reached out to steady herself with her right hand. For a moment that seemed much longer than it was she hung in the air. Then she fell the last seven or eight feet to the ground. She landed hard on her ass, but the snow cushioned the impact.

"Son of a bitch." She squirmed a bit and used the tree to pull herself to her feet. She rubbed her sore backside and glanced accusingly at the old rungs. She smacked the tree playfully. "Good one. You almost had me." She started back for the house.

It was the footprints in the snow that stopped her. They came from behind her and led deeper inside the woods. The person who left them seemed to have paused at the tree house; the impressions in the snow were deeper in one spot. Cynthia's eyes narrowed. She knelt in the snow and looked more closely. The footprints were small, definitely made by a child. And they had not been present when she arrived, she was certain of that.

"Megan." She whispered the name without knowing she spoke at all. Cynthia stood and followed the tracks.

The child had wound her way around the trees and a few boulders jutting from the frozen ground. Cynthia followed them, her heart matching the quickening pace of her feet. She moved through a dense patch of trees and emerged into someone's backyard.

The house was a split-level and not in particularly good condition. Even from sixty feet away Cynthia could see the paint peeling from the old siding. The roof looked like it should have been repaired perhaps ten years before. The shades and curtains were drawn in all the windows. Several toys were scattered about the yard and covered with snow. Cynthia could see parts of the Big Wheels and bicycles that jutted from the snow as well as the rusty, ancient swing set in the corner and to her right.

"Just kids," she said. She was not certain why she was disappointed. Had she really expected to find Megan here? That was ridiculous and she knew it. Cynthia let out a long, slow sigh and headed back for the house.

****

She curled up in a high-backed chair in the living room with a fire crackling in the fireplace and the TV droning in the background. She flexed the fingers of her right hand and wished the pain would stop. She was at a loss to explain why the phantom pain had left her alone the first three weeks after the accident but now seemed utterly reluctant to leave. Cynthia hoped this was not to be the norm. She popped some painkillers when she returned to the house, but they seemed completely useless against the maddening onslaught working its way up her hand and into her arm.

She wished she still had some of the kid's joint left. Even more, she wished she had said something to him at the supermarket. She was fairly certain she could have convinced him to stop by with more, if only to stop Cynthia from telling his mother what she had witnessed in her backyard. But she had not, and she had no idea how to get hold of him, or anyone else who might keep the supply line going.

Cynthia made herself some hot soup and sat back down in front of the television. She caught the tail end of a story about the young girl abducted right in Dennisport. She

173

was able to glimpse the child for only a moment before the photo was replaced by a video of a three vehicle collision on U.S. Route Six. Cynthia looked away from the TV and fumbled with the remote until the channel was changed. She did not need to see any images of wrecked automobiles. The phantom throbbing in her missing hand had subsided, but now it began to pick up the pace again.

She shook her arm. The throbbing continued. She ignored it and ate her soup and watched some *Family Feud* before she decided to take a nap. Three minutes later she was upstairs and in her rented bed.

Cynthia tossed and turned for perhaps two hours. She alternated between staring at the framed photos she brought with her from her old life and out the window at the cold January sky. The sunlight was already fading and she could see the barren branches of trees swaying in the wind.

The gun was in the nightstand drawer. She went so far as to open the drawer, but she stopped herself from reaching inside. Blinking back tears, she swore loudly at the ceiling. She slid the drawer closed and lay flat on her back. With her eyes still red and her heart pounding in her chest, Cynthia nodded off.

****

This dream was the most realistic one yet. She could not see Megan, but she knew it was her daughter who clasped her right hand and coaxed her from the bed. Cynthia allowed the little girl to lead her down the stairs and out the back door. The wind which swayed the tree branches earlier was picking up and it tossed her hair about. Cynthia absently brushed it from her eyes with her free hand.

Her bare feet crunched through the snow. "You should have given Mommy a chance to put some shoes on, honey." Megan made no reply, simply continued to lead Cynthia across the yard. By the time they reached the woods Cynthia's feet were numb. The top coating of snow had crystalized and the icy edges of her footprints scraped at her legs, drawing blood. *Good thing this is a dream*, she thought, *'cause I didn't pick up any peroxide or Band-Aids at the store.*

Megan led her into the woods. Cynthia was certain her daughter was taking her to the tree house and she was surprised when they trudged past it without pause. "Where are we going, honey?"

The little girl's invisible little hand wrapped its fingers more tightly around Cynthia's invisible hand and continued forward. Cynthia looked down and saw they were following her own tracks from earlier in the day. "That old, run-down house? Is that where we're going?" The cold wind whistling through the skeletal trees was the only reply Cynthia received.

The wind was starting to cut through her. In addition to having no shoes Cynthia was also short her coat. Her sweatshirt was thick and offered some protection but it was becoming as cold as the wind. Cynthia began to shiver. Only her right hand remained warm, clutched in the little girl's fingers.

They reached the edge of the woods and Cynthia was once again looking at the dilapidated house. A sliver of light escaped from the off-center shutters enclosing a set of windows on the ground level. Cynthia noticed for the first time all the windows facing the backyard were shuttered. That single ray of light shining onto the snow was the only indication the house was not deserted.

Cynthia felt a tug on her missing hand. Megan was urging her forward, into the yard. "Why are we here, honey?" Cynthia whispered. *For that matter, why am I whispering?* Her invisible daughter continued to tug on her hand and Cynthia allowed Megan to guide her toward the house.

The footprints led to a set of clamshell cellar doors. The window with the light seeping through the old shutters was directly above her head. Cynthia tried to see through the small breach, but there was too much grime on the glass. She instead regarded the cellar doors.

A padlock and chain that looked new and out-of-place secured the doors. Cynthia reached for the padlock with her free hand and scooped it up. The chain clinked its way across the metal handles through which it was looped. The lock was cold and seared her left hand. Cynthia gasped and nearly dropped it. She returned it gently to its former place.

She let out a slow breath and watched it frost the air in front of her. "Now what, baby?' she whispered.

Megan obligingly tugged on her hand and guided her around to the driveway. The snow was partially cleared from the driveway but someone really half-assed the shoveling job; there were some clear patches of blacktop but not many. An ancient single-car garage stood to Cynthia's left. The structure had no windows. Cynthia looked at the house and saw a side door which led into the room from where the light originated. Four panes of glass were framed in the center of the door. They appeared black as the night sky. Megan was coaxing Cynthia to the steps which led to the side door. Cynthia got as far as the base of those steps before she stopped herself.

"I can't go in there, honey," she whispered. "That's against the law. C'mon, Mommy's cold and tired. Let's go back to the house."

Megan tugged on her hand again, more forcefully this time. Cynthia gasped at the strength her daughter displayed; the tug nearly caused her bare feet to slip out from under her. Cynthia leaned against the pull. She felt her feet skid across the patches of ice on the driveway.

"Megan, we have to stop," Cynthia said, her voice no longer a whisper. "We can't just walk into someone's home, honey."

Megan continued as if Cynthia had not spoken. They reached the base of the stairs and Megan continued up. Cynthia had no choice but to allow her daughter to lead her. They ascended the short set of steps and Cynthia found herself standing in front of the door.

Cynthia felt her right hand reach for the window glass. One finger touched the glass and drew a straight line down its length. She saw that her missing hand had left a streak on the glass, a streak that was blacker than the rest of the window. Cynthia's brow furrowed. She inspected the glass more closely. "It's painted?" This time she touched it with her left hand. Another black steak appeared next to the first. "Who paints their windows black?"

Vampires, said the voice in her head helpfully.

"Shut the fuck up," Cynthia replied. Then, to the invisible girl with her: "Sorry, baby. Mommy shouldn't swear like that."

Megan placed Cynthia's right hand on the doorknob. "No, honey, this is as far as we can go. We have to go back to the house now." Cynthia felt her hand turning the knob; it was ice-cold in her grip. To her surprise the knob turned slowly and freely. When the door cracked open and her phantom-fingers released the knob Cynthia saw the warm impression made by her ghost-fingers on the brass. Her lips parted but she remained silent. Cynthia pushed the door open a bit more with her left hand and peeked inside.

She was looking into someone's kitchen. Plates were stacked in the sink and on the counter. They were caked with congealed food. More plates were on the small table to her left; they were in the same shape as their brethren. The smell was overpowering, especially following the fresh winter air outside. Cynthia gagged and held her hand to her mouth. She stifled a cough and blinked tears from her eyes. "Christ," she whispered.

Megan gently pulled her inside the kitchen. Cynthia had the presence of mind to keep the door open an inch or two. Dream or not, she felt she might need a fast escape.

They wound their way through the kitchen. A hallway revealed itself on her right. Ahead of her was an arched doorway that led to what Cynthia assumed was the living room. She could hear a hockey game on the television. The only furniture she glimpsed in the room ahead of her was a couch that might have been new when Hitler was still among the living.

Against her will, and against Megan pulling her hand toward the hallway, Cynthia crept closer to the living room. The picture window was draped and revealed nothing from outside. She advanced enough to see a man's meaty arm splayed on the armrest of a recliner. He grasped a beer can in his bear paw and she could now hear the sound of deep snoring coming from him. Cynthia retreated slowly and silently.

Megan was headed for the hallway and Cynthia followed her. It was dark, too dark for Cynthia to see anything. She allowed her dead daughter to be her eyes. After a moment they came to a stop. Cynthia felt Megan guide her hand to another doorknob. This one refused to turn for Cynthia's missing hand. She used her left hand and it turned easily.

She pushed the door open slowly. The door may have led to the Abyss for all Cynthia could see. Megan reestablished her grip on Cynthia's ghost hand and coaxed her forward. There were steps beyond the door. Cynthia felt along the wall with her left hand and descended into complete darkness. The stairs creaked under her weight and she could hear dust and dirt fall onto each step below. She whispered, "Where are we going, Megan? What's down here, baby?"

The stairs paused at a narrow landing and then continued at a right angle. Cynthia continued down. She stopped suddenly when she felt dirt beneath her feet. It was nearly as cold as the snow outside. Cynthia gasped. "Where are we?"

There was another sound from somewhere in front of her and to her right. It wafted through the darkness and made Cynthia's heart speed up. She went silent, refusing to even breathe. Megan wanted her to advance into the dark but Cynthia remained rooted in place. She strained her ears to pick up any sound at all and willed her eyes to pierce the darkness.

The sound repeated itself. It could have been a mouse, and if Cynthia had her way, it would have been. But she knew it was not. "Where are you?" Cynthia whispered. "I can't see you."

Cynthia held her arms out in front of her and she took a step forward. Her frozen feet moved slowly across the frozen dirt of the basement. She had been in the cellar for over a minute now but her eyes had yet to adjust. She was in a starless void bereft of all light.

Her right foot struck something. Pain shot through her toes and Cynthia stumbled back with a short, sharp yelp. Something metallic clanged in the darkness and she heard someone take a quick breath. That was followed by the sound of a young girl whimpering.

Cynthia forgot about the pain in her foot and limped forward, arms outstretched. "Megan? Is that you, baby? It's Mommy, honey, where are you?"

Cynthia followed the soft whimpering until she felt something cold and hard in front of her. She knelt on the cold earth and extended her hand. It was a cold, thin metal of some kind, probably steel. Steel bars. The whimpering was coming from directly in front of her.

"Megan?"

Light suddenly and unexpectedly blossomed overhead. Cynthia shut her eyes against it, but only for a moment. She opened her eyes a slit and looked about.

There were work tables strewn about the large cellar. Most held tools and devices the use of which Cynthia could not guess. The floor was indeed dirt and the walls appeared to be a mix of stone and cement. Along one wall was a cork-board of some kind; newspaper clippings were taped to it like insects caught on flypaper.

Directly in front of her was a cage large enough to hold a Saint Bernard. There was a little girl inside. She was not Megan; she was the little girl Cynthia saw on the news and on the front page of the *Beacon*. Her face was dirty although tears had cleaned some of the flesh on her cheeks. Her eyes were wide, terrified. She gasped at the sight of Cynthia, but her eyes looked beyond the woman kneeling in front of her.

Cynthia heard heavy footsteps on the stairs behind her. The blood drained from her face and she felt her heart leap into her throat. Her eyes darted about the room, settling on a large table cloaked in darkness in the corner closest to her. She dove for it.

She rolled under the table and tucked her arms beneath her. She was a good eight inches into the darkness of the corner. She hoped it would be enough.

Very large feet attached to very large legs entered her field of vision. The man from the recliner paused at the bottom of the stairs. Cynthia got the impression he was looking about the basement until his eyes settled on the little girl in the cage. He took a few steps forward until the cage's occupant began to cry. Her cries turned to shrieks. The man laughed, a guttural, animal sound that chilled Cynthia more than the temperature in the room.

The cage rattled and the girl screamed more loudly than before. The man crossed in front of the table under which Cynthia lay. She held her breath and prayed he could not hear her heart hammering away inside her ribcage. He walked past the table to the wall beyond, paused, and then retraced his steps. He rattled the cage again, causing the little girl to scream, and headed for the stairs.

Cynthia heard his ascent and then the basement was plunged back into darkness. The door at the top of the steps closed.

Sweat dripped from Cynthia's hair and stung her eyes. She blinked it away and released a shuddering breath. The frozen earth beneath her left palm scratched her skin.

God Almighty, she thought. *This isn't a dream.*

****

Her heart threatened to burst right through her chest. Cynthia tried and failed to slow her breathing. The last time she felt anything approximating this was when the airbag deployed in front of her and the whole side of the car crushed her against the center console. Her mind raced and nearly shut down. Somehow she remained conscious.

She became aware of the little girl's rapid breathing and diminishing sobs.

Cynthia crawled out from under the table on her elbows. The stump of her right arm scraped along the cold dirt and sent lightning bolts of pain into her shoulder. She ignored it as best she could until she was clear of the table.

"I'm here to help you," she whispered into the darkness. "Be very quiet and I'll get us out of here. Okay?"

The little girl said nothing; her breathing quickened and she let loose a whimper.

Cynthia crawled across the floor to another table. She thought she saw an old Zippo lying among the scattered tools when the man was terrorizing the child. She bumped into the table with her head and suppressed a scream. She felt along the tabletop with her hand until she found it. She opened it against her leg and flicked the flame to life. It sputtered and burned low. It was not much but after the absolute darkness of the basement it would be enough.

Cynthia crawled back to the cage. She held the flame in front of her face, and said, "My name is Cynthia. What's yours?" She extended her hand closer to the cage so she could see the little girl's face.

The little girl stuttered several times before she got out, "Marcie."

"It's nice to meet you, Marcie. Now let me see about getting you out of here."

She held the flame to the latch and saw what looked like a brand new padlock blocking her way. It looked identical to the padlock which secured the basement doors from outside. Cynthia's lips pressed into a thin line. She placed the lighter on the floor and gently tugged at the lock. It held fast.

"Are you Megan's mommy?"

Cynthia stopped short. She turned slowly back to the cage. "What did you say?"

The little girl sniffled. "She came to see me last night. She said she would get her mommy to help me."

Cynthia covered her mouth with her hand and blinked the tears from her eyes. It was several long moments before she regained a semblance of control. "I'm gonna do my best." She swallowed. "Okay, there has to be a key around here. Let's hope he doesn't have it with him."

She struggled to her feet and brought the lighter to the closest table. She searched among the tools, some of which were stained with something dark and dried, but she came up empty. There were likewise no keys present on the next one or the one under which she hid.

Cynthia turned toward the corkboard. More tools and implements covered the old wood of the tabletop. She put the Zippo down and felt her way through the objects until she felt a key ring. She scooped it up and held it to the lighter. There were three keys on the ring, any of which looked as if they would fit the padlock. Cynthia placed the ring between her teeth and grabbed at the Zippo.

On the way up she caught a glimpse of the newspaper clippings on the corkboard. They were all of missing children. A few were local but most seemed to have come from all over New England. One was from Syndey, Australia. They had been abducted from various points around Cape Cod, everywhere, it seemed, except Dennisport.

Cynthia licked her lips and turned back toward the cage. The lighter gave up the ghost and went dark.

Cynthia flicked it a dozen times but it remained dark and dead. She dropped it on the floor and made her way back to the cage. She fumbled for the lock until she felt Marcie's small hands steady it and hold it in place. "Thanks, honey." Cynthia cycled through the keys until she got the correct one for the padlock. She heard the lock disengage. She turned it in her hand and removed it from the cage. The lock followed the lighter onto the dirt.

Cynthia swung the door open. She heard Marcie move forward slowly. When the little girl was close enough Cynthia wrapped her arm around her and kissed her forehead. Marcie hugged her as if Cynthia were the last life vest on a sinking ship. The girl began to cry and it was all Cynthia could do not to join her. After a moment she held the girl at arms-length.

"Okay, Marcie, listen to me. We're gonna leave now. But you have to be *very* quiet. Like in a library, okay? No noise. We don't want him to hear us, do we?"

"No," she whispered.

Cynthia nodded. "Okay, now hold my hand. Try to step where I step. And no matter what happens, don't say a word. Understand?"

"I understand."

"Okay, let's go."

****

Each stair creaked under her weight and Cynthia fought the urge to stop each time. She craned her neck toward the ceiling, trying to gauge their distance from the living room, where she hoped the man was, and hoped the sound was not significant enough for him to hear them. They reached the small landing and turned in the direction of the door at the top of the stairs.

The next step creaked loudly and this time Cynthia did stop. She held her breath and listened for the sound of footsteps from above. She heard none. After a moment she started moving again. They continued up until they reached the door.

Cynthia gently withdrew her hand from Marcie's and she tried the knob. It, too, squeaked, but it turned easily enough. Cynthia opened the door a crack and peered through. She was looking into the kitchen. There was no sign of the big man. She could hear the sound of the hockey game coming from far away.

There was enough light filtering through the open door that Cynthia could see the vague outline of the little girl behind her. She held a finger to her lips and Marcie nodded. Cynthia took her hand again.

She opened the door enough to get a look at the entire kitchen. The man was nowhere in sight. Cynthia took one, then two steps into the room. Marcie followed in her footsteps. Cynthia could just about hear the announcers calling the game between the Bruins and Red Wings.

Just watch your game for another minute, she thought. *That's all we'll need.*

They advanced into the kitchen slowly, one step at a time. The meager light was an assault on their eyes after the darkness of the cellar. Cynthia would have shielded her eyes had she two hands. Instead she simply led their slow advance toward the side door.

When they stood in front of it Cynthia once again withdrew her hand from the girl's. She reached for the knob but her hand stopped short. The door was closed and locked. Her heart leaped back into her throat. Her head snapped back in the direction of the living room.

The man stood in the arched doorway. Now that she could see him, she recognized him immediately as the big, ugly man who confronted her at the tree house in her dream. He leered at her and his lips pulled back from the stubs of his teeth. Drool beaded on his lips and dripped onto the ancient linoleum.

"Ain't you a pretty sight," he said. "A little old for my tastes, but I think I can manage."

Cynthia screamed and fumbled for the lock. Marcie hunched down behind Cynthia and began to cry. The big man stepped into the kitchen.

When she finally succeeded in unlocking the door, she threw it open. The man's expression changed from delight to anger. He roared and surged forward at a far faster rate of speed than Cynthia would have thought him capable. She screamed, then scooped up Marcie and hurled both of them through the open door.

The man crashed into the doorframe somewhat drunkenly. He swiped at Cynthia, and would have had a lock on her wrist had she possessed a right arm. Instead he lost his balance and toppled onto the floor.

It was blind luck his hand found her ankle. He grasped it with enough force to make Cynthia cry out. Without thinking she kicked down with everything she had. Her bare foot collided with the man's jaw in spectacular fashion. He howled and released his grip on her ankle.

Cynthia screamed again and grabbed Marcie. She hurried the little girl down the steps and into the driveway. The street was a little darker than Cynthia would have liked, but there were other houses nearby. She was confident they could reach one. They started down the driveway as fast as they could manage.

Cynthia stopped and whirled, off-balance, when Marcie grabbed her hand roughly and pulled her toward the backyard. "What are you—" Cynthia stopped herself. Marcie looked as surprised as she did, and the little girl had not pulled her at all. The tug was coming from her right hand. "Megan?"

Cynthia looked in the direction of the street, then into the darkened backyard. "We can't go that way, baby. This way is safer." The dead girl tugged her again. Cynthia pulled back and succeeded in freeing herself. She whirled back in the direction of the street.

The man stood at the end of the driveway. Something sharp in his hand gleamed in the meager light. Had they run that way he would have had them easily. Cynthia could see enough of his face to know he smiled at them.

Marcie screamed. Cynthia grabbed her and lifted the little girl and held her to her chest. They took off toward the tree line.

****

She stayed within her own footprints to increase her speed. It would matter little and she knew it. They did not have a large enough head start, and the little girl in her arms was both slowing her down and throwing her off-balance. The adrenaline allowed her to momentarily forget about the sharp edges of her footprints scraping the skin off her legs and the numbness returning with a vengeance to her feet. Branches clawed at them as they passed and tore at their clothes and skin. This, too, she was able to ignore, if only for the moment.

The single shot she was able to deliver to the ugly man had not, unfortunately, been to his legs or even his groin. *Should have gone for his balls. We could have strolled to a neighbor's house.* But she had not, nor had it occurred to her until this very moment.

The voice in her head inquired, *Why are you running away? Don't you want to die? This is even better than doing the job yourself. No one will have any idea you took the punk way out. You should let this guy do it and thank him for it.*

Cynthia gritted her teeth. "Shut up."

They reached the tree house and Cynthia spared a glance over her shoulder. The man was still there but she had managed to open a bit of a lead on him. His breathing was labored; the breath blew out of him in great puffs. He went down in the snow, swearing loudly. Cynthia regarded the tree house. If she could get Marcie up the ladder quickly enough he would not see. Then she could get him to follow her to the house where the Dennisport police were a phone call away.

She leaned toward the lowest rung on the tree. "Climb up, honey, fast so he won't see you."

"No!" Marcie shouted into Cynthia's ear. "He'll get me! I wanna stay with you!"

"Shh," Cynthia soothed in a tone she had not used in weeks. "You have to be quiet. Get up there and hide. I'll get him to chase me. He won't even know you're there."

Cynthia leaned again toward the rung. She felt Megan's hand pulling on her ghost arm, pulling her toward the house. Cynthia looked longingly at the tree house before glancing back at the ugly man. He lifted himself off the ground and wiped the snow from his eyes. He glared at her and roared.

Cynthia swore and abandoned her idea. She sprinted for all she was worth for her rented Victorian.

****

She did not expect to reach the house before he caught up to her, but she did. The back door was open, as she left it. She ran for it, out of breath and pain lancing into her right side. The little girl sobbed into Cynthia's chest.

Cynthia put Marcie on the stoop and shouldered the door open the rest of the way. "C'mon, honey, c'mon, quick!" She hustled the girl into the house and slammed the door shut behind them. She threw the deadbolt and peeked through the curtains. The man was no more than thirty feet from the back door.

Cynthia backed away and ran for the phone. "Hide, baby, hide real good and don't come out until I tell you to. Understand?"

Marcie nodded and ran for the living room.

Cynthia dialed 911, but her fingers were numb and she pressed too many buttons. She swore, turned the phone off and then on again, and tried a second time.

The window in the back door shattered. Glass pelted her and skidded and bounced across the kitchen linoleum. Cynthia screamed and dropped the phone. She looked wide-eyed at the door. The man's meaty arm snaked through the broken pane and fumbled with the deadbolt. She heard the tell-tale *click* of the bolt sliding free. The backdoor opened.

Cynthia gasped and ran for the living room. She saw no sign of Marcie and that was good, at least. Her cell was on the end table next to the sofa. She snatched it up as she ran for the stairs.

The man ran into the living room. He stopped and smiled when he saw her. "You're not getting away, bitch. Me and you and that little twat are gonna get down and dirty tonight. You wait and see." He paused and smiled at her. "I never had a cripple girl. This is gonna be a treat."

"Fuck you!" Cynthia screamed at him. She bolted up the stairs two at a time.

She slipped on the blood from her feet and went down in the hallway. She crawled as fast as she was able to the bedroom. When she reached it she slammed the door closed behind her. The large dresser next to the door was heavy; she thought her adrenaline would allow her to move it, and perhaps it would have had she possessed two arms. As it was she roared as new pain found its way into her lower back when the dresser refused to move.

Cynthia ran for the bathroom and locked the door behind her. She heard the bedroom door fly open hard and fast enough it slammed into the wall behind it. Kneeling by the keyhole, she peeked through. He took one step into the bedroom and paused.

What the hell is he waiting for? There's only one place I can be. Was it possible he did not see the footprints in blood leading to the bathroom? No. He saw them and his eyes followed them.

She remembered the cell in her hand. She nosed the power on and tried to work the buttons with her numb fingers. She nearly dropped the phone twice. She managed to hold onto it, but her fingers would not work properly. She misdialed twice before she heard the footsteps stop outside the bathroom door. Cynthia's breath caught in her throat.

The doorknob turned right and left slowly, almost gingerly. When the man on the other side knocked gently, Cynthia screamed. "Come out, come out, wherever you are," said a soothing voice. "Or shall I huff and puff and blow your door in? What'll it be, little piggy?"

Tears streamed down Cynthia's face. Desperately her eyes went to the small window to her right. She could probably squeeze through it but she was on the second floor. If there was nothing to step on to...She looked out the window anyway. One of the spires stood sentry perhaps ten or twelve feet from the window. It was a leap she did not think she could make, especially with her feet slippery with blood, but what choice did she have?

Cynthia used the sink to pull herself up.

"Well, well, well," said the man on the other side of the door. "What do we have here? Someone else for me to play with. I'm a very lucky man."

Cynthia knelt back down so quickly her knees cracked on the floor. She gasped but managed to stifle a scream. She peeked through the keyhole again.

She could not see Marcie, but she knew the little girl had to be in the doorway. The man obscured her view as he faced the new arrival. Cynthia slammed her palm against the door. "No, no, no, you cocksucker! Here! Come and get *me*!" She fumbled for the doorknob.

"Aren't you the precious one?" the man said. "I'm gonna take you back home with me and we're gonna have cookies and hot chocolate. How does that sound?"

Cynthia got the door open and hurled herself at the man's back. He turned at the last minute, but he was too slow. Cynthia clubbed the man's jaw with the stump of her right arm and used her left hand to grab hold of his arm. She dug her nails deeply into his flesh and drew blood. The man howled and flung Cynthia away. She bounced on the bed and then vanished over the side nearest the wall.

Cynthia landed on her right side and screamed. The stump of her arm took the brunt of the landing and it felt like she had dipped the thing into molten lava. "Marcie! Get out of here now! Run and hide!"

She clutched the stump and felt it throb in her hand. The bandage was gone, who knows where. She looked at the scars and saw some of the stitching had opened. Blood beaded around the thread in some spots.

"Don't you listen to her, Marcie. Is that your name? Marcie? That's funny, I have another Marcie you can meet. The two of you will be great friends."

Cynthia got her right arm onto the bed and used it to haul herself to her knees. "Leave her alone, you fucker!" She meant to scream but she managed little more than a hoarse croak.

Let it go, the voice whispered to her for the last time. *Let him have the girl and then yourself. It's what you want, isn't it? What you came here for? It won't be as quick as the gun, sure, but—*

Cynthia pawed at the nightstand drawer. It slid open easily enough for her. She rooted around inside until her fingers brushed the handle of the gun. She closed her fingers around it and withdrew her hand.

The man loomed above the little girl in the doorway. Cynthia aimed the muzzle at his back and squinted at the target. "Hey, dickhead."

"With you in a minute, darling," he said without turning in her direction. "First I have to see to little Marcie here. I have to say, she's being more cooperative than her mother."

Cynthia pulled the trigger. The gun's report was loud, much louder than she expected. It stung her ears and sent tremors up her arm and into her shoulder.

The bullet disappeared into the man's right shoulder. The impact spun him like a giant top. Blood fountained from the wound and splashed onto the walls and the hardwood. He steadied himself and faced her. His expression was altogether uncomprehending. He looked like a caveman trying to puzzle through Fermat's Last Theorem.

His hand drifted slowly to his wounded shoulder. The move looked subconscious to Cynthia; she doubted he realized he moved at all. His fingertips were covered with blood when he examined them. His eyes moved from the blood to Cynthia.

His expression remained confused for only another moment. Then his lips pulled back from his teeth and his eyes narrowed. Cynthia identified the look in his eyes as murder.

"Marcie, get out of the way now!" But she need not have spoken at all; Marcie was gone from the doorway.

The man charged forward. Cynthia pulled the trigger again. And again. And again.

He pirouetted with each impact, a monster performing a ghastly ballet. More blood spurted into the air; it stained the walls and floor. Cynthia fired the gun dry and waited for the obscene dance to reach its end.

The man stutter-stepped until his knees hit the side of the bed. He went down on the comforter and bounced. Cynthia backed away from the bed and put her back to the wall. She aimed the empty gun at the man's head. He managed to get through a few large, ragged breaths before he lay still.

When it occurred to Cynthia he was through moving she crawled around the bed to the open doorway. "Marcie?" Her voice was still a hoarse croak but she was able to add some volume to it. "Marcie, are you okay?"

Cynthia propped herself in the doorway and looked back at the man on her bed. He remained still. She noted with some relief he was no longer breathing. Then she heard the sound of small feet ascending the stairs. She watched as the little girl she had found in a cage reached the second floor landing. "You all right?"

"Is the bad man gone?" Her voice was soft and full of hope.

Cynthia looked again at the corpse before she nodded. "Yes, sweetie, he's gone."

Marcie ran the rest of the way to Cynthia and collapsed into her arms. Cynthia dropped the gun and held the child's head to her chest. They were both breathing heavily and sobbing and Cynthia waited until they caught their breath. When the shaking had subsided a little for both of them, she said, "I told you to stay out of sight. You could have been hurt, baby. You should have stayed hidden."

The little girl tilted her head but kept it resting on Cynthia's chest. "I did stay hidden."

Cynthia brushed at her hair. "You came up here, stood right where we're sitting right now. It helped me, but it was a very dangerous thing for you to do."

"I didn't do it," Marcie said softly. "I was gonna come look for you, but Megan told me to stay behind the chair."

"Megan told—"

Cynthia looked again at the bare stump of her right arm. It bled a little and it throbbed but not as it had the past few days. She tried for several moments to flex her fingers but she felt nothing below the stump. Cynthia leaned her head back against the doorjamb and closed her eyes.

****

The Dennisport police were only too happy to buy her story. With the child abductor dead and his latest victim safely back with her parents they had no inclination to delve too deeply into Cynthia's official story.

The little girl thanked her profusely as did her parents. The staff at Dennisport Memorial took good care of Cynthia's wounds and pronounced her fit. She declined an interview with the *Beacon* mostly because she wanted to get the hell out of town and back to her life in Rahway. She told the reporter he could find what he needed in her statement. The man was gruff, but she stood her ground.

She was packed and the car was loaded when it occurred to her she had one task left to perform in Dennisport. She walked back to the tree house and gingerly climbed the rungs. She wrestled the photo of Megan from its frame and placed it on the one remaining bench. Her eyes welled up with tears and she made no effort to control them. They spilled freely from her eyes.

Cynthia smiled. "I love you, baby."

There was no reply, neither a spoken word nor a grasping of her missing hand. She was not okay with that, not by a long shot, but she thought perhaps someday she would accept it.

Cynthia drove south alone.

The Frenchman

The guy who answered the door was so mobster he was nearly a cliché. Grossly overweight, pinstriped suit and a tie, thinning black hair slicked back with more grease than you'd find in all three of my cars. If not for my flawless professionalism, I would have laughed in his face. He regarded me for a moment, then held his palms up and lifted his fingers in unison several times. I stood just inside the door, and briefly considered allowing him to search me. I rejected the idea, and simply stared at him.

He looked over his shoulder at the man seated in the high-backed chair. I waited patiently, somewhat curious as to how my scene with Fat Boy was gonna play out. If the boss decided I needed to be searched, this was going to get ugly very fast. My profession demands I be armed at all times, and these guys would know that. I didn't know if the boss was armed, but I had already seen the bulge in Fat Boy's jacket. Small caliber, if I'm any judge of weapons. And I am. You can bet your life on it.

The boss shook his head. Fat Boy turned back to me, clearly displeased with the decision. He shouldn't have been; his boss saved his life. He looked at me and I could see the anger in his eyes. Normally, I would deal with this idiot in one of two ways. I would simply pull my piece and splatter him, or I would grab his own gun and beat him with it. And then splatter him. I did neither. I'm good, maybe the best out there, but even I don't want to go to war with one of the Five Families. If Fat Boy turned out to be a blood relation of the boss's, their code would force Gugliotti to come after me. Besides, better to find out what they want first. I can always kill Fat Boy later if the mood strikes.

"You're the Frenchman?" Fat Boy asked.

"I am."

"You don't look French."

"'I'm not." Frankly, I don't know why people are surprised about this. Contract killers are not known for using their Christian name.

"Please, come in and sit down." The boss gestured to the sofa across from his chair.

As I crossed the room, I noted the brandy glass on the end table next to him. The bottle stood next to it, and it was three-quarters empty. He wasn't drunk; a large man such as he probably needed to down a couple bottles like that one just to get a buzz. I sat on the sofa, placed my laptop case on the floor beside me, and looked him over. I'd seen his picture on television every now and then, as I'm sure you have as well. Everyone has; you don't become boss of one of the Families and remain unknown to the media. He looked thinner in person, but he could still stand to lose about forty pounds. He was bald but for a crown of close-cropped salt and pepper hair. His feet shifted every few seconds, and it dawned on me he was anxious. I'm used to that reaction, but not from a potential employer. They're usually cooler than that.

"You know who I am." It was not a question.

I nodded. "Yes." Behind me, Fat Boy closed the door and I heard the lock engage. I did not turn to look at him.

"I would like to partake of your services. One time job." He reached into the pocket of his sports coat and pulled out a wallet-sized picture. He held it up, placed it on the coffee table between us, and slid it in my direction. "My daughter."

I leaned forward and took the picture. The girl was perhaps twenty-one or twenty-two. Long, straight jet-black hair, thin (*wait a few years, kid*, I thought), and gorgeous. She was sitting on a swing in someone's backyard with the sun behind her. "Very beautiful," I said.

"She was."

I put the picture on the table and looked at him. "She's dead." This, too, was not a question. I realized two things at that moment: The first was this was a revenge job. The second was he wasn't anxious about meeting me; he was grief-stricken. I'm usually a better judge of people than that. I'd have to watch that in the future.

"Three weeks ago. She left work and never came home. The cops found her body two days later." He took a long breath. "She'd been dumped in a trash pile in an alley off Eighth Avenue." He clenched his teeth. "My little girl."

"And you want me to find out who did this and deal with them?" I kept my voice level, professional. I don't get emotional on the job; it doesn't pay.

"We already know who did it. It was a street gang, the Broadway Vampires. We got one of em and made him talk." He leaned forward in the chair, and it creaked. "No matter what we did, though, he wouldn't give up their hideout. He was more scared of their leader than he was of us. I don't like that. And it's their fucking leader I want, anyway. His name is Shrek. Like the ogre in the kid movie."

"I think it's Schreck, actually. Max Schreck. He played Count Orlok in the 1922 film *Nosferatu*. If they're using a vampire theme for their gang, that's probably who their leader named himself for. Just a theory."

He waved his hand dismissively. "Do I look like Roger Ebert to you? I don't give a shit about his name or where he got it. I just want him."

"Dead or alive?" I already knew the answer, but professionalism demanded I ask.

"Dead if necessary, but alive if at all possible. I'd like to meet this son of a bitch myself."

"That's understandable." I cleared my throat. Now we were getting down to business. "Look, Mr. Gugliotti. I think perhaps this is something you should handle in-house. This will likely result in more than a few deaths, and my fee is non-negotiable. This will be expensive."

He didn't miss a beat. "You think money matters to me? This is my *daughter* I'm talking about. The cocksucker who killed her is out there somewhere, him and his little gang of wannabe tough guys. And I want them dead. I want them *all* dead. Except this Schreck."

I folded my fingers together and placed my hands on my lap. "Very well. How many members of this gang?"

Gugliotti looked at Fat Boy, who walked to him and handed him a scrap of paper. Fat Boy reoccupied his position next to the door and Gugliotti looked at the paper. "As close as we can tell, fifteen more. We took care of one of them already."

I nodded. "And since they fancy themselves vampires, I assume they only come out a night?"

"No, we caught ours around ten in the morning. He was pretty drunk, stumbling down the sidewalk." He leaned forward again and tapped his left shoulder. "They wear matching leather jackets, if you can believe that. With a patch on their shoulder that says *Broadway Vampires*." He scowled. "Like they were in a fifties motorcycle gang. After what we did to their buddy, though, they may not want to advertise their identities no more."

"Probably not," I said, and I believed that. No matter how tough you think you are, if you piss off a mob boss, do you really wanna broadcast yourself as a target? "Can I at least assume they operate around Broadway? Or is that bullshit as well?"

"No, they're around there someplace. The one we caught was right in that area. We just can't find their leader. Fucker's pulling a Claude Rains."

"I'm not worried about that." I leaned back and looked at him. "My fee is five hundred thousand per target, plus expenses, and as I said a few minutes ago, it is non-negotiable. That's what I charge for persons who will not be missed. Fortunately for you, these gents qualify as such. You said there are fifteen of them. That's seven-point-five million. Half now, half upon completion." I hesitated to allow that number to sink in. "Do we have a contract?"

Gugliotti stroked his chin for a moment before he nodded and stuck out his hand. I shook it and then pulled my laptop case onto my lap. A few moments later, I had the appropriate screen up and placed the laptop on the table. I spun it around to face him. He read the money transfer page, typed in his code and a very large number, and spun the laptop around so I could see. TRANSFER COMPLETE it said in big block letters. $7,500,000.00 U.S.

"I'd rather pay the whole thing upfront. If it turns out there are more than fifteen, we'll settle after the fact."

I nodded, closed the laptop, and replaced it in its case. He had stood and looked down at me. "Remember, if you can take this Schreck asshole alive, do it. I'll throw in another three for your trouble."

"I'll do what I can," I said, and I meant it. If someone promised you a bonus of three million dollars, wouldn't you try for it?

"My associate here has some information for you," Gugliotti said as he stood. "When you're done with these cocksuckers, contact me." He walked to the door and disappeared through it.

I watched him leave and Fat Boy closed the door behind him. He pulled a small pad from his jacket pocket and held it out to me.

****

As it turned out, daddy's little girl was a stripper. Gugliotti probably hadn't wanted to admit it to me face to face, and I couldn't blame him. I've seen *The Sopranos*; if that's how mob guys treat strippers, it's no surprise the boss didn't want me to know about his daughter's occupation while he was in the room. What amazed me was that the old man allowed this. I'd have expected him to have a talk with the owner of the joint and straighten out a few things. Maybe he hadn't known about it until after she went missing. Whatever. It was none of my business.

Fat Boy had given me the name of the joint she worked at (Lucky Lenny's? Really?) and the address. He had also provided me with the name of one of the dead girl's friends who had left work with her the final time. The boss had left out another detail during our chat. Fat Boy said the girl's throat had been ripped out. My only reaction was a raised eyebrow. In truth, I was pretty happy to learn of that. It meant these guys did more than just call themselves vampires. They tried to live the lifestyle, as well. That could come in handy. After I secured my laptop at one of my safe houses, I took a cab out to Eighth Avenue. The cabbie knew the address, and I had to wonder if he had spent any time inside watching a mob boss's daughter writhe on the floor wearing a smile and not much else.

The neon sign above the door flashed LUCKY LENNY'S at me. Just below it, in smaller but equally obnoxious letters flashed, LIVE GIRLS. *As opposed to dead ones*, I thought. I entered, paid the ten dollar cover, and got my first look at Immaculata Gugliotti's former place of employment.

It was a dive, in every sense of the word. Despite the smoking ban, men puffed on cigarettes and cigars like the world was about to end. Fat guys in business suits sat at the bar and next to the stage. They waved dollar bills at the two dancing girls, laughed, drank, and dared one another to acts of indecency. There were two bartenders. The man was burly, tattooed and wore a scowl that dared anyone to fuck with him. The woman had probably danced here in her younger years, and was now relegated to serving drinks to the same men who had once shoved money into her g-string with much enthusiasm.

I took a bar stool and ordered a beer. I don't usually drink on the job, and I'm not a beer guy, but I didn't want to stand out. I watched the show for a few moments, eyed the men in the crowd. There were a few leather jackets in the room, but none had a Broadway Vampires patch. My twin nine millimeters remained in their holsters beneath my jacket.

A slinky, sleazy song I never heard before blared from the speakers. As it neared its end, the disc jockey in the booth said, "Give it up for Miss Sapphire, ladies and gentlemen!" The crowd roared, the girl waved and ran off the stage. "A nice round of applause. She'll be back here tomorrow, same time, same crime!" More applause from the men in the audience.

I eyed the door through which Miss Sapphire had disappeared. Fat Boy had given me the real name of Immaculata's friend, but he had neglected to provide me with her stage name. Sapphire fit the description, but then, so did the dancer still on stage, and the new one who made her way up there now. I sighed and thought about smashing Fat Boy's face.

Miss Sapphire approached the bar. She had put on a gown over her miniscule wardrobe, and a pair of glasses which made her appear like a college professor in a porn movie. "Red Death," she said to the burly bartender. She reached into her purse, threw a fiver on the bar, and pulled out a cigarette. She fished around in her purse for a moment before I took out my Zippo and flicked it for her. She backed up a step, looked at me with the cigarette dangling from her lips, and leaned into the flame.

"Thanks," she said, and exhaled toward the ceiling.

I put away the Zippo and took a sip of my beer. "Anytime. How are you today?"

She looked at me again, clearly having expected me to try to talk with her, and just as clearly dreading it. And why not? She probably got hit on by all sorts of scumbags on an hourly basis. I was certainly no different in her eyes. Better dressed, perhaps, and not stuffing a wedding ring into my pocket, but a scumbag nonetheless.

"I'm doing great. You?" She tried to sound interested, but I could hear the resignation in her tone. *Occupational hazard*, it said. *Even when I'm not on stage I have to put up with assholes like you.*

"I'm well." I tried to sound charming, and I suppose I was successful, but her guard was up. I couldn't blame her. "Do you give lap dances?"

Burly, who I came to find out later was Lucky Lenny himself, put a glass full of something red in front of her. He eyed me for a moment before seeing to another customer.

"I'm off shift," she said, and reached for her drink. "Sorry."

I reached into my pocket and pulled a wad of bills. I peeled off two Ben Franklins and placed them on the bar.

She looked at the cash, then at me. She reached for the bills, but slowly, as if expecting me to snatch them away before she could touch them. I allowed her to take the money, and she turned back to me with a smile. "Standard rate is fifty for fifteen minutes. No physical contact."

"What does two hundred get me?" I asked, and polished off my beer.

"Fifteen minutes," she said and stuffed the bills into her purse. "No physical contact."

"Sounds like a bargain," I said with a smile.

"It is." She put her cigarette out in an ashtray, downed her drink in one long gulp, and put the empty glass on the bar. "Follow me."

Bargain Lady took me to a side room and closed the door behind us. There was a red velvet sofa against one wall, and a small, square, raised platform in the center of the room. She pointed at the sofa and mounted the small stage. "There are cameras in here, and believe me, someone *is* watching. So don't get any ideas."

"Wouldn't dream of it," I replied, and sat back on the sofa.

She went to work. I have to say, for a minute there, I actually forgot I was on the job. That doesn't happen to me very often, almost never, in fact. But this girl, well, she was something. Her robe wound up on the floor twenty seconds into her act. Her top followed it a moment later. She made eye contact, and must have seen me losing myself in the movements of her body. The slinky siren stepped off the platform and danced her way toward me. Once in front of me, she shook her ass with practiced ease, and I admit, I felt a tingling south of my belt buckle. By the time she turned and faced me, though, I had remembered why I was there.

She straddled me and rubbed her tits across my face. When she squished them, they made a sandwich out of my face. I kept my arms at my side, more out of professionalism than an adherence to the rules. She must have sensed my pulling away from her, because she paused in her performance and looked down at me. Her eyes searched mine for the least bit of interest (or lust), but she came up empty. "What's the matter, honey?"

"Your name is Shannon Dimecco, right?"

She stopped, but only for a moment. She went back into her act as if I had not spoken at all. "Sorry, you have the wrong girl."

"I don't think I do. You were friends with Immaculata Gugliotti, weren't you? I'm a friend of hers. I just want to ask you some questions about the last time you saw her."

"What are you? A cop?"

"Most definitely not," I said.

Sapphire stopped, took a few steps, and reached for her robe. She slipped it on and turned to me. "Sorry. If you wanna talk, that's extra. And besides, it's been fifteen minutes."

"It's been more like seven," I said, and stood. I guessed, correctly, as it turned out, that she knew what her late friend's family did for a living. She put two and two together and probably figured out why I was there. Scooping up her purse, she got a step toward the door before I grabbed her arm.

"Hey!" she said, and tried to pull away. "Hey, let go of me, you asshole!"

"I need you to talk to me about Immaculata." I tightened my grip on her arm, just enough to show her I was serious. "I'm not here to hurt you, but I need information. Please."

She tried to yank her arm free, but I held her in place easily. "Let go of me, *goddamnit*!"

Burly came through the door like he'd been fired from a cannon. The guy who watched the front door was behind him. They outweighed me by four hundred pounds, easy. They knew it, Sapphire knew it, and so did I. They probably thought I'd be intimidated enough to release her instantly. I don't work that way.

"Lenny!" Sapphire shouted. "Lenny, get this guy off me!"

Lenny and his doorman stepped into the room and the door closed behind them. I frowned. They weren't leaving me much choice.

"Drop the bitch, now," Lenny said. "I said *now*, jerk-off. You're in a world of shit."

"I don't want trouble. I just want to ask the lady a few questions and I'm outta here." I knew it wouldn't work; I could see the bloodlust in their eyes. They probably looked forward to this sort of thing. It was probably something they laughed about after hours when they had the place to themselves.

"You're gonna be carried outta here," Lenny said, and lunged for me.

I threw Sapphire to the floor to get her out of harm's way. I stepped back and landed a haymaker across Lenny's jaw. He went down hard and fast. He pulled himself to his knees with assistance from the raised platform, shook his head and looked at me. He pushed himself to his feet and tried for me again. He swung his fist in a wide arc, child's play for me to dodge. When he was off-balance, I smashed my first into his face as hard as I could. Blood flew in all directions from his broken nose and he went down again.

The bouncer took a couple steps toward me and I pulled one of the nines from its holster. I pointed it at his head and he stopped in his tracks. His hands went up like a bank clerk's in an old western. I looked at Lenny, who rolled onto his back. His hands covered his nose and blood seeped between his fingers. He groaned, and perhaps tried to speak, but he was unable to produce anything beyond a pained gurgle.

Sapphire had crammed herself into a corner and held her hands out. She was more than scared; it occurred to me she had probably lived in terror of Lenny and his temper. She looked horrified, as if envisioning her boss's wrath for the result of his coming to her defense.

I kept the gun on the bouncer and knelt in front of Sapphire. "Look, I'm not here to hurt you, Shannon. I just need to know what you know about that night with Immaculata. Here, I'll make it worth your while." I pulled a few more Franklins from my pocket and dropped them into her lap. "Yours, just for coming with me. Please."

Her eyes went from Lenny to me to the bouncer. After a moment, she picked up the money I had dropped and held it in front of her eyes, as if she did not know what it was. Finally she focused on me, and whispered, "You have to get me out of here. He'll kill me for this."

I shook my head. "No he won't. Not while I'm around. Let's go."

I stood, held out a hand and she took it. I helped her to her feet and eyed Lenny. "If you fuck with this girl in any way, shape, or form, ever again, I'll come back. You won't like what happens then, I promise you."

I don't like to bluff, but it was highly unlikely I'd ever step foot inside Lucky Lenny's again. After I got what I needed out of Sapphire she was on her own. But there was no reason I couldn't play it up, at least a little. And who knows? Maybe the prick would buy into the threat.

Lenny gurgled again, but made no move. I looked at the bouncer, who still had his hands high above his head. I motioned him to the side as we made for the door. He moved farther away, the very picture of cooperation. We were out the door a moment later.

I holstered the nine millimeter and Sapphire led me to the dressing room. There were three girls inside in various stages of dress. They eyed me, but the only reaction was a knowing smirk from one of them. I don't know if they saw the expression on Sapphire's face, or if perhaps a man being led into the dressing room was a common occurrence. Either way, no one spoke to us or got in our way. Sapphire took a moment to grab her street clothes from her locker. She slipped into a well-worn denim jacket, and led me to the back door.

****

Her hands shook so much she was unable to light her cigarette. I took the lighter from her hands and did it myself. She took a long pull on it, inhaled deeply, and thanked me. "You're welcome," I said, and led her up the alley and back onto Eighth. The sun was high in the sky and too bright after the darkness of the club. I slipped my sunglasses on, and took my first real look at Sapphire.

Away from the flashing lights and perpetual smoke cloud of Lucky Lenny's, she was actually quite beautiful. I pegged her age around twenty-two, twenty-three at most. Her hair, which had looked black in the club, was light brown in the afternoon sun. A streak of bright blue ran back from her temples. It was long and straight, just as Immaculata Gugliotti's had been. She was short, no more than five-one, guaranteed, and could not weight more than a hundred pounds, at best.

She was sobbing, but by the time we reached the next block, she had gotten it under control. She took her sunglasses off and wiped at her eyes. They were red and puffy, and she looked scared, but she also looked like she was getting her shit together. I was happy for that. The last thing I wanted was to attract the attention of some cop walking the beat. I had never killed a cop before, although I had come close a few times. Better to let that particular sleeping dog go on sleeping.

"God, I'm such an asshole," Sapphire said. "One fuck up after another, that's me."

"What do you mean?" I had my hand on her arm and was guiding her along Eighth. I wanted to get to Broadway as soon as possible, but not so soon that I wouldn't have a chance to talk with my new companion.

"You know how many strip joints there are in Manhattan? Lots. You know how many I've been fired from? Almost all of em. I mean, there's no way I can go back to Lenny now. Not after what you did to him."

"I'm sorry," I said, although I wasn't. Not really. "I might be able to help you with that, but first we need to talk. About Immaculata."

She sniffled and lit another cigarette. This time she was sufficiently calm to do the job herself. "Who are you? A relative?"

"No. I am currently an associate of her father's. I'm looking for the guys who killed her. I think you know something, and I want to know what."

"She never liked her father, you know." She coughed, the kind of wet cough you expect to hear from someone in their nineties after a lifetime of smoking. "She started stripping because he told her she couldn't do it. That's it. That's all it took. Just her asshole father forbidding her to do it. She was good, too. Made a lot of cash, made a lot of friends among the girls."

"Uh huh."

"Let me tell you something, that's not easy to do. Making friends with the girls, I mean. Most girls who dance are very territorial. They don't like each other very much. As a rule, I mean. Immaculata was different. Just about everyone liked her."

"Including you?"

She nodded. "Including me. Sometimes, if we got off at the same time, she'd come back to my place. We'd hang out, get high, fool around." She took a deep breath. "I really miss her."

We turned onto 42nd Street, and at the end of the block, I could see the insane traffic that was Times Square at late-afternoon. "Then tell me what you know about the night she was killed." Our pace had slowed somewhat, so I picked it up and all but dragged Sapphire with me. Her feet skidded on the pavement but she got them under her and kept up.

"We got off at midnight on the nose. I wanted to get her back to my place, but she wanted to go out clubbing. We hit a couple spots, nowhere special. We had a few drinks, did a couple lines with some guys who tried to pick us up."

"Who were these guys?"

"College geeks. Nobodys." She paused to puff on her cigarette. "I was trying really hard by then to get her to come home with me, but she wanted to keep partying. So I went home. Alone."

"And that was the last time you saw her?"

"Yeah. Well, kinda."

We emerged into Times Square. The electro-kinetic Coke sign seen by the world on New Year's Eve flashed at us. People walked in every direction, seemingly oblivious to the traffic whipping by them. *This is the single most chaotic place on earth*, I thought. *How people aren't being run over every minute is one of the great mysteries of our time.*

"What do you mean, 'kinda'?" I proceeded to guide her toward the main intersection.

"Well, I saw her talking with a couple guys in black leather jackets. One of em had his arm around her, and the other was just kinda there. That was the last I saw of her." She tossed her cigarette to the ground and stepped on it. We continued walking toward the Square.

"So that was it? Two guys in black leather jackets."

She stopped so unexpectedly I was nearly yanked back. My first impulse was to pull her forward and continue walking, but something in her expression stopped me. Even through her sunglasses she looked confused, but also as if she were concentrating on something I could not see. I'd seen that look before, mostly from someone staring down the barrel of one of my nines, and trying to come up with something that would save them. I decided it might be important enough to allow her a moment.

"Wait a minute," she whispered. "Wait a fucking minute."

I could actually see her working it out in her head. People walked around us the way water flows around some new obstruction dropped in its path. No one paid us any mind, despite the fact that I was clearly a few decades older than this girl. She was obviously distressed, but the foot traffic kept to its pace and ignored us. *Gotta love New York*, I thought. Still, I saw no reason to press our luck. It would be a bad time for some well-meaning passer-by to poke his nose into our particular relationship dynamic. "They had shoulder patches on their jackets, right?"

"Yeah, yeah," she said, and waved a hand dismissively. "But that's not it. Christ, if I hadn't been so fucking high I woulda remembered." She looked at me with wide eyes. "She came over to me as I was leaving. Wanted me to go with her. She said those guys were having a party and they wanted us to go. Fuck, why didn't I remember that?"

"Go where?" I started walking again and was relieved she followed. I didn't want to have to drag her through the busiest intersection on the planet in full view of a thousand people. That would be a little too obvious, even in New York.

"Let me think," she said.

By the time we reached the center of the Square, she was snapping her fingers over and over. "It was a theatre, I remember that much. But not one of the big ones." She looked up Broadway. Her brow furrowed, and if she wasn't trying her hardest to cut through the fog of that night, she deserved an Academy Award for her performance. Her lips moved, but I could not hear what she said over the traffic and street noise. It took me a moment to realize she was talking to herself. "The Olympic!" she said at last, triumphantly. "The Olympic Theatre. It's right up the street!"

I looked to where she indicated. I saw a few theatres, but I was at too odd an angle to read any signage. "Okay, let's go." I started in that direction.

"Wait a minute," she said, and pulled back.

"What's the problem?"

"You said you wanted information. I gave it to you. That's all I know. Now let me go."

"You're coming with me," I said. "To confirm what you told me. If you're telling the truth, you're free to go with my blessing." I padded my pocket. "And a fistful of cash. But if you're lying, well, that's a whole different story."

"I'm not lying," she said, and tried to pull away.

I hoped for both our sakes she would not create a scene. *Remember what happened to your boss*, I thought, and wished for telepathy. I didn't know precisely how much I could get away with. There were too many civilians around, and while I didn't see any cops, I knew they were there. They had to be. If she started screaming or hitting me, I'd be in a bad spot. I strengthened my grip on her arm and pulled her closer.

"Listen to me," I said through clenched teeth. "The last thing I want to do is hurt you, but I will if you make me. All I want is for you to take me to this theatre. If your story checks out, you're free to go." With my free hand I reached into my pocket and pulled out my billfold. I held it in front of her eyes, and shoved it into the breast pocket of her denim jacket. "Do we understand each other?"

She stopped struggling, and her hand went to the new bulge in her pocket. I have no idea how much I stuffed in there, two or three grand perhaps. Considering what I was going to make on this job alone, I could afford it. And it's not like she didn't need the money. Strippers, especially those with a coke habit, were always short on cash.

She settled appreciably. "Okay. Okay, I'm with you. I'll show you the theatre, then I'm gone. That's the deal, right?"

"Get me inside the theatre, *then* you're gone. *That's* the deal."

She frowned but said nothing. A moment later, we were making our way up Broadway.

****

The Olympic Theatre had seen better days, I could tell that much from half a block away. Unlike the glittery theatres we passed as we made our way up Broadway, the Olympic was dark and shuttered. Its marquee sign looked as if it had last been lit around the time LBJ was in the White House. Letters that might have been red at one time hung on the marquee like dead, pink bugs on a windshield. CL S D it proclaimed. The display windows on either side of the pair of double doors at the front contained posters so faded as to be all but illegible. I wasn't certain, but I thought I could make out the name of Rosemary Clooney, and I whistled through my teeth. Could this place really have been sitting there abandoned for that long? In the middle of the theatre district? It didn't seem plausible.

The sun had disappeared behind taller buildings to the west. It was still daylight on one of the busiest streets in the world, but the shadows had lengthened. People walked past us and never looked in our direction. We were holding hands, something I had suggested which Sapphire had gone along with. We wouldn't look like a couple, unless someone took a glance at us and figured me for a millionaire (which I am), and her for a gold-digger (which she may have been, for all I know). But I didn't look the part. At best, we probably appeared like a father and daughter walking along the Great White Way. And that's me being generous to myself. I am nearly old enough to be her grandfather.

"This is it," Sapphire said. "This is the place."

216

"Uh huh." I tried the first set of double doors, then the second. All locked, hardly surprising. I walked around to the end of the building and looked down the narrow alley. Old boxes and all sorts of garbage had accumulated there, but my eyes went to the two side entrances. I wondered if Rosemary Clooney had used these to escape from the theatre undetected by her adoring public. "This way." I headed down the alley, Sapphire in tow.

The first door was locked. I looked at the dirt and grime that had settled in front of the door, and saw no footprints. A light sconce still bolted to the building above the door held an ancient light bulb I guessed hadn't worked in decades. I tried this door for the hell of it, and found it locked.

The second door proved more interesting. There was a new padlock threaded through the steel arm. It told me all I wanted to know. I looked back toward Broadway. Foot traffic continued to pass by the alley in both directions, worker bees on their way home from their various hives. No one even glanced in our direction.

The lock was solid but hardly an obstacle. I could have smashed it open with one of my nines, but the noise might have attracted some attention from the street. Instead I used my lock picks. It took less than a minute and the new padlock was on the alley floor. I wrapped my fingers around the handle and it turned easily for me.

You can tell a lot about someone by looking at how they defend the ole homestead. A single padlock was all that stood between these guys and the outside world. It told me they were overconfident, too sure of themselves and their superiority. Sometimes, such people needed a lesson in humility. I was willing to provide them with one, but it wasn't something they would be able to put to use when the lesson ended. It happens like that sometimes.

I considered waiting for dark. If these guys fancied themselves vampires, they would probably be asleep or at least not very active until later. It would ruin one of the more positive aspects of my job. I liked watching their expressions change after I put a bullet in them. Everyone, from professional to civilian, always got the same look on their face as they realized their life was over. Some of them even pleaded, which made no sense. Why would you plead for mercy *after* you've been shot? And from the man who shot you, no less. In their last moments, people were seldom logical. Ultimately, I decided to go in right then and there. If I caught most or all of them asleep, that would be fine. It was at least fifteen to one against me, after all.

I pulled the door open and looked inside. Dark, but some light spilled in from the alley. There was a wide open space on the other side of the door. Piles of boxes were everywhere, and I saw more than a few rats scurry for cover from the unexpected intrusion. I was thankful Sapphire hadn't looked inside yet; if she saw a rat and screamed, my job would be that much more difficult. I looked back at her, took her hand again, and stepped inside.

It smelled old. It's a tough smell to describe, but I'm sure you know what I'm talking about. It was the kind of smell that took a very long time to generate, and once it was there, it took twice as long to get rid of it. Sapphire stepped through the door behind me, and immediately put a hand over her mouth. I couldn't blame her; I'd been to places less pleasant than the Olympic Theatre, but not many.

The sound of our footfalls died at the source, and I noted this approvingly. Whatever covered the floor deadened any sound of footsteps. It made sneaking up on someone so much easier, although I was aware the reverse was true, as well. I kept my eyes and my ears open. The rats made no further appearances, a fact for which I was grateful. I had Sapphire's hand in my own, and my other rested on the butt of one of my nines. Just in case.

"Mister, please let me go."

Her voice was barely a whisper, so at least she had sense enough for that. But that she had spoken at all irritated me. I looked back at her and glared. Her face fell but her feet kept moving. She got the message.

There was a door, slightly ajar, at the other end of the room. I gripped the butt of the nine a little tighter and made my way to it. I peeked through the crack and saw two men seated in chairs, one on either side of the door. One was clearly asleep; his chest rose and fell in quiet rhythm. The second was throwing pebbles at an empty can a few feet away. BROADWAY VAMPIRES read the patch on each man's shoulder.

I turned back to Sapphire, held a finger to my lips, and locked eyes with her until she nodded her understanding. I let go of her hand and reached into my pocket. I pulled out the coiled piano wire which had served me well so many times. I spooled out the whole thing, wrapped it around my hands and tugged on it, once. Then I reached through the door with both hands.

I had the wire double-wrapped around the man's throat before he knew I was there. He gasped, or tried to, and reached back with both hands. I ignored his blows, which were weak and off-target. The chair tipped back but I wedged my leg against it to keep it from falling over. In his desperation, he reached out for his sleeping companion. I twisted my upper body and pulled him away from the man. His eyes rolled back into his head, his arms stopped flailing and dropped to his side. I released the wire, and caught him before he could hit the floor. I reached out and put a hand on his neck. No pulse. One down, half a million in the bank.

I stepped through the door and stood in front of the sleeping man. Oblivious, probably dreaming of the women he would rape or kill when he woke up. If he proved helpful, perhaps I'd allow him a look at Sapphire before I killed him.

I took my nine and placed it in his mouth. He woke up right away. His eyes went wide, and he reached for the gun in his mouth. I froze him by pulling back the hammer. His breathing had quickened, and sweat beaded on his forehead. It was almost comical. I leaned in close to him, so our noses almost touched. "How many?"

His eyes went to either side. I'd seen this enough to know he was looking for a way out. I gave him a moment to realize there was none before I pulled the gun from his mouth and centered it in front of his face. "I won't ask again."

"F-fifteen…No, wait, sixteen. *Sixteen!*" His voice was an excited whisper. Clearly, he was no stranger to having a gun on him. Just as clearly, he recognized the futility of shouting for help. It's like that with predators, sometimes. Like they go through life expecting to one day meet someone bigger and meaner than themselves. For the Broadway Vampires, this was the day.

"Get up," I whispered. He got to his feet slowly, keeping his hands up. His eyes never left the gun. "Show me."

He said nothing, but he began to walk, very slowly, toward the other side of the room. Another door, this one closed, awaited us. I turned and looked back at the door I had come through. Sapphire stood in the doorframe, a silhouette from a forties gangster flick. "You can go," I whispered. She nodded and disappeared from the door. I could hear her retreat, but just barely. She was most assuredly running, probably at full speed, but that floor deadened the sound. I returned my attention to the man in front of me.

He paused at the door, and turned his head slightly. I stayed well enough behind him that he couldn't see me. "They're here," he said. He wasn't stupid, so kept his voice low.

"Open the door."

He pulled the door open slowly and peeked inside. Flickering light spilled into the room through the crack, light which could only have come from a fire. I caught a faint whiff of smoke, and decided it made sense. The theatre was officially closed down. How else would they be able to see? It's not like they could call ConEd and have the power turned back on.

"Look out!" he screamed, and dove for the door.

I didn't think, simply fired two shots from the nine. Both slugs caught him in the back and propelled him forward with a bit more force than his legs were capable of producing. He crashed into the door, and it flew wide open. He landed in a heap on the floor and stopped moving.

I pulled the second nine millimeter from its holster and jumped through the door. I was in the main theatre. The old stage stood directly in front of me, and rows of ancient seats stretched back an impossible distance. The room was mostly lost in darkness, but there were several ash cans placed around the room, and all sent flames and smoke toward the ceiling. I coughed at the unexpected assault on my lungs, and scanned the room.

Guys in black leather jackets, too many to count at a glance, hollered and jumped behind seats and pulled weapons. Two such men were on my right. They were caught in the open, stunned into inaction. They looked at me with gaping eyes. I fired the twin nines, the sound like thunder in the acoustics-friendly room. Both men backpedaled and went down.

I dove to the floor and rolled until I reached the closest row of seats. They stunk of old farts and age. I put my right arm on the top of the seatback, and a plume of dust billowed out. I swung the nine slowly, seeking the next target. Several muzzle flashes came from various points around the room, and the sound of the gunfire was especially loud. None of the shots came close to me. They were panicked, firing blind. They weren't used to being challenged in their own home, and it threw them off their game.

I dropped a fourth man, then a fifth in quick order. One of them was panicked enough that he ran for the stage. He fired his weapon dry before he reached it, and went on pulling the trigger right up to the moment I put him down. The others continued to fire away, and I paused long enough to watch them for a moment. They were in full panic mode, firing in all directions and throwing away bullets like they were old ticket stubs. Jackets rained down on the decaying carpet and wood floor and made a tinkling sound. I almost felt sorry for the assholes.

I took aim again, and dropped two more. One of them twitched and fired several shots into the floor before he fell.

That was when someone got lucky and a slug buried itself into the seat in front of me. Old padding flew up from the seat cushion, and something hard and tiny found its way into my left eye. I dropped to the floor and tried to blink the thing out, but it was in there good and deep.   I crawled to the next aisle and sat with my back to the rest of the room.

The Broadway Vampires continued to fire away, hitting everything but me. Light sconces flew off the walls, explosions of stuffing plumed up from seats, even the old piano on the stage took one. *How did these morons survive on the streets so long?* I wondered.

One of them stepped cautiously into the aisle and saw me. He shouted something unintelligible and leveled his weapon at me. He got off one shot, then his gun went empty. He took his eyes off me and looked at it, as if wondering how it could have betrayed him. I gave him two in the chest and one in the head. Unfortunately for me, the others now knew precisely where I was. Bullets chewed up everything around me, and I crawled forward, half-blind. It snowed dust and bits of cushion on me, and it must have been one hell of a sight.

I counted nine dead, including the two men in the first room. That meant seven more still out there, at least. I had no idea if that included Schreck or not. I would certainly try to take him alive, but only if I could do so safely. Assuming, of course, I hadn't already put him down.

I reached the front row of the auditorium. The left side of the stage was dead ahead. A short set of stairs directly in front of me led to the stage, and I eyed the old curtains hungrily. *Good cover*, I thought. They had ceased fire, probably waiting for me to reveal myself. I sprung up and fired both nines while I flew up the stairs and dove behind the curtain.

I slid across the stage, and my momentum carried me much farther than it should have. I stopped only a few feet shy of the piano, fully exposed to the gangbangers in the auditorium. I swore and rolled for the piano. It was old, decayed, and probably wouldn't last more than a minute or two, but it was my only chance. I got behind it and bullets bit into the stage around me. Tiny pieces of wood flew in all directions.

I swung up the nines, and one nearly flew from my hand. I maintained my grip on it, but only just. I looked at my hand, and saw it was covered with blood. There was no pain, no sensation of having caught a stray. I noticed my jacket sleeve was dripping with the stuff, and I looked at the stage. A wide streak of gore led from behind the curtain right to me. *That's why I slid so far*. There must have been a pool of that shit on the stage and I hadn't seen it. But whose blood? I hadn't nailed anyone on the stage. Not yet, anyway. Immaculata's? No, too long ago. Another victim's? Now we're getting somewhere. Fuckers probably killed her (I was positive it was indeed a female) onstage, maybe after acting out some scene from a play. Or a horror movie.

The piano sounded a recital written by a madman as the gangbangers emptied their clips into it. Wood and piano keys rained down on me, and one side of the thing collapsed. I took a breath, waited for the gunfire to end. In truth, in took only a few moments more, but it felt like hours as my only source of cover was rapidly chipped away.

"Check it, Gibby, we'll cover you," I heard one of them say. Gibby uttered a sound that showed he was less than enthusiastic about his new assignment. But since the order wasn't repeated, he must have agreed. I took a moment to try to clear my left eye, but whatever was in there had no intention of leaving. It hurt like a motherfucker every time I tried to open that eye, so I clenched it shut and hoped my tears would wash it out. I was in a tough enough spot without being half-blinded.

Gibby's footsteps ascended the stairs, but slowly. I had to turn my whole head since the stairs were on my left. My field of vision was still obscured, but it was better than turning my whole body around and making enough noise for them to know I hadn't assumed room temperature yet. I held both nines close to my chest but aimed them as best I could at where I thought the stairs were located. First one foot, then its twin reached the stage. Gibby held his position a moment, obviously looking for any sign of me. I didn't think he'd be able to see me from that angle, and I was correct. He took a few steps to his left, walking a straight line from the stairs, and came directly into my field of vision.

Gibby yelped and brought up the barrel of a shotgun. I fired both nines, but my aim was off. The shots went wide of the target and disappeared into the darkness beyond the stage. The gun in my right hand went dry, so I dropped it into my lap and put both hands on the other. Gibby got off a shot, and the part of the piano between us disappeared in an explosion of rotted wood. I shielded my eyes, leveled the nine, and fired three shots. The first missed, but the second and third took up residence in Gibby's chest. His arms flew up, the shotgun sailed through the air and exited stage left, and Gibby collapsed.

There were shouts from his buddies, and the air around me erupted again. I pulled my legs in close to my chest and reached into my jacket pocket. I pulled two fresh clips from inside the liner and scooped up the nines. The piano at my back ceased to resemble a musical instrument and became a thing of dead wood. Worse, several shots made it through the thing and continued on. I reloaded the nines, pulled back the slide on each, and waited again for them to run out of ammunition.

The cacophony lessened but did not end. *They finally got smart*, I thought. They were taking turns now, slowing their rate of fire so they wouldn't all run out at the same time. Worse, I had lost track of how many were left. Was Gibby the ninth or tenth Vampire I dropped? *You're getting careless, old man. You* never *lost track of your targets before.*

I got my feet under me and eyed the curtains on the right side of the stage. Ten, maybe twelve feet away. May as well have been a mile, but I had no choice. I took two steps and dove for the curtains. The gangbangers opened up with everything they had, and it was blind luck I didn't catch a slug. I fired the nines and saw one of the Vampires take one in the head. It was pure luck and I knew it. I reached the curtains and scrambled a few more feet until there was a solid wall between me and them.

They continued to fire for a few more moments before realizing they couldn't get me from there. Since this was their hangout, they would know about the wall between us. And if there was a way around it, they would know about that, too. I could hear muffled voices from the auditorium, and although I could not understand the words, I picked up on the meaning.

Heavy feet mounted the stage and made their way in my direction. I was in the shadows; behind the curtains, the ash can fires did nothing to illuminate the backstage area. An old desk that would have looked at home in JP Morgan's office was behind me. Old, but it appeared to be made of solid oak. I slid across the desktop, hunched down behind it, and aimed at the stage.

I fired at the first man I saw, and he collapsed. The man behind him fired a few shots, but the old desk absorbed them. My first shot at him missed, but my second put him down. Two more Vampires charged the stage and dove for cover. They used the remains of the piano, and the bodies of their friends as cover. More gunfire chewed into the desk, but the old thing held.

I tried again to clear my left eye, and succeeded in making it worse. This was going to require the services of Doctor Hogun. I kept him on retainer. His fee was somewhat steep, but he knew about discretion. And besides, I rarely had to call on him. As I blinked the pain away, I noticed for the first time the rope tied off to a wall fixture next to me. I followed the rope up into darkness, and my good eye contin-ued to trace what I hoped was its path. A lighting fixture above the stage, and almost directly over two of the vampires. I hate clichés as much as the next man, but my eye was killing me and I was already sick of these assholes.

The knot in the rope had been there for so long it re-fused to budge. I put the barrel of a nine against it and fired. The rope shot straight up into the air, and left a plume of dust behind it. It also took with it a good patch of skin from my palm. Blood welled up and it stung like hell. I ignored it.

The rope had, indeed, been connected to the lighting fixture. It crashed to the stage with a tremendous noise I hadn't expected. It crushed one man completely, but the second had been on its outer edge. He was pinned, but not dead, and I didn't have a decent angle on him. He cried for help, but his buddies weren't buying.

"Fuck this, Cisco, I'm outta here!"

The voice had come, not from the stage, but from the area in front of it, I was certain.

"Get back here you piece of shit!" another voice said, the same voice which had ordered Gibby to his death. "We got him now. He's pinned, for Christ's sake!" Then, a moment later, "You fucking coward!"

I heard no more voices, save for the trapped man on the stage crying weakly for help. Cisco, it seemed, was alone. I checked my nines; more than enough ammo for two more guys. I got up from behind the desk, kept both guns level and the hammers back. I eyed the man pinned under the lighting fixture. As I had expected, he was no threat. He was nearly dead, and his gun lay on the stage a good six feet away. His eyes widened when he saw me, but I paid him no mind. When I reached the edge of the curtain, I peeked around the corner.

Cisco had been waiting for me. He was in the small orchestra pit, his arms resting on the stage and his gun pointed at the curtain. He fired five or six shots, and again, it was blind luck he didn't hit me. I hit the deck and stayed there. Bullets continued to tear holes in the curtain and Cisco kept shouting something in Spanish, but I couldn't make out any words over the sound of the gunfire. I remained where I was until I heard the dry click that told me he was out of ammunition.

I stood up, straightened my jacket, and walked calmly out from behind the curtain. I eyed Cisco, who was frantically trying to drop the spent clip from the weapon. I kept my gait casual, like a man strolling through a park. I didn't look at the man trapped under the lighting fixture when I put a bullet into his skull. I kept my eye on Cisco.

He had taken a step back from the stage, exposing more of his body. The clip dropped from the gun and he fumbled for a second. I raised one of the nines and put a bullet into his shoulder. He spun in place, dropped the weapon, and sank to his knees. I walked to the edge of the stage, sat down, and dangled my legs into the orchestra pit.

"How's it goin', Cisco?" My tone was so conversational even I could almost believe I wasn't about to kill the piece of shit.

"Fuck you, man!" He spat at me and missed.

"Indeed." I stayed like that, like a man dipping his feet into a pool, and looked at Cisco.

"Why, man? What the fuck did we do to you?" He was trying to reason his way out of it. I'd seen this type of thing before, all too often. It didn't surprise me one bit.

"Three weeks ago. You and your boys killed a stripper." I shook my head slowly. "That might not have been the dumbest thing you've ever done, but I'm betting it's pretty close." I leaned forward a little. "Am I right?"

"Go fuck yourself!"

I put a bullet into his other shoulder and waited for the screams to stop. He was breathing heavy, and his eyes were alive with hatred. Had his eyes been capable of firing on me, I'd be Swiss cheese. His arms hung useless at his side. Cisco had murdered his last stripper.

"You're alive for one reason and one reason only, Cisco. Tell me where I can find Schreck."

Cisco spat again, this time on the floor of the pit. "I ain't tellin' you jack shit."

"Very well." I put the next bullet directly through his forehead. Cisco looked at me incredulously for a moment. He went down face-first and stopped moving.

I scanned the room with my good eye, but I already knew I was alone among the living. If any of the gangbangers had been in any condition to fight, they would have taken their shot while I was sitting on the edge of the stage. I looked at Cisco's body while I released the spent clip from the nine in my right hand. Time to count the bodies and see if Gugliotti still owed me anything beyond his deposit.

****

I had counted five when the clapping started. Lucky for me I was in a row of seats. I dropped to one knee and pulled the nines again. The damn acoustics of the room made it nearly impossible to tell where the clapping was coming from. It was one guy, of that I was certain. *Must be Schreck. Why is he applauding the slaughter of his gang?* My good eye moved over every row of seats and came up empty. I looked back at the stage, but other than the dead Vampires there was no one there. The clapping stopped and the mystery man whistled his applause. Then the clapping resumed. "Bravo! Bravo!" he said in a deep baritone.

My gaze darted to the balcony. It was shrouded in darkness; I could just barely make out the ghostly outline of some of the seats in the first two rows. *Christ, I'm a fucking amateur.* Of course *he'd go for the high ground.* I couldn't see him, but I was positive he was up there. The applause continued for another moment before the man came into view. He walked down the steps of the balcony and emerged from the darkness like he had been a physical part of it. He reached the edge of the balcony and placed his hands on the safety rail.

"I admire your form," he said in a tone that was not unfriendly. "I've been watching you since you got here." He surveyed the floor of the theatre. His eyes lingered on each corpse before he returned his gaze to me. "Well done." He smiled.

"Thank you. One tries." I stood and kept the nines trained squarely on his head. I walked into the center aisle, and toward the back of the theatre. I stopped when I felt I was at the optimum firing angle. "You Schreck?"

He bowed from the waist. "At your service."

"Not your real name, I take it. Max Schreck, the actor from *Nosferatu.* Right?"

He smiled. "Smart *and* good with a gun. Very impressive."

There wasn't a condescending note in his tone. He sounded like a teacher being impressed by a C student who just scored an A on an exam. I tightened my grip on the nines.

"I assume you employ a professional name as well? I've known assassins in my time, and they all favored an alias. May I know yours?"

"The Frenchman."

He tilted his head like a puppy. "Funny. You don't look French."

"I'm not." I raised one of the nines an inch. "Someone is very interested in meeting you. It's against my better judgment but I'm going to give you a choice. You can come with me on your own or I can wait til dark and carry your corpse out of here. Your call."

He brought a hand up and began to drum his fingers on his cheek. His eyes upturned, a cartoon picture of someone making a decision. When the drumming stopped he returned his gaze to me. "Hold on. I'll be right down."

He jumped. He brought his knees to his chest to clear the safety rail, arms straight out from his sides like a bird's wings, or a bat's. He back-flipped in midair, a somersault worthy of an Olympic medalist. I backed up a few steps, more from instinct than anything else. He landed in a crouched position no more than ten feet from me. He remained like that for a moment, and raised only his head so I could see his eyes. Yellow contact lenses. Appropriate if unexpected.

I backed up a few more steps as he straightened to his full height. No biker jacket for this guy. He wore a black trench coat, with matching leather pants and boots. His shirt was dark gray, but what drew my eye was the gold cross on a chain around his neck. It caught the light from the ash can fires and all but glowed. *So much for the vampire theme.*

"There. Now we can chat face to face."

"I'm not interested in chatting. My employer is, though. He's *very* interested. You killed his daughter." I shook my head without taking my eyes from him. "Off-hand, I'd say that was a huge mistake."

"That depends on one's point of view, no?" He took a few steps forward, but casually. I thought for a moment he was about to try for me, but nothing in his body language suggested hostility. He put a hand on the top of a seatback and trailed his fingers lazily across its surface. "I can use someone like you. You're smart, professional, non-emotional. And brave. Let's not forget about bravery. It's very underrated, especially these days." He stepped behind the first seat in the aisle and put both hands on the seatback. "What do you say?"

"I'll have to pass. Sorry. As you said, I'm a professional. Are you going to come along quietly or do I have to kill you?"

He grimaced and shook his head. "That's too bad. But very well. We'll do this the hard way."

As soon as he said it I opened fire. The bullets destroyed the seat in front of him. A blizzard of dust and stuffing erupted and blocked my view of him, so I never saw him drop. I took a few steps forward, nines pointed in case there was still some life left in the asshole.

He was gone. There was nothing on the floor behind the tattered seat, and no body in the aisle, either. I looked up and in every direction. He was seated on the edge of the stage, precisely where I had been when I killed Cisco. He sat with his arms folded across his chest and a smile on his face.

"Nice trick," I said, and fired again.

He leaped up, straight up, and moved so quickly for the side of the stage I lost sight of him. I fired the nines empty at where I thought he would be, but I hit nothing. I dropped the two empty clips and inserted new ones. My last ones. Twenty-two bullets. More than enough.

Something big shot past me so fast all I saw was a blur. Even that didn't register until after the pain hit me. My feet left the ground and I sailed maybe fifteen feet through the air. I bounced off a seat and landed awkwardly in the center aisle. My right side felt like it was on fire, and for a moment I thought perhaps I had landed in one of the ash cans. But no, I rolled onto my back and felt something warm and wet on the right side of my torso. My left hand went there and came back bloody. I rolled onto my left side and took a look. My shirt and jacket were torn, and so was my skin, nearly to my ribs.

Blood flowed freely from five slash marks that began just below my pectoral and continued diagonally around to my back.

I grunted and tried to get up. I had to use the seat just to get to my knees, and it was then I realized I had lost my nines. I searched frantically for them, and became aware of the laughter which echoed from all around me.

"You should have accepted my offer, Frenchman," Schreck said. His voice was lyrical, happy. It seemed to come from all around me. "You've left me little choice, I'm afraid."

I tried to stand, but I couldn't get my legs to work properly. My right side hurt like hell, and it occurred to me there was almost certainly some muscle damage there. My right arm felt dead and refused to follow any orders issued by my brain. I crawled away, down the center aisle and toward the spot where I had been struck. My guns had to be there somewhere. The sooner I found them, the better I'd feel.

I pulled myself along the ancient and worn carpet using only my knees and my left arm. I was moving in slow motion, and the blood leaking from my right side looked like a rapidly flowing river of red. It was the single most disconcerting moment of my life.

One of my nines was on the floor, perhaps fifteen feet away. It had flown from my hand and landed at the base of an aisle seat. I picked up the pace, or tried to; frankly, my head was getting fuzzy by then and I can't say with certainty I increased my pace in the slightest.

"I have to say, I admire your don't-quit attitude," Schreck said. I looked up and saw him sitting atop the seat-back, his feet planted on the armrests. My nine rested on the floor no more than two feet below his boots. "It's wasted, of course, but still, quite admirable."

He hopped down and stood in front of me, above me. If I'd had any doubts about what had hit me, a look at his right hand got rid of them. His fingernails were impossibly long. Blood still dripped from them and hit the carpet in front of me. I put my head down, a combination of weakness and frustration. "I don't know if your attempt to retrieve your weapon is bravery or stupidity. But I'm in a generous mood, so let's call it bravery. What do you say?"

I felt his hand on the back of my jacket, up high, close to my neck. He pulled me up, lifted me high enough that I looked down at him. My feet scissored the empty air. My left hand clamped down on his arm and I was surprised at how much strength I was able to muster. He pulled me in, just a few inches, and looked straight into my good eye. I was close enough to see the yellow in his eyes was not the result of colored contacts. His lips pulled back from his teeth, and as I watched, his canines elongated. When they stopped their expansion, they must have been three inches long. If that doesn't sound long to you, you haven't seen what I've seen.

The good humor was gone from his eyes; he was in full predator mode. I'd seen that look before, but this was the first time it ever frightened me. I tightened my grip on his arm, but if he noticed, he gave no indication. He tilted his head again, but there was no puppy quality to the gesture this time. This time it was all business, an entomologist studying a new species of insect.

"I have good news and bad news," he said. His tone was still light, almost jovial. "The bad news is you've seen the sun for the last time. The good news? Well, you're about to discover that for yourself."

My eye went to the cross, which still dangled from its chain around his neck. I took my hand off his arm and batted at it. It bounced away more than once, but I managed to get a grip on it. I held it up to his eyes.

He laughed. "Oh, Frenchman, you are *priceless*!" He laughed again, a full-belly laugh that did nothing for my confidence. He wiped tears from his eyes with his free hand. "Religious symbols don't work unless the bearer believes. That's why I can wear the thing. I don't believe in that bullshit. Looks like you don't, either."

He laughed again. When he finished laughing, he pulled me in too fast for me to do anything. I was aware of the blinding pain in my neck. After that, I wasn't aware of anything.

****

As much as the job went tits-up it was nothing compared to the dreams I had afterwards. No, that's not quite right. *Dreams* might not be the correct term. *Visions* comes closer, although I'm not certain that's accurate, either.

First, dehydration. It builds slowly until it reaches a crescendo and I'm ready to drink my own piss if necessary. Anything, as long as I can get some fluids in me. So thirsty I feel I will die. But I don't. I'm in a desert and there's simply nothing to see for miles in any direction. I don't even see a mirage to get my hopes up. Just me and endless miles of sand. And, of course, the goddamned sun beating down on me like the hammer of Thor.

Then, drowning. I gulp down water against my will. It's salty as hell, so clearly I'm in the middle of the ocean. I try to close my mouth but for some reason I can't. The water finds its way down my throat and into my belly and I am powerless to stop it.

The sudden and unexplained shift in setting and situation is what tells me these are dreams or visions or whatever you want to call them.

Years later, I get curious enough to do some research online. I find that the visions, for lack of a better word, comprised my mind's attempt to interpret actions that it could not handle. It created an illusion to mask a truth that would have driven me insane at the time. Funny thing, the human mind.

They also tell me I'm still alive. Dead men don't go through this shit. So Schreck didn't finish the job, after all. That was the first mistake he'd made since I first saw him. As I started to come to I had a single thought in my head: Recover my nines, place them on opposite sides of Schreck's head, and pull the triggers until they go dry. After that I'd find something to drive straight through his chest. If he fancied himself a vampire I'd treat him like one.

This *was* a dream but it was a happy one. I bet I even smiled in my sleep.

****

I woke up in a dark room with no windows. It was small, and aside from a pile of garbage in the corner, it was empty. I was naked, and the old rotted timbers of the floor were cold to the touch. There was a single wooden door across from me, and I calculated the odds of finding it unlocked. *Sucker's bet*, I thought. I crawled across the floor to the garbage pile, intent on finding something I could use to cover myself, at least until I could get out of the room and find my clothes. As it turned out, it wasn't a pile of garbage, after all. Or maybe it was. Depends on your point of view, I guess.

The body belonged to one of the Broadway Vampires. The patch on the jacket told me that much. His eyes stared vacantly at the ceiling. Blood had trickled from the corners of his mouth and stained his teeth and beard. His throat was ripped apart. I had a feeling if there was any light in the room, I'd be able to see clear through to his spine. I imagined this was how Immaculata Gugliotti had appeared when her body was discovered.

The guy was almost twice my size, so his leather pants weren't much use to me. I took the jacket from the body, and considered the shirt before rejecting the idea. It was saturated with blood, and who knew what diseases this asshole had had. I slipped on the jacket and felt better. I put my foot up against the bottom of his boots, and saw his feet were three, maybe four sizes too big. Great. *Of all the assholes to find in here, I get stuck with a colossus.*

The fight with Schreck came back to me all at once. My hands flew to my right side, and although I couldn't see, I felt the scars from Schreck's nails on my skin. Healed, almost completely. *How long have I been down here?* I was no doctor, but I knew those gashes had been deep and wide enough to require stitches. I didn't feel any thread or even a sign that I had received medical attention.

It occurred to me my left eye was pain-free. I touched the area gently with a finger, ready to pull back at the slightest sensation of pain. Whatever had found its way inside my eye was gone. I decided to be thankful for small blessings.

The door opened and a blast of light hit me. I backed away, threw a hand in front of my eyes and squinted. A man stood silhouetted in the doorway, and it didn't take my amazing powers of observation to know who it was. "Schreck."

"Indeed." He stepped into the room enough for me to get a decent look at him. He stood with his hands behind his back, at parade rest. He smiled at me. "How are you feeling today?"

"Fuck you," I said. But I backed up nearly to the wall when I said it.

"That's not very nice. I came down here for no other reason than to check on your well-being. And all I get is 'fuck you'?" He shook his head in mock-sadness. "You really are quite ill-mannered, aren't you?"

"What do you want with me?" I didn't say the words so much as I spat them. They hung in the air like dead things.

He ignored me and walked (*strolled*) to the corner where the dead body lay stripped of its leather jacket. He stood next to the body, looked down on it, and shook his head slowly. "Blonsky," he said. His voice was neutral. "He's the one who ran when you were on your rampage in the main theatre. He chose the better part of valor. Took me two days to track him down." He turned his head slightly in my direction. "I knew you wouldn't let me down. Welcome to the club."

"What the hell are you talking about?"

He held his hand out in the direction of the body. "You, you don't think *I* killed him, do you? Oh no, no, no. All I did was bring him here. Alive. To you. Then I locked the door and walked away." He turned his head the rest of the way and looked me square in the eyes. "You did this."

"Fuck I did." My hands clenched into fists without my knowledge. "I *would* have killed him, but the chickenshit ran away. Besides, if I killed the asshole, I think I'd remember."

"No one remembers their first," Schreck said. "You're so lost in the thirst your mind shuts down. You do what comes naturally, with no conscious thought or memory. It's been a long time since I went through it, but I do recall the sensation of dying of thirst, followed by the absolute certainty I was about to drown." He searched my eyes for confirmation, and nodded at what he saw. "See? Told you."

I put my back to the wall and shook my head until I nearly fell over. "No. No fucking way."

"I'm afraid so. How do you feel?"

My head was spinning. The room, already dark, threatened to go darker. I sucked in air like it was on sale. My heart thundered in my ears. My heart—

"I'm not a vampire," I said triumphantly. Suddenly, nothing in the world seemed as important as proving him wrong. The sense of triumph pulled me back into the world and slowed my breathing. "My heart's beating. Everyone knows vampires are undead. They have no heartbeat." I suppressed the urge to add a *Ha ha!* at the end of my exclamation.

"Stoker didn't get everything right," Schreck said. He turned and walked back to the door. "I have something for you. A present. Took me four days to find it. But I think you'll like it." He disappeared beyond the door but came back into the room a moment later. There was a sack over his shoulder, and I have seen enough body bags to recognize one when I see it. "Here." He dumped it on the floor, and I heard the muffled cry from inside the bag. "For you. Enjoy." He walked out the door and closed it behind him. I heard the lock engage from the other side, and his footsteps recede into the distance.

I looked at the bag, which had begun to writhe on the floor. The person inside was clearly trying to escape. I saw the knot tied into the top of the bag and knew he had no chance. I walked to the bag and regarded it. Whoever was in there was certainly not a friend of Schreck's, which made him a friend of mine. I untied the knot.

Sapphire spilled out of the bag and gulped air. I jumped back, surprised. She was, frankly, the last person I expected to see. She freed her arms and slid and kicked the bag until she was free of it. She backed away on all fours until she reached the far corner of the room. She was panting, crying, and rubbing her arms and body as if trying to clean herself. I could relate.

"Sapphire," I said, and took a step toward her.

She shrieked and crawled even more into the corner. With the door closed, the room was once again in darkness. Curiously, I found I could still see as if the door were open. With Sapphire, this was clearly not the case. She held her arms out, fingers splayed and probing. Her eyes were wide, the widest I'd ever seen. But she could see nothing.

"Sapphire, it's me. Immaculata's friend. Are you okay?"

She screamed again at the sound of my voice, and her arms crisscrossed in front of her. "Wh-where are you?"

"About ten feet in front of you. I'm going to come to you. *Don't* scream. We're alone in here."

I crossed the room and reached for her. My hand found one of hers and she screamed again. "It's me, it's me.

Calm down. You're okay." She whimpered but was able to stifle another scream. I was thankful for that; she was making my head hurt. I sat next to her, and my bare ass felt the rough wood of the floor. I took her hand and sandwiched it between mine. "It's okay, it's okay. I'm here."

"It's not okay," she said through her sobs. Tears flowed down her cheeks in a steady stream. Her breath hitched in her throat every few seconds. I could smell her blood, feel her heartbeat when I pulled her close. She trembled in my arms and I knew it was not because the room was cold.

"He *shredded* them," she said when she had regained some control. "Lenny and Mikey and Saul. He didn't just kill them. *He tore them apart!*" She dissolved into hysterics again, crying so hard I thought she might pass out. She remained conscious, and after a while, her sobs quieted down some.

"Shh, it's okay. Don't you worry, Sapphire. We're gonna get out of here. I promise." I rocked her back and forth, slowly, gently.

"Shannon," she said. "My name is Shannon. I'm not Sapphire anymore."

"That's good," I said. "That's very good."

She lifted her head from my chest and said, "What's your name?"

"Christopher," I said without thinking. It was the first time in years I had spoken my real name. It surprised me how easily it came from my lips. *Strange bedfellows, indeed.*

She lapsed into silence. A few moments later, she was sound asleep. To my utter astonishment, I joined her shortly thereafter.

****

I woke up to pain. My stomach felt as if it had been stabbed with a hot poker. Sapphire had fallen asleep with my arm around her, and I pulled that arm back and felt the pins and needles sensation of blood rushing back into the limb. I fell onto my stomach, then doubled over and wrapped my arms as tightly around my midsection as I was able. It was excruciating, and the tiny part of my mind not dealing with the (*thirst*) pain tried to recall if I had ever experienced anything like this. It came up empty.

I moaned, then screamed. Every muscle in my body contracted, and I became the world's most gifted contortionist. The blood pounded in my ears and blotted out everything else. Faintly, as if from a great distance, I heard a girl's voice. I could not understand what she was saying, but the voice was there and it wouldn't go away.

I became aware of a bright light. I mustered every ounce of control and lifted my head and opened my eyes. The door was open, and Schreck stood there. He looked at me, and I swear the son of a bitch was smiling. He said something, but it was overpowered by the pounding in my ears.

My body convulsed again, spittle flew from my lips, and I might have pissed myself. That female voice was back, and I could hear it a little better. It was calling to me and sobbing, and a dim part of my brain labeled the voice *Sapphire*. I searched my memory for an image to go along with the name, and eventually I found one.

I opened my eyes and there she was. She was still in the corner of the room, looking at me with eyes that were wide with terror. She shrieked my name, and drew her hands up to her mouth.

"Saff. Ire." I said it as if it were a foreign word I was learning to pronounce phonetically. I got one arm under me and pulled myself a few inches closer to her. The blood was still pounding in my ears, but it had subsided enough for me to hear her clearly. She was crying, screaming nonsense words. My heart ached (*the blood*) to protect her, to do anything (*THE BLOOD*) to comfort her and tell her (***THE BLOOD***) it was going to be all right.

"Yes, my brother," Schreck said from someplace behind and above me. "Take her. Take her and the pain will go away."

I was moving a bit faster now, although I still felt as if I were crossing the floor in slow motion. Sapphire cowered in the corner, terrified beyond the capacity for rational thought. Her arm shot straight out, as if to ward off an assault. Her eyes darted from me to the monster behind me. *Just a few more feet. Just a few more feet and I'll be between her and Schreck. That cocksucker isn't touching her. No way, no how.*

I reached Sapphire and put a hand on her shoulder. She screamed, and I thought for a moment she would pull away. But she didn't. She remained perfectly still. I applauded her bravery.

"Christopher," she said. Her voice was barely a whisper. Her breathing had slowed somewhat, but I could hear and feel her heart pounding in her chest. "Please, don't hurt me." Her voice was unsteady, and it pained me to think she expected me to hurt her. "Please, you don't have to listen to him."

I looked into her beautiful, big eyes, and didn't like what I saw there. They were red, pregnant with tears, and I hated the idea of her being so frightened. I hated Schreck for striking such fear into her. What kind of a monster...? I pulled myself up a bit more until we were eye to eye.

She cupped my face in her hands. "Christopher, please. Help me get out of here. I have a little boy. Who will take care of him if you do this?"

"Shh," I said, my own voice soft. I almost didn't hear it myself. "It's okay. Everything's going to be okay. We're gonna get out of here."

I pulled her close and she wrapped her arms around me and her tears returned. I nudged her chin, just a little. She obliged and I kissed her newly-exposed neck. She smelled of sweat and fear and adrenaline. I felt a tingling south of where my belt buckle would have been.

Sapphire screamed. I winced at the pain. Her mouth was only an inch or two away from my ear. That scream filled the world and drowned out everything else. I wondered what had caused her to produce such a sound. I kept right on wondering even as the first gush of her blood made its way down my throat.

****

The old fisherman's shack was about as out-of-the-way as you could get, even for upstate New York. The unpaved road which led to it had more dips and bumps than perhaps any road in the continental U.S. I thought about the man in the trunk and hoped he was enjoying the ride.

The road cut through the woods, which could more accurately be described as a forest, and the trees on either side seemed to press in on the Buick the closer we got to our destination. The moon was behind those trees somewhere, and it was full, but you wouldn't know it. Not that I needed it (or the headlights) anymore. I found I could see just fine in total darkness these days.

The road opened up into a clearing, and at the far side stood the shack. Two men sat on the meager porch and smoked. Light spilled out from the two facing windows, and I could see, quite clearly, two more figures pass in front of them. That made four, at least. I felt naked without my nines, but I suspected that feeling would fade over time. The two men on the porch stood and regarded the Buick as I approached. I put it in park a few feet short of them and killed the engine.

One of them approached the driver's side, and I saw right away it was my old buddy Fat Boy. His companion kept his distance and eyed me suspiciously; his hand rested inside his sport jacket.

Fat Boy opened my door and looked at me. "Where is he?"

"Where do you think?" I asked, and inclined my head toward the trunk.

He held out his hand. "Keys."

I obliged and dropped them into his hand. He walked around to the back of the car without another word, and I got out and stretched my legs. It had been a hell of a long ride and my muscles felt stiff. I looked at the second man, Fat Boy's buddy. Tall, a solid 220, with a scowl I knew right away never left his face. I nodded at him. He didn't nod back.

Fat Boy opened the trunk and reached inside. With much more force than was necessary, he pulled Schreck from the trunk. He stood the prisoner on his feet and surveyed the knotted rope which bound his hands behind his back. A fresh bruise discolored the right side of his face, and dried blood marked the corner of his mouth and his chin. Schreck looked at Fat Boy and smiled.

"Let's go, tough guy," Fat Boy said, and shoved Schreck toward the shack. His partner took Schreck by the arm once he had passed the car, and I fell into step behind them. We mounted the steps and paused while Fat Boy opened the door. I was the last one in, and I closed the door behind me.

Gugliotti was there, which surprised me a little. Men in his position were rarely present when scores were settled, owing to the need for an alibi. The second man in the room looked like a younger version of the boss, and could only have been his son. The last person was more than a surprise; she was a shock. A woman in her late-forties, dressed to the nines and wearing enough jewelry to sink a ship. Of them all, her stare at Schreck was the coldest. *The girl's mother*, I thought.

Fat Boy and his buddy stood behind Schreck, each with one hand on his arm. Gugliotti approached him, looked him up and down, and turned to me. "This him?"

I nodded once. "That's him."

"You murdered my daughter," Gugliotti said. His voice was level, low. Ominous. Even the old me might have been intimidated.

"You fucking piece of shit!" Mrs. Gugliotti screamed. She lunged from her chair and slammed her fist across Schreck's jaw. She pulled her hand back and clutched her wrist. I'd heard the bones snap on impact.

Her son grabbed her by the shoulders and led her to the back of the room. "It's okay, Mom, it's okay. This cocksucker is gonna get his. Don't worry about that."

Mom didn't look worried, she looked homicidal. She allowed her son to escort her back to her chair. She sat there and cradled her broken wrist and glared at Schreck. One of her rings had opened a small cut on his face, and fresh blood trickled from the wound. My stomach grumbled.

Gugliotti never took his eyes from Schreck. He held his arm out behind him. Junior reached under the decrepit sofa and withdrew a suitcase, a *large* suitcase. He lugged it across the room and placed it on the floor at my feet. "Three million," Gugliotti said, still staring at Schreck. "Plus a little extra. I trust our business is concluded?"

"It is, indeed," I said, and picked up the suitcase. The ease with which I did so drew a curious expression from Fat Boy and a startled one from Junior. I walked the suitcase to the door and placed it on the floor.

"Then your job is finished. Contract complete. You can go. We'll be in touch if we need your services again."

I folded my hands in front of me and faced the room. "I'm afraid it's not that simple."

For the first time, Gugliotti took his eyes from Schreck. "What did you say?"

I didn't repeat myself. I was too busy enjoying the confused looks I was getting from Gugliotti and the rest of his crew.

Schreck smiled. "He said it's not that simple. And he's right." Schreck turned to me. "You can have the bitch and the boy. Consider them my gift to you. The rest are mine."

"Deal," I said.

Schreck snapped the rope with effortless ease.

We went to work.

Old Ghosts

1.

Wherein the Prodigal Son Returns At Last

Scott Booker looked at the highway sign through his windshield. He had seen it hundreds of times, thousands, but that was a lifetime ago. In truth, he could have lived the rest of his life without seeing it again, or the town that spread out before him. The trees on either side of Route 6 had yet to give way to the houses on the outskirts of Deacon's Landing, but they would in another minute or two. He wondered how much the place had changed since he had last seen it. He wondered if he would even recognize those changes. The former resident had not spent the past forty-six years trying to forget about the little town by committing its layout and architecture to memory.

He eased off the gas and applied his foot gently to the brake. The rent-a-car slowed and then stopped next to the small green sign that read: *Deacon's Landing Welcomes You!* Beneath that in smaller letters: *Founded 1698.* He lowered the passenger window and leaned over and looked at the sign more closely. He hated it immediately. He would have spat on it if he had any saliva, but his mouth had gone dry. Instead, he put the Chrysler in park and opened the driver's door.

The asphalt was smooth beneath his shoes and he walked to the front of the car until he stood nearly even with the road sign. He looked at the ground. No line on the blacktop to mark the boundary of the town. No interruption to the tree line on either side of the road. The cables strung from telephone pole to telephone pole did not cease suddenly in midair.

But he could sense the invisible membrane that separated Deacon's Landing from the rest of Connecticut as well as the rest of the world.

One more step, he thought. *Just one and you'll be back home.* He scoffed at himself. This had, indeed, been his home, but that was a lifetime ago. Deacon's Landing did possess a certain resemblance to his adopted town of Wilmington, North Carolina, but it was superficial at best. The people would dress and speak differently here, and they moved at a faster pace, but he doubted he would even notice. The differences between his first home and his present one would be more subtle. Like walking into a room where the corners were not quite ninety degrees and the windows were not quite square.

He drew in a long, slow breath, held it, and released it just as slowly. He lifted his foot perhaps eighteen inches off the ground, aware of the fact he probably looked like a member of Hitler's SS, and goose-stepped across the boundary into Deacon's Landing.

Nothing happened when his foot touched the asphalt. Day did not become night, a volcano did not spontaneously rise from the ground in front of him, no commercial jetliners plunged from the sky. The breeze remained constant and cool. He lifted his other foot and gingerly placed it next to its mate. Booker took in another slow, deep breath. The air tasted no differently. He released that breath and breathed normally.

He stood and looked about. The trees that lined Route 6 continued for perhaps another two hundred yards or so before the first house intruded into his sightline. Beyond it he could see a few more houses. They appeared to be of the Cape Cod variety and in that, at least, things had remained the same. He grew up in one himself, which most likely explained his utter refusal to even entertain the idea of buying one when the time came to provide his family with a permanent roof over their heads.

He thought of Lisa and the roughly fifteen-hundred miles that now separated them from each other. It was the farthest they had been apart from one another in all their life together. In point of fact, aside from a sales conference he once attended in Atlanta, this was really the first time they had been separated by more than fifteen or twenty miles since the night they met back in the fall of '75. That was in Selkirk, New York, another three hundred miles or so north of Deacon's Landing and that much farther away from Lisa.

He had been staying with Smokescreen, who was better known as Michael Catalina to those who had not flown with him in the skies over North Vietnam. Smoke had dragged him to the town's harvest fair. There would be dancing, of which Booker was not a fan, given his utter lack of anything resembling rhythm, and beer, of which he was a huge fan. There was also the promise of many fine, unattached ladies who would be in attendance. He was a fan of that, too.

When they arrived he knew Smoke had not exaggerated about the dancing, beer or unattached ladies. The place was full of all three. The music was something of a surprise. Smoke had described it as traditional (meaning shitty) country-western. The sound that greeted their ears was more like something that was popular in San Francisco back in '68. They spied no flower children, for which he was grateful, but the music would have been to their liking. He watched with some amusement the older residents of Selkirk grumble and point disgusted fingers in the direction of the stage where hippie musicians in bellbottoms tuned in, turned on and dropped out. The younger contingent among Selkirk's citizens seemed to dig it; they danced (if it could be called that) in front of the stage and hooted and whistled at the long-haired hooligans jumping around and playing their instruments with much more volume than was necessary.

Smoke led the way to the nearest concession kiosk and bought them a couple of brews. They stood to the side and drank from their Styrofoam cups and watched the denizens of Selkirk pass in front of them. Other than the stage where the hippies played, there were some games of chance and a few animal stalls near them. The pumpkin judging contest had not started yet, but several farmers dragged their best and biggest pumpkins toward another, smaller stage. A group of kids who appeared to be of junior high age had gathered near a fenced-in area where several vintage cars from the twenties and thirties were showcased. His eyes lingered on the pre-World War II relics that made him think of his paternal grandfather's '32 Chevy sedan. The old prick managed to keep the thing in pristine condition until his health deteriorated and forced him to spend his last four years in a hospital bed.

Booker forced the image of his dying grandfather from his mind and took in more of the fair. His eyes stopped when he saw Lisa. She was young then, twenty-three, but looking more like nineteen at most. She wore cutoff jeans and a light green tank top that contrasted nicely with her dark skin and also showed off her impressive bosom. (Normally, he would have labeled them "boobage" or simply "big-ass titties" but she was far too beautiful for such terms.) Her hair was jet-black and spilled down her shoulders in a decidedly un-70s style. Her eyes were the same color and appeared larger than normal. He noticed her, not simply because of her appearance, but because she seemed to be looking him over as well.

She was with four or five other girls, none of whom even came close to her in terms of physical beauty. He looked to see the wedding ring that was surely on her finger, but that hand held a Styrofoam cup similar to his and he could not see it. He looked away eventually but only because Smoke was pointing out some of the local attractions and seemed to be a bit offended that he, Booker, was not giving them his full attention.

Someone tapped him on his shoulder and he turned and his breath caught in his throat. Lisa stood in front of him, a wry and beautiful smile on her lips. A long and elegant cigarette holder extended from between her fingers. He remembered this vividly, mostly because the prop seemed so out of place given their surroundings. It also made her appear like Audrey Hepburn in *Breakfast at Tiffany's*. She brought the cigarette holder to her lips and asked, in a soft and quite seductive tone of voice, for a light. He fumbled for the lighter in his back pocket but there was something wrong with his fingers. It took him three tries to bring out the lighter and two more before the flame came to life. She smoked beautifully, as women were allowed to back then. It would be twelve years and three kids later before both of them decided to quit for good.

The rest of that night was a blur to him. What he remembered was being unable to sleep. He stared into the darkness of Smoke's spare bedroom with images of Lisa playing on the ceiling like a movie. She had given her phone number to him and it would be two days before he got up the balls to actually dial that number.

Their first official date was to the drive-in. He had to borrow Smoke's old Camaro, but at least they had a good time. Lisa could remember the movie they saw; he had forgotten completely. There were many dates to follow and when he eventually asked her to marry him, she had smiled her beautiful smile and nodded with tears in her eyes.

The wedding was small, mostly because Lisa's family had not taken to him particularly well and also because he had not invited anyone from his own family. His parents had, in fact, not heard from him since he left Deacon's Landing. Smoke was the best man over the objections of Lisa's father, who wanted one of his sons to serve in that capacity. Booker gave somewhat less than a shit what the old man wanted; he was not going to accept Booker regardless of who assumed best man duties at his daughter's wedding. They honeymooned on Martha's Vineyard and it took most of Booker's savings to do it. But they enjoyed themselves and that was all that mattered to them.

Their first child, Roger, arrived one year later. Two years after that Lisa had the twins, Lawrence and Lorraine. His job moved them from Selkirk to Wilmington in eighty-eight. They lucked out on a nice Colonial and paid off the mortgage the same month Aaron Boone broke the hearts of Red Sox Nation. It was the same year Roger and his girlfriend Amanda gave them their first grandchild. Their grandson had since been joined by two more from Roger and Amanda, as well as three girls between Lawrence and his wife and Lorraine and her husband. Lisa was retired and he figured he was two years away from his own. They planned to travel, mostly through Europe and South America. He had seen enough of Asia during his years in the Air Force.

And then he received the call. He had no idea how his cousin Steven had tracked him down, and the news he brought made Booker temporarily forget to ask. "Sorry, man. Just wanted you to know your mother passed away last night."

Booker had, in fact, assumed his mother had been dead for years. Her side of the family was notoriously short-lived. With Steven's voice droning in his ear he made some quick calculations and discovered his mother must have been eighty-nine or ninety. That was surely a record among the Clan Coolidge. Steven continued to give him information (heart attack, found by her neighbor, nothing the doctors at DLH could do for her) and then he surprised Booker by asking, "Are you going to come up for the funeral?"

Before he even realized his mouth had opened he heard himself say, "Yes, of course. I'll get a flight up tomorrow morning." He remained silent for a few more moments as he tried to discover from where that answer had come. Had he actually agreed to return to Deacon's Landing? For, of all things, his mother's funeral? He returned to the present in time for Steven's offer to pick him up at Bradley International, but Booker refused. He would rent a car and make his own way there. No, he would not stay at Steven's house. The local Holiday Inn would serve well enough. He thanked his cousin for the information and hung up the phone.

He paused to look at the half-decorated Christmas tree. It stood in front of the living room bay window. Lisa was still placing bulbs in strategic areas. Next would come the garland and, finally, the icicles. The small plastic manger set (a gift from Lisa's mother) sat beneath the tree. The stockings were not yet hung above the fireplace but they sat draped over his armchair awaiting Lisa's attention. Bing Crosby crooned on the radio and Lisa hummed along with him.

Booker took his keys from the small basket near the side door and walked outside. Then he did something he had not done in twenty-five years. He drove to Melton's Service Station and bought himself a pack of Salems. He bummed a light from a kid in the store's parking lot and sat in his Lexus and smoked. The first one tasted like total shit, but it felt good going down. He chained another one before he started the car and headed home.

He took a long, hot shower when he arrived. It was as much to hide the smell of smoke from Lisa as it was to clear his head. Afterwards he sat at the computer in his home office upstairs and booked himself a flight. By then it was no longer Bing Crosby he heard down in the living room but Burl Ives. He listened while he located a convenient flight. Then he went downstairs and told Lisa he was heading to Connecticut the following day and the reason for said trip.

She was conciliatory and supportive and offered to go with him. He turned her down and promised he would be back home by tomorrow night. She did not ask why he felt the need to return, which was fortunate because he had no answer. Lisa knew of his family history, of course, but this *was* his mother, after all. She said she would tell the kids and he nodded and went into the den to watch the Jags pound the Cowboys.

To his surprise he slept like a baby in its crib after the game ended. He awoke in plenty of time for his flight. Lisa made breakfast for him and walked him to the car. His ticket said he would return to Wilmington International at eleven and he would be back home by midnight, give or take, depending on traffic. They kissed good-bye and he put the old Colonial in his rearview.

The flight sucked, as most did. It was cold at Bradley International, and he should have expected as much. Among the many things he did not miss about the northeast was the cold weather. He was kept warm by the knowledge that he would not be there long enough to need a heavier coat. He picked up the rented Chrysler and headed south for Deacon's Landing.

Now he stood on the shoulder of the two-lane blacktop and looked down the road into his hometown. It struck him as strange to think of Deacon's Landing in such a way. Booker had long since come to think of Wilmington as his hometown. And before that, it was Selkirk he thought of as home. But not the quiet town with its stereotypical New England appearance spread out before him. *Besides,* he thought, *after forty-six years, it's not like I'll recognize anything, anyway. Even this burgh will have changed with the times. It'll be like I've never seen this place before.* "I wish," he said.

Booker got back behind the wheel of the rental. He put it in gear and headed into Deacon's Landing.

2.

Wherein Booker Breaks the House Rules

The houses gave way to the retail area of Route 6. The first thing he saw was Biello's Chevrolet. It had apparently taken the place of Biello's Pontiac and it was much larger than he remembered. He was certain there had been a house on either side of the dealership when last he saw it. Different, too, were the cars that populated the lot. The Firebirds, Bonnevilles and GTOs had been replaced by Cruzes, Equinoxes and Silverados. A giant inflatable Santa beamed happily at him, standing among that greatest of all automotive travesties, the minivan. Even the old station wagons his father favored were better than those mom mobiles in his opinion.

Past Biello's he found a few strip malls and he was pleased to see a number of mom and pop operations still clinging to life despite the ridiculously large box stores that dominated the landscape on the right side of Route 6.

He passed the old town hall and it looked precisely the same as he remembered, from the large, ornate double doors to the bronze statue of Robert James Deacon on the lawn. It was bereft of the Christmas decorations he remembered from his childhood. Three police cars were parked in front of the building, but their drivers were not in evidence. Two blocks farther south a rather large building was under construction. The sign proclaimed *The Deacon's Landing Police Dept Will Rebuild!* Several large construction vehicles had assembled around the slowly-forming brick façade and numerous men in hardhats and heavy coats moved about the area. Booker continued on his way.

His GPS guided him through the town but he found himself relying on it less and less. He activated his turn signals when he needed to even before the mechanical female voice instructed him he was approaching the turn. He was of two minds on this. His first feeling was pride in that he remembered his way despite the decades that had passed since last he saw these streets. The second was darker and more troubling. He felt he had put the town and all that happened there behind him for good. In this, apparently, he was mistaken.

He saw Baron's Funeral Home on the left and he pulled up to the curb and stopped. According to his cousin this was where his mother's wake would take place. He was positive her body was already there, possibly even lying in state in one of the viewing parlors. He sat in the rental and looked through the window at the old Victorian someone had converted into a very large and gothic funeral home.

It was perfect, really, the precise image of a New England funeral parlor. The front doors, most likely oak, were painted a warm, if somber, shade of crimson. Large windows on either side of the doors revealed nothing of the inside due to the presence of what appeared to be thick, dark green drapes. Several smaller windows on the next three levels of the façade likewise concealed the building's interior. Twin spires, almost minarets, stood guard on either side of the building. The driveway was long and disappeared behind the structure.

Booker found himself turning the steering wheel toward the driveway before he stopped himself. He would eventually make his way inside, but before he did he would drive to his old house. His cousin would probably be there. He was correct.

The old Cape Cod looked somewhat different from how he remembered it. It took him a moment to realize it was the siding. In 1968 it had been wood slats painted generic white. They had been replaced with what he took to be vinyl that someone, probably his mother, had chosen in a sickly yellow that clashed with the maple trees that dotted the yard and the side of the driveway. A green VW Passat sat parked in front of the garage, a good thirty feet from the street.

Booker parked the rental in front of the house and killed the engine. He stepped out of the car and looked again at his childhood home. His eyes were drawn to the second floor window on the left. It had been his room once, a thousand years ago. He could almost see his ten year-old self looking through that window at the world outside and waiting most impatiently for the time he could escape. He smiled then, although he would be hard pressed to explain why. Nothing about his old home, or even the whole town of Deacon's Landing, had ever made him smile, not even the few times he had thought of the place since making good his escape. It was not an environment that lent itself to smiles and happy thoughts, certainly not for him, at any rate. Yet he smiled nonetheless.

The front door opened and an old black man poked his head out. "Scotty? That you?"

Of course it was Steven, had to be. No one outside his family had ever addressed him as "Scotty". It made his smile vanish. He waved and said, "Yeah, it's me. How you doing?" He walked around the car and gave no thought to Steven's reply. By the time he reached the front door, which his cousin helpfully held open, Steven was expressing his condolences for Booker's loss. Booker nodded and stepped to the door.

He paused at the threshold. Was he truly about to enter his mother's house? He remembered, quite vividly, the last time this particular roof had been over his head. He remembered the song that was playing on the stereo in his room and the droplets of blood that stained the poster of Jim Morrison on his wall. There had been no hesitation on his part when he walked (ran) out of the house. And he had been a kid then.

He was not a kid now and the reason for his leaving was one day away from spending eternity with six feet of dirt between her and the sunlight. He ignored the gooseflesh on his arms and entered the house.

"Good to see you," Steven said. "I just wish it was under better circumstances. Christ, it's been a long time."

Booker looked about the living room. It was typical of any old person's home. The furniture looked thirty years out of date, although it was all in good shape. A long shelf high up on the wall held numerous porcelain cats in various poses. He did not remember his mother displaying any fondness for the animals, and they had had no pets while he had lived there. Perhaps she had developed a fondness for them after his father passed away.

A grandfather clock stood to his right. It *tick-tocked* a rhythm that was much slower than his own heartbeat. He glanced at it and found he had a vague memory of the thing. It had been a gift from someone, but he could not remember who. He did not think it had been positioned next to the front door, but he could be mistaken.

The fireplace was clean and looked as if it had not been used in decades, which may well have been the case. A poker-and-shovel set stood on the raised dais next to the red brick. The implements were coated with dust.

There were few photos and he could find himself in none of them. Most were old black and white portraits of his parents. One was of his father standing in front of the doors of the Foy factory, where he worked until the heart attack side-lined him and eventually killed him back in '71. The only reason he knew of the old man's death was the USAF chaplain who informed him after a mission debriefing. It was the one and only time he considered returning to Deacon's Landing, but in the end he remained In Country.

The stairs which led to the second floor were ahead and to his left. He swallowed and found he had no desire to mount those steps. He wondered, briefly, what his old room looked like before he decided he did not care. His heartbeat, already in fourth gear, beat even faster at the thought of seeing the bedrooms. No, those stairs would not be climbed by him. Not now, not ever. He swallowed.

"Scotty? You in there?"

Booker became aware of his cousin's hand on his shoulder. He pulled his eyes away from the staircase and looked at the old man in front of him. He saw concern in Steven's eyes and it made him want to smash his fist into his cousin's face. He did no such thing, of course, but the impulse remained. He tried to offer a smile but even that was beyond him. Instead he simply nodded. "Yeah. Yeah, I'm okay. Just zoned out there for a minute."

Steven's look of concern became a look of sad under-standing and it was all Booker could do not to throttle him. "Totally understandable," Steven said in a calm, measured tone. "We're never really ready for shit like this, are we?" He removed his hand from Booker's shoulder and took a few steps toward the kitchen. "My mom's eighty-nine and in a home and I know how I'll feel when she goes. It's shitty but it's a fact of life, I guess. Just sucks that it had to happen during the holidays." He nodded in the direction of the kitchen. "There's some coffee made. Want a cup?"

Booker nodded wordlessly and followed Steven into the kitchen. The table and chairs were old but in decent shape. Booker sat down while his cousin poured two cups of coffee and continued to drone on about how death takes all too soon. Booker did not agree with that particular opinion; often he felt the opposite was true. Sometimes death took its sweet fucking time getting around to some people. That, *my friend, was a fact of life.*

He looked at the cabinets and drawers and wondered which one held the wooden rolling pin his mother favored whenever she felt the need (or desire) to administer some parental discipline. He was certain it was there somewhere although he would most definitely not look for it. He had seen enough of the fucking thing during the first seventeen years of his life. The last time he had seen it, in fact, a small piece of his skin had become embedded in the grain of the wood. He wondered, too, if that was still there as well. Probably not. Mary Ellen Booker was nothing if not meticulous; it would not do for someone to see something like that while she flattened the dough for whichever bake sale in which she had agreed to participate.

Booker fished a cigarette and his lighter out of his jacket pocket. Steven placed the two cups on the kitchen table, saw Booker about to light up, and said, "Hey, man, you know your mother didn't allow smoking in the house. She couldn't stand it."

Booker nodded and lit up. He slowly and happily exhaled a cloud of smoke toward the ceiling. "You don't say."

The corners of Steven's mouth turned down. "She didn't even own an ashtray. The last time I was here, this past summer, she made Billy and Erica—that's my son and his wife—go outside in the pouring rain to smoke. That's how much she hated it."

"Well, she's not here right now, is she," Booker said, and took another satisfying puff. "So I guess I don't have to worry."

Steven's frown increased, but he said no more about it. Booker used the saucer Steven provided with the coffee as his ashtray. The two men sat at the table in silence until Booker finished his cigarette. He toyed with the idea of chaining another, just to piss off Steven, but he decided one was enough. Besides, he did not want to return home having rejoined the ranks of smokers.

When they finished their coffee, Steven said, "I told you the wake will be at Baron's, right? The place on Main a few blocks from city hall?"

Booker nodded. "Yeah. I passed it on the way here."

"And the funeral will be the next morning at Lichgate. Do you remember where that is?"

Booker nodded again. "I'm kinda surprised at how much I remember about this place. The town, I mean. I was a teenager the last time I was here, but I didn't even need the GPS to find my way around. Weird, huh?"

"Not so weird when you consider this was your home for, what, seventeen years?"

"Anyway, I won't be at the funeral." Steven opened his mouth in surprise but Booker continued. "Right after the wake I'm heading back to North Carolina. My plane leaves at nine."

Steven either did not or could not hide his surprise and disappointment. "What the hell are you talking about? Scotty, she's your *mother*, for Christ's sake. You have to go to the funeral."

"Actually, I—"

"And then there's the matter of the will. I imagine all this will be yours now. You have to be there for that."

Booker's lips compressed into a thin, dark line on his face. When he spoke, his voice had dropped an octave. "No, I don't. Listen, let's not pretend here. I haven't been back since '68 and there's a reason for that. It's the same reason I had no idea she died until you somehow tracked me down and told me. It's also the same reason I didn't bring my wife and kids up here for the funeral." He realized his hand had curled into a fist. He willed that fist to open and he flexed his fingers. "The fact is she's been dead to me since I left. The wake tonight is just a formality as far as I'm concerned." He leaned a bit closer to the table. "Understand me?"

Steven sat back in the chair. The look of surprise had turned to disgust and he made no effort to hide it. "No, I don't understand, but I guess that's your business."

"You're damned right it is." He pushed himself back from the table. He reached for the empty coffee cup and saucer-turned-ashtray but Steven held up a hand.

"I'll take care of that."

Booker nodded and made for the front door.

3.

Wherein an Old Acquaintance Says Hello
And Booker Hits the Strip Club

He made the mistake of walking past the bay window and when he did he stopped in his tracks. Outside, across the street, sat what looked to be an old muscle car. He could hear the throaty growl of the idling engine through the window. He could not identify the make or model, only the bright yellow paint job. For no reason he could pin down, his hand shook as it moved to the funeral shroud curtain and drew it back.

The car was a '65 Pontiac Tempest. The windows were tinted too dark for Booker to see the driver. Whoever was behind the wheel must have seen him, however, for as soon as Booker got his first good look at it the driver hit the gas pedal and the growl became a roar. The car rocked on its suspension as the V8 under the hood strained to be let loose.

The sudden increase in volume made Booker pull his hand back from the curtain. He took an involuntary step away from the window.

The Tempest's driver gunned the engine a few more times before he popped the clutch and the car surged forward. It picked up speed rapidly and was down the street and out of sight a few seconds later.

Booker stood a few feet from the window for a moment before he was able to move again. He pulled the curtain back and looked down the street. He saw no sign of the Tempest; indeed the street was deserted even of pedestrians.

He had seen a car just like that back when he still lived in this house. The owner of the car was in Booker's class at DLHS despite his being three years older than his classmates.

His name was Samuel Jacoby and he was universally recognized as bad news. The rumor was the school board had voted to graduate him despite his failing grades simply to get him the hell out of the system. Being a student was, Booker figured, the only reason Jacoby had not been drafted and sent to Nam. Booker was positive some of the teachers and school board members secretly wanted the guy shipped overseas, perhaps to meet his end at the hands of the Vietcong or his fellow GIs. It was Booker's secret wish as well. Jacoby was consistently in trouble with both the school administration and the police department. It was whispered a town-wide celebration would ensue should Jacoby be drafted. Booker and his friends would certainly celebrate such a wonderful bit of news.

But Samuel Jacoby never got to graduate. He and his Tempest were removed from the mortal plane at the same moment, a moment witnessed by young Scotty Booker. It was something to which he had given no thought since his deployment to Nam. Of course, that could not have been Jacoby's Tempest. The rational part of his mind knew that. Unfortunately it was having a difficult time convincing the rest of his mind that it was correct. It was the bright yellow custom paint, unavailable from GM in '65, or any other year, that stuck with him.

He became aware of the sweat on his brow. He wiped his sleeve across his forehead and it came away wet. His breathing was fast, much faster than it should have been. He closed his eyes and willed himself to calm down. When he felt he was once more in control he opened his eyes and looked outside again. The street remained deserted. "Get a grip, old man," he said.

"Did you say something, Scott?" Steven asked from the kitchen. Booker heard the sound of the tap running and pictured his cousin washing away all traces of their conversation.

"Just that I'll see you at the wake."

"Yeah, I'll see ya there."

Booker opened the front door and checked the street again. Empty, except for his rental. He walked to it. Once he was down the street he felt a little better. He lit up a cigarette (a direct violation of the rental agreement) and he felt better still. But what he really wanted, *needed*, was a drink. He wondered if any of the bars were open yet.

He kept a lookout for the yellow Tempest, but it did not make another appearance. He glanced at every car he passed, looked into every parking lot, but it was not in evidence. Despite the rational part of his mind he kept looking.

The mall, big and ugly and built sometime after he had made his great escape from Deacon's Landing, had a few restaurants. He drove through the parking lot and stopped in front of a Ruby Tuesday's but he opted against it. The last thing he wanted was to be in a family environment. He needed to get his drink on and he would feel better if he did not have to be surrounded by mothers with their small children. He needed something more adult.

Spotting a sign for Lucky's Gentlemen's Club, he thought that would work just fine. Booker pulled into the parking lot and turned off the engine. Inside the door was a rather large gentleman who asked for the five dollar cover. Booker had little interest in partaking of the club's primary reason for being, but he paid the cover without comment.

The club was small, dark and smelled of spilled alcohol and stale tobacco. Despite the statewide indoor smoking ban several patrons puffed away. Booker had no problem with that. Christmas lights hung from various places along the walls and a plastic, grime-covered Santa stood on one of the shelves behind the bar. He took a seat at the bar and ordered a whiskey from another large gentleman, this one with a dirty dishtowel slung over his shoulder.

He lit a cigarette and downed his whiskey and asked for another. The DJ introduced, for their viewing pleasure, Autumn. Booker glanced over his shoulder and saw a young, pretty blonde girl take the stage. Her outfit was nearly non-existent, although the Santa hat was a nice touch. *Because nothing says "Merry Christmas" like a young girl shaking her tits in your face.* Several men seated along the stage hooted and hollered and Autumn launched herself into her act. Booker returned his attention to his whiskey.

He was not alone at the bar, but he was the only one not turned toward the stage. He could live with that. The bartender, whom someone called Max, filled his glass again. Booker could feel the alcohol burn its way down his throat and settle in his stomach. He could have one more, perhaps two, before he would have to stop. The last thing he wanted was to be caught driving drunk. How could he explain that to Lisa? And when she asked why he was drunk, and she would, what could he tell her?

I'm sorry, honey, but I saw a car that was probably compacted forty-six years ago and since turned into paperclips. It was sitting outside my mother's house waiting for me. More accurately, its driver was. And he's been in the ground since 1968. If that's not a reason to down a few, I don't know what is.

Of course he could not say that. But it was true nonetheless.

4.

Wherein the Lizard King Ignores Him And Jacoby Does Not

It turned out to be the last time his mother beat him. She had not used the rolling pin that time. Oh, no, that would have required her to run down to the kitchen and then back up the stairs again. She was only a week out of the hospital and she was still having a bit of trouble moving about. So she settled on using her hands that time.

He could not remember what offense he committed and it was entirely possible there had been no offense. His mother was so fucked up on painkillers and alcohol it was likely she had imagined he had done or said something out of line. It did not matter, not in the end.

He was listening to Creedence. He remembered that like it was yesterday. Yet another example of how amazing is the human brain. Like much of his childhood, he had not thought of that particular day in decades. But he remembered listening to the first track, the old Screamin' Jay Hawkins song "I Put a Spell On You" when his bedroom door flew open and his mother charged in.

His first thought was he was somehow playing the music too loud, but that could not have been the case. He managed to get out, "What did—" before her backhand caught him on the left side of his head. He tumbled off the bed and it was blind luck his head landed on the thick throw rug instead of the hardwood. He tasted blood and his eyes suddenly brimmed with tears. He got one hand on the bed and was pulling himself up when she grabbed his arm and hauled him to his feet.

She screamed at him, though he could not remember what, and hit him again. He saw a mixture of blood and spittle sail through the air and land on the wall and his poster of Jim Morrison. The Lizard King looked at him with neutral eyes and somehow that made him angry. He looked again at his mother.

His mother's brow was bathed in sweat. Her eyes were wide and furious. A thick vein stood out on her forehead and throbbed. Her lips had pulled back and she bared her teeth. She had pulled her hand back and was ready to land yet another blow and that was the moment something inside his head snapped. It was sudden and entirely unexpected. It would be hours before he was calm enough to try to figure out what had happened.

His fist shot forward and caught her arm inside the elbow. Her yes went wide. She dropped him and backpedaled, clutching her wounded right arm. Behind the anger, the rage, something else had taken up residence in her eyes. It was something he had never seen there before. He mistook it for fear at first, but it slowly dawned on him what he was seeing. It was more than disbelief, it was shock.

She stood her ground a few feet from him, still clutching her wounded appendage, and stared at him with eyes as wide as saucers. Her lips moved, but no sound escaped them.

The needle had skipped across the record when he impacted the floor and he realized he had missed the second song entirely and was listening to the musical outro of "Suzie Q." Absently, and with no idea why he was doing so, he walked to the stereo and pulled the needle from the record. He looked back to his mother.

Her hand massaged the area he had struck but the shock had left her eyes. The only emotion he saw there was rage. Her eyes were nearly red with it. Tears spilled from them and worked their way down her cheeks. She seemed not to notice.

"You…" Her mouth continued to work and it seemed she was slowly regaining the ability to speak. "Fucking…" Her fingers drove themselves into her arm and produced crescent moon-shaped beads of blood. *"Cocksucker!"*

She hurled herself across the room at him. Calmly, as if it were the most casual move in all the world, he sidestepped her charge. She landed on the bed with enough force she bounced. He bolted for the door.

Booker was down the stairs and out the front door in seconds. He ran down the street as fast as he was able. He had passed three houses by the time he heard his mother scream, "Get back here you fucking cocksucker! Get back here and take your medicine!" He never looked over his shoulder.

He did not stop running until he made it to Marcelina's on Piedmont Street. The small corner store was usually a haven for teens and younger kids, given the ample racks of candy and comic books. Mr. Marcelina was an older man who ran the store with his wife. Booker went there occasionally after school for a grinder or maybe just a pack of gum or some other sugary concoction which he would either consume before he got home or hide under the t-shirts in his dresser.

He stopped outside the door and put one hand on the side of the building and breathed heavily. He was shaking, he was thirsty, and when he spat on the ground it was more blood than saliva. He straightened and walked back and forth across the parking lot a few times, willing his heart to slow down. When he felt he had collected himself enough, and with one more sleeve wipe across his mouth to clear away any blood, he made for the store's front entrance.

He went straight for the cooler and pulled a bottle of Coke from its rack. Mr. Marcelina regarded him with some suspicion, doubtless because of his frazzled appearance, but he said nothing and accepted the fifteen cents. Booker exited the store and twisted off the cap and downed half the bottle with one gulp. The cold liquid stung the inside of his mouth but he did not care. It was the best tasting Coke he had ever had. He sat on the bench next to the door and drank his Coke and watched the street intently for any sign of his mother. She did not appear. He tossed the empty bottle into the garbage and began to walk up Piedmont.

He had no idea where to go. Home was absolutely out of the question. He could try his grandmother's house but he had reason not to trust her. She was his mother's mother, after all, and was likely to simply call home and report his whereabouts. That would bring his mother running. He had taken her by surprise in his bedroom but that would not happen again. If she caught up to him she would most likely beat him senseless for what he did. She might even be so filled with rage that she would not stop beating him until he was no longer recognizable as a human being. So returning home was not an option. Ever again.

He ran down the list of his friends, but his mother had the same list. She was doubtless calling them and telling their parents to call her if he showed up there. He stopped in front of a row of track houses and began to pace the sidewalk. After a few moments of that, and having thought of nowhere he could go, he stopped his pacing and simply sat. He draped his arms across his knees and sat and watched what little traffic there was pass in front of him.

He lost track of how long he sat there. The sun had disappeared behind the tall trees across the street but there was still plenty of daylight left. He wondered where he would spend the night and hoped the temperature would not drop enough that home started to look like an option.

He heard the car before he saw it. There were a number of hotrods in Deacon's Landing, but only one sounded like a wild beast chasing down its prey. He craned his neck and leaned forward and tried to see around the corner. There was no mistaking the sound of the machine coming toward him. The last thing he wanted was for the owner of that car to see him sitting on the curb so Booker climbed to his feet and leaned against the telephone pole and hoped he looked casual. He began to sweat and it felt cool on his arms. *Let him be alone, let him be alone*, Booker thought. He repeated the mental plea a few times before the car rounded the corner.

He was right about which car it would be, not that he entertained the idea he was wrong. The Tempest took the corner at what was a leisurely pace for Jacoby, meaning that all four tires remained in contact with the pavement. The bright yellow paint had been custom made to Jacoby's specifications, or so the story went. In daylight the car was painful to look at; the color seemed somehow…*wrong,* as if no human mind could have conceived it. Anyone unfortunate enough to see it in full sunlight was forced to look away; the color was simply too bright and hurt the eyes. Or was there something more to it? Booker suspected it was not simply the Tempest's color which made most people avert their eyes when they heard it coming. What that other reason might be he did not know, but he felt it and he was willing to bet everyone else did, too.

There were two others in the car with him, possibly three, but Booker could not see through the dark tint and into the backseat too clearly. He knew Wilson would be riding shotgun because he always did. The kid in the backseat was either Finlay or Turner, possibly both. He hoped they had other things on their mind than making trouble for him. He willed the bright yellow beast to continue on its way.

It did not.

The brakes locked up and the Tempest slid a little and came to a jolting stop a few feet from the curb. Booker stepped away from the telephone pole and dropped his arms to his side. He still could not see if there was a fourth person in the car but it made little difference. Jacoby apparently decided to make some trouble and odds of at least three-to-one were not in Booker's favor.

Both doors opened at the same time. Deacon's Landing's Bad Boy Number One stepped out, as did Wilson, who was indeed riding shotgun. Jacoby rested his arms on the car's roof and treated Booker to his gap-toothed grin. "Hey, Booker, how's it hanging?"

Wilson stepped to the side and Booker watched the front seat fold down and Turner wrestled his bulk from the obscured backseat. Booker backed up a step and waited to see who else would emerge but it seemed the Tempest had finished regurgitating its passengers. The three of them regarded Booker with what he felt was plain and unmasked loathing.

"Down to my knees," Booker said to Jacoby. He tried to keep his voice level and in this he succeeded. He sounded calm and not the least bit concerned about their sudden arrival and clear intentions, to his own ears, at least. "What's happening?"

"Little bit of this, little bit of that," Jacoby said. He drummed his fingers on the Tempest's roof as he spoke. "Me and the boys here were just cruising around, seeing what's what." He nodded. "Wanna join us?"

Turner reached into the inside pocket of his leather jacket and Booker leaned in the direction of the track houses at his back. Beyond those houses were woods and if he managed to get a big enough lead he knew he could lose them. Unless whatever was in his jacket turned out to be a gun. Booker doubted it; the street was too busy and there was still plenty of daylight left. Turner could not be that stupid. Besides, as much as these guys were assholes he had never heard of any of them being so armed. Booker relaxed somewhat when Turner produced a fat joint and held it beneath his nose. He sniffed it dramatically. "This is some good shit, Booker," he said. "Care to partake?" He laughed and high-fived Wilson.

Booker had never smoked pot before although he had been tempted the previous summer when he dated Barbara Meehan a few times. All that girl did, morning, noon and night was get high. But he had resisted the urge and saw no reason to sully his streak now. He shook his head slowly. "I'll pass, thanks."

"Fucking pussy," Wilson said. "I thought all you brothers were into this shit."

Jacoby held up his hands. "Hey, if the cat don't wanna smoke he don't wanna smoke. No need for name calling. And you can knock off that 'brother' shit, too, ya fucking mick."

A look of anger flashed across Wilson's eyes, but he said nothing.

Jacoby returned his attention to Booker. "What do you say, Booker? Hop in. We'll cruise."

Turner returned the joint to his inside pocket and folded his hands over his crotch. "C'mon, Booker. We're cruising for chicks. Even you should be interested in that."

Wilson tilted his head at Booker as if he were a scientist studying an unfamiliar specimen. "Maybe he don't like chicks." He looked over his shoulder at Jacoby. "Maybe he don't wanna smoke a joint because he'd rather smoke some dude's dick." He returned his eyes to Booker. "You a fag, Booker?"

"Ask your mother," Booker said and smiled inwardly when Wilson took an angry step away from the Tempest. His eyes flared and threatened to shoot flames. Booker took two subtle steps toward the houses behind him.

"Cut the shit," Jacoby said, as much to Wilson as to Booker. "Why is everybody so fucking hostile all the time?"

"You heard what he said. *Nobody* talks about my mother and gets away with it!" Wilson was furious and did not bother to hide it.

"I talk shit about your mother all the time," Jacoby pointed out.

The anger in Wilson's eyes was joined by impotent frustration. If Jacoby was not a confirmed badass and the undisputed leader of their group Wilson might have had something to say about that. As it was he gave a strangled grunt and put his head down. His hands remained curled into fists.

When Jacoby seemed satisfied Wilson would keep his cool, he turned back to Booker and said, "What do you say? Wanna cruise?"

He was almost certain it was a trap. But the little voice in the back of his head urged him to go along. If he went with them and it turned out they did what they said they would and cruised for chicks he might get lucky. Not with the ladies, mind you, he was not thinking about that, although he would not turn down an offer from a girl he found attractive. But he thought he might be able to crash at someone's house for the night when Jacoby had had his fill. It beat the shit out of sleeping on a bench in Misset Park. Or returning home.

He felt himself nod. "Yeah, okay," he said. He tried to sound excited but he was simply not that good an actor.

"Outstanding," Jacoby said. He turned to his cohorts. "Let's roll, gentlemen." Then, to Booker, "You can get in on my side. You'll never be able to squeeze past Turner's fat ass." He laughed.

Turner looked pissed but he only grumbled and slid his bulk back into the Tempest. Booker walked around the back of the car and a different voice inside him screamed, *Get out of here, man. Get out of here right now. Make a break for it. If you do it now you'll catch them flatfooted. You'll have a good fifty, sixty feet on them before they can react. Just move now!*

Shut up, he told the voice. *Either we take our chances with them or we freeze our asses off tonight in the park.* The voice mumbled something which Booker could not (or refused to) understand.

When he reached the driver's door Jacoby nodded and favored him with a toothy grin. "Glad to have you aboard, m'man," he said and clapped Booker on the back. "Get on in."

Booker took another look at the Tempest with its too-bright yellow paint, swallowed, and slid into the backseat. He did not have much room. Turner did indeed take up most of the seat. Jacoby plopped himself behind the wheel, closed his door, and fired up the V8. The sound was not as loud as Booker expected within the car but it was still enough that he was unable to hear the AM radio clearly. Jacoby threw the transmission into first and they pulled away from the curb.

The inside of the car was not nearly as difficult to look at as was the outside. The seats were black leather and comfortable. He noticed the instrument panel numbers were yellow, even the numbers on the speedometer, and he found that disturbing for reasons he could not articulate. Turner fired up the joint, took an enormous hit, and passed it to Wilson up front. Booker was thankful for the open windows; he was well aware of the precariousness of his situation and the last thing he wanted was a contact high.

Jacoby turned around in the 7-11 parking lot and headed back toward Main Street. Booker watched the pedestrians and other drivers turn their head at the Tempest's approach. The sun was well behind the rise of the foothills that bordered the west side of the Naugatuck Valley and the sky had just begun its transition to purple. In another hour it would be dark. For the first time in his life Booker wondered where the night would find him.

5.

Wherein Doors Are Opened

Max tapped on the bar and said, "Want another one, mister?" He held the whiskey bottle in his hand.

Booker looked at him and it took him a moment to remember where he was. He licked his dry lips and blinked the past away and nodded. "Yeah, thanks." He pushed the glass toward Max.

Max looked at him with a raised eyebrow, but he said nothing and refilled the glass. He moved on to the other customers who had come in while Booker was busy in 1968.

Booker looked about. The bar had filled in without his notice. All the seats around the stage were occupied and two new girls danced and gyrated to a song Booker had never heard. He gave the crowd a cursory glance before he returned his attention to his glass.

"Got my check, Max?" asked a soft, female voice from behind him.

Booker turned and saw Autumn standing behind him. She had changed into street clothes and put on a pair of glasses. The Santa hat remained on her head. Her pocketbook hung over her shoulder and she held a long cigarette between her slender fingers. She regarded him briefly before returning her eyes to the bartender.

"Sure do." Max reached into a small leather case beneath the bar and rummaged through its contents. After a moment he produced a folded slip of paper and handed it to her.

Autumn puffed on her cigarette and looked over her paycheck. She seemed satisfied and smiled at Max. "Thanks. I'm outta here, Max. See ya on Friday."

Max nodded and returned his attention to the customers at the bar. Booker watched Autumn saunter her way out the door. Daylight invaded the club when she opened the door and for a moment she was framed as a black silhouette surrounded by white smoke. It made him think of Lisa back when they were dating.

In that moment Booker decided he could not wait until after his mother's wake to return home. He needed to be back with Lisa *now*. Fuck the wake, fuck the reading of the will and fuck Deacon's Landing. It was time for him to return home. With something approximating renewed purpose he downed the whiskey and slid the glass toward Max. He put two singles on the bar and made his way toward the door. The bouncer looked up from his magazine long enough to utter a "See ya later," and then Booker was outside once again.

He got into the rental and fired it up. A moment later he was on Main Street and making for Route 6. He passed a cop sitting in the parking lot of a boarded up storefront and he glanced at the speedometer.

He nearly lost control of the car. The speedometer had changed quite drastically from the last time he looked at it. The numbers did not stop at 100 MPH (a *very* unlikely top speed for such a vehicle) but instead went to 150 MPH. The mileage counter was no longer digital; it was six digits long with the last digit in black and it read 28,122.6. Most troubling, however, was all the numbers and the needle were bright yellow.

Booker was startled enough to hit the brakes. The rental did not swerve, a fact for which he was grateful, and he managed to stay in his lane. He looked up at the police car and saw the officer was speaking into his mic. He did not activate his lights or siren and Booker realized the cop had seen nothing out of the ordinary. He was thankful the cop took no notice; he was not drunk but that did not mean his blood alcohol level was under the legal limit. He passed by the cop and continued down Main Street.

He wiped his sweaty hands on his pants and after a few moments he dared to look at the speedometer again. It was the same one he had kept an eye on during the drive from Bradley International to Deacon's Landing. The digital odometer was back and read 86,596. The speedometer ended firmly at 100 MPH. The numbers on the gauges were uniformly flat gray.

Booker licked his lips and relaxed his grip on the wheel. He resisted the urge to smoke another cigarette (because that was the real horror of the things, how easy it was to embrace them even after years away) and concentrated instead on getting to Route 6.

He almost passed the funeral home, but he pulled to the curb before he knew what he was doing. His hands tightened on the wheel once again. Why had he stopped? He had no desire to remain in Deacon's Landing for another moment, let alone to visit the funeral parlor. Against his will he watched himself put the car in park and turn off the engine.

"No," he whispered. He unlocked his seatbelt and then the door. The keys went into his jacket pocket and he stepped onto the street.

There was a loud blast from a car's horn and a silver blur streaked past close enough for him to feel the breeze.

Booker stepped back instinctively and threw his hands up. The car slowed considerably until it came to a jarring stop. The driver, a young man in his twenties, leaned out the window and screamed, "Watch where you're going, asshole!" He got back inside the car and drove off. He flipped Booker the bird as he did.

Booker stood still for a moment. His heart pounded a heavy metal beat in his chest and his hands shook. His breathing was shallow and fast. He stutter-stepped behind the car and then put it between him and the street. Several more cars moved in both lanes past him. He watched the traffic move along Main Street for several more moments before he turned and faced the funeral home.

The position of the sun in the sky had changed from this morning and the building's façade was slowly being consumed by shadow. Some of the windows on the ground floor were lit up; the top two levels of the structure were dark.

Just get in the car and go, he told himself. *Put this whole fucking town in the rearview and don't stop til you hit the airport. Forty-five minutes to get there and about two hours flight time and you'll be back home. With Lisa.* Which was exactly what he wanted. Except his legs apparently did not agree. He found himself moving up the walkway toward Baron's.

He felt cold, much colder than could be blamed on the temperature. Yes, it was freezing but he felt colder still. His joints ached in a way they never had before. He wished he had remained in the strip club or even at his mother's house. Anywhere would be preferable. *Shoulda stayed in Wilmington,* his brain told him, and he could not argue the point.

The wide steps which led to the ample front porch (more of a deck, really) were made of wood. They were weather beaten but did not sag nor creak when he stepped on them. Several chairs were arranged on the porch and two cigarette caddies were positioned on either side of the front doors. He reached for the doorbell before he stopped himself and simply opened one of the doors.

The foyer was brightly lit by a large and elegant chandelier. Several sofas and armchairs were scattered about what must have been someone's living room when the house served as a residence. A fireplace dominated one wall; it was large enough for several men to stand shoulder-to-shoulder within its confines. The carpet was dark green and old but it still gave a little beneath his weight. A wide staircase led to the second floor; the rail looked to be solid oak and had obviously been hand-carved by a master artisan a century ago. *You don't see work like this anymore*, he thought. He would appreciate the craftsmanship more had the hair on his arms not been standing at attention.

He did not want to be inside this house any longer but he could only watch himself close the door behind him. A small bell hanging from the ceiling jingled when he shut the door. He did not remember hearing the rather unpleasant sound when he first opened the doors. It was probably intended to sound cheerful or at least consoling. To Booker, it sounded somehow…final.

He swallowed and looked about. There was a sign on the wall next to the doorway to his right. **Parlor A**, it proclaimed, with an arrow pointing the way. Beneath that in much smaller lettering was a removable, hand-written placard that read *Mrs. Miller*.

Booker peeked inside the room and saw it had been prepared for the night's viewing. Several rows of chairs led to a podium with a gold cross stamped upon its face. Half a dozen flower arrangements were lined against the wall. The casket which sat upon the dais was closed and an old black and white photograph of the deceased sat perched atop it.

Booker moved deeper into the house.

He found the sign indicating **Parlor B** and beneath that the smaller sign which read *Mrs. Booker*. He paused and licked his lips. The double doors which led to the parlor were closed. Booker reached for the handle and stopped himself. *She's really in there. Nothing between you and her now but a simple door.* He tried to swallow but his mouth had gone bone dry. He reached for the handle again and this time he got all the way to resting his hand on it. He could not bring himself to turn the handle and open the door.

"This is a bad idea," he whispered. He took his hand from the door handle and turned toward the front entrance when he saw a man in an expensive suit standing in the foyer. Booker gasped.

The man appeared to be in his early-fifties. His salt-and-pepper hair was short and neat. His suit looked as expensive as it was impeccable. A thick gold wedding band was wrapped around his ring finger. It caught the light from the chandelier and gleamed quite brightly.

The man smiled faintly but politely. It was a gesture he had no doubt practiced in front of a mirror. He approached Booker slowly, his hand stuck out in front of him. "How do you do, sir. Is there something I can do for you? If you're here for Mrs. Booker I'm afraid the viewing is not until five PM."

Booker shook the man's hand and nodded in the direction of the closed doors. "She's my mother." His voice was quiet, subdued, although he had no idea why. He seemed to have trouble speaking clearly.

The man heard him and the polite smile lessened somewhat. "I'm very sorry for your loss," he said. He even managed to sound sincere. "Of course you can go in."

He reached for the door handle and before Booker could stop him the man opened the door. For a moment Booker's mind went blank save for a single thought: *Now there's nothing separating us.* The man said something else, most likely some mindless platitude, but Booker could not hear him. The only sound of which he was aware was the pounding of the blood in his ears.

He turned slowly in the direction of the open door. The room itself was a carbon copy of the other viewing parlor. An identical podium with an identical gold cross stood to the side of the room. Behind it and lined up along the wall were a few flower arrangements. Absently, Booker wondered who would send flowers to the old lady's wake. *Probably whichever companies made her favorite vodka and whiskey,* he thought. *I hope their CEOs haven't made any large purchases lately.* It was a cruel thought, he knew, but he did not care.

Someone, probably his cousins, had put together a corkboard filled with photographs of Mary Ellen Booker. It stood on an easel to the left of the doorway. Many of the photos were black and white but a few were in color. Although they were too far away to see clearly he thought he spied his father in some of them. It made him realize he almost forgot what the man looked like. He wondered, briefly and absently, if any of those photos held the image of a young boy. Not that it mattered.

Unlike Mrs. Miller's casket in Parlor A, his mother's was open. He could not see her from this distance. Even so the hair on the back of his neck joined its comrades on his arms and stood at attention.

The funeral parlor man was still beside him, still droning along in his quiet, conciliatory tone. Booker picked up on the last few sentences. "So if you need anything, please do not hesitate to come to me personally. The name is Andrew Baron. My office is straight down this hall, last door on the right." He retreated a few steps before he stopped and said, "Again, I'm very sorry for your loss." He did not wait for a response. A moment later even the sound of his footfalls was silenced.

Booker looked again into the viewing parlor. Against his will he crossed the threshold. He tried to stop himself but found his legs were of a different mind. They continued their slow advance.

He passed the corkboard with its photos. He willed himself not to look at them and in this, at least, he was successful. He walked around the perimeter of the room, past the flowers (*From Your Friends at de Ville Market* read one; another proclaimed *Condolences From Sophia's Hair and Nails*) before he stopped at the last arrangement.

It was large and beautiful and clearly expensive. A yellow ribbon with the word *Sympathy* emblazoned upon it caught his attention. He stopped and reached for the card. It read: *Sorry for your loss, brother*. It was signed Michael Catalina and Family. "Smoke," he said to the flowers. He looked at them again and a faint smile spread across his lips.

However you found out, thanks, man. I owe ya one. Not for the flowers, not exactly. But Booker felt energized by the gift from his old friend. It was as if a lifeline had been cast from outside the border of Deacon's Landing and someone was trying to pull him back to the real world. He suddenly felt better than he had since before Steven's call.

He turned with purpose toward the casket. It was no more than ten feet from him. He covered the distance easily and casually. He reached the casket and looked inside.

His mother had aged significantly since the last time he had seen her. *Well, that's only right. So have I.* Her hair, black as the day is long, was now the color of snow. Wrinkles had taken over her face, most noticeably around her lips and eyes. The makeup used by the mortician softened them but could not erase them completely. Her hands were folded across her chest and a rosary was wrapped around her fingers. *Should be a rolling pin. That would be more authentic.*

Her funeral dress was a white/pink ensemble. It wrapped itself loosely around her small frame. She had shrunk, or perhaps she had always been this size and he simply did not remember. Whatever the reason he now had trouble imagining how she had managed to terrify him so much during his childhood and teen years. *For Christ's sake she looks like she weighs about eighty pounds. I was more than that by the time I was ten years-old.* "I shoulda left a lot sooner than I did," he said, the first words he had spoken to her since 1968. "Why the fuck did I stay in that house for so long?"

His mother did not have an answer.

"Well, this is it, mom. I'm not coming back here again. This is the one and only good-bye you get from me. And frankly, it's more than you deserve." He reached for her hands, the same hands she used to dispense her mysterious brand of parental discipline on him, but he stopped short of touching them. He swallowed and turned from the casket and he did not look back.

That's it, run away, said his mother from the casket. *It's the only thing you were ever good at, Scotty.*

Booker froze halfway to the door. He knew the voice was in his head and that the ancient corpse in the casket had not uttered a sound. Yet his mouth was suddenly dry and his forehead was suddenly wet. He turned his head slightly and peeked over his shoulder. He could see the end of the casket but not the body that lay within. "Shut up," he whispered. "You're dead and it's about fucking time. You don't get to say shit to me anymore."

Your friends in the Tempest are dead, too, she cooed. *I bet they have plenty to say.*

"How do…" His voice hitched in his throat. Was he really going to have a conversation with a corpse? This one, in particular? "No, I'm not," he said. He squared his shoulders and turned his head back to the door. It took a bit of willpower but he got his feet moving again.

He felt better immediately after exiting the parlor. He wiped his sleeve across his forehead and he felt the dry mouth dissipate somewhat. He took in a few slow, steady breaths and leaned against the wall with his eyes shut. After a few moments he felt himself again. He made for the door without looking back into the viewing parlor.

6.

Wherein An Invitation Is Extended

The yellow Tempest sat parked behind his rented Chrysler. It was not in direct sunlight but the bright yellow seemed to gleam nonetheless. When Booker closed the front doors of the funeral home behind him the Tempest revved its engine. It sounded like a thunderclap directly overhead. The sound vibrated its way through the old porch and up into his legs. It made the fillings in his teeth hurt.

Booker shielded his eyes with one hand and tried to peer through the dark tint of the passenger window. He could see the driver as a vague silhouette, a darker shadow within the dark interior of the vehicle. He thought perhaps the driver was motioning to him, waving him to approach. Booker did so.

He moved steadily along the walkway and down to the curb. He approached the Tempest but at the last moment he continued on past it. He used the keychain remote to unlock the Chrysler and he opened the door and slid behind the wheel. The Tempest's driver gunned the engine again and Booker could feel the vibration even through his own steering wheel. He started the rental and put it in gear. He pulled away from the curb and watched the Tempest in his rearview. The too-bright antique remained at the curb until he crested a short hill and it was lost from his view.

Booker allowed himself a sigh of relief. He expected the car to follow him, perhaps even try to cut him off. When it was at last gone from his rearview he felt the hair on the back of his neck settle back down. He nodded and gripped the steering wheel a little more tightly. It seemed he would miss his mother's wake as well as the funeral, and that was all right with him. He had seen her, paid what he felt was the proper amount of respect (which was little to none), and now it was time to go back to Lisa.

He headed north on Main Street and waited for it to turn back into Route 6.

He stopped at a four-way intersection and saw the Tempest sitting at the opposing light. It idled loudly and belched thick gray smoke from its duel tailpipes. The car behind it, a dark green SUV of some kind, was nearly obscured by the cloud emanating from the back of the Tempest. The driver gunned the engine and the car rocked on its suspension. There was no direct sun glare and the sky was well on its way to dark purple and yet Booker had difficulty looking at the Tempest for more than a moment or two.

He licked his suddenly-dry lips and returned his attention to the stoplight. When it turned to green Booker hit the gas a little harder than he meant to and the Chrysler lurched forward. He watched the Tempest from the corner of his eye until he was through the intersection. His eyes moved to the rearview and he lost sight of the car behind the cloud of exhaust. He drove a bit faster than the posted speed limit but he did not care. The urge to evacuate Deacon's Landing (and that was the proper way to put it, he thought) was nearly overwhelming and it was all he could do to stop himself from mashing the gas pedal.

"Leave me alone, Jacoby," he said. "Just get lost. You're dead and I'm not and I'm never setting foot in this fucking town again for as long as I live. So back the fuck off."

Booker guided the Chrysler up Main Street until he saw the sign that indicated he was on Route 6. He checked the rearview again, saw no sign of the Tempest, and allowed himself a smile. For reasons he could not articulate he felt he was safe once he crossed the town line. As if Jacoby (and he was convinced that was the identity of the man behind the wheel of the fucking thing) would be unable to follow him once he left the boundaries of Deacon's Landing.

Except he had not left Deacon's Landing. He had yet to see the sign marking the border of the town. He had seen it on the way in and he knew it was there. So why did it seem to be missing? His smile faltered but he kept a steady speed and looked for the sign. The next sign he came across was another marker for Route 6. Booker looked closely at the sign. His eyes widened and he eased off the gas and pulled the car onto the shoulder. He stopped in front of the sign and looked at it again.

He activated the headlights even though he knew the added light would not change the sign. It did indeed inform him he was on Route 6. Directly below the blue number was the word *South*.

"That can't be right," he whispered. "That can't be right at all."

He checked his rearview again and saw it was clear of any traffic. The houses and businesses along Main Street had long since given way to trees and the occasional streetlight. He recognized the strip of road despite the decades that had passed since last he saw it. He was fortunate he realized where he was before he continued much farther. Woodbury was in that direction but there was something between Deacon's Landing and Woodbury that he had no desire to see. He breathed a sigh of relief even as he berated himself for his stupidity.

"I'm on the wrong side of town." He swallowed and nodded at the sign. "Somehow I got turned around. Too fucking distracted by that yellow Tempest, Scotty," he continued to no one. "Gotta watch where the fuck you're going, old man."

He pulled a cigarette from his pocket and lit it and flopped back into the driver's seat. "Christ, that was dumb," he said through puffs of smoke. He slapped the side of his head. "Wake the fuck up, idiot." He sat back in the seat and smoked and did not move until he felt calm once more. He pitched the cigarette out the window and sat up again.

He thought of Baron's. When he first saw the funeral home he had just entered the town. It was on his left which was one of the reasons he had continued past it. When he left the old Victorian it was on his right and he had made no U-turns since then. His heartbeat picked up and his eyes went wide when the realization hit him. He had not gotten turned around at all; he retraced the road he took into Deacon's Landing and it should have put him on the way to the airport. Instead north had somehow become south. He shivered and it had little to do with the cold.

"No," he whispered. "Come on, don't do this to me." He took a few deep breaths to try to steady himself again but it only half-worked. "I'll feel a hell of a lot better when I'm outta this fucking town." He knew that was true; he simply did not know how to accomplish his goal. He felt he had no choice but to turn around and head back through the town. If he kept a close watch on the street signs he felt he could make it out. The road was wide enough for him to make the turn. He checked his rearview, saw it was clear, and pulled onto the street.

The last moment before impact he heard the roar of the big block V8. Instinctively he braced himself and slammed on the brakes. He caught sight of a bright yellow streak as it zipped past his window. The streak clipped the Chrysler's front fender and sent the car into a spin. He heard the sound of plastic and aluminum shattering around him. The muscles in Booker's arms corded and he held himself as far from the steering wheel as possible. The airbag blossomed from the center of the wheel and blinded him and for a moment the world was whited out. After a moment the car came to a stop. The noise and chaos around him did not lessen gradually but stopped all at once.

The airbag had not yet deflated but Booker had the presence of mind to push the thing away from his head. His hands moved quickly over his body while his mind sought out any injuries. He came up empty. The airbag, it seemed, had performed as intended. He scanned the road in both directions and knew what he would find. The sky was darkening rapidly but he found the Tempest easily enough. It sat in the middle of the road perhaps two hundred feet from where his Chrysler came to rest. It faced him and rocked gently on its suspension as the driver revved the engine. Even in the waning light the bright yellow was enough to sting his eyes. There was no discernable damage to the Tempest's front end; the paint was unblemished and stung his eyes and the chrome was perfectly intact. The old muscle car showed no sign of the impact with Booker's car.

The Tempest started forward, but slowly. The engine's roar became a low-key, menacing growl. Booker watched it for only a moment or two before he remembered how to move. He opened the driver's door and tried to pull himself out of the car but the seatbelt restrained him. He cursed himself and fumbled with the lock and watched the old muscle car continue its slow advance. The seatbelt unlocked and he threw it aside and stumbled from the rental. He went down to one knee before he was able to regain his balance. He grabbed onto the mangled front fender and used it to pull himself to his feet.

The Tempest pulled even with the Chrysler and came to a stop. Booker used the wrecked fender to hold himself steady and he looked at the old muscle car and through its tinted windows. The proximity allowed him to see some detail from within the car. Aside from the silhouette that was the driver there were two others in the backseat. He could see just enough to know that all three paid him little attention; they seemed to stare straight ahead. The passenger door opened seemingly of its own volition.

Booker held his ground but only for a moment or two. He walked around the front of the Tempest and to the open door. There was a large dent in the passenger door. He thought at first it was from the impact with his rental. He quickly abandoned that idea. They had sideswiped him; this looked more like a direct impact. And besides, the sheet metal skin of the Chrysler was hardly capable of leaving much of a mark on the solid steel body of the old Pontiac. Jacoby kept the thing cherry, as they used to say. The dent had not been present the last time he found himself a passenger in the Tempest, of that he was certain.

He eyed the two kids in the backseat. Wilson and Turner sat in complete shadow. They might have looked exactly as they had four and a half decades before. But he caught sight of something hanging from Wilson's cheek.

Booker thought it was a flap of skin. They took no notice of him.

Jacoby sat behind the wheel. He, too, had not aged since the last time Booker had seen him. He turned his head slowly in Booker's direction. His neck creaked as he moved. He said nothing, simply sat and looked at him.

Booker slid into the front passenger seat. He reached for the door handle but he needn't have bothered; the door shut on its own.

7.

Wherein Booker Receives a History Lesson
And Jacoby makes A Mistake

He had a sinking feeling in the pit of his stomach when Jacoby turned south on Main Street. Even before they left the center of town and he saw the sign that read *Woodbury 8 Mi.* he felt he knew their intended destination. He kept quiet about it mostly because he had allowed himself to be cornered. He had decided to take a flyer on Jacoby on the off-chance he could wrangle himself a place to spend the night. Now the thought of a bench in Misset Park did not seem so unappealing. If anything it was preferable to what he was sure was Jacoby's destination.

His heart sank a bit more when Jacoby continued onto Route 6. They passed the last side road for the next seven miles without slowing. Since it was well known there was nothing of interest in Woodbury unless one was fond of antique stores (something Booker seriously doubted when it came to his present company) that left a single possible destination. There was only one thing to see along this section of Route 6. It was something Booker had seen any number of times when his father drove the family to his aunt's house for the annual July Fourth get-together, but he had never set foot inside the place himself. And why would he? There was simply no reason anyone outside of the town historian would have for entering such a place.

At least Turner finished the joint, he thought. He had managed to come through it without a contact high and he felt he had his wits about him. If it came down to him making a break for it he figured he could get a decent enough head start to outrun them. On foot, at least. It was nearly dark and the absence of any streetlights on this section of Route 6 could help him. The stretches of empty land gave way to heavy woods on both sides of the road. With luck he could lose himself in there and Jacoby and his crew would simply give up the chase and go find someone else to abuse. *Just be cool,* he thought. *See what they're on about before you do something stupid.* And on the heels of that: *Getting into this car was pretty fucking stupid.* "Shut up," he whispered. Between the roar of the engine and the Troggs belting out "Wild Thing" on the AM radio no one heard him.

Jacoby and Wilson were talking over something in the front seat but he could make nothing of their conversation. Turner simply sat back in his stoned stupor and enjoyed the ride. Booker watched the trees go by on both sides of the road and prayed he was wrong about where Jacoby was taking them. As it turned out, he was, indeed, correct.

Jacoby pulled onto the dirt shoulder on the right side of the road. Across from them and barely visible above the stone wall that surrounded the place stood Old Lichgate Cemetery. The wrought iron gate, straight out of an old Universal horror movie and gothic as all hell, stood closed and locked. An old and rusted chain looped through the bars and he could just barely see the lump which he took to be the padlock that secured those chains. It would have been quite an imposing obstacle if the gate and the stone wall were more than five feet high. The sky was transitioning from purple to black. Even with what little remained of the light he could see the dark shapes of the headstones on the far side of the cemetery; the wall hid those closer to the road.

Jacoby killed the engine and all sound left the world. After becoming accustomed to the roar of that big block V8 it was quite a change. For the first time since he sat outside the 7-11 Booker could hear his own heartbeat again. It was fast and hard and unsettling. Evidently his physiology had no more love for the cemetery than did he.

Wilson turned and looked him over. "All out," he said. He opened his door. "Booker, you ever been here before?"

"Been by it a few times," Booker replied. "Never been inside."

Wilson's smile grew and he shared it with Turner. They exchanged a quick, knowing glance before Wilson returned his attention to Booker. "Then you're in for a treat, m'man. Let's go."

Booker followed Jacoby out of the Tempest and they waited for Turner to squeeze his bulk out of the backseat. Jacoby lit a cigarette and offered one to Booker. He took it without comment and leaned forward when Jacoby offered his lighter. It did not taste particularly good and the smoke burned his throat on the way down but somehow it made him feel better. Booker stood beside Jacoby and smoked and looked at Old Lichgate.

"What do you know about this place, Booker?" Jacoby asked.

Booker shook his head. "Not that much. Just what Mrs. Burke told us about it in history class back in eighth grade. I know the place is old and it's not used anymore. Beyond that… " He shook his head and let his voice trail off.

Jacoby allowed himself a smirk that was just enough for Booker to see. "Oh, it's old, all right. There are some cats in there from the Revolutionary War. But there's one in particular that I want to show you. It's pretty fucked up. You'll see." When Wilson and Turner at last joined them Jacoby said, "Let's go."

They crossed the road. Jacoby and Wilson barely paused at the stone wall before they climbed over. *Now's my chance*, Booker thought. *They're on the other side and there's no way Turner can catch me. If I break for it now I'll have at least ten seconds on them.* He looked at Turner and for an awful moment he thought perhaps he had spoken aloud. The fat kid looked at him with a suspicious, sideways glance. He held that glance for an uncomfortable few seconds before he nodded in the direction of the wall. "Over you go, Booker."

Booker nodded. "Right." He hoisted himself up the wall and landed gracefully on the other side. Jacoby awaited him but Wilson had already begun to walk casually around the old headstones. Booker looked at them. They were short and thin and very weather-beaten. He had no idea what they were made of but it was definitely not marble. He could find no rhyme or reason to their placement; it seemed the bodies were buried wherever someone pleased. It was small, much smaller than Booker had thought; the stone wall bordering the grounds was already visible as a dark mass at the far end.

A large and out-of-control tree stood next to the wall on his left. The branches hung low enough to the ground that at first Booker thought it had toppled over. Some of the branches had apparently been hacked away. There was an ill-defined path which led into the branches. Booker could imagine it being used as a party area by the older kids in town. To back up this image, several old and crushed beer cans littered the ground around the tree.

There was little in the way of grass but some stubborn patches were evident here and there. They were not over-grown which led Booker to conclude someone was taking care of the grounds, at least on occasion. That made him feel slightly better about standing in the cemetery. At least there were others with enough balls to enter the place.

"Check the place out, man," Jacoby offered. "There's some pretty funky shit in here."

Booker heard loud grunts from the other side of the stone wall and realized Turner was attempting to scale it and join them. He eyed the far side of the cemetery; if he could get there without appearing like he was about to bolt he could make his move before Turner got over the wall. He started in that direction.

He paid no attention to the first few headstones he passed, but he realized it might appear too obvious. He slowed his pace and paused at one of the stones. The engraving was almost gone and he could not read it. The next one was in slightly better shape. The name was illegible but he could still make out the date: 1792. Booker assumed that was the date of death. He clasped his hands behind his back and tried to appear casual as he continued on his course toward the cemetery's far end.

He was even with the large tree. There were more graves on the other side, hidden by the tree's bulk. That area was out of Jacoby's line-of-sight. Booker made for it, doing his best to move casually. He chanced a quick look over his shoulder. Jacoby remained by the wall and Turner straddled the top of it. He was panting with the effort and swearing up a storm. Jacoby looked amused. Wilson was across the cemetery and wandering around the headstones. He was paying no mind to Booker.

Booker somehow maintained his casual pace but his heart was hammering the inside of his chest. A few more steps and he would be out of Jacoby's view. Beyond the stone wall was perhaps fifty feet of open ground, and beyond that the woods began. He calculated the time it would take him to get over the wall and reach the woods. He felt he could do it.

There was a thud at the wall near the front of the cemetery and he knew Turner had finally joined them. That was all right; Turner was hardly his main concern, anyway. He was even fortunate the fat kid was there; it kept Jacoby on that side of the cemetery. He estimated he now had at least one hundred twenty feet between him and Jacoby. It would be enough.

The instant he was out of their view he bolted for the wall. The grass was a bit higher in this area, *quite* a bit higher, in fact. Booker did not let that slow him. He slogged through the tall grass and was nearly to the wall when his left foot struck something hard and unyielding and he went down with a yelp.

"Booker, you okay?" Jacoby called. "Where you at, man?"

"He's near Edgar," Wilson called from across the cemetery.

Booker got his hands under him and pushed himself onto his knees. He could hear Jacoby and Turner coming his way, and the dark silhouette that was Wilson was running in his direction. There was no way he could break for it now; he climbed to his feet slowly and brushed the dirt and grass from his clothes. His left ankle throbbed, but did not feel broken.

He tested his weight on it and found himself to be unhurt. He looked down into the tall grass to see if he could find what had tripped him up.

There was another headstone roughly six feet away. It could not be what he tripped over; it stood nearly a foot taller than the grass around it. Something in front of it, perhaps. A toppled headstone? He nearly looked past the tall headstone before he realized it was different from the others he had seen. He looked at it more closely. It was thicker than the others and made from a different type of stone. There was something engraved on the headstone's surface but the tree blocked what little moonlight there was and he could not read it.

Jacoby joined him at the same time Wilson arrived at his side. Turner was still thirty feet away and closing the distance at what for him was full speed. "You okay?" Jacoby asked.

"Hey, man, you found Edgar," Wilson said.

"Yeah, I'm okay." He looked at Wilson. "What?"

"Edgar," Wilson said, as if the name alone was explanation enough. "You found Edgar."

"Who the fuck is Edgar?"

Jacoby walked an odd half-circle around the area in front of the unusual headstone and brought out his lighter again. He flicked it to life and held it in front of the headstone.

It did not appear to be made of marble but it was in much better shape than the other headstones he had seen. The stone was discolored in a wide swath across the front. He would not have noticed it if not for Jacoby's lighter. In the flame the discoloration appeared to be bright yellow paint. He knew, although he did not know how, that it was the same yellow that adorned the Tempest.

The engraving was deep and clear and showed no signs of wear. It might have been inscribed earlier that day. Booker read it aloud. "'Edgar Sleeps.'" He looked up at Jacoby. "Edgar sleeps? That's a fucked up thing to put on someone's grave."

Turner had joined them. He clapped Booker on the back with much more force than was necessary. Booker held in a cry of pain but glared at the fat kid. "If you think that's fucked up, wait'll you see the rest of it."

"Got that right," Wilson agreed.

"Follow my path, Booker," Jacoby said. "Follow it precisely."

Booker's back still stung and he still wanted to level Turner but he did as Jacoby asked. He stood next to him and waited for whatever Jacoby was going to do. He prepared himself to break for the wall the instant Jacoby made a move he did not like.

Instead, Jacoby reached down and pulled out a handful of the tall grass by its roots. "Start pulling." Jacoby gathered another handful.

Booker glanced at Wilson and Turner, but they simply stood and watched him. The first move would be made by Jacoby. Booker prepared to run. He grabbed up some of the tall grass and tossed it aside. "And why am I doing this?"

"Because there's something very cool here," Jacoby answered. "Something not too many people know about. I wanted to show it to you."

Booker looked again at Turner and Wilson. They alternated between talking among themselves and watching him.

He returned his attention to the grave and its tall grass. As more of the stuff was pulled away he saw what looked to be rusted metal bars beneath the grass. Another few handfuls of grass removed and it appeared to be a cage which covered the grave. It looked to be of the same wrought iron as the cemetery's gate. It was obvious he had tripped over this in his run for the wall. "What is this?"

Jacoby stood straight and swung the lighter in a slow arc over the cage. "Pretty cool, huh? They call it a *mortsafe*. They did this kinda thing sometimes in the Middle Ages in Europe. Can you guess why?"

Booker had never seen such a thing, nor had he heard of it. He thought for a moment. "To prevent grave robbing?"

Wilson and Turner laughed but Jacoby silenced them with a quick stare. They went back to standing and watching. Jacoby seemed satisfied his two companions would remain silent. He returned his attention to Booker. "Well, that's not a bad guess, actually. That's even the official reason you'll find in an encyclopedia. But that's not the *real* reason." He leaned a few inches closer to Booker. "Wanna know what its real purpose is?"

Booker swallowed. He did not, in fact, give a shit about the thing's real purpose. And that sloppy swath of yellow paint was somehow making the hair on his arms stand up. He took a slight and (he hoped) unnoticed step toward the stone wall. "Sure. Tell me."

Jacoby leaned in closer to him. When he spoke again, his voice had dropped a full octave. "It was to stop the corpse from climbing out of the grave."

Booker swallowed. "Is that a fact?"

"Oh, it's a fact," Wilson said and laughed loudly.

"They had a real fear of vampires and shit back then," Jacoby continued. His voice dropped another octave and he sounded like the bass voice in a doo wop group. "So they came up with a way to keep them from climbing out of the grave. Pretty cool, huh?"

Booker dropped all pretense of putting some distance between him and the three assholes with whom he shared the cemetery. He backed away slowly but steadily. "Pretty cool," he agreed. Cold sweat broke out on his arms and coated his back. It felt like ice in the sudden and cold breeze that wafted through the cemetery. "Pretty cool."

"Say, where ya going, Booker?" Turner asked. "You thinking of leaving?"

"He's not going anywhere," Jacoby said. "Not until he's seen the king."

"Yeah, you have to meet the king," Wilson said with another laugh. "You'll like the king!"

"I think you'll *love* the king," Turner added.

Booker's mouth went dry. His breath frosted the July night air. He said nothing. He kept his eyes on the three kids in front of him and backed up toward the wall. His arms felt, not just cold, but frozen. He spared a single moment to look at them. A thin layer of ice coated his skin. It cracked but remained in place when he flexed his arms. He glanced over his shoulder. The wall was no more than fifteen feet away. He continued his retreat.

"You can't leave now, man," Jacoby said. "And if you try to run we'll have to catch you and drag you right back here."

"Yeah, Booker, c'mon," Turner pleaded. "Don't make me run after your black ass. Be a man!"

Jacoby let his lighter go out and the cemetery was plunged into darkness.

Booker turned and bolted for the fence at full speed. He heard the kids behind him swear loudly and come after him. He reached the stone wall. He leaped for it and hurled himself over the top. He landed hard on the ground and felt some of the ice on his arms crack and fall away. He was on his feet in an instant. He ran as fast as he could for the tree line. It seemed impossibly far away, as if the open area between it and the cemetery wall had somehow expanded in the past few moments.

He heard but did not see Jacoby and his friends scale the stone wall. Two separate thuds told him Jacoby and another, certainly Wilson, cleared the wall. He did not look back.

He reached the tree line and did not slow. He whipped past branches that scratched him and tore at his clothes. He jumped a fallen tree and kept going. He knew he was parallel with the road, more or less, but he could not stop to get his bearings. He heard Jacoby and Wilson enter the woods somewhere behind him. They sounded far back and he allowed himself the hope that he had opened up an insurmountable lead. He was in good shape, relative to the kids behind him, anyway, and he felt that gave him an advantage. He just had to stay ahead of them long enough to get back to Deacon's Landing. The thought of spending another night in his parents' house suddenly seemed tolerable, even preferable. More branches tore at him, but he did not care. The cold he felt in the cemetery was a distant memory; if anything he thought he might overheat in the warm July air. He would need to stop eventually, if only to catch his breath and slow down his heartbeat.

The opportunity to do just that came a few moments later. He paused just long enough to take in a great gulp of air. When he did he listened for sounds of pursuit. He heard nothing. He found a large boulder in his path and he stumbled to it. He propped himself against it and breathed heavily and listened.

His legs shook, his arms shook, and his knees threatened to buckle at any moment. He knelt in the dirt and closed his eyes and listened intently. He heard nothing but the sound of his own labored breathing and his heart pounding in his chest. He was covered with sweat and it dripped from his hair and stung his eyes. Of Jacoby and his buddies there was no sound.

Booker stayed that way for some time. When at last he was confident he could move again he pulled himself to his feet and trotted in the direction of the town. He felt he could move a bit faster, but he wanted to hold that in reserve should Jacoby suddenly appear in front of him. He did not need to worry; he saw no sign of Jacoby or the others.

The woods gave way to open fields. Booker stood at the tree line and looked at the road eighty or ninety feet to his left. It was free of traffic. He took a first hesitant step from the safety of the woods. Jacoby did not show himself, nor did his friends. Booker jogged in the direction of town. He knew there were a few homes on the outskirts of Deacon's Landing and he thought perhaps he could talk his way inside one of them and call his father. Walking back into that house did not seem like such a bad idea, at least compared to running into Jacoby again.

Once outside the woods he was bathed in moonlight. The road contained too many twists and turns yet for him to see the lights of Deacon's Landing, but he knew he was getting close. *Two miles*, he thought. *Can't be more than that.* He trusted his legs to carry him that far.

The first house he came to was abandoned and falling apart. Its windows were smashed, its paint had peeled almost completely off the wooden slats and numerous roof shingles dotted the overgrown yard. He considered for a moment spending the night in the house, but only for a moment. Only God knew what was living in there. And it was entirely possible, perhaps even likely, Jacoby would check the house, anyway. Best to keep going, especially this close to town. He left the old house behind.

He saw the headlights of an approaching car on the road. He dropped to one knee and listened carefully. He could barely hear engine noise which meant it was not Jacoby's Tempest. "Thank God," he said. He ran up the slight incline to Route 6. His legs felt like jelly and threatened to give at any moment but he willed them to keep moving. He stumbled perhaps fifteen feet from the road and saw and heard the car pass. He shouted, nothing coherent, nonsense syllables, but he shouted nonetheless. The car kept going. He crawled the rest of the way up the incline until he reached the side of Route 6. He looked after the car and saw its taillights disappear around a corner in the road. Booker's shoulders slumped and he pounded his fist on the pavement. "Dammit!"

His breathing was labored and his arms and legs shook. He had never felt more exhausted in his life. He used the last of his strength to gently lower himself to the ground. He lay there on the side of Route 6 and tried to get his breathing under control. It took several moments during which he nearly fell asleep twice. He managed to stay awake, however, mostly by thinking that Jacoby could pull up on him at any moment. He was too close to the fucking road. He propped himself up and started for the open field before him.

There was a sudden and entirely unexpected roar from directly behind him. Booker screamed his surprise and threw himself down the incline. He rolled most of the way down until the field leveled. He sprang up onto one knee and looked at the road.

The Tempest sat on the side of the road, directly across from him. Its rough, loud idle was interrupted only when Jacoby revved the engine. The passenger door opened and Wilson stepped out. "C'mon, Booker, you ain't getting away. Get in the fucking car." Turner also said something but it was lost to the Tempest's growl.

"Fuck you," Booker said.

Wilson turned away a moment, looked into the Tempest. A moment later he turned back to Booker. "Last chance, man. Don't make us come after you."

Booker knew beyond doubt they would catch him. He did not have the energy to outrun them a second time. He looked about for anything to use as cover. He was in an open field; the nearest house was the one he passed perhaps five minutes before. He looked in that direction; the house was a dark shape too far away to be of any use. He took a deep breath and pushed himself to his feet.

"I can do this all night," Booker lied. "Seriously, how do you out-of-shape assholes expect to catch me?" He turned in the direction of the old house and got into a sprinter's position. He hoped they bought it.

Wilson had another brief conversation with Jacoby before he got back inside the Tempest and closed the door. The car sat there for several moments. Booker could imagine the conversation taking place. He hoped it ended with them deciding they could not catch him. He would welcome the sight of the Tempest leaving the area at a high rate of speed.

The engine revved several times. Booker remained in the sprinter's position. His muscles, coiled and locked, began to protest the lack of movement. "C'mon, leave," he whispered. "Give it up."

The car surged forward and then made a hard right turn into the field. It took Booker a moment to comprehend what he saw. When he realized what was happening and the ridiculous position in which he now found himself, he shouted, "Shit!" and ran.

He felt a surge of energy he did not expect from his legs and he used it. He could not reach the abandoned house and there was nothing in any other direction. He sprinted up the incline toward the road. It occurred to him, in some dark corner of his mind, that he was moving faster than he had ever moved in his life. The Tempest had slid a bit on the grass and Jacoby was having some trouble controlling the car. It bought Booker a few seconds, nothing more, but he thought maybe it would be enough.

He reached the road and ran straight across it. This section of Route 6 was bordered on one side by what the local kids called Mount Phoenix. It was not a mountain, certainly not in the sense of the Sierra Madres or the Rockies; it was more of a craggy jutting of rock that towered over the road. Booker had climbed it once on a dare when he was thirteen years-old. He knew it could be done; he did not know if he was in any condition to attempt such a climb at present but he was about to find out.

He looked over his shoulder. The Tempest had spun out in the grass but was muscling its way up the incline. The rear wheels machine-gunned grass and dirt behind the vehicle. The engine screamed its rage. Another few seconds and it would be on pavement again.

Booker had no choice.

He picked a spot on Mount Phoenix that looked as good a starting point as he would find and he ran for it. He got perhaps seven or eight feet off the ground when he saw the lights of the big rig taking the turn up the road. His eyes darted to Jacoby's Tempest. The front wheels found purchase on the blacktop and its rear wheels would at any moment.

Booker's eyes went wide. He held out a hand and screamed, "Stop!"

The Tempest did not stop. Its rear drive wheels grasped pavement and the car shot across Route 6.

For a single moment he saw Jacoby and the others through the dark tint of the windows framed in the eighteen wheeler's headlights. The truck's air horn sounded and its brakes locked up.

Jacoby ignored it. His eyes were fierce and full of hate and focused entirely on Booker.

The big rig broadsided the Tempest and shoved it sideways violently. Sparks flew in all directions. Booker heard the Tempest's engine roar even above the sound of the big rig jackknifing across Route 6. The truck came to a stop, but the Tempest did not. It continued its sideways skid across the blacktop until one of its tires of the right side gave up the ghost and exploded. The car tipped onto its side. It had enough momentum that it began to somersault its way down the road.

Booker watched with wide eyes as the mangled piece of steel (he could no longer think of it as a car) continued its wild and uncontrolled course along Route 6. He climbed back down and took off down the road after the Tempest.

It came to a stop on the passenger side. Bits of glass crunched beneath Booker's sneakers as he ran for it. The Tempest sat in the middle of the road. Smoke drifted slowly into the sky from something within the engine compartment.

A hand which likely belonged to Jacoby grasped onto the side of the driver's door. The hand was covered with blood. The pinky and ring fingers appeared to hang by a single flap of skin.

"Hang on," Booker shouted. "Just hang on."

He was nearly to the Tempest when it exploded.

The force and heat of the blast knocked him onto his back. Booker held his arms in front of his head to protect himself. He had the presence of mind to roll away from the inferno. His hands picked up numerous small cuts from the glass that littered the road, although he would be unaware of the wounds for some time.

He climbed to his knees and surveyed the wreck. Flames consumed the Tempest. The entire rear portion of the car was gone and burning pieces of debris littered the road. The flames burned along what remained of the fuel line and licked greedily at the engine. The front tires remained in place; they crackled and hissed as they burned. Jacoby's hand no longer jutted from within the car. Booker thought for a moment he heard screams coming from inside the Tempest but it was most likely his imagination. Anyone who survived the collision would have been killed instantly when the gas tank went.

His eyes were drawn to the big rig. It sat jackknifed in the middle of the road perhaps forty feet from the remains of Jacoby's Tempest. The driver was still behind the wheel. The light of the flames allowed Booker to see the man's wide eyes. His hands remained on the wheel; his knuckles were bone-white.

Booker walked slowly to the big rig. He reached up and opened the driver's door. The man behind the wheel did not react. Booker reached across him for the CB mic.

Hours later with his statement given to both the DLPD and the state troopers Booker made his way to Misset Park. He found a bench near the fountain and curled up and fell asleep. The following day he walked into the United States Air Force recruitment office, lied about his age, and signed up.

He would not step foot in Deacon's Landing again for forty-six years.

8.

Wherein Booker Meets the King
And Receives An Invitation

Booker held his silence for the first few moments. He was certain his new/old travelling companions would have much to say. He was somewhat surprised when they said nothing. He looked over his shoulder more than once but Wilson and Turner did not even move their eyes in his direction. They seemed content to ride in silence.

Even Jacoby seemed to have nothing to say. He turned the steering wheel and shifted the transmission when he needed to but beyond that he may as well have been alone in his car.

Booker sat back and simply watched the world outside the windshield grow darker and less distinct. The open fields gave way to the woods which still dominated the landscape along this section of Route 6. Ahead he could see the start of Mount Phoenix. As they approached the spot where the Tempest and its occupants shuffled loose the mortal coil, Booker expected Jacoby to stop the car. He did not. They continued south on Route 6 past the location where three kids died in 1968. None of them so much as glanced out the window.

They passed the open field where the dilapidated house once stood. A large and (to Booker's eyes) pretentious condo complex stood there now. "Where were you when I needed you?" Booker asked aloud. The kids in the car ignored him. He watched the condo complex recede from his field of view. He sat back in the seat and waited for the Tempest to reach Old Lichgate.

His eyes were drawn to the large crack in the dashboard. He had failed to notice it before. Had it always been there? Booker doubted it. Like the large dent in the door this, too, was new. Jacoby would never have allowed that kind of blemish on his pride and joy. Something about that crack gave Booker hope. He did not know why, but he felt it nonetheless.

There were still no streetlights along this section of Route 6. The road snaked its way through the woods on both sides. They saw no other vehicles. After a few more moments he caught sight of the cemetery on the left side of the road.

The stone wall had crumbled in an area on the north side. The opening looked large enough to accommodate the Tempest, although Jacoby did not seem inclined to make use of it. The giant tree was still present and much bigger than Booker remembered. Free of leaves its skeletal branches clawed at the night sky. He could see several graves through the opening in the wall and even more when Jacoby pulled up to the wrought iron gate. The gate itself was visibly rusted; several of the bars were either broken or missing. The grass was severely overgrown around it although the cold weather had beaten it down somewhat.

"Not much in the way of maintenance being done around here, is there?" He received no answer from anyone in the car, nor did he expect one. It was more to break the silence than to invite conversation.

Jacoby turned off the ignition. The engine stuttered a few times before finally shutting down, something Booker was sure it had never done in its life. He became aware of the overwhelming silence around him. He was used to quiet, living as he did in a small, somewhat isolated neighborhood in

Wilmington. This was something else entirely. He did not believe he had ever experienced the complete absence of sound as he did now. His own breathing, slow and steady, sounded as loud as a Deep Purple rock concert to his ears.

When Jacoby opened his door the sound made Booker jump; it creaked like Dracula's coffin in an old Lugosi movie. He chastised himself immediately and silently. It was precisely the type of reaction that would have produced insults from the others in the car back when they were among the living; none reacted save Jacoby, who half-turned and regarded Booker with what might have been a knowing smile.

"Let's go," Jacoby said. His voice was deep, gravelly, Darth Vader with throat cancer.

Booker reached for the door handle. It was loose in his hand. He glanced again at the crack in the dash and found it had travelled all the way to the top of the glove compartment. When he opened his door the handle came off in his hand. He tossed it noncommittally onto the front seat and stepped out. He waited to see if Wilson and Turner would join them. He had to stifle a scream when he saw them.

Wilson's jaw hung far too low and at a very odd angle. Booker could not see his left eye but his right had vanished into the recesses of his skull. The skin on his cheeks was rotted. Turner appeared in even worse shape. His ample stomach hung over his belt; the skin was rotted and Booker could see something red and wet dripping onto the leather seat. They seemed content to remain in the back, unwilling or unable to exit the vehicle. Booker took a moment to get over their appearance before he closed the door.

He walked around the front of the Tempest and stood as close to Jacoby as he could bring himself. He spared a quick glance at him. Jacoby did not mirror the appearance of his friends but he moved stiffly. He stood beside the car and stared straight ahead. He remained that way for a moment before he inclined his head toward the cemetery.

"In there. You remember the grave?"

"Edgar Sleeps," Booker said. He was surprised to find he did remember. He had actually forgotten about the strange headstone until that very moment.

"Yes. The king awaits you."

"Elvis is dead, man. Maybe you didn't hear."

Jacoby did not reply.

Booker took a few steps toward the old and rusted gate. He stopped in the middle of the road and turned and looked back at Jacoby. "You know I never wanted that to happen to you." It was not a plea; it was a simple statement of fact.

Jacoby remained silent. He simply stood by the Tempest and looked into the cemetery. One of the car's headlights winked out, cutting the available light in half.

Booker swallowed and turned back toward Old Lichgate.

Upon closer inspection the gate was in even worse shape than it looked from the road. He had noticed several bars missing but now he saw those that were still present were in terrible shape. There was no paint in evidence, merely rust. Flakes of the stuff fell off the bars in the slight breeze that sprung up. Small mounds of them dotted the ground below the gate. Booker took a deep breath, held it for a moment, and swung the gate open enough for him to squeeze through.

The headstones themselves did not look much the worse for wear since last he saw them. They remained weather-beaten and appeared fragile but they jibed with his memory of the one and only time he saw them up close. He fixed his eyes on where he remembered Edgar's grave to be and set off in that direction.

He walked slowly past the giant tree. Bereft of its leaves he should have been able to see through the branches to the massive trunk; there were simply too many branches for him to see anything. He could not venture a guess as to its age but he could imagine the thing being planted when the cemetery was established. Or perhaps it had been there even then. The lower branches scraped the ground and wore away some of the topsoil; the marks in the dirt appeared as if they had been made by fingernails.

He could see the outline of the east wall opposite the entrance. He stopped and regarded it. It would be a simple enough matter to scale the wall and try to get away from Jacoby and his dead buddies. He rejected the idea the moment it entered his head. He had been unable to outrun them when he was seventeen and in good shape. Although he kept himself more or less fit he knew he had no chance of outrunning them now. Not that he had anywhere to go, anyway. Even if he made it back to his rented Chrysler he could not hope to keep ahead of Jacoby's street beast until he reached Deacon's Landing. It seemed he had little choice but to do as Jacoby told him and meet his mysterious king.

Whoever the fuck he was.

He saw the bars of the cage perhaps twenty feet away. He walked toward it and tried to remember what Jacoby had called it. After a moment it came to him. A *mortsafe*. It was something else he had forgotten about completely until that very moment. The memories were coming back to him faster and with much more force than he would have expected or liked. He was troubled by how easily the memories returned. He had spent more than four decades forgetting about Old Lichgate and Jacoby and Deacon's Landing. Silently he cursed his cousin for the phone call that brought him here. He cursed himself, as well, for stupidly leaving Lisa to attend the funeral of a woman he had assumed to be dead for decades. *Should have just stayed in Wilmington, Scotty.* Yeah, no shit.

He stopped before the grave and saw the inscription was as clear as it had been in 1968. Edgar continued to sleep. The bars of the *mortsafe* appeared to grow out of the weeds that had long since taken custody of Old Lichgate. The bars looked strange to him although he did not know why. He fished his lighter from his pocket, knelt by the cage and brought the flame to life. The cold breeze picked up, but only slightly. The lighter's flame sputtered but did not go out. It took Booker a few moments to see what a part of his mind had already recognized. "No rust," he whispered. It was true; the *mortsafe* might have been installed the day before for all the damage it had taken from the elements. That fact alone made him reconsider making a mad dash for the east wall.

He remembered something else, the swath of bright yellow someone had painted across the front of Edgar's headstone. He held the lighter up and saw it was, indeed, still there. It looked as fresh as the *mortsafe*.

Booker let the flame die and he put the lighter back in his pocket.

He shifted his weight but remained kneeling by Edgar's grave. The cold wind picked up a little more and it made him shiver. He felt he would shiver even had he not been acclimated to North Carolina temperatures. The cold, he knew, had little to do with the wind. He remained kneeling for several more moments until his legs started to protest. He stood slowly and flexed his leg muscles. "What now, your majesty?" he asked the grave.

He remained there for perhaps five more minutes. Nothing happened, no king presented himself, nor did Jacoby and his dead friends enter the cemetery. Booker looked toward the road but the slight down slope of the cemetery caused the stone wall to block his view. He could not see if the Tempest was still there. He had not heard the car leave, but he might have been too distracted by Edgar's grave to notice.

He had waited long enough. He calculated the distance to where he left the rental and figured it to be a mile away, maybe a little more. He would be tired when he got there, but he could make it. He turned from the grave.

The wind picked up significantly as he did. It rippled both his jacket and his khakis. He shoved his hands into his pockets against the sudden assault and put his back to the wind. The dead and dying grass around him undulated like the waves of the ocean. It whistled through the barren branches of the great tree to his right. The branches themselves creaked their protest.

The wind lessened after a few moments and Booker took his first step in the direction of the gate when he realized the whistling he assumed to have come from the tree contin- ued. He looked closely at it and saw the branches had stilled. At the same moment he noticed his shadow upon the ground in front of him. It was wreathed in yellow light.

He tried to swallow but his mouth was suddenly dry. His first thought was to run, Jacoby and his friends be damned. Indeed he would have had his feet not inexplicably grown roots into the ground. He tried to turn back toward the grave, but his feet simply refused to move. He managed to turn his head in that direction. His eyes widened even against the bright yellow light.

It came from the headstone. He could no longer see the face of the stone nor its engraving. It seemed as bright as the sun but the light did not hurt his eyes. If anything it seemed a calming force on his nerves. He felt his heartbeat and his breathing slow to nearly normal levels. The chill which had settled in the base of his spine vanished. He felt better, in fact, than at any time since his cousin's phone call. After another moment he found he could move again. He turned and faced the headstone.

A warmth that did not fit into early December in southern New England radiated from the light. Booker noted, with some gratitude, that his breath no longer frosted the air. Within a few moments he wondered why he wore a jacket. He took his hands from his pockets and held them, palms out, toward the grave.

The light grew in size and he found he could no longer see the outline of Edgar's grave at all. The light retained its oval shape but it was much larger. It no longer resembled a headstone but a large oval door.

The yellow light intensified and now it did begin to hurt his eyes. He held a hand in front of his face and turned his head slightly to the left. There were new sounds coming from the light; he could not identify any of them. They may have been voices or something mechanical, he could not tell. The volume of noise grew louder with the intensifying light. Booker turned his body away from the door and used both hands to cover his ears. He squeezed his eyes shut and gritted his teeth. He could feel warmth at his back as if winter had become spring and then summer. He began to sweat. The heat, light and noise formed a trinity that threatened to overwhelm him. Booker staggered and went down to one knee.

The assault lessened in intensity until he could hear and see again. The heat remained at his back but it had become pleasant. It reminded him of early summer nights when he was in grade school. He turned his head back toward Edgar's grave but only a few inches. He kept his hands near his ears in case the noise resumed its assault.

Edgar's headstone and *mortsafe* were gone. In their place was a large, open doorway. On the other side of the glowing, golden arch appeared a town much like Deacon's Landing. He could see little detail beyond the homes that dotted the sweeping hills and valleys. One distant building, much larger than the others and apparently constructed of bright yellow stone, made Booker think of church. If that was indeed the building's purpose he could not imagine the sermons that would be recited within. The building possessed a steeple and there appeared to be something perched at its top. Perhaps he was too far way or his eyes had yet to adjust to the muted daylight spilling through the open doorway. Whatever the reason the object atop the spire was blurred.

Booker climbed back to his feet and took a single step toward Edgar's former grave. The sky on the other side of the doorway was indeed brighter than the sky above the old cemetery but its sunlight was mostly hidden by a type of cloud Booker had never before seen. The clouds were dark, blacker even than the thunderheads that preceded a late-summer hurricane in North Carolina. What he assumed to be lightning lanced through the clouds but produced neither rain nor thunder.

Closer to the doorway, much closer, were trees and grasses that looked as if they had been pencil-drawn by a madman. The grass was a shade of gray that Booker was certain did not exist within nature. The trees were of the same color and the leaves (if that's what they were) appeared to be the color of dried blood. Some type of flowery fruit dangled from some of the branches. Booker had never before seen their like.

A weak current of air emanated from the doorway. Booker caught a whiff of it and recoiled. He could not describe the smell, never having encountered anything similar. The closest he could come was *rot*. Wet rot, but that did not do it justice. He backed up a step.

He bumped into someone at his back. He yelped and whirled. Jacoby stood directly behind him. He said nothing, did not seem to notice him at all. His dead eyes were focused intently on the doorway. Booker got the distinct impression, although he did not know how, that Jacoby awaited something. He had no desire whatsoever to see who or what would come.

He tried to sidestep him but Jacoby got in his way. He tried to shove past him but Jacoby placed his hands on Booker's arms and held him fast. "Let go of me," Booker said and struggled to free himself. Jacoby did not reply, simply held him in place. "Let go of me, you asshole." To his own surprise he was no longer afraid of Jacoby or his dead friends; in place of the fear was a growing anger, even rage. "Fuck off, Jacoby! I'm leaving right now and you won't stop me."

Booker spun quickly enough that Jacoby momentarily lost his grip. Booker drew back his fist, ready to throw the best haymaker of his life. His arm froze in midair.

Deacon's Landing's Former Bad Boy Number One no longer resembled the punk kid who had so intimidated Booker when they were young. He did not even look the same as he had a few moments before in the car. His skin was gray, almost the same color as the strange grass on the other side of the doorway. His hair had thinned considerably; it blew in various directions with the wind coming from the strange land before them. His eyes were no longer brown but milky white. His lips pulled back from his rotted teeth.

Jacoby whispered, "He comes."

For a reason Booker could not articulate that simple phrase drained all the strength from him. He went limp and would have collapsed to the ground had Jacoby not held him up. He struggled to get his feet under him and when he did he turned back to the doorway.

A man approached. He walked along the gentle slope of the gray grass. He wore what appeared to be a robe; it was bright yellow and not easy to look at, especially in contrast to the drab colors around him. As the figure drew closer Booker realized he had been mistaken; the man did not walk at all. Booker got a good look at his feet. They hovered perhaps five or six inches above the ground. More so, his robes had seen better days. The edges were frayed, even torn. Loose threads dangled from the cuffs and the collar and the golden sash that acted as a belt. The man's face was hidden in the darkness of his hood. Although he had no evidence of this, Booker felt the man was either severely disfigured or he wore a mask. He did not know why he received that impression, but it was strong and he knew he was correct.

Booker no longer felt the hands on his arms. He cast sideways glances at the kid next to him. Jacoby dropped to his knees and knelt in the cold dirt with his head bowed. Booker looked at him for several moments and contemplated his chances of making it out of the cemetery before Jacoby could catch up to him. *Just run, old man. Run and don't stop. Leave this dead asshole to his king.* But no. He would make no such move, *could not*, in fact. It appeared Jacoby would get his way after all. Booker was about to meet the king.

Booker turned again and regarded the man in the ragged yellow robes. He stood now no more than ten feet from the doorway. His feet remained several inches above the ground. He was tall, much taller than Booker expected. It was difficult to say with certainty because he continued to hover, but Booker estimated his height to be better than seven feet. His robes were the same color as the church in the distance, the same as Jacoby's Tempest.

The King's arms were folded and the robes hid his hands. Suddenly and slowly he unfolded his arms and cast them open in what might have been a welcoming embrace. Booker could see the King's hands and wrists. They appeared emaciated and scabrous. It made him examine the robes a bit more closely. As he suspected the robes seemed to cling to the King's bones. Booker doubted the man weighed one hundred pounds.

"Have you come to petition for a place in our fine city?" the King asked. His voice was melodious and deep, too deep for the frail form beneath his robes.

"What?" The word was a whisper; Booker barely heard it himself. His mouth was dry and tasted of the strange breeze that emanated from the doorway.

"He does," Jacoby said.

"We have room for many," the King informed Booker. "All are welcome."

"I don't…" His voice trailed off. He felt dizzy, light-headed. The one time he felt anything even approximating this was when he and Smoke indulged in some killer weed when they were in Nam. Two hits of that crap had made Booker nearly incoherent for two hours. This was much worse. "I don't know," he managed.

The King extended a skeletal hand. It brushed the edge of the threshold between Booker's world and the other side of the doorway. "Come, Scotty."

Booker tried to swallow but his throat had sealed shut to anything but air. The world around him swam; only the land behind and around the King seemed solid and real. "How do you know my name?" It was a stupid question but it was all he had.

The King tilted his head slightly. "Come and I will show you."

Booker watched his hand move of its own accord toward the King. He tried to stop himself, but his hand continued on its path. His feet joined the conspiracy and moved him closer to the doorway. "Yes," he whispered.

Something rippled beneath the King's yellow robes. At first he thought it was the strange-smelling wind that caused it but a dim corner of his mind recognized it as something else. He was absolutely certain he did not want to see what caused the King's robes to move in so unnatural a manner.

He commanded his other hand to move. It was sluggish and disobedient. He willed it more forcefully and felt his fingers curl reluctantly into a fist. He brought his fist up hard and fast before that hand rebelled as well. His knuckles collided quite dramatically with his nose. Blood spurted and Booker backpedaled and nearly lost his balance. Tears streamed from his eyes and he tasted hot copper at the back of his throat. He went down on one knee before his strength gave out and he lay on his side on the dead cemetery grass.

He felt the euphoria/dizziness lift from his mind all at once. The strange smell from the other world intensified and Booker vomited onto the ground. He could not tell from the darkness around him but he was willing to bet there was a fair amount of blood mixed with the bile. The wind coming through the doorway picked up and tore at Booker's clothes. He wanted to curl into a fetal position and stay down. A voice in his head, a voice that sounded suspiciously like Lisa's, shouted, *Get up now, Scott, or you'll never see home again.* He did not know where the voice came from, but he believed it. He got one hand beneath him and pushed himself to his knees.

Rough hands grabbed at his arms and hauled him to his feet. The sudden and unexpected movement made his stomach convulse. Booker vomited again. Fresh tears spilled from his eyes and blinded him. He was aware of the person who had hold of him. He struggled in Jacoby's grip but he could not free himself. He was turned around. He lost track of his position in the cemetery but he could guess in which direction Jacoby dragged him. Booker dug in his heels and pulled against him. He managed to slow their progress but he could not stop it. He felt the breeze from the King's land intensify on his face and body. He must be very close to the threshold.

Booker tensed and put everything he had into a final push. Jacoby managed to keep one hand on Booker's shoulder but the other one was gone. Booker flailed his arms and felt his hand mash Jacoby's jaw. Jacoby spun away. The hand remained on Booker's shoulder. He turned quickly, expecting to see Wilson or Turner. It was neither. The hand belonged to Jacoby, as did the arm at the end of it. It was severed above the elbow. Rotted flesh hung in thin strips from the break. Booker got it together enough to fling the arm away from him. He took two steps toward the cemetery gate.

Wilson had made it over the wall. He shambled slowly in Booker's direction. Like Jacoby, he had changed drastically in the short time he had been in the cemetery. Wilson looked like a long-dead corpse under the control of an insane puppeteer. His body spasmed and jerked with every movement. His jaw was gone completely and he seemed to rot before Booker's eyes. Even as Booker watched one of the dead kid's legs snapped at the knee and he went down on the grass.

Turner scaled to the top of the wall and remained there for a moment. Unlike Wilson he still had his eyes. They burned into Booker's with unmasked hatred. The fat kid rolled off the wall and landed a few feet behind Wilson. Turner's body exploded in a spray of blood and bone when he hit the ground. In the light from the doorway the blood appeared black.

Wilson managed to raise his arm in Booker's direction. Turner lay perfectly still.

Booker swallowed and resumed his course for the gate. Jacoby's remaining hand grabbed his arm and spun him back in the direction of the doorway. Booker gasped and nearly lost his balance. His eyes went from the doorway and the King to Jacoby.

The dead kid's jaw hung crookedly from one hinge. When he spoke his words were garbled but Booker could still understand him. "Don't fight it, Booker," Jacoby whispered. "He has so much to show you. That place was made for people like us."

Jacoby had him perhaps six feet from the doorway. The wind pouring into Booker's world had become both more foul and more forceful. It whipped along his scalp and tossed his jacket about him. The King held both hands before him. His body language made Booker think of the families who welcomed home the soldiers and airmen who returned from the war. The embrace appeared both warm and loving, but Booker did not believe the King capable of either emotion.

Booker pivoted away from Jacoby. With only one arm, and a swiftly-rotting one, at that, Jacoby could not maintain his grip nor did he keep his balance. He staggered toward the doorway.

What happened next remained with Booker for the rest of his life. The King's robes rippled again and something that looked suspiciously like a tentacle snaked its way out between the King's feet. It shot forward, crossed the threshold, and wrapped itself around Jacoby's remaining arm. The kid had no time to react. In the time it took Booker to blink his eyes the tentacle retracted and Jacoby shot across the threshold. He did not scream; he did not utter a sound. He simply vanished, quickly and completely, within the King's robes.

"Jesus Christ," Booker said. His legs gave out and he simply sat on the grass, a few feet from the doorway. *That was supposed to be me. If I hadn't put Jacoby between me and the King...*

Before the King's robe fluttered closed once again Booker caught sight of something beneath it. There were more tentacles hidden within the darkness of those yellow robes. They coiled about each other and writhed restlessly. He got the distinct impression there was something else behind the tentacles, beneath them. His mind either could not or would not identify whatever it was. He thought perhaps he should be grateful for that.

Behind the King the landscape of his unnamed realm had become more vivid, more real. The bright yellow structure was indeed a church although it resembled no church Booker had ever seen. The architecture was wrong, somehow, although it took Booker a moment to identify what was out of place. The windows were of irregular size and shape and their placement made no sense. It looked more like a child's drawing than a combination of brick and mortar.

Other structures, houses, dotted the landscape in almost a grid-like pattern. Some larger square buildings lay on the outskirts of the land. It resembled, although Booker did not know how he knew this, the layout of Deacon's Landing. It was not exact but the resemblance was too close to be random.

He was even able to spot the other world's version of his mother's house. That angered him for reasons he could not articulate. He pulled his eyes from the structure and gritted his teeth. His anger returned a modicum of strength to his limbs.

He stood slowly and brushed the cemetery dirt from his clothes. The warm air of the alien world caressed his scalp and produced beads of sweat on his forehead.

Booker looked up in time to see the King's robes whip open. One, then two tentacles revealed themselves. They writhed their way out of the yellow robes and slithered across the strange grass at the King's feet. Their movement was similar to a snake's with a slight difference Booker could not identify. Later he would be thankful for that; he felt any serious study of the King would likely result in him losing his mind.

He spared a quick glance at the wall where he had last seen Wilson and Turner. They remained where they fell. Wilson might have still possessed one eye; his skeletal hand remained raised in Booker's direction. Turner seemed truly dead.

Booker stepped away from the threshold. He started to bolt in the direction of the road. The sight of someone approaching from behind the King stopped him in his tracks. He knew immediately the identity of the woman in the white and pink funeral dress. What he did not know was why he stood in place and waited for her to take up position beside the King.

"Hello, Scotty," his mother said.

Booker did not reply. He remained frozen in place.

"Come join us, son. We're all waiting for you."

He did not believe the apparition beside the King was truly his mother, even when she attempted a warm smile. The corners of her mouth struggled with the gesture and worked against the creases in her skin. She held out her hand and gestured him forward.

Booker took a single step toward the threshold. *This is how she could have been,* he thought. Warm, loving, the type of mother who populated the television shows of his youth. But that was not Mary Ellen Booker. He thought of the single drop of blood working its way down the wall and down Jim Morrison's chest. Booker retreated a step.

He looked at the King, who remained in his original spot. "You screwed up, your majesty. That's not my mother and we both know it."

His mother stomped her foot. "Scott Terrance Booker, you heed me."

"Fuck you both."

The King lifted his head and screamed. His robes flew open and a mass of tentacles shot forward across the threshold.

Booker dove to his left and hit the ground hard. The tentacles passed over his head close enough for him to feel the breeze. They clipped the top of the nearest headstone and pulverized it. Booker was pelted with bits of old stone.

He rolled away as fast as he was able and hoped none of the tentacles found purchase. He calculated he was perhaps fifteen to twenty feet from the doorway. It would have to be enough. He leaped to his feet and sprinted from Edgar's grave with as much speed as his legs could generate.

He was closest to the east side of the cemetery. He raced for the section of the wall which was collapsed. He scampered over the fallen stones. He heard the King scream again and the inhuman sound was joined by his mother's bellow of rage. The sound was enough to make his bladder let go. Booker threw himself across the cemetery's border. He landed hard on the ground and the breath was driven from his lungs. He felt two ribs crack.

He did not tarry. He was on his feet in an instant. His fractured ribs brought pain with every shallow breath. It took him a moment to realize the air had changed. It no longer smelled foul and unnatural. He whipped his head around and looked back at the cemetery. He could see no individual graves but the large tree was backlit by the yellow glow of the alien world. Several tentacles whipped through the air and reached a height several feet above the tree.

Booker tore his eyes from the cemetery and ran for all he was worth up the incline and toward the road. The returning cold seemed to energize his muscles and give him a second wind. He made it to the road and started north. He made it no more than ten feet before he realized the night had returned to total darkness.

He stopped and turned his head back in the direction of Old Lichgate. There was no yellow light, no magical doorway and no sign of the King or his new consort. The cemetery sat dark and quiet within its boundaries.

The adrenaline surge left him all at once and Booker allowed himself to drop to one knee. His lungs took in great gulps of air and his muscles shook. He remained on the shoulder of Route 6 and took several moments to catch his breath. He waited for some of the strength to return to his limbs. After some time he was able to slow his breathing and his heart stopped trying to hammer its way out of his chest. A measure of strength returned to his muscles, but he felt tired in a way he never had before.

When he felt he was ready, he pushed himself back to his feet. He winced when his fractured ribs protested the move but he otherwise ignored the pain. He looked a final time at the old cemetery. It was dark and deserted and free of anything that lived.

The Tempest remained where Jacoby left it but it was in bad shape. Most of the chassis was gone, as were the seats and floorboards. The frame was supported by four flat tires. The giant engine block sat at an odd angle between the front wheels. Booker watched small pieces of rotted steel blow away from the frame on the slight breeze.

He turned north and started to walk back to where he left his rented Chrysler. He wished there was another route he could take back to Bradley International that would allow him to avoid Deacon's Landing entirely but if there was he could not remember it. So he would see his old town one last time.

And then he would return home to Wilmington and Lisa. He would not spend a single moment of the rest of his life thinking about the small town in Connecticut where his parents lived and died and were buried. Nor would he think about Jacoby and his dead friends.

He could not control his dreams, however.

And therein ruled the King.

Thank You

The author wishes to thank:

Jeff Melton
Theron Johnson
Denise Malione
Julie Filippone Aresco
Vin DiVergilio
The POWER Players Guild
Elizabeth Fortin

About the Author

Author photograph by Taria A. Reed

Joseph J. Christiano is the author of
The Last Battleship, Moon Dust and
Dark Annie.
He resides in Connecticut.